"Come on," Jenna whispered as she crouched, then stood, putting out both arms like a blind woman. When she blinked, there was no change in the total blackness. "Hold on to me."

But when they finally found a wall and started to move, Mandi tripped. Jenna bent to help her sister up, getting her fingers snagged in the chain that held Mace's ring around Mandi's neck.

A shuffling sound. They both froze again. Light curled around a corner, then shone in their faces, blinding them. Jenna shaded her eyes, then threw herself knee-high at whomever held it. The man cursed, jumped away. His light went out, plunging them into utter blackness again. He shoved Jenna facedown on the stone floor and put a knee between her shoulder blades. But Mandi must have run, because all Jenna could hear was the distant echo of her scream.

"Ms. Harper's tale is full of twists and turns...."

—*Romantic Times* on *Shaker Run*

Also available from MIRA Books and
KAREN HARPER

SHAKER RUN
DOWN TO THE BONE
THE BABY FARM

Watch for the newest novel
of romantic suspense from
KAREN HARPER

THE FALLS

June 2003

KAREN HARPER

THE STONE FOREST

ISBN 1-55166-909-9

THE STONE FOREST

Visit us at www.mirabooks.com

Printed in U.S.A.

Although I completed this novel four months
before the terrorist tragedies at the
World Trade Towers and the Pentagon,
I want to dedicate this book to the memory
of the many people who lost their lives there.
The Pentagon, like many famous American
buildings, is made of Indiana limestone.

"Murder may pass unpunished for a time,
But tardy justice will o'ertake the crime."
—John Dryden

"When I try to imagine a faultless love
Or the life to come,
What I hear is the murmuring
Of underground streams,
What I see is a
Limestone landscape."
—W. H. Auden, *In Praise of Limestone*

Prologue

June 6, 1985

''Nice party, but I thought they'd never leave,'' Mandi said with a sigh and a yawn.

''I never wanted it to end,'' Jenna protested.

''You never wanted that *kiss* to end.''

Sweet sixteen birthdays were supposed to be special and Jenna's had been, mostly because Mace—her older sister Mandi's boyfriend—had kissed her.

Now that the guests had gone home, Jenna and Mandi kissed their mother good-night and went upstairs, leaving most of the mess for the maid to clean up in the morning. Mother called their home Kirkhall, as if it were some grand mansion, instead of just the biggest house in little Ridgeview, Indiana, where nothing much happened anymore. The limestone quarries that surrounded the town were in a decades-long slump, and the town still seemed petrified in the sixties.

The girls paused at the top of the curving staircase.

''Your face only got about as red as my dress when he kissed you,'' Mandi added, her voice more piercing than teasing.

''You're not mad?'' Jenna blurted out, before she realized that was a stupid thing to say.

After all, eighteen-year-old Amanda Leslie Kirk was

Ridgeview High's golden girl, cheerleading captain, and homecoming queen. With perfect teeth and naturally curly blond hair, the five-foot-five-inch Mandi was her own Farrah Fawcett poster—if Farrah had just stepped out of a romantic Laura Ashley ad. Lace-edged linen printed with roses for dress-up, or Calvin Kleins when she was really down-and-dirty—that was Mandi. Her style might have set her apart from others but she attracted folks like flies and graciously included them in her world.

Jenna was the daddy's girl of the family, an old-time tomboy. Tall at five feet seven inches already, she was as lithe as Mandi was shapely. She tried to make light of her braces by calling them "mousetraps." Jenna excelled at softball, track, and swimming. She didn't have half as many friends as Mandi, but she was closer to the few she had. Although she'd worn a bright blue dress to her birthday party, she was more at home in loose Levi's. Jenna wore her straight auburn hair short and sleek, like Mary Lou Retton, who'd earned all 10s in the Olympics last summer. The 10s Mandi won were the kind guys gave out, like in that movie with Bo Derek running down the beach.

Mace MacCaman was Mandi's steady, but Jenna had secretly, achingly adored him for as long as she could remember. And she'd never forget his kiss today, the way his narrowed green eyes had assessed her before he'd hugged her hard. He'd meant, no doubt, just to peck her on the cheek. But Jenna had been so swamped by his touch that she'd turned her head, and his firm, warm lips had caught the corner of her mouth. The impact of that had flashed clear through her and made her legs go wobbly. It was the first time she'd realized what adults saw in kissing, other than as a friendly or comforting gesture.

"Mad about Mace giving you a birthday kiss? Me?" Mandi said, as she pulled Jenna into her bedroom and closed the door behind them. *"Hardly."*

Mandi's room, which, when she was in one of her moods, was off-limits to Jenna, displayed collections of everything she loved. Photos of friends, arranged in perfect order, were framed and hung on long, wide velvet ribbons, not just stuck on the mirror or wall. Three posters from her all-time favorite book and movie, *Gone with the Wind,* covered another wall, with the one of Rhett carrying Scarlett up the staircase in the center.

Glass and porcelain ballerinas danced, and painted china and stuffed cloth cats preened on built-in shelves. Her Siamese cat, Pert, slept on her bed amid twenty heart-shaped pillows, each with a different saying. The cabinet by her stereo speakers boasted tapes and albums, including everything ever recorded by Barry Manilow. She used to play his song "Mandy" for days straight, until Jenna almost threw up. Secretly, though, she wished she had a song titled with her name, too. Barry Manilow's top-of-the-charts hit "Jenna" would have some boss lyrics like, *"Oh, Jenna. You grew up, and I knew that I loved you. Oh, Jenna. I realize how much I need you. We've got to break it to others that there is no other for me but you, Jenna..."* Of course, the song was written from Mace's point of view, but if he chose to keep their love a secret till she was grown, Jenna would wait for him that long—or forever.

Jenna was startled from her thoughts as Mandi pulled her over to the cushioned window seat and sat her down hard. "I need your help, Jen."

"I'm not lying to Mom to cover for you again."

"You don't have to lie. If she ever sees I'm not here, you play completely dumb. I'll just tell her I couldn't sleep and had to go out to get some air."

"Oh, sure. With the chain lock on the door from inside?"

"I can handle it. I'll tell her I went out a downstairs window or something. I've got to get out tonight."

"You're meeting Mace again?"

Mandi looked as if she wanted to say more, but instead she only looked down at her knees and half nodded, half shrugged. She dragged Mace's class ring back and forth on the chain around her neck, making a clicking sound in the sudden silence.

The mere thought of sneaking out to meet Mace MacCaman after dark excited Jenna as much as it must have Mandi, however cool and calm her big sis always acted about it. Their mother had an eleven o'clock curfew for Mandi, unless it was a special school or church event. On the nights she sneaked out, Mandi waited until their mom, Cynthia Kirk, was busy in her office downstairs, making late-night calls for donations for her Right-A-Wrong Association or talking to the other township trustees about trying to keep outsiders from swimming in the empty, off-limits quarries.

Mandi would go out the back door—Mom sometimes called it the servants' entrance, though they only employed one woman as a part-time cook and maid—and Jenna would lock it behind her, including the chain lock Mom always checked before going to bed. Then Jenna set an alarm clock under her pillow for 2:00 a.m. to sneak down to let Mandi back in.

Sometimes, when she couldn't sleep, Jenna sat in her own bedroom window seat and stared out at the tree house Dad had built for them years ago in the big oak.

Usually, she tossed and turned, wondering what Mace and Mandi were really doing out there. After all, nothing was open in little, boring Ridgeview at night.

Mandi had confided that she and Mace went down to Green Eye and skinny-dipped or just went for rides in Mace's car and made out. But Jenna, even if she'd only had a grand total of two fix-up dates so far, knew better than that. The past few months, though Mandi had hurried past Jenna in the dark when she came in, she had looked all messed up, as if she'd been wrestling—or worse.

Tonight, Jenna almost told Mandi to let *herself* out and in. "You will, won't you, Jen?"

"Yeah, but this is the last time. Since you're graduating soon, you can just tell Mom that eleven o'clock is—"

"I knew you'd help! We have to stick together, no matter what," Mandi declared with a toss of her hair. She jumped up to disappear into her walk-in closet. Jenna stared at the bulletin board on the wall by the closet door. Tacked to it were several large samples of the way Mandi always signed her name: Mandi Kirk, with big, hand-drawn hearts instead of dots over both *i*'s.

Watching Mandi slip outside, Jenna did not close the door behind her but stood staring out. This night of her sixteenth birthday was breezy and balmy and salted by a sprinkle of stars. She smiled, pleased with that wording—*salted by a sprinkle of stars.* She'd have to tell Mace's sister, Cassie, her best friend. Cassie was the best writer in the whole sophomore class, if not all of Ridgeview High. *Salted by a sprinkle of stars.*

Suddenly, she was seized with the urge to go out, too.

Not to get a glimpse of Mace from afar, like those glances she cherished and always wrote about in her diary, nor to spy on them. Just to be out in this fragrant, special night, maybe to pretend she was meeting someone she loved, or starring in her own romantic adventure movie, like *Romancing the Stone.*

They had tons of stones around Ridgeview, but they were monolithic blocks of limestone and hardly romantic. Yet tonight she felt like running clear out of town, through the Stone Forest to Gram's house, which sat guarded by Grandpa's stone carvings. She could pretend she was meeting Mace in the moonlight, and they'd go skinny-dipping under a *sprinkle of stars* in a limestone country quarry.

She strained to listen for the murmur of her mother's distant voice. Yes, Mom was still talking on the phone. Of course, Jenna told herself, she'd come right back to the house. She had no one to meet, and she wasn't really going far. Jenna closed the door quietly behind her and walked away from the muted window lights. Mom's office was around the other side of the house, but the bright light mounted on the roof by the side yard cast sharp shadows on the grass, especially of the big black square form of the old tree house. She craned her neck to look up at it. That's what she could do. Just like when Dad was alive, she would climb up there and lie on her back, surveying the stars through the spring leaves.

The crude staircase that curved around the thick trunk was creaky now. She was only four steps up when she heard something. Her mom's voice? Had she been caught? If so, could she cover for Mandi? But the muffled woman's voice seemed to come from the bushes beyond the driveway.

She felt herself flush. Maybe Mace had hugged Mandi

so hard she'd let out a little cry. Or was that what passion really sounded like? But it hadn't sounded like a cry of pleasure. It was more like surprise—or pain.

Jenna swung from a low branch and dropped quietly to the ground. She froze, listening, then started in the direction of the deeper shadows, toward the driveway and the street. It was not too dark, once her eyes got used to it; the moonlight was pale but street lamps splashed puddles of gold.

Pushing through the thin bushes, she gasped at the sight of Mace and Mandi, locked in a fierce, rocking embrace. Mesmerized, yearning, she stood silent a moment. But was Mandi hugging or fighting him? Mace must be hurting her.

"Mace, don't!" Jenna cried, stepping toward them.

But it wasn't Mace, was it? Then everything went black, but she still saw stars.

Had she fallen from the tree house and hit her head? Her daddy was dead and couldn't catch her. Or was she under those stone blocks that the fireworks had loosened when Daddy died? But certain parts of her hurt more than others, so she must be alive.

She tried to move. Her hands and feet were tied tightly together and to a chair by ropes. She fought to open her eyes. Taped? Something was even in her ears, muting sounds—unless that was because she'd been knocked out. She felt so swimmy-headed.

"Where am I?" she demanded, but her voice sounded like she was in a barrel or had a bad cold. "Mandi?"

A leather-gloved hand pressed her lips to her front teeth once, then twice. She felt a fist—no doubt from the same hand—tap her jaw. The message was silent but clear. She kept quiet but fought to open her eyes again, despite how her eyelids and long lashes stuck to the blindfold. Duct or electrical tape, wide and heavy. And the chair felt like woven plastic—a lawn chair that would fold up. But where was she and why?

Her thoughts cleared even more. Mom would be frantic when she found them both missing, but she might not know until morning. No, she'd figure it out when she checked the back door locks. She'd see they were gone and maybe call the county sheriff. Jenna hoped Mom didn't phone Gram, because it might make Gram have another heart attack. The man with Mandi must not have been Mace. Mace would never do this. The stranger had been dressed in some sort of loose coat, and Mace just wore jackets, even in cold weather.

Jenna was sure of one thing. Before someone hit her and she fell, she saw that the man holding Mandi must have worn a hood or ski mask, because he had no face but blackness.

Carefully, quietly, Jenna tried to move her feet. Yes, they were tied, not taped, to the aluminum legs, but it was duct tape that held her hands and feet together. She let herself think it then: she and Mandi had been kidnapped.

Oh, dear Lord Jesus, please protect us! Please, please, Lord. Please!

Her heart began to beat faster. She was sure she could taste blood in her mouth, coppery and sickeningly sweet. She sucked in air through flared nostrils. A stale smell, yet a slight draft blew from somewhere. Despite her earplugs, she was sure she heard the murmuring of distant voices. Tears prickled her eyes behind the tape, and she sniffled. Thank God, she wasn't gagged and that she could breathe. But the walls, which she could not see, and the entire roof of the world seemed to be closing in. Like an overheated animal, she began to pant.

"What do you want?" she finally whispered, unable to bear the silence.

No reaction this time, neither through sound nor touch, but she sensed someone close, just standing there, watching. Despite the cool temperature, she began to sweat. She was going to die. Mom didn't have money to pay the ransom for her daughters, despite the large house Dad had built for them. Or did someone think that, as a candidate running for state senator, Cynthia Kirk had some kind of power or influence? Or had someone wanted to play a horrible trick on the woman who had become a national spokesperson for victims' rights?

Or was Mandi about to be raped, when Jenna stumbled on the crime? She couldn't fathom why anyone would want to kidnap her for that.

In her growing frenzy, Jenna began to wheeze. She felt something cold on her bare upper arm, then a pinch, a jab. Someone was giving her a shot. To calm or kill her?

She began to buck in her bonds. Her chair tipped over, and her head slid down someone's legs, also taped, before she hit a cold concrete floor. *Mandi.* Mandi was right next to her.

The lights and pictures in Jenna's brain started to go out, like the big, old curtain at the Bijou that covered the movie screen. Drugged. So scared. *Save Mandi. Save myself…*

Jenna swam upward again from sodden sleep. She was still tied but had been laid in a warm, cloth cocoon. Odd, but the first thing that came into her head were ancient mummies, which spent centuries in a dark tomb.

She began to panic again, but forced herself to lie still. And then she felt the big, double-sided zipper on the inside of the flannel sleeping bag, and began to slowly saw her wrist bonds against its metal teeth.

Still drowsy, she slept off and on, but kept sawing layer after layer of tape between times, through the smothering darkness of her panic. She was given water and fed soda crackers. Her heart thrilled once when she was sure she smelled Mandi's perfume—actually Mace's English Leather. Mandi was still here, nearby, and she was going to get loose and somehow save them both. *We've got to stick together no matter what,* Mandi had said.

Hours or days dragged by. Thank God, she didn't have to go to the bathroom, despite stomach cramps from the raw fear that pressed her down. Sometimes she sensed that their captor or captors left the room, and then she sawed even harder. And, finally, her wrists popped free.

She remained curled on her side, as she had been since she'd started sawing, and prayed she was facing away from her captors. Slowly again, so slowly, she raised her numb hands to her face and painfully pried the tape from her eyes.

Even when she was sure she'd lifted her sticky blindfold far enough to see, the room was utterly black.

She almost shrieked. Were they underground, trapped with just a little air? They'd read about that in tenth-grade Lit—that awful buried-alive story by Edgar Allan Poe, where the so-called corpse awoke and tried to claw his way out. She'd heard about a kidnapping case like that on the evening news. But no, there was a slight air movement. It must be night, that's all. But why was there no glimmer of light? Were they in a cellar or a cave? What could be *this* dark?

Drenched in sweat, with her blindfold still stuck over her eyebrows like the visor of a baseball cap, she unzipped the bag the rest of the way and yanked at the tape that bound her feet until she was free of it. She pulled plastic plugs from each ear. Still, no sounds. Praying she wouldn't come upon her captor in the blackness, she felt across the stone floor for something to use as a weapon. Maybe she'd find a light. Or anything, before this terror of being closed in made her go completely crazy.

She touched a soft form. A woman's body. Dead?

"Mandi?"

"Jen? Oh, J-Jen, where are w-we?"

"I've got to rip off your tape. Where is he?"

"Don't know, but they t-took the l-light."

Jenna could feel her sister shaking with cold or fear.

"I could see a little under my blindfold. T-t-two men. One in Western b-boots."

"Are we in a cellar or warehouse?" Jenna asked.

"A cave, I think. I'm scared of a rock slide. Mace loves caves. He t-told me about a rock slide underground, just like at the p-picnic."

"We can't be too far in. I felt air. If we stick tight to the wall, we can find our way out before they come back."

"I can't see anything. We might run into them or fall."

"Maybe they got what they want and left us here to die. You've got to come with me, 'cause I've got to get out."

They scrambled on hands on knees, discovering by touch what was left on the cave floor immediately around them. An empty cracker box. One more sleeping bag. No flashlights or lantern.

"Come on," Jenna whispered, as she crouched, then stood, putting out both arms like a blind woman. When she blinked, the total blackness never changed. "Hold on to me."

But when they finally found a wall and started to move, Mandi tripped. Jenna bent to help her up, getting her fingers snagged in the chain that held Mace's ring around Mandi's neck.

A shuffling sound. They both froze again. Light curled around a corner, then shone in their faces, blinding them. Jenna shaded her eyes, then threw herself knee-high at whomever held it. The man cursed, jumped away. His light went out, plunging them into utter blackness again. He shoved Jenna facedown on the stone floor and put a knee between her shoulder blades. But Mandi must have run, because her distant scream echoed, echoed.

Jenna alone was returned to Ridgeview the next night, still drugged, dumped in a way she could not recall, near her grandmother's house in the Stone Forest. Her mother had managed to scrape together the ransom that had been demanded, but no one had claimed it. No one was sure why her abductors gave Jenna back. Dead or alive, where was Mandi? Jenna knew she should have saved her. No trace was found, no matter how many leads were followed or suspects questioned.

Finally, people whispered, something had happened in little Ridgeview. The police, the press—another nightmare began for Jenna. And each person—every officer, her psychiatrist, even her mother—marveled and questioned why Jenna came back alone. Alone but haunted, always, by her losses and her loves.

1

April 22, 2000

A baseball bat in one hand, thirty-year-old Jenna Kirk hung fifteen feet up in a tree. She'd climbed the self-rigged rope with the intention of checking the solidity of the upper trunk of a big hickory, where she was planning to build a prototype of a children's tree house. But the balmy breeze, the clear open sky and sun of the late April Saturday had lured her into enjoying the ride. Secure in her seat harness, she pumped her legs back and forth and surveyed her little kingdom.

From this height she could see the edge of the cemetery and the rims of the abandoned quarries that hemmed in her four acres of land to the west and north. The one filled with spring water was Green Eye; the dry one, which was much newer, had been dubbed The Campus by the high-school kids of her era, partly because many of the massive blocks used for Midwestern college buildings had come from its depths. Mostly, though, the name came from the fact that it, along with Green Eye, had been the best hangout, make-out, or cut-school location around. She sighed as she swung more slowly. The high school she had attended—*We are the stonemen!*—had been closed and students were now bused to a consolidated school in a larger town. So much had changed.

Her view was especially spectacular today since the leaves were just starting to emerge. It was the best month to build a tree house. You could clearly see the structure and strength of limbs, and the weather was reasonable. In the year she had been back in Ridgeview, living in the house on these grounds her maternal grandmother had left her, Jenna had begun her own business, Out On A Limb, through which she designed and oversaw the building of luxury adult tree houses.

More than once she'd told herself that she should have started the business building smaller houses for the children's market and expanded from there, but it had taken her this long to even think about tree houses for kids. Living and playing and dreaming aloft was for happy times, and the two tragedies of her childhood had made her memories anything but happy. Yet she was now ready for this new step—branching out, no longer up a tree, she thought with a grin.

She twisted around to look at the old Victorian home she so loved, her shelter in childhood and this past year. It needed a lot of work, as it hadn't been repaired since Dad died. But she was skilled with tools and was making progress with renovating the place. Like many houses in this hilly region of south-central Indiana, the long porch and wooden eaves were adorned with ornate gingerbread called carpenter's lace.

Only the wealthiest homes, like Kirkhall where she had grown up, were constructed mostly of cut stone. Yet even the poorest local dwellings boasted fancy bird baths, urns, or other decorations carved by the old stonemen of the once flourishing area. The woods that surrounded her home were filled with so many charming, unique statues, carved by her long-deceased grandfather, that it was known locally as The Stone Forest.

Jenna noticed a large black car, creeping down the crushed limestone road which shone stark white in the spring sun. A chauffeured government car, distinctive and recognizable. Her mother's car.

Since she'd taken quite awhile in rigging a safe climb up here, Jenna hastily finished her task, knocking the bat against the trunk to make certain it was solid this far off the ground, where the umbrella supports for the main floor would go. It sounded good and looked good, this venerable hickory. She patted it like an old friend, then heard the metallic slam of the distant car door and shouted, "I'm out here, Mom!"

Dropping the bat to the ground, she let herself down slowly, her lower hand controlling the speed of descent and her upper guiding the rope through the brake bar rig. She savored the bird songs and sweet soughing of the wind as her mother made her way down the crushed-stone path into the forest. Her mom's driver stayed by the car, leaning nonchalantly against it. For once, it seemed, Cynthia Kirk, the lieutenant governor of the great Hoosier State of Indiana, had ridden the fifty miles from Indianapolis to Ridgeview alone. She'd probably been on her cell phone or dictating letters. Lt. Gov. Kirk had never been one to waste time, effort or purpose.

"I didn't know you were coming!" Jenna said, hastily unfastening and stepping out of her harness.

"Or you'd have baked a cake instead of climbed a tree," her mother said. "You looked like Peter Pan soaring around up there."

Jenna clapped dirt and bark from her hands before she hugged her mother, even though the black outfit Cynthia wore wouldn't show marks. Platform heels and a sleek pantsuit with shoulder pads—Cynthia Kirk was a pioneer of power dressing, even in a forest.

"Speaking of Peter Pan," Jenna said, "I've just added a quote from *Peter Pan* to the new children's page on my Web site. Something like, 'I shall live with Tink,' said Peter Pan, 'in the little house we build for Wendy. The fairies are fixing it high up beside their nests in the treetops.'"

"Mmm," her mother said, rolling her dark blue eyes. "Swiss Family Robinson and Christopher Robin lived in trees, too. I'm starting to think you should have gone into elementary teaching instead of high school English and then that environmental education office job. I still can't believe you're sticking to all of this," she concluded with a sweeping gesture at the surrounding trees, especially the one that held Jenna's small but lofty office and the three oaks that shared the weight of her masterpiece tree house.

"Mother, I'm just starting to build my dreams here. Surely you understand that."

"But who's going to come traipsing to Ridgeview to see your models?" she demanded. "I only want what's best for you, and to protect you."

"First of all, most sales will be from the Web site. But if clients want to see these models—and some already have driven in from as far away as Chicago and Columbus—this isn't Outer Mongolia."

"Even if you don't want to live with me anymore, at least come back to Indianapolis, darling. Get a condo in the suburbs and build tree houses there, where—"

"Where the local authorities would plague me with zoning or permit restrictions."

"Now, you know I could take care of that. A few well-placed words here and there..." Her mother heaved a huge sigh. A silence stretched between them, so familiar it was hardly awkward anymore. They had started to walk toward the house, through what Jenna had always called Rabbit Run, because of the stone faces with long ears peeking from rocks in this section, when her mother stopped abruptly. Placing her hands on Jenna's shoulders, she turned her daughter to her.

"I'm not just passing through, Jenna, though I have a meeting in Bloomington this evening."

"The day before Easter? Can you come back, then, and stay here for part of the holiday weekend? We could go to church, and could fix dinner here."

"You see, if you were still in Indianapolis, we wouldn't have this scheduling problem. But I have something to tell you, something absolutely thrilling," she rushed on, her classically beautiful face lighting. "I'm on the short list—the *very* short list—for vice president. That's *the* vice president of the *U.S. of A.,* darling, if Hal Westbrook gets the presidential nomination at the party convention this summer! So you see, I'm going to need you for another campaign. Well?"

Jenna covered her surprise with another hug. "Congratulations! Even if it doesn't all work out in the end, that's great!"

"I'll accept nothing but positive thinking," she declared, rocking Jenna slightly. "I think we could win. When Geraldine Ferraro was on Mondale's ticket in '84, the times weren't right for a woman in the second highest post. But they are now, and *I'm* the ticket to the women's vote, the victims' rights vote, *and* the conservative Midwest vote."

Sincerely happy for her mother, Jenna held to her until her mother set her back at arm's length. "So you can see, if that happens, you can't be hiding out in the woods building tree houses, luxury versions or not."

"I'm not hiding out. Actually, I think I'm finally ready to face some things."

Her mother shook her carefully coiffed head sharply. Frown lines creased her oval face, always the echo of what Mandi would probably have looked like if they had gotten her back after the abduction. After years of desperately hoping the abductor would release Mandi, or at least that her body would be found; after countless crank calls, hours of police and FBI work, and the fruitless searching of many local caves, her mother had given up and had her eldest daughter declared dead. Jenna, though, had never accepted that.

As their feet crunched along to the intersection of the path and the driveway where her car awaited, her mother said, "If you mean you're ready to face or relive the family tragedies we've shared, I don't want you trying it without at least Dr. Brennan's help."

Garth Brennan was a psychiatrist whom Cynthia used as an advisor for her victims' rights work and as a longtime family counselor. "You know he's always urged me to live my life and not look back," Jenna pointed out. "Can't you see I'm doing that now? No more single or joint sessions with Dr. Brennan."

"Jenna, after we lost Mandi, we used to be a team, you and I."

Jenna faced her talented, strong mother, who had made so much good from the bad that had befallen the Kirks and little Ridgeview. She was deeply proud of her and loved her more than her mom would ever know. But the controlling charisma that had made her what she was remained something to be battled.

"No. I'm determined to stay here and build this business and face Ridgeview and the past. That's the healthy thing, the right thing for me now."

"For Pete's sake," her mother muttered, turning away, "then I'd better get elected vice president so I can get you some secret service protection out here—" Jenna had to stretch her strides to keep up, despite the fact she wore work boots and her mother was in high heels. "You have a perfectly beautiful, four-bedroom stone home sitting empty on the edge of town, where you could at least live on the second floor, instead of in this ramshackle, hard-to-heat Victorian that wasn't even new when your grandparents bought it. Do you know how high heating bills may be next winter?"

"As usual, you have insider information? And as for memories—" she plunged on "—I have happy ones here. Kirkhall's the place we were in before Daddy was killed, the place Mandi and I were taken from—"

Her mother stopped with a crunch of gravel, her arms straight at her sides and fists clenched. "You were taken from the dark outdoors, where neither of you would have been if you'd listened to me!" she cried. "You're still not listening to me now, not admitting that you could get hurt out here alone. Oh, I just mean fall out of a damn tree, into a sinkhole or something, or knocking around using your father's old power tools. I worry about you, baby," she pleaded. "You're all I have now."

Tears from a woman so strong she almost never cried, Jenna marveled, blinking back those that prickled her own inner eyelids. Real tears, though not enough to run the waterproof mascara that perfectly highlighted her mother's eyes. Mandi's eyes. They hugged again, while the driver, twenty feet away, pointedly looked in the other direction. Jenna saw it was Vince Sabatka, who often drove her mother and sometimes served as a bodyguard.

"Insider information aside, needless to say, what I confided to you today is embargoed information," her mother said, sniffling. Before Jenna could dig out a wrinkled tissue, her mother produced an initialed handkerchief from the pocket of her pantsuit and blew her nose delicately. "But if I get that call," she whispered, "I'll need you beside me at the convention, and I could use your help in the campaign."

"I'll find a way to be there. Of course I will. No way I'd let you down—not intentionally."

"Not till now. Oh, Jenna, I didn't mean that the way it sounded. It's just...I worry about you, alone in this town without my protection. A town this small and inbred never lets things—scandals—go. You know that."

Cynthia Kirk cocked her head as a muted phone rang. It wasn't Jenna's, tucked in the pocket of her denim jacket, nor was it on her mother. "Mrs. Kirk, your private line," Vince called, producing a cell phone from the depths of the car and holding it out, stiff-armed.

Her mother hurried to take it. Jenna watched her intent expression as she listened to the caller. Whirling, she walked away a few steps, one hand on the trunk of the car. Her shoulders slumped, then squared. She nodded and kept talking. The only words Jenna caught in the blur of them were "nearby now."

"Is something wrong?" Jenna asked when her mother punched off and turned back around. Her face looked strained but stoic, stony. "Something about—what you told me?" Jenna prompted.

She shook her head. "I've got to go check out a situation right now, that's all. I'm sorry I can't stay longer. Vince, the meeting in Bloomington will have to be delayed.'' A man of few words, he opened the back door, his ebony hair gleaming to match his polished shoes. Her mother got in, then rolled down her window.

''Sweetheart, I'll see you later,'' she told Jenna with a tight smile that showed the little web of lines around her mouth and eyes. ''We can talk more about the future. And maybe just one little visit from Dr. Brennan, yes?''

''No,'' Jenna said as the window rolled up and she saw her own face reflected where her mother's had been. As Vince got in and the motor purred to life, Jenna figured her mother hadn't heard her and, even if she had, wouldn't heed her. Not when business demanded the lieutenant governor's presence anywhere but here.

Crossing the Indiana state line on I-70, Cassandra MacCaman pulled her new PT Cruiser into a fast-food restaurant parking lot and headed inside for more coffee. She reminded herself never to do a cross-country drive alone again—but then, who would she bring with her? Divorce had its benefits, but there were drawbacks, too. Besides, she needed the time by herself to think and plan. In the stretch between Albuquerque and Chicago, she'd figured out her entire strategy for the book.

She hit the rest room, then ordered carryout coffee and a Danish. It was such a lovely day that she ate a few bites by her car, then threw the rest of the sickeningly sweet roll in the trash can. Flipping open her cell phone, she scrabbled for her billfold to get her note to herself and punched in Jenna's number at her grandmother Darva's old house. She ran her free hand through her short, spiky red hair as she counted the rings. Two, three, four...

''Hello.''

''You up a tree or something?'' Cassie asked at the

sound of her childhood best friend's voice. ''Jennie, it's me.''

No one but Cassie called Jenna ''Jennie,'' not even Mandi, who had stuck stubbornly with ''Jen.'' But Jennie was a nickname born long ago when, as an eight-year-old, Jenna had protested that Amanda was Mandi, Cassandra was Cassie, Daddy called Mommy ''Cindy,'' and she was the only girl without a cute name. Cassie and Jennie had been best friends since they could recall, even in the early days before the Kirks built the big house. Though events had taken them separate ways, their common losses had also bonded them for life, for they had both lost a parent in the Ridgeview rock slide. And Cassie was the only one who knew how much Jennie had adored her big bro, Mace.

''Cassie? It's so great to hear your voice! No tree houses right now, but I am cleaning house, believe it or not.''

''Not. Listen, I'm back home in Indiana—'' she sang those four words of the old state song ''—about two hours away.''

''I heard about your father's illness. I'm so sorry. The whole town's in shock. Can you stay for a little while?''

''I've taken a leave from work for at least six months. Time to be with him—and to write.'' She raked her fingers through her hair again. ''I should have called you earlier, but I had so much to do—leasing the condo, getting my leave, packing my car to the teeth. I've taken my maiden name back, too.''

''It's under terrible circumstances, but I'll be so glad to see you, to have some time together after so long. If things get tough, you know my doors—house *and* tree house—are always open.''

''That's just what I was getting to. You mind if I stay

with you tonight—since I'll get in a bit late to be crashing in on a sick man…a tough, sick man…''

When her voice caught, Jennie gave her a moment to compose herself. ''Advanced lymphoma is very serious, Cassie, but he's a fighter. I hear he's still going into MacCaman Stone everyday, running the place with an iron—well, a stone fist.''

''I was going to say nothing changes, but I'm praying some things do. See you in a couple of hours.''

Cassie jammed her phone back in her purse and fished out her lipstick, accidentally snagging the articles from the thick stash she'd printed out from the major Indiana newspapers, dated June 6th, 7th, and 8th, 1985. She muttered a curse as she chased the blowing paper across the parking lot. She'd had the originals once, until Mace had thrown them all out when he'd left home, saying they had to get over it somehow.

Finally, she retrieved the paper and stuffed it in her purse. She'd better hide all these somewhere before she stayed with Jennie.

Jenna made certain she had all the ingredients for *pasta putanesca,* then dusted the guest room, which was the bedroom she'd always used when she'd stayed here as a child. She'd never really known her grandfather, one of the last great Ridgeview stone carvers, who had died when Jenna was two. Her mother seldom mentioned him, but Jenna had learned from town talk that he had been strict and stern. Cynthia had been Darva and Cletus Crandal's only child, and Grandpa had been disappointed she showed no artistic talent, because he was sure it would be inherited.

Well, Jenna thought as she moved a tiny vase of violets from her room into Cassie's, it sure was inherited that children disappointed their parents. It had been six days since she'd seen or spoken to her mother. And poor Cassie—Mace, too—with their father…

After shoving the dust mop over the hardwood floors in her own room, she pulled open her bottom dresser drawer. Now that Cassie was coming home and Rod MacCaman's days were numbered, the precious pile of postcards in the old Christmas card box drew her. She dug it out from under her winter sweaters, sat in the padded rocker by the window and opened the box on her knees.

Mace's postcards. Ten, sent in the fifteen years since she'd last seen him, after the day he'd had some blowup with his dad and left home the year Mandi was lost. He had sent these off and on, always to her correct addresses, as though he were watching over her. To the condo in Indianapolis she and her mother shared when Cynthia first became a state senator. To her different dorm rooms at I.U. in Bloomington. And then, this past year, to 1008 Cutter's Camp Road. It was no mystery how he knew where she was, for Cassie was their common bond.

Jenna went through the cards again in order. The first few came while he was getting his geology and business degrees in New Mexico, working two jobs to put himself through college. But some were from all over the country and the world—places where Mace had led caving expeditions or taken *National Geographic* teams of photographers, or later for his job of cave surveying and mapping. The terse notes, though, didn't mention that. They only said things like *In memory,* or *For our shared loss.* Or once, *Remembering the good times.* But they were all signed *Mace* in that bold, unmistakable signature.

She shuffled through them again as if they were playing cards, staring at the glossy photos. Moana Loa Volcano in Hawaii. A pride of lions in Kenya. An ocean scene with palm trees in the Canary Islands. Amazing that there were caves in the Canary Islands, Jenna mused.

Some postcards were sent from closer to home, like Arizona. There were more non-caving scenes from places where, if she couldn't casually ask Cassie about the local caves Jenna researched until she found out. West Virginia had the dangerous Schoolhouse Cave; South Dakota had delicate Jewel; and New Mexico had Lechiguilla, which Cassie said was America's greatest underground wilderness. Mace had even done what was called urban caving in the old water system pipes beneath New York City. A postcard from Wyoming depicted a cave called Great X, for Great Expectations.

"Great expectations..." she whispered, cradling the thin stack of postcards to her breasts. She knew why he never mentioned the caving, which Cassie said was the only passion of his life; he had never married. He knew Jenna had gone through hell in that cave, and she'd told him the last time she'd seen him about her rampant claustrophobia. He wanted to protect her, and he still cared.

She closed her eyes and pictured him, bad-boy handsome, as she'd seen him last, like some kind of rebel *with* a cause. He'd worn leather when it wasn't in style; he'd forgotten to shave before grunge and worn his hair only a bit shaggy when other guys wore theirs long. Black T-shirts, not white, and jeans that always showed dust or mud from his rock climbing. Hair so black it looked blue in the sun, in contrast to those startling green eyes. A rugged, older face, even in his high-school years.

Six-foot, squared-jawed and big-shouldered, but graceful for a man. His voice had gotten deep and raspy, compared to her memories of him as a lanky, curious and stubborn boy, a bit of a loner.

She jumped straight up when the doorbell rang its old-fashioned three-note chime. That couldn't be Cassie already, and she wasn't expecting anyone. She put the cards back in the box and dropped them in the open drawer, closing it with her foot. From the window she could see a small, square U.S. mail truck parked below.

She hurried downstairs and opened the door. Russel Pierce, Ridgeview's postmaster, held a cardboard box slashed with a red, white and blue tape that read PRIORITY MAIL.

"How's it going, Jenna?" Russ was a townie who had never lived far from home, and the nasal Hoosier hills twang always sang through his speech.

"Hi, Russ. Are you driving the rural routes now?"

Russ had been two grades ahead of her—the nerdy math genius of those days. He was a small, sinewy man who ran cross-country in high school and now jogged miles each day when he wasn't coaching the local Little League baseball teams. He had sharp brown eyes that his tinted glasses magnified. He was already going bald and combed his thinning hair forward. He was fully attired in his blue-gray postal uniform, which looked a few sizes too big for him.

"I like to get out and about now 'n' then," he explained. "'Sides, I was heading home and didn't want to leave something that looked this important in your mailbox on the road. Too big to fit in it by four-and-a-half inches. You usually get smaller boxes."

Russ Pierce knew everyone's business in and around town. Jenna always thought he'd be a better editor for the weekly *Ridgeview Reporter* than Mary Drout was, but she supposed he contributed to that impression.

"I really appreciate your dropping it by. Do I have to sign?"

"Oh, yeah, here." He produced a pen and clipboard from beneath the box. "It's too bad about the Godfather getting the Big C, isn't it? But if anyone can lick it, it's Rod MacCaman," he told her as she wrote her name.

"I surely hope and pray so," she said, handing back the pen and clipboard.

Most Ridgeview townies had called Mace's father by the affectionate but respectful nickname of the Godfather since he'd taken over failing MacCaman Stone from his father. The sobriquet was double-edged: Rod ran the only family-owned mill that had survived in these parts, and, like many other men who started out as cutters in the noisy mills, he whispered, much like Marlon Brando's character in the movie *The Godfather*. Cutters were notoriously hard of hearing and too proud to wear hearing aids. Rather than shout like many people who were partly deaf, Rod deliberately talked in a whisper. In the few fights Jenna had seen of the many between Mace and his dad, Mace had been shouting and Rod whispering.

She looked down at her package. Seattle? Who did she know in Seattle?

"I hear Cassie's coming home for a spell. Mace, too?" Russ asked.

Her insides flip-flopped. "I really don't know about Mace, Russ, but Cassie will."

"The thing is," he said dropping his voice, "though I personally think it's a bunch of hooey, some folks still think..."

She stared him down because she knew what was

coming. "...you know," he went on, "that he was somehow...involved."

He didn't need to say more. That was one of the painful things about returning to Ridgeview. Her roots were here and she cared for the people, however eccentric, but even though folks were kind, she'd catch them staring or whispering. Sometimes she felt she might as well wear a sign that labeled her as The Abducted, Surviving Sister Of Missing Girl And Daughter Of A Rock Slide Victim And Ridgeview's Most Famous Woman.

"It's been established Mace wasn't involved. He had an alibi," Jenna countered more sharply that she meant to.

"Well, yeah," he drawled, "guess everybody in the whole school and town had an alibi. See, it wasn't me been talking about Mace off and on."

"No, it was 'folks,' as you say. Honestly, Russ, if you're going to pass on old gossip, at least say from whom."

He shuffled his feet. "Frank Connors, that's who. Don't tell him I said that, since you been seeing him."

"I have not been seeing him. When I first came back, he was nice enough to take me out to dinner a few times. That's all." She didn't mention that Frank had kept calling after that and she'd turned him down. She knew she'd hurt Frank's feelings, but she couldn't see the relationship going anywhere and felt it wasn't fair to him.

"Like Frank says," Russ went on, obviously trying to extricate his foot from his mouth, "it's just so sad Mace been gone all these years."

"Gone on the run, you mean—or did Frank imply that? Doesn't the manager of the only bank in the area and the postmaster have something to do besides rehashing old events?"

"Didn't mean to get you all het up. Really, Jenna," he said, holding up one hand and the clipboard as if she might jump him. "Just passing the time o' day. Frank and Mace were good friends once, but they had their differences over—over things, too."

"I really think all of us have enough to worry about, with problems we have here and now, that we don't need to be resurrecting past griefs," she added, unwilling to let him off easily. But saying that made her feel like a fraud. She had finally figured out that by resurrecting the past, she might be able to look it full in the face, and then—finally—bury it for good.

"Sure, sure, didn't mean nothing different," he said, passing the clipboard from hand to hand. "Well, I was fixin' to get on home quick for an early Little League practise, and here I am yakkin'. See you."

Gratefully, she closed the door behind him and put the lightweight package on the big kitchen table. Grabbing a pair of scissors, she cut the box open. The address still puzzled her; she couldn't recall a client in Seattle, nor had she ordered anything from A Stitch in Time Shop, listed on the return address. Of course, with online and phone ordering these days, anyone could buy anything from anyplace.

She checked the sender's name on the return address label. Alice Kirwin. She didn't know any Alice Kirwin. She hoped it wasn't a mistake, or she'd have to send it back.

A few packing peanuts fell on the table as she lifted out the item. She could read the cross-stitched words before she could see what it was. A mauve background with purple writing. *Laugh and the world laughs with you. Cry and you cry alone.* She saw what it was then.

Inside a clear plastic bag was a heart-shaped pillow, much like the ones Mandi used to collect. And the enclosed gift card read not *To Jenna,* or even *To Jennie,* but *To Jen.*

2

Jenna paced across her big, sunny kitchen, wrapping the phone cord one way, then the other, around her index finger. She knew she shouldn't be tying up her phone in case Cassie called again. But A Stitch in Time had kept her on hold, and now the Seattle operator was taking her good old time, too.

The shop had not been some little establishment where a salesperson might recall a face. Instead, it was a catalog house, with an operator who, even with coaxing, could give Jenna no information on Alice Kirwin beyond the address she had listed on her order.

Jenna jumped when the Seattle operator came back on the line. "Ms. Kirk, I find no Alice Kirwin at that Seattle address in our master directory."

"Then, she could have an unlisted phone number?"

"I can check that, but of course cannot give you the number, should it be unlisted. Do you wish me to check that, anyway?"

"Yes!"

Her nerves were fraying over a simple mistake someone had made in sending her that pillow. But who would mail her something that would have fit so perfectly Mandi's collection of heart-shaped pillows? And what did that embroidered message mean? *Laugh and the world laughs with you. Cry and you cry alone.* Was that a threat? A clue? To what?

But what really rattled her was that the initials of this perhaps bogus Alice Kirwin were A.K., the same as Mandi's Amanda Kirk. It was a long shot, of course, but—

"Ms. Kirk, we have no one with that name, nor any Kirwin family at the address you gave."

Jenna thanked her and cut the connection. She finally realized she was still holding the phone in her hand when it began to beep its warning. She hung up, but she wasn't giving up. She'd call the Seattle police and explain the circumstances. They could go to the address, ask a few questions, describe this Alice Kirwin to her. The smell of the sauce for the pasta began to make her queasy, although she knew she was starved.

She heard a car door slam close by. It was so quiet back in the forest, several hundred feet from the road, that sounds carried. Unless some visitors had driven back here because they'd heard about the stone carvings, it must be Cassie. Forcing a smile when she wanted to explode in tears, she rushed to the front door.

Jenna gasped to see how thin Cassie looked, but when she hugged her and felt each bump of her backbone, she was staggered. Cassie had always been slender, but now she was bony and gaunt. Of course Cassie had problems of her own. A difficult divorce, a father dying. Jenna stifled her instinct to spill her worries about a stupid package with a pillow. She even considered not mentioning Cassie's appearance at all, but they had always been up front as well as supportive of each other.

"Good Hoosier home cooking's going to feed you up, girl!"

"A tough divorce after a bad marriage is not a diet plan I'd do a book on," Cassie kidded as she carried a carpetbag purse and Jenna toted a small suitcase into the house. ''Remember that pillow Mandi had—I think the quote was by the Duchess of Windsor—that said, *You can never be too rich or too thin?* I'm too thin but the other part of that hadn't worked out yet.''

''*You* sent me that pillow!'' Jenna cried, both relieved but puzzled. ''But why didn't you sign your na—''

She stopped in mid-word, for she saw instantly that Cassie had no clue what she was talking about. Surely her bringing up Mandi's pillows right now couldn't be mere coincidence?

''What pillow?'' Cassie asked, looking not at her but at the refinished wicker porch furniture.

''Nothing important,'' Jenna said, realizing she was already going against how the two of them used to share everything. ''Just a gift from an admirer.'' No way she was going to unload all her sudden angst on Cassie when she had so many of her own problems—not quite yet, at least.

''Oh, Jennie, you've done wonders with this place,'' Cassie cried, looking around the high-ceilinged living room with its fireplace, big oval hooked rugs and comfy, overstuffed country furniture.

''There's still a lot to do—refinishing the tables, wall-papering, putting new Formica in the kitchen. I started with the rooms on this floor, but the upstairs is still pretty retro.''

''Heck, this whole damn town is retro, so I keep telling myself I'm gonna love it. Your return to Ridgeview must have been good for you.''

Cassie's beaming smile reassured Jenna that her friend's strong spirit hadn't shrunk, even if her body had. Yet, up this close, Jenna noted that the distinctive, flaming red hair had been colored, so it's natural brilliance must have faded. Cassie had always been so cute, with a pixie face, pert nose and Cupid's-bow mouth to go with the freckles. Now she had bluish hollows under her eyes, as well as smile wrinkles and tiny crow's-feet. Cassie looked older than her thirty years. And she looked as if she was still out west, dressed in a long, full denim skirt and jacket, moccasins, and heavy turquoise-and-silver Navajo jewelry. She should have ridden in on a stagecoach instead of in a car.

"Let's say I'm still working on settling in," Jenna said. "I just hope your homecoming will be good for you, too, despite the fact your dad's so sick. It's a blessing for both of us we're back together for a while. Random phone calls and e-mail just don't make it."

Leaving Cassie's things at the bottom of the stairs, they walked arm in arm through the dining room into the kitchen. The rays of the setting sun had turned the oak floor, cabinets and harvest table a rosy gold.

"My dad was a bear to live with even when he was hale and hearty," Cassie said, accepting the glass of Merlot Jenna poured her. "I'm pretty scared about what he'll be like now."

"I haven't seen him since the diagnosis—well, I hardly ever see him. But maybe facing a serious illness—"

"It's fatal," said Cassie.

"But the point is, maybe it will change his outlook on life, his type-A, authoritative—"

"As much of an optimist as ever, aren't you," Cassie interrupted, her voice bitter. "Since mother died in the rock slide, he's been an overbearing, dictatorial son-of-a-gun, to put it politely."

"But he could still realize how precious time, and you—and Mace—are to him..." Jenna's voice trailed off. She took a big swallow of her wine, then put it down. ''So, I bet you'd like to wash up first, but I figured you'd be starved. After the pasta and salad, we can take our dessert out and eat it in the tree house, unless you don't want to climb the ladder after dark.''

Cassie leaned forward and touched her arm. ''Do you go out after dark, Jennie? How are you...that way, really?''

''It's not the dark that gets me—not if it's outside,'' she confided as they leaned against the kitchen counter in the sun that streamed in over the sink. ''It's closed places—even the cellar, which has electric lights on the ceiling.'' She nodded toward the basement door. ''It's a great storage area and I keep my dad's old tools down there. But it has those thick stone walls and it's almost windowless. Even in daylight, I—I hate to use it.''

''But you've faced losing Mandi? You've accepted it? And the fact your mother's triumphed over it and gone on to new heights?''

Jenna nodded. She almost told her friend about the next lofty rung of Cynthia Kirk's political ladder, but she'd promised she wouldn't. ''At least,'' Jenna assured her as she walked to the stove to stir the *putanesca* sauce, ''I'm working on it. I came home partly to face it and go on.''

She almost blurted out about the pillow, about how it goaded her to do some investigating of who had kidnapped Mandi and her fifteen years ago. But there would be time for all that later. Tonight she would not dump on Cassie, who, if she wasn't anorexic, sure looked it. Tonight they were going to be together, after all these years, and build each other up. Their friendship had always done that when they were kids, so surely it would again.

''Gotta tell you one thing before I go wash up,'' Cassie said, taking another swig of wine. "Well, maybe two."

Jenna looked at her instead of the pasta sauce. "Shoot."

"First, I'm going to take this six months to write a book I've had in my head for a couple of years."

"That's great, I'm proud of you," Jenna said, seizing on the positive note and clinking her goblet to Cassie's. "What about?"

"I hope you'll help me when I tell you, Jennie. It's about your mother. Are you—you look surprised."

"If I am, it's only because no one else has done it yet. And who knows where she'll end up? It could be a great book."

"Is she going to run for governor?" Cassie asked, her voice suddenly professional instead of personal.

"I'm sure you'll be doing interviews with her for this, so you can ask her."

"Higher than governor? Someday, at least? Jennie, Cynthia Kirk is the best and biggest political story ever to come out of Indiana and I'm sure as heck including our illustrious Indiana-born-and-bred vice president, Dan Quayle, in that!" Cassie laughed, but Jenna didn't.

"You *do* mean you'll stick with her political career?"

"A life story, all of it. A biography—an authorized one, I hope. After all, just like you, she's survived two terrible tragedies, so it will be an inspirational book, too. I'd really be grateful for your help with it. What you know, what you can remember—the good *and* the bad."

Jenna put her goblet down on the stovetop again and went back to stirring. Although she knew dredging up the past for Cassie's book might be painful, it could also help. Maybe they would find out some things together.

"I'd like you to check with her first, to see what she says," Jenna said.

"I'm determined to do this," Cassie countered, raking her fingers through her short hair hard enough to make her silver hoop earrings bounce.

They stared at each other for a moment. Cassie crackled with that electric element of personality that emanated from Cynthia, too. Not just strength or stubbornness, for Jenna shared those things. More like raw, run-you-down ambition.

"You had a second thing to tell me," Jenna prompted.

"Maybe you'd better be sitting down for this one. Like what I just said, it could be good news or tough, depending on how you look at it."

"You're not sick, too?"

"Jennie, Mace is coming home. I talked to him last night. He's coming home today."

Mace MacCaman tried to keep his thoughts on factual observations so he could control his damn emotions. Ridgeview had not grown much, though it now had its own Kmart. His truck passed a new trailer park. The sign read Enchanting Acres, though it hardly looked enchanting. Hell, if Dad didn't take him back, maybe he'd live there in a tin trailer and set up local caving expeditions for college kids from I.U.

The outskirts of town sported a few more billboards than he remembered. He noted satellite dishes in yards instead of antennas on roofs. A spiffy-looking sign at the city limits proclaimed Ridgeview, Home Of Indiana's Lieutenant Governor, The Hon. Cynthia Kirk. He shook his head at that, not in disbelief but to cast off the memories that threatened to swamp his courage.

Mace avoided driving by either his childhood home

or Kirkhall, but drove past the old high school. The houses around it looked smaller and dingier, if that was possible. Its windows were boarded up—just as well, he thought. *Rest in Peace, Ridgeview High.*

The old sign in front that had once announced game days, drama productions and vacations now advertised some sort of flea market held in the old stadium where he'd been the heir apparent for quarterback. That is, until he'd quit the team his junior year to have more time for caving. No one in town, especially not his coach, his dad, or Mandi, had ever forgiven him for that, though he guessed Jenna might have understood. And if his mom had been alive then, she'd have stood up for him.

He drove west out of town, away from MacCaman Stone and into Sunset Cemetery. Parking near his mom's grave, he let his truck idle and got out. He'd been back to Ridgeview five times during the past fifteen years, but no one except Cassie knew that, since he'd only come here. Now he had the crazy urge to hug his mom's headstone, so he knelt and wrapped his arms around it and pressed his face to the cool, chiseled letters: *Susan L. MacCaman, April 6, 1942–July 4, 1979.* Many of the tombstones here were carved of limestone into tree stumps, distinctive in the area. But this was of Italian marble Dad had ordered, with garlands of stone roses curled around the edge. Mom had once had a great rose garden and she'd wanted to see Italy, and Dad admitted he'd never paid enough attention to either of those things. At Cassie's suggestion, under the name and dates was a quote from a Wordsworth poem, which read *"But she is in her grave and, oh, the difference to me."*

"I'm back, maybe for good," Mace said aloud. "I'm gonna try like hell to live with him for the days he's got left."

A jet roaring high overhead jolted Mace. His whole body lurched before he realized what had startled him. Not the plane, but the memory of the roar on that dreadful day.

The town's Fourth of July celebration had seemed as much a company party as a patriotic picnic, that year when he and Mandi were twelve and Cassie and Jenna were ten. The parade of several floats, the high-school band, and numerous kids on decorated bikes or in wagons their mothers pulled had begun at the town square and ended up at MacCaman's Deep Heart Quarry. The profits from it had been keeping most Ridgeview residents financially afloat, and the MacCamans were footing the whole celebration today. Catered food for four hundred stretched down plank tables covered with plastic tablecloths; cans of pop and beer swam in sweating galvanized tin tubs of chipped ice. When the fireworks began after dark, some climbed the stone slabs or piles of grout for a better view.

At first, when the rumbling began, Mace thought it was a big fireworks blast, maybe a display that just hadn't been launched yet. And it took a moment—he'd gone to sneak another beer—for him to realize the shrieks and screams were not cries of awe or delight. A couple of limestone blocks, each weighing tons had given way, slipped and crashed—

Flashlight beams popped on and stabbed the darkness. Shouts, panicked ones: "Someone's pinned by the blocks! Dear God, I think someone could be under there! Anybody missing? Check around—anybody not here?"

Cries, names being called.

"Jenna, Mandi!" Mrs. Kirk screamed, dragging both girls past Mace, who stood suddenly frozen with fear. "Your father—your father was standing right up there!"

"Where the hell's your mother?" Dad asked him, running past him in the chaos. "I thought she was over there with Cassie!"

Then Mace went berserk, running, hurling himself at a massive block, clawing at limestone until his hands were bleeding and he was choking with dust, gasping, sobbing. Finally, his frenzied father hauled him away.

It took an eternity for the shrieking, blinking emergency vehicles to arrive, but it was the MacCaman derricks and massive machinery that were ultimately needed to move the monoliths and rubble that had slid and settled. His father was even at the controls of the derrick that moved the last block, uncovering what was left of the five missing, including John Kirk and Mace's mother.

Shaking his head to drag himself back to the present, Mace stared at the empty plot next to hers, then lifted his eyes to the crest of the hill where lay Mandi and Jenna's dad's grave, close to the other three from that disaster. He knew he partly went caving—sometimes extreme caving—in defiance of that day and its earthshaking tragedy. Daring the tons of rock over his head to harm him was the only way he knew to face and fight his fears that the catastrophe had somehow been his family's—his father's—fault.

Mace was glad they hadn't put the town memorial here, where tourists would come traipsing through to ruin his privacy. The Ridgeview Rock Slide Memorial sat in the middle of the old town square, a tribute not only to the five dead but to Cynthia Kirk and his dad, who had headed up the committee to raise the money and had chosen the unique design.

He got back in his truck and started to drive, but stopped again where the cemetery gate met Cutter Camp

Road. He craned his neck and squinted to peer into the fringe of shadows at the edge of the Stone Forest that surrounded what was now Jenna Kirk's home. He knew that forest, with all the stone animals and fantastic carved scenes, like the back of his hand, even in the dark. He imagined her now, coming through the trees, waving and glad to see him, forgiving him for running away—but he kept picturing her at sixteen, the day he'd said goodbye. She had tried to smile for him, but tears had run down her cheeks as he left.

Thudding his fist on the steering wheel, he crossed Cutter Camp and turned down Chestnut, smiling grimly at the three right-angle turns it took to get into town by skirting the old Mother Lode quarry. If a car ignored the barrier wall, with its glow-in-the-dark decals, and crested the earth embankment, it would free fall two-hundred feet. In the fifties, two teens had died drag racing when their car didn't handle the first turn. To the north lay Pioneer and Big Apple, the latter so named because limestone blocks from it had been used to erect several New York City buildings.

Though few outside the Hoosier state knew it, stone from south-central Indiana had built such American edifices as the Empire State Building, the Pentagon, the interior of the Lincoln Memorial, and Rockefeller Center, not to mention numerous churches, stores and campus buildings across the fruited plain.

His truck bumped over the unused railroad tracks that once spiked out toward the working quarries. These days trucks did the stone hauling. At least his dad had modernized the business, but Mace was somehow certain the old man hadn't changed in the ways that mattered. And sadly, he was sure as hell his dad would never beat advanced lymphoma, no matter how well he'd beaten other odds in his sixty years of life.

Mace turned down the long gravel driveway past the simple sign that read MACCAMAN STONE, EST. 1946. Actually, the stone mill on this site was a lot older, but the year after World War II was when his grandfather, Mason MacCaman, took over, riding the business through boom times to the devastating bust in the glass-and-metal skyscraper era of the seventies. His father had taken up the MacCaman mantle in hard times and hung on, and he'd expected the same from his only son. Today, mostly because Mace couldn't bear another death where he couldn't say goodbye, he was coming to wave the white flag, if not of surrender, at least of a clean start.

He parked in one of the newly lined visitor spaces and walked in. So that the old man didn't drop dead at the sight of him, Mace had planned to phone from outside town. But Cassie had told him that, according to Jenna, his dad was going to the office every day. Even though it was almost dusk outside, he figured he'd still find the old slave driver here.

"Yes, may I help you?" an attractive blond receptionist in her twenties enquired in the front office. The place was still laid out the same, though the floors were carpeted in place of the old linoleum. Mace noted a fax machine, a computer and new furniture, too.

"I'd like to see Mr. MacCaman."

"Do you have an appointment, sir?"

"One of long-standing. Tell him the prodigal son, Mason the third, is here."

"Oh!" she said, breaking into a big smile. "I knew you weren't one of the salesmen, and the architects always come in with big briefcases. You know, you do resemble him. Have you just—yes, of course I'll tell him,'' she interrupted herself and turned abruptly away to punch a button on a phone panel.

His stomach knotted even tighter as Mace glanced around. No more crude collection of stone samples glued to a Peg-Board. Backlighted glass boxes with blowups of buildings hung from the walls. Glossy brochures and copies of *Architectural Digest* were arranged on the veneer-thin polished tabletop of Salem buff limestone. He glanced out the new picture window, which overlooked the outside of the mill, with its familiar piles of huge cast-off stone known as grout. Multi-tonned blocks leaned like kids' toys, seasoning in the sun; the massive stone-moving equipment was new and there was less of it, just as there were fewer men working the quarries in these times of computerization and cutbacks.

He looked at the receptionist again—Rita Carlson, the nameplate on her desk read—to see if he was even going to be invited in. But before she could say anything, the door behind her banged open. His father stood there, thinner, grayer. But he filled that door and the room as he'd once filled Mace's life.

''Well, I'll be damned,'' came the familiar whisper Mace had not heard in so long. ''Thought I told you not to come back 'less you were ready to walk into MacCaman and work to take it over someday.''

''I finally heard you.'' Mace spoke loudly, noting how his father watched his mouth intently as if he were reading his lips.

''Then, I'll kill the fatted calf—if you're not just passing through.''

''That's up to you. I was hoping you'd be willing to hire and train a geologist with a business minor who can spot limestone outcrops better than you ever did.''

"That'd be the day hell freezes over! Better come on in," Mason Rodney MacCaman, Jr., told his son. "You got here 'fore Cassie showed up, but the three of us gonna have us a real whing-ding."

Mace saw that just gesturing him forward made the older man totter against the door frame. Despite the powerful persona, the physical shell was frighteningly frail. The shock of that kept Mace rooted to the spot. Then he went to his father. He wanted to hug him, but he only took his arm.

"I'm fine," Rod whispered, but he didn't pull back. "My docs say this new chemo stuff's gonna help better'n a shot of prime booze—which they told me to lay off of. Wait till you see the place, 'cause it's night and day since you left."

Mace saw tears in Rita Carlson's eyes. He turned away to follow his father down the hall to a redecorated office, with two glass walls that overlooked the interior of the noisy mill. But it was the tears in his own eyes that almost made him trip.

3

Although Jenna and Cassie had talked until past midnight, Jenna couldn't sleep. She sighed and tossed, pummeling her pillow and churning her blankets to waves. For years, she'd slept with a light on. Finally, she got up to pace, hoping to make herself at least as tired physically as she was emotionally.

Mace was coming back, just as she had, to face everyone—to pick up the pieces. Only, he had returned to be near his father, while she had returned, at least in part, to escape her mother's dominating influence in her life. Jenna couldn't believe she would soon see Mace, talk to him. Cassie had said he was coming home today.

Jenna tried not to make movies in her mind of their reunion. Should she give him a sisterly kiss? Did he still love Mandi? Although he had never married, had he fallen in love with someone else? Cassie said he had lots of friends, but no one in particular. Of course, she could never tell Mace she still had feelings for him, when he'd never been hers in the first place. He had been Mandi's.

And if he asked if she'd been seeing anyone? Not that it would matter to him, but she'd probably better mention that his old friend Frank Connors had taken her out to dinner when she first came back. Mace and Frank had been best buddies for a while, but were fiercely competitive, too.

Though Jenna had never admitted it to Dr. Brennan,

she worried that the traumatic childhood roller coaster she'd been on had stunted her emotional growth, and she'd never get over the adolescent crush she'd had on Mace. Surely that's all it was. In trying to hold on to Mandi, she held onto Mace, too. When she saw him again, she'd know it was over. They would talk about the good times and the bad. Maybe they could be friends.

Her thoughts rolled on and on. But that heart-shaped pillow was bothering her, too. Scaring her. She'd call the Seattle police tomorrow for sure. No one but Mandi had ever called her Jen.

At 2:00 a.m., she got three flashlights from her bedside table—she was always prepared, in case one or more failed—and stepped out into the upstairs hall. Leaving the hall light off so she wouldn't wake Cassie, whose door was slightly ajar, she went into the third bedroom. She quietly closed its door and turned on the light. Though it was the smallest bedroom, it had three doors, one leading to the hall, one to the closet, and one to the attic. Unfortunately, the attic had never been wired for "the electric," as her grandmother used to say, so Jenna usually only went up there during the day. As she opened that door, a cold draft wafted past her.

She froze, feeling again that breath of the cave so long ago. "That's all over. Go on," she whispered to herself, even as the spring wind howled around the lofty eaves.

With two flashlights on and the third in her robe pocket, she went up the stairs, stooping under the slanted roof at the top. During the day the four narrow windows made it quite bright up here. The attic was not insulated, so it was cold in cool weather and "hotter than the hinges of Hades," as Gram used to say, in the summer. Maybe it was stupid to do this right now in the dark, when the slanted walls seemed to be leaning in, pushing her down.

"No, you're fine," she told herself. "This is a big attic. *Your* attic."

She marched straight to the cardboard box she was sure held the heart-shaped pillows—but when she opened it she saw she was wrong. This was the one with Mandi's china cats and stuffed cat pillows. She'd packed them together, the stuffed felines acting as padding for the breakable ones. When Jenna had returned to Ridgeview, Mom had asked her if she wanted Mandi's things, instead of leaving them in Kirkhall—and Jenna had said yes. She had boxes of her sister's goods in both the attic and the cellar, but she hadn't found the time or the courage to put any of them out yet.

Annoyed that she hadn't remembered its location, she finally found the carton that held the pillows in the other corner. The noise seemed incredibly loud as she ripped the masking tape from the top of the carton. Resting one flashlight on another box, she shone the second beam on the contents of the open box. She lifted the pillows out, each in the plastic bag her mom had put them in long ago.

Mandi's pillows were varied colors, and all but a few had words on them. *I Shot J.R.,* the top one said, then in smaller print, *Watch the premiere of Dallas.* The second one read, *You've come a long way, baby! Virginia Slims.*

This was like opening a time capsule Jenna thought. Mandi's life—at least, her life in Ridgeview—had stopped in 1985. So much had happened; so much had changed. What would she ever think if she came back?

Sharing a plastic bag were two small pillows that used a heart in the place of the word *love.* Mandi always used to say "heart," anyway. One read *I "heart" my cat,* another, *I "heart" Trivial Pursuit.*

Beneath them was the pillow Cassie had mentioned, about never being too rich or too thin. It didn't say here that the quote was by the long-dead Duchess of Windsor. Leave it to Cassie, reader and researcher, to know that. Surely it was mere coincidence that Cassie and the pillow arrived the same day. She had always trusted—still did trust—Cassie with her life.

Next, she saw the large pillow Mandi had given Mom, which Cynthia had put with the others when Mandi was lost. In bold fuschia and fringed with pink, old-fashioned lace, it declared, *A woman's place is in the House—and in the Senate.* Cynthia hadn't become a state senator until three years after Mandi was lost, but this pillow was a prophetic, feminist statement that her mother had delighted in.

Jenna held it to her for a moment, as another memory assaulted her. Her mother, usually so calm and controlled, had become hysterical when Jenna was the only one released that night in the Stone Forest. Though she'd been half drugged and exhausted, Jenna recalled how her mother had grabbed her shoulders. Sobbing, she shook her and shouted, "Where's Mandi? Mandi! No, dear God, no! We've got to find her. It can't...can't be just you! Where's Mandi?"

Dr. Brennan had counseled Jenna more than once that her mother would have screamed just the opposite if Mandi had been found and Jenna remained missing. He'd always urged her to look ahead, not back.

Playing her light beam into the carton, Jenna stared down at the two pillows in the bottom. Gram had embroidered the smaller one for Mandi. It showed Mandi's own signature, with the heart-dotted *i.* The other read *Absence makes the heart grow fonder.*

"I thought Sunday was supposed to be a day of rest!" The man's shout, coming from behind and below, startled Jenna. She grabbed for the ladder and jerked around, balancing her small portable chain saw before she turned it off.

For one moment she had thought it might be Mace. She didn't recognize the voice, but she'd been thinking—hoping—he'd come over sometime in these two days since he'd been home. But below her, looking up, stood Garth Brennan.

"Dr. Brennan, you startled me. With this saw going, I didn't hear you. Never call out to someone up a ladder, especially someone holding an instrument of destruction."

"I've been watching for a while and can't stay long. Are those limbs all dead?"

"I need a few removed before I put a children's tree house here. The wood and glass will be delivered this week. Later, I'll photograph it, put it on the Web site and in the brochures, and invite some of the local kids to enjoy it, too."

"Always the altruistic angle, just like your mother."

"It's not an angle with me, and I hope not with her."

"I didn't mean that as it sounded. You know, Jenna, she's worried these risks you're taking are going to backfire." He stepped forward to take hold of the bottom of her extension ladder as she came down.

"I take precautions," she said, stopping and looking down at him until he stepped back so she wouldn't descend into his embrace. "I don't want to hurt your feelings, but I really need to work out being back here on my own. No more counseling sessions, formal or informal.''

''So Cynthia said,'' he replied, taking his pipe from his pocket and tamping tobacco into it with a golf tee. ''I'm merely stopping by today to tell you I consider myself always on call for you. I'm actually here,'' he added, as she put the saw on the ground and he lit his pipe, ''to see my aunt Mary.''

That made her feel better. Mary Drout had been the editor of the *Ridgeview Reporter* for as long as Jenna could recall. Garth had not been reared in Ridgeview, but had often visited over the years. At least he hadn't made a trip down here to see her, Jenna thought. She tried not to feel indebted in any way to him, as Mom had paid his fees over the years, but he always made her think she should be. Part of his psychiatrist couch-side manner, she supposed.

Then, too, he exuded trustworthiness, maybe because of the deep voice and calm demeanor. He was her father's age, so he always made her wonder if Dad would have aged so well. The dove-gray eyes, prematurely silver hair and professorial good looks made Garth Brennan seem like someone you could always confide in.

He and several other doctors had an established family counseling practice in an Indianapolis suburb, but it had been his willingness to testify in high-profile court cases about victims' rights that put him in her mother's orbit. For a while, Jenna had thought the two of them might become romantically involved. But amazingly, her mom had never become serious about anyone after Dad died. Seven or eight years ago Dr. Brennan had married an attractive, much younger lawyer, and they now had a daughter in elementary school.

''Actually, I'm doing what you suggested more than

once—coming back here and starting over,'' she told him as they walked toward the house together. Though she didn't approve of smoking, his pipe gave off a pleasant tang.

''Jenna, I never meant you should come back to the very place that has traumatic memories for you, and people who might not be willing to let the past rest in peace.''

''I'm fine here, forging ahead and not looking back unless I absolutely must.''

He pursed his lips and nodded in one of his noncommittal gestures, half questioning, half accepting. Let him think she was still not looking back, she thought. The caveat she'd tacked onto the end of her promise was the key: *Unless I absolutely must.*

She'd received a return call from the Seattle police department early yesterday evening. The sergeant had told her that no residence existed with the address Alice Kirwin had given for A Stitch in Time. Jenna had to admit she'd hit a dead end, but it had made her more curious than ever to start looking at the past here again.

Later that sunny Sunday afternoon, Jenna stopped studying the diagram she'd made of the children's tree house and walked to Green Eye. She loved the forest, but sometimes needed a bit of open sky. The heavens over this particular quarry always seemed as vast as the huge, rectangle of emerald water itself. The quarry was where Ridgeview kids went swimming and fishing, and lazed the summer days away. Her property line stopped at the edge of it; the land beyond still belonged to MacCaman Stone, however derelict it now was as a quarry.

She climbed the familiar, tilted giant block hanging

partway over the water, from which everyone used to dive. Everyone but Mandi, that is, who feared she'd looked like a drowned rat when all that thick, curly hair got wet. Mandi looking like a drowned rat—that was a good one, Jenna thought, and laughed. At least she could take joy in some of the past.

She was about to stretch out against the sun-warmed limestone when she gazed across the green glint of water and saw a man on the rocks. The far sides rose up much steeper than these. He was not sitting or standing, but edging precariously along a lofty ledge, his face toward the stone. In a black sweatshirt and jeans, with arms outstretched, he literally clung to the buff-hued, vertical rock face, high above the cold water.

Mace. It might be—*must* be Mace.

She stood and watched as he inched confidently along the cliff the old-time cutters had made using huge dinosaurs of machines called channelers. The limestone had been quarried in layers, each leaving a ledge about a foot wide before a twelve-foot drop-off to the next level. The man was five layers above the water. Mace, and sometimes Frank Connors in a challenge, were the only ones who used to dive off the ledges instead of the big stones that lay lower on this side. Over there, they had to turn carefully on the narrow ledge and dive out far and hard to keep from hitting the other ledges on the way down. Surely he wasn't going to dive today.

Jenna left the heated bed of her block and started around the closest end of the quarry. She had considered just watching him until he climbed back out, but her feet took her toward him, past the rusted derricks that had once hauled blocks up the cliff face. Out of breath, her heart beating hard from her exertion—or from his nearness—she stopped on a tilt of stone slightly above but beyond him. He seemed so intent, his arms spread out either to get handholds or for balance. Though he was tall and broad-shouldered, he still seemed graceful.

As if he sensed her presence, he slowly turned his head and looked up. "Jenna!" he called, and his voice echoed back and forth across the stone and water.

"I'd say be careful, but I recall you know what you're doing."

"Stay there. I'll be right up."

She held her breath when he disappeared, but he had only gone into a narrow cleft in the stone. His head appeared, then he hoisted himself up and clapped dirt off his hands. As he started toward her, a smile on his face and squinting into the sun, wearing no sunglasses to obscure his eyes, she needed to fill the air with talk.

"How did you do that without a rope?"

"It's called chimneying. Like a crab-walk, only you go up or down in a narrow place."

His deep-set eyes were the color of the water, and she wanted to swim in them. He was so tanned that his teeth looked stark white. His ebony hair was not quite short enough to be a military buzz, but was what her father used to call a "businessman's cut." More lines and angles than she remembered etched his strong-willed face. He looked bulkier in the chest and thighs than before—but what did she expect after fifteen years? She could tell exactly how much she'd grown since she'd seen him last: her eyes used to be level with his shoulder, but now she gazed directly at his mouth. When he spoke, his dark eyebrows lifted.

"Jenna."

When he hugged her hard, the sky seemed to cartwheel over the solid stone on which they stood.

* * *

Mace could not believe how she'd blossomed. Not lanky anymore, Jenna was both svelte and athletically shapely. Curly auburn hair, which glinted almost red in the sun, framed her oval face and highlighted her wide-set, dark blue eyes. Either she was blushing or her healthy sun color made it look that way. The once-thin face with a hundred expressions had softened to a distinctive, mature beauty. She seemed steadier, too, although she trembled in his arms.

He didn't kiss her, though he wanted to. He was afraid it would be the wrong kind of kiss. Cupping her face in his hands, Mace studied her, but he didn't want her to think he was searching for resemblances to Mandi, so he let go. Jenna had never looked or been like anybody else. He wished Cassie had not let it slip years ago that Jenna had had a wild crush on him. Then it had amused him; while he'd been away it had touched him; but now it intrigued him. Yet, he lectured himself, he'd better keep his distance. There were definitely things about the past she didn't need to know.

"I was coming over to see you, but figured I'd better call first," he said lamely as they stepped apart. "With the family reunion, I've been busy. I wouldn't have gone out today either, except Dad was sleeping and Cassie went into town for groceries and some stuff."

"And you had to see Green Eye again," she finished for him. They jumped off the rock and walked back around toward her side of the quarry. "Cassie told me you and your dad are getting along pretty well."

As they started into the fringe of her forest, he nodded and shrugged. "Better than I'd expected. Listen," he rushed on, "I'd like to see your tree houses. How about a quick tour? Since I'm going back to work at MacCaman—"

"It's true? You'll be staying in Ridgeview?" She looked and sounded so transparently excited that his pulse picked up its beat.

"You think I shouldn't, or can't handle it?"

"I didn't say that. If I can flourish here, you can, too."

"Jenna, no one thinks *you* had a part in your own abduction."

"That's water over the dam here, Mace—"

He touched her lips with his fingers, then withdrew his hand. "It might be water over the dam with you and Cassie, but I'm not an idiot. I'm going to try to make a go of this, but I don't ever want you or anyone else lying to me, even to protect me. I've got to admit, caving's my passion, and it's also been my great escape. But there's nowhere to run anymore."

He was surprised at all that had fallen out of him, when he hadn't shared it with anyone else. His fellow cavers called him Caveman, instead of MacCaman, because he spoke only when he had to, at least underground. Nods and grunts often suited him. But here, at home, back at Green Eye with Jenna...

"I didn't mean to mislead you," she said. "I've faced up to a lot here, too, and there are still ripples in Ridgeview about everything. I *do* understand," she said earnestly. "I guess my tree houses are my escape, a perfect place for privacy, only aboveground, not under."

"You know, from the time I was a kid I wanted this forest," he admitted, forcing himself to look around instead of at her. "I sometimes wandered through it at night when I shouldn't have been out. With all the carved treasures here, it was almost like Disneyland—or like exploring a cave, with all its special stone features."

"I do love it, even if it's a bit lonely sometimes. I

have more good memories than bad here,'' she added, almost defensively.

''If I had your acres, I'd eventually own not only Green Eye but everything that surrounds it, except the cemetery. You just let me know if you want to sell—as if I had that kind of money right now.''

''Mace MacCaman, no way you're getting my land!''

They grew silent, walking through the forest and looking up at the large tree house wrapped around several sturdy trunks. Their feet crunched last autumn's leaves in unison.

''That other smaller one beyond,'' she said, pointing, ''I use strictly for an office in good weather. Have laptop, will climb. And I'm building a model for a classic children's tree house beyond that.''

He put a hand on the railing of the narrow, open stairs that circled the tree. ''Let's go up,'' he said, and smiled.

''What does this remind you of?'' Jenna asked Mace as they stood on the narrow porch that wrapped around two sides of the tree house.

''It reminds me of 'Me Tarzan, you Jen.'''

''You mean Jane,'' she said, grinning.

He gave a half yodeling, half screeching Tarzan yell until he had her laughing so hard she had to hold her sides.

''No chimps or bananas hanging up here,'' she told him when she caught her breath, ''but I do have a stash of wine and chocolate. I guess that's my adult version of the fruit juice and graham crackers Mandi and I used to have in our tree house.'' She sobered at last. ''This tree house always reminds me of the one my dad built Mandi and me once. I believe you even slept up there more than one night when your dad threw you out— Oh, I'm sorry to bring up that memory.''

''This tree house is a mansion next to that thing,'' he protested, leaning on the railing to survey the view before he looked back at her. ''You know, I was always afraid you'd worry I was spying on you, since it was outside your bedroom window at Kirkhall, when I was just trying to be...''

''Close to Mandi,'' they finished in unison.

They gazed out into the verdant, new leaves of the tree canopy. ''You're right about the change from primitive to palatial, as tree houses go,'' she admitted. ''I guess this reminds me of that old one because the feeling is the same. A closeness to nature, escape, freedom— like what you said about caving. Let me show you the inside.''

She unlocked the front door of the building she'd called Home Tree Home in her publicity. She loved this place and could live up here for weeks. With Mace, maybe years.

She was so aware of herself physically with him: the way she climbed the two sets of open stairs to the landings ahead of him, the way she positioned herself in relation to his body, the way the breeze blew her hair against her cheek and mouth.

''The wood is cedar, including the shake shingle roof,'' she began, once again needing to fill the silence between them with rational words. ''I chose materials to blend in, not stand out.''

''It's great the way two of the trees come right up through the middle of it, as pure as any giant stalagmite column I've ever seen. Amazing, what fits in here—even a kitchen counter, a chair and a bed, a big one.''

''I can't stand small beds, even up here,'' she blurted,

"but the chair and table are downsized. I built the table myself with leftover wood."

"I'm impressed. How much of the construction for these do you do yourself?"

"Most of it is assembled on the ground and then winched up. I brought a local team in for this, but I supervised—and pounded as many nails as they did. What? Why are you looking at me like that?"

"As I said, I'm impressed." He had been looking her over head to toe, but now he glanced out each window. "I might just have you build something like this for me someday. I'd want to design my own, though, because I've always known what I wanted."

Jenna realized she had been holding her breath, and she let it out carefully.

"Deal?" His thick eyebrows lifted, and he grinned at her across the foot of the quilt-covered bed.

"Deal," she said, and they shook hands. But it was Jenna's entire being that he really shook. So much for her being over him. So much for being able to separate the past from the present.

Subj: Children's Tree House
Date: 4/30/00 10:24:47 p.m.
US Mountain Standard Time
From: alkin@pittfreenet.com
To: outonalimb@ind.net
Re: A custom-designed child's tree house

I have seen your sample and would like to order a child's tree house. Single ladder approach, floor 8' x 8'. Roof of light brown asphalt shingles from an old garage. Room for 2 sleeping bags. Wooden bin lined with plastic to keep squirrels out of graham crackers and apple juice. Material—old clapboards from my dad's lumberyard.

This would be a dream place for me—hope for you, too.

Alicia Kincaid

Jenna was puzzled, then horrified by this message among the business e-mail sent last night. She printed it out for evidence—of what, she wasn't sure—in her tree-house office the next morning. But in reading it in black-and-white, she handled it as if it would burn her, barely touching the edges of the page.

This must be some sort of sick joke. Who was tormenting her? This was no legit order, but a description of the tree house her dad had built at Kirkhall for her and Mandi the year before he died.

Jenna got hold of herself. She wasn't going to back off. She stopped pacing in her tiny office loft, sat back down at her laptop and clicked the reply icon. Though she wanted to flame the sender into oblivion, instead she typed in Please include your phone number and snail mail address on all orders and hit the send button.

It couldn't be Cassie, or even Mace, teasing her, could it? She shoved her hair back from her face, both hands gripping her skull. Suddenly, her head felt as if it would explode. Yesterday afternoon, she and Mace had reminisced about the old tree house and talked about her building one for him someday. But many had been up in that Kirkhall tree house over the years. The number of people who knew about the stash of crackers and apple juice she and Mandi used to have there, though, would be far fewer.

She agonized as time slipped by, then jumped as the online voice declared, *You've got mail.*

There, she thought, as the new message line appeared. At least Alicia Kincaid, who was probably also Alice Kirwin, was going to answer her. It wasn't some dead end, like trying to trace who had sent the pillow. But then she saw the subject line read mailer daemon. Trembling, she highlighted the new message and clicked the read icon.

Your e-mail is being returned to you because there was a problem with its delivery. The address alkin@pittfreenet.com had permanent fatal errors.

She stared at those last three words until her eyes teared up and the whole screen blurred. For the first time in years she surrendered to soul-wrenching sobs.

4

"I'm putting you in good hands for a tour this morning, Mace," Rod MacCaman told his son and gave him a feeble slap on the back. Mace blinked back tears at the thought of the years he had missed with his father, who might not even have another year left.

"I'd show you around the mill myself," Rod went on, "but need to get a little more strength back after that last round of those chemo poisons that pass for medicine these days. Clay, you remember Mace, don't you?" Rod asked, when his mill foreman appeared in the door of the office.

"Sure do. You're a blast from the past," Clay Henshaw said with a taut grin. "Tall and skinny, running errands in the summers before the entire business changed. Glad to see you back, Mace."

Mace shook hands with Clay. Mace had noted, while immersing himself in everything he could read about the company this weekend, that Clay now held the title vice president of operations. Even the term *foreman* had been updated around here.

"Good to be back," Mace told Clay, then realized he might not be the only one putting on a front. Clay's cold, pale blue eyes did not match the tight tilt of his lips.

Clay Henshaw was a thickset redhead whose hair color had faded, unlike the temper that Rod MacCaman claimed went with it. Yet Rod had also said that Clay had a good rapport with the men, both the young techies hired right out of college and the veteran mill locals. Clay looked straight yuppie white-collar to Mace, with his wrinkled chinos and tieless white shirt. Only a slight beer belly made him resemble the T-shirted workers on the mill floor.

"Give him the dollar tour, Clay, not the cheapo one," Rod said as he sank into his leather desk chair. "And save the big news for me."

"What big news?" Mace asked as he took off his jacket and laid it over a chair. He unbuttoned his shirt, which felt like a straightjacket, anyway, and began to roll up his sleeves.

"Naw, after you look around, get a grasp of things," Rod whispered, and Mace knew that was the way it was going to be.

"Dad says you have three sons," Mace said, as Clay led him from the office and down metal stairs onto the floor of the noisy mill.

"Great kids, ages fifteen, twelve and ten," Clay told him, raising his voice to be heard above the din of machines. "After dealing with that bunch, keeping these guys here in line's nothing. We live in the old Gray homestead on Cutter Camp."

"That would make you Jenna Kirk's closest neighbor."

"Yeah, but still distant. Not even a stone's throw would get us there. She said the boys can hike in the forest, but I told them to watch out for wolves now."

"Wolves?" Mace demanded, swinging around to face Clay at the bottom of the stairs. "Does Jenna know that?"

"I dunno. Haven't spotted any, and just heard it myself a couple days ago. It'll be in the *Reporter* soon enough."

From makeshift shelves of planks, Clay handed Mace a hard hat and put one on himself. Clay's read Floor Boss. "There're actually timber wolves making a comeback in some rural areas," Clay went on. "I hope no hunt-happy idiots go gunning for them and hit something else, but we don't need the wolves picking off pets or farm animals, either."

At least timber wolves didn't climb trees like human wolves did, Mace thought, recalling only too well how attracted he'd felt to Jenna when she showed him her tree house. He shook his head at another thought. Jenna, living at her Gram's house in a forest with wolves, like in some Grimms' fairy tale. But he knew it would take more than timber wolves to scare her off. He wondered exactly what it would take.

"You're about thirty now, right?" Clay asked as he handed Mace a pair of ear protectors. Clay didn't put his on, but instead shoved them through his belt so they could hear each other, and Mace followed suit.

"Thirty-three," Mace corrected him. "And you're about ten years older, with a lifetime of experience at MacCaman, right?" He could see where Clay was going with this. He understood, even sympathized. He'd come home to learn the stone business, but it was still a tough man's world, and he was going to have to assert himself early to avoid being sabotaged.

"You got it," Clay said in a clipped tone, taking a wider stance and crossing his arms over his barrel chest. "Just like my father—and yours—I worked my way up and know this mill, its feeder quarries and the whole shebang like the back of my hand."

Mace saw that hand had become a fist as Clay spun

away to lead him first down the massive concrete floor between the painted yellow safety lines. But they soon turned off toward the huge conveyers, which took raw slabs of limestone through a dozen grinders, sawers and polishers until they emerged as flat, gleaming wall panels at the far end.

"No place here for human carvers and very few for cutters anymore," Clay told him gruffly as they watched. "Instead of the entire skeleton of the building being thick stone now, it's only the thin skin on top of the steel bones."

"What keeps the dust down?" Mace asked. "Everyone in here used to look like ghosts."

"Water sluices at each function—like everything, controlled from up there," Clay said, and pointed at a balcony area where two men ran the entire operation from their computerized control panels. "And learning about that's a whole new ball game."

After he brusquely introduced Mace to everyone, Clay's tour ended in the massive yards, where blocks that had been cut from below the water table were arrayed in rows until the air cured them of their quarry sap. Dry stone was the buff hue of ripe wheat; wet stone was more bluish. This lot was drying to what Clay called a Rolls-Royce gray.

The smell, the sight, the solidity of the stone lured Mace, who even now half wished that he was caving. While Clay obviously stood clear of tilted blocks, Mace got close to them, touching them and walking under them as if they were gigantic animals he could pet.

"Can't believe you do that, after the rock slide at Deep Heart, however long ago it was," Clay told him as they started back to the offices. "If I were you—or Jenna Kirk, either—I wouldn't have come back."

Mace turned to face him just outside the building. That had almost sounded like a threat. "I appreciate your sharing your expertise here today, Clay. I'd like to think you and I will be able to work well together."

"I'll be here. I'm not running."

Their eyes met and held. His dad hadn't said so, but it was blatantly obvious that Clay Henshaw had been in line to take over MacCaman Stone, if the heir apparent hadn't come back to ruin things. Maybe, somehow, he'd like to ruin things for the heir.

"Me, neither," Mace muttered. "From anything or anyone."

"Sure," Clay said, his eyes narrowing and a little tic jumping at the corner of his left one. "Just watch your step around here. I suppose caving can be dangerous, but this line of work's no picnic. Let's see now, what's that Bible quote my wife's always throwing at me 'stead of telling me outright to be careful?"

He paused a moment as if he couldn't recall it, then recited, "'He who quarries stones may be hurt by them.'"

Mace was back at his dad's office by eleven, only to find two lunches laid out on the desk. "It's early, I know," Rod said, gesturing him in, "but I eat early—or when food looks any good at all. Deli sandwiches Rita sent out for. Since you took a long run early, like you're training for some damn Olympics, you're probably ready, too."

Mace had to admit the sandwiches, coffee and chocolate chip cookies smelled good, but he needed to watch his weight. Since he was tall for a caver, he couldn't crawl or wriggle through some passages, and he didn't need to make it worse by adding pounds. He'd overeaten since he'd been back, even if it was partly to get Cassie to eat more. And he'd get more wired than he already was with this caffeine.

"So what's the big news?" Mace asked as he sat down across from his dad and unwrapped his sandwich.

Rod waited until he took a bite.

"I'm gonna reopen Deep Heart."

Mace gulped down the bite before he could choke. "You said you never would." His heart kicked into a faster beat. "I know the memorial's on the town square, but it's at Deep Heart, too, where they died. Mom—"

"Would want me to reopen it if it's good for the business, and you gotta learn to think that way, too. I know I never wanted to look at the place again after the slide, but a lot of great stone's still there, and I've got an order that will be perfect for it. Look at it this way, Mace. To cut out solid stone, we'll have to remove all the rock that slid."

"You don't think it could go again?"

"Hell, no. I know this may be tough for you, especially as a first assignment, and I'd do it if I could—oversee the safety of the place, the cutting there. Can you do it for me and MacCaman, or not?"

His gaze slammed into his father's. "I see business is business here, no matter what," Mace said.

"We gonna have us a wrassling or shouting match, like in the good old days?" Rod demanded, leaning forward, his chin thrust out, although his hands on the chair arms shook.

"Sure, I can do it, but no one's going to like it, including me. And, of course, it will get me off to a great start in town," he added, his voice sharp with sarcasm.

"And don't you go telling Jenna Kirk. I already ran it by her mother and had Cassie ask Jenna to supper at the house tonight so we can tell her—and Cassie—together."

"You've covered all the bases."

"Like I said, you better learn to think that way, too. Now, eat up."

"I'm not hungry. I'm going out by the slag piles for some fresh air."

"We gonna make it, boy?" he heard his father's whisper, half question, half taunt, as he went outside into the sun and air. He heard that challenge again and again in his head as, ignoring his hard-soled shoes and new slacks, he climbed the pile and sat on a ledge, both loving and hating the monoliths that had been torn from the flesh of the earth.

Jenna had surveyed the kids'-tree-house materials that had been laid out by the deliverymen on the ground under the tree. She had checked things off her list, then sketched how they should be assembled when she got the construction team here. Hungry now, she went back to the house for lunch and saw a note stuck in her front door.

Warily—that pillow and e-mail had made her really jumpy—she glanced at the envelope. Cassie's handwriting. If Cassie'd stopped by, why hadn't she come out to find her? What was with the sneaking around? Maybe Cassie was just in a hurry, she thought, taking the letter in with her. But Cassie had phoned this morning to ask her to dinner. So why had she stopped by, too?

"You're getting par-a-noid," Jenna warned herself in a singsong voice.

She opened the envelope at the kitchen table and saw that it contained several double-spaced, typed pages. She started to skim them, then read the note Cassie had stuck to the top of the first page:

I know you were a little tentative about my resurrecting the painful past in a book about your mother. I thought I would share this section with you, so you can see how honest and heartfelt it is—I just want you to trust me and help me. Cassie

Pressing the knuckles of both hands to her mouth, Jenna began to read:

It was still the era of *Happy Days* and *The Brady Bunch,* an attempted return to simpler times in the aftermath of the Vietnam War and the Iran hostage crisis. In Ridgeview, Indiana, which was always a bit behind mainstream fads, teens still wore mood rings and had pet rocks. Jimmy Carter was in the White House, the country was in an economic depression, and nobody worried about AIDS, certainly not in little Ridgeview, on that Fourth of July, 1979.

People were excited about the ox roast, the games and the big fireworks show at Deep Heart quarry that night. Though times were tough, Ridgeview was proud of the fine grade of limestone being cut from Deep Heart. No one, especially not Cynthia Kirk and her two young daughters, knew that their lives were about to be crushed; as always, though Cynthia Kirk's bedrock strength would pull them through.

Jenna's hands had begun to shake and sweat. Yet, in dreadful anticipation, she read on.

Everything went well until the fireworks finale that night. It was to be the culmination of a fun day for so many in Ridgeview. A continual cascade of rockets and twirling spires were accompanied by big booms. Kids squealed or hushed in awe. Very few even reacted when the slide started. They learned later that it was caused by the strong vibrations of the fireworks—almost like TNT—placed upon what must have been a freakishly unstable balance of stones. Yet the four-hundred-twenty townspeople at the celebration that day could have climbed those same stones and nothing would have moved.

But move they did. Shook free and shifted. Half-harvested Deep Heart stones slid and settled upon themselves and those who were too close. Some said it was a blessing in disguise that only five of the attenders were caught and killed under the tons of rock. But to the five families who lost loved ones, including Cynthia, it was no blessing. It was four days before her beloved husband John was pulled…

That was only the first page, but Jenna couldn't read the rest. Tears streaming down her face, she jumped up, refolded and stuffed the pages in the envelope. She didn't know how Cassie could get through this. Maybe it was catharsis for her, a way to actually control the memories of the horror.

Cassie came out to meet Jenna the moment she pulled up at the MacCamans' house that evening. The sprawling, stone-and-wood ranch design that wrapped around the edge of a cliff above a crooked stream was the most modern one in the area. It had been built about the same time as Kirkhall, but the styles were day and night. No view in the area could beat the one out the back windows of the MacCamans'.

"I couldn't wait to see what you thought of that part of the book," Cassie blurted as the evening breeze whipped her full broom-stick skirt around her Western boots. "Did you get to read it?"

"Powerful stuff," Jenna managed to say, as they went up the flagstone walk together, "I think for anyone, not just me. But I couldn't get through all of it, just enough to know how you—"

"I want people to grasp how strong your mother's been through everything," Cassie insisted. "She bends but won't break. Jennie, to do this book, I need to think like her—to *be* her—and I know you can help."

"Sometimes I want to look back, but it's so hard. I'll help, but if I say 'red light,' that's it."

"Sure, sure!" Cassie held up her palm as if taking a solemn oath.

"Oh, and to prove my good faith, here's a key to my tree house, the big one, in case you want to escape there to write."

"You're the best!" Cassie said, and hugged her. "I won't mess up a thing, and I'll see some flowers and food gets up there, too! And, Jennie, I'm not going to lean on you for a lot, I swear it. I'm going to do independent research and I'm going to see your mother tomorrow in Indianapolis. I hope to get—well, you know..."

"Royal dispensation?" Jenna suggested.

"*You* said it, not me. I hope she'll be pleased and honored."

"And if you quote me in that book without permission, I'll have your head."

"What book?" Rod asked as he opened the door. The two women almost fell into him.

He gave Jenna a weak hug. She hadn't seen him for over a month and, despite his height, it seemed as if a breeze could blow him over. Seeing him, she prayed that Cassie, thin as she was, didn't have some dire illness, too.

"The book I told you about—a biography of Cynthia Kirk, past, present and future," Cassie told her father.

"I said it's not a good idea," Rod muttered with a downward slash of one hand as if the subject were closed.

"I think it is," Cassie argued, not raising her voice. "Dad, I'm a professional journalist, not a kid writing lovelorn poetry or half-cocked adventure stories anymore."

"Yeah, well, the lieutenant governor will be glad to hear that, but you'd better clear things with her. I'm telling you, she'll think it's as bad an idea as I do."

"I say she's a savvy politician on the way up who will appreciate the publicity!" Cassie cried. "Besides, it will be an inspirational book about rising above tragedy and loss."

"All right, you two," Jenna said, taking each of their arms, "I didn't come here to referee."

Rod looked as if he wanted to say more, but instead he rolled his eyes at Jenna and motioned them into the living room. The view of the pink and orchid sunset outside the picture window, overlooking the back deck, was stunning. Where was Mace? Jenna wondered. Then, as if her question had conjured him up, he joined them from the hall that led to the bedrooms.

It was only seeing him in these surroundings, after so long, that she realized how much Mace's strong features resembled his father's, however wan and wasted the once powerful Rod MacCaman looked now.

"Jenna," Mace said and kissed her cheek, just as a brother might. "Have you heard about the timber wolves in the area?"

"Yes, but I haven't seen a sign of them yet," she said, sitting on the sofa with Cassie. "And I do have a rifle in the house."

"No kidding?" Cassie put in. "And you can use it? Does your mother keep a gun?"

"It's my dad's old shotgun, but I can do whatever I have to do with it. As for my mother, that's her business."

"So how is your mother?" Rod asked, sipping a soft drink while the rest of them had wine. "Haven't seen her for a while."

"Busier than ever," Jenna said. "On top of everything else, she's chairing a committee for the Republican convention this summer."

A smile lit Rod's face. For one moment, Jenna almost thought he knew about Cynthia's prospects for the vice presidency—but of course, he couldn't.

Though the sun had long set, Mace, Jenna and Cassie had an after-dinner drink on the deck. Rod had not eaten much and had begged off after dinner, giving Mace a pointed look.

"What is it?" Jenna asked him as they stood at the railing, gazing off into the darkness. "Maybe it's none of my business, but are you and your dad still get—"

"The company is going to open Deep Heart for more stone." Jenna's insides went into free fall.

"What?" Cassie exclaimed. "He—you can't do that!"

''He just told me today. Evidently, my first 'Sir, yes sir!' test is to oversee the site.''

''Oh, I don't know,'' Cassie said, her voice bitter. ''The way he set you up and deserted you tonight, I'd say having to tell both of us is your first test.''

''Jenna?'' Mace said, turning to her and taking her arm.

At his merest touch, sparks shot through her. ''I don't blame you,'' she said, trying to keep calm. ''I'm sorry it isn't going to be left as a natural memorial, but if it has to be...''

Cassie turned as if to embrace her, but Mace got there first. He hugged both of them. Cassie clung to his left shoulder, Jenna his right. They stood like statues.

''I suppose it's going to stir up a lot of things around here again,'' Mace said, turning his head to watch Jenna. His mouth was so close to her ear and temple, she could feel his warm breath.

''If it does, I'll get a lot more fodder for the book,'' Cassie put in.

''And I'll have to face *that* past, when it's the other part,'' Jenna said, ''being trapped in a cave, that I've been preparing to face again...''

Mace's arm tightened around her. She leaned slightly into him, so grateful for his strength.

''Face again how?'' Cassie asked. Mace jerked his sister's arm, but she ignored him and stepped away. ''Jenna, after all this time, you're going to look into your and Mandi's kidnapping?'' she demanded. ''I'll be glad to help. I'm planning to—excuse my wording—turn over some rocks around here, anyway, when I get to that part of the book.''

Jenna almost blurted out about the pillow and the e-mail, but something held her back. As she had told her mother and Dr. Brennan, she wanted to face things on her own, however much she longed to cling to Mace.

She, too, stepped back from him, though reluctantly. "I guess I can handle Deep Heart being quarried again," she said. "For me, the other's much harder to face, because there was someone evil behind it." She tried to explain, gripping the railing and staring off into the night. "The rock slide was an accident or act of God, but Mandi and I being taken like that...and then her disappearance..."

"Disappearance?" Cassie echoed. "You don't think she just went missing, do you? Not after all this time, at least? I mean, your mother had her declared dead and—"

"Not now," Mace put in so forcefully that Cassie quieted in midsentence.

Jenna turned to give Mace a weak smile. In the dim reflection of house light, she studied her friends. Cassie looked disturbed; Mace determined, maybe even deeply angry. She loved them both in different ways, but she wasn't sure if she could truly trust even them. Someone who had known her and Mandi intimately was trying to scare her, trying to make her desperate, maybe trying to make her think Mandi was alive. But why? Was it just some distant, sick mind at work, or worse—someone very close and very smart?

5

First thing the next morning, Mace drove into town to pick up the weekly MacCaman Stone payroll checks. Ridgeview stone workers had traditionally been paid on Tuesdays instead of Fridays for as long as he could recall, though he had no idea why. Maybe in the old days it was harder to go on a drinking binge on a weekday.

He parked along the town square, which looked like something out of a Currier and Ives print: the painted store facades, an elevated band gazebo, the Civil War monument. Only the rock slide memorial looked modern, with the five polished metal doves taking flight from the tilted limestone monolith beneath it. Years ago he and Cassie had decided that their mother's spirit was the highest of the five birds, but he'd once heard Jenna telling Mandi that their dad was the top one.

He sat in the car, looking around. The Kmart on the outskirts of town had evidently killed the Five-and-Dime; TV and video stores had long ago done in the Bijou Movie Theater where they used to go as kids—but other than that, things looked pretty much the same. A couple of antique shops, a pizza parlor, a Dairy Queen, two down-home restaurants, the small storefront library, and a newly renovated bank building.

Establishments were just opening; he'd probably be the bank's first customer. It annoyed him that he felt nervous about facing Frank Connors. The guy had once been his closest friend, but they hadn't parted on the best of terms. Hell, he hadn't parted on the best of terms with anyone in Ridgeview, except Jenna. A lot of folks remembered her deposition about Mandi sneaking out to meet him the night of the abduction. He'd never corrected Jenna on that and he never would. Certain things—at least one—she must never know.

Some folks had theorized that his dad was trying to cover up for him by claiming he and Mace had argued the night of the Kirk kidnapping. Mace's father had told investigators he'd locked his son in his room, where he'd stayed until the next morning. But locals knew that nobody—not even "The Godfather"—could keep Mace MacCaman in his room, or in this town, if he wanted out.

Of course, those who swore that Mace was guilty had never come up with a logical person to be the accomplice Jenna had described, but that hadn't stopped the rumors. Two possible motives had been promoted and argued. Some folks thought Mace wanted that $50,000 ransom to get away from his dad, but he'd been too scared to pick it up and had just taken off for years, anyway. The other theory was that he and Mandi, wanting to elope, had planned to stage the kidnapping together, but their scheme had fallen apart when Jenna stumbled on them. Then things had turned tragic and Mandi had been silenced, either deliberately or accidentally. According to Cassie, gossip on the unsolved crime was endless and varied to this day.

"Damn it all to hell!" Mace hit the steering wheel with his fist. He shuddered and shook his head. Would he ever be able to squelch the spoken and unspoken mistrust and become part of the community again? He hoped he had the guts to get close enough to Jenna to find out if she'd moved beyond her losses—and close enough to discover if she blamed or suspected him. If she did, he'd have a big decision to make about what to do with her.

He finally got out of his truck and headed for the bank. Ridgeview Trust, the sign read. Despite the warmth of the day, he put his suit coat on as he went in. Frank, who still sported a head of thick blond hair, was out of his office, talking to his two tellers about some procedure. Tall and well-built, he'd been a fanatic about working out long before it was fashionable. He wore what Cassie called the Regis Philbin millionaire look, which she'd urged Mace to try. Frank's shirt and tie were a silky material in the same dark gray as his suit.

Frank evidently noticed his tellers staring over his shoulder, and turned around. "Frank," Mace said, and thrust out his right hand. They shook firmly but briefly.

"Mace. I heard you were back. I was going to call you. Come on in."

Minutes later, Mace sat across a huge, polished desk from his old friend. Frank's computer screen glowed blue behind his head. Photos of three kids and framed civic awards lined one wall, alongside a polished plaque announcing that Frank was a Ridgeview Township Trustee. Mayors meant nothing in this part of Indiana; here, trustees were the civic leaders. The decor of the office was rich-looking, though the piped-in Muzak killed the ambience.

Frank Connors was good-looking in a strong, Nordic way, but his face was puffy, and dark circles edged his light blue eyes, as if he didn't sleep at night. Or maybe, Mace admitted to himself, they were all just getting older.

''You're really back to stay?'' Frank asked, leaning forward and steepling his fingers in front of his mouth.

''If I have enough staying power,'' Mace told him with a tight smile. ''But yes, I'm not just here while Dad is ill. I'm going to put down roots and pick up the pieces.''

''Will one of those pieces be Jenna?''

Mace sat up even straighter. ''Meaning what?''

''I heard she had dinner with you last night, that's all.''

''I keep forgetting I'm in the gossip capital of the Midwest, if not the world. Cassie invited her. You know how tight they were.''

''Jenna's got some problems, Mace.''

''Don't we all?''

''I think everyone around here feels protective of her, that's all I meant.''

''You feel protective of Jenna, Frank? Maybe like you felt about her sister?''

Frank look shocked he'd brought that up. ''No, but I've been keeping an eye on Jenna, and not just because she's got her small business loan with me—with the bank, I mean. She's been through a lot and doesn't need more crap.''

''Let's get back to her current problems. What are you talking about?''

Frank shifted his weight in his big leather chair, and it squeaked. ''Her adjusting to being back, after everything. The Honorable Cynthia isn't too happy she's here, either. She wants to hold on to her.''

''So, what else is new. Besides, can you blame her? Despite the powerful politician facade, Cynthia Kirk's lost her husband and her other daughter. And it sounds like she's never remarried. She's married to her career. On the personal front, Jenna's all she's got."

Frank changed his position, hunching forward to drum his fingers on the desk. "Sure. I understand being possessive—very possessive—about someone you care for."

They stared at each other across the desk, silent for a moment. It was what went unspoken that screamed at them.

"So," Frank said, "you're here for the MacCaman payroll." He spun around in his chair and took a thick envelope from a file. "I hear you've lived all over the world. 'Down under' in more ways than one," he went on in a rush. "I've always wanted to visit Australia—can't wait to see the summer Olympics—but I'm pretty busy here with my kids. I'm divorced—my ex lives in Indianapolis, but I see the kids a lot. Want me to go over with you how we lay this payroll out?"

"Our accounts guy already did," Mace assured him, astounded by how Frank had tried to change the subject in several directions.

"Hey, let's get together sometime for lunch or some golf, get caught up," Frank said, standing and extending the thick padded envelope across the corner of the desk. "You know, it's ironic that you became a professional caver, and here Jenna can't stand the thought of caves. She's a pretty bad claustrophobic, you know."

Mace took the envelope and stood, deciding not to discuss Jenna any more with this man. "It's also ironic that you were the only one in Ridgeview besides me who used to like exploring caves and taking risks at the quarry—and now here you are, all safe and sound behind a desk," Mace threw over his shoulder as he headed out the door.

To get off on the right foot around here, the last thing he needed was to deck the bank president.

"I'm honored—deeply honored—by your request to do an authorized biography of me, I really am," Cynthia Kirk told Cassie. Sitting in a small café one block from the statehouse in downtown Indianapolis, Cassie leaned a bit closer to Cynthia over their table. She had been up before dawn, driving through rush-hour traffic to meet Cynthia at this early hour, who claimed this would be a nonstop day for her. Cassie had asked if she could meet with her when Cynthia came to Ridgeview for Pioneers Day this weekend, but Cynthia had said her schedule was just too full, especially because she wanted some quality time with Jenna.

This small place was evidently fashionable, for it was filled with more than the smell of java. Lawyers juggled briefcases under tiny tables, secretaries and paralegals stood in line for takeout for their bosses who, like Cynthia, had already started their workdays. A cacophony of conversation was like background music. Cynthia was talking low, and although Cassie was used to that with her dad, it was hard to hear her.

"Eat your bagel, Cassie," Cynthia told her with motherly concern. "You are as thin as some of those television actresses and models, and believe me, in their case, fashion cannot be healthy."

But Cassie was not to be deterred by more small talk. Ever since she'd explained her idea for the biography, Cynthia had been giving her advice on her weight, her hair color and her dad.

"I am totally dedicated to doing this book, Mrs. Kirk, which means I'm really here to inform you—and, of course, request your cooperation."

"And you'll request the help of many Ridgeview citizens, I suppose? Not to mention Jenna?" she said as she tore off hunks of her blueberry muffin and nibbled at them.

"Absolutely. I want a fair, multifaceted presentation of a multifaceted woman, one I'm sure is climbing further yet, toward..."

Cassie intentionally hesitated, smiling.

"Fill in the blanks for you?" Cynthia asked, drizzling more honey on her muffin. "I hope and pray the best is still to come, but you'll not get predictions from me yet. Maybe soon. But as for grilling Jenna, she's shaky. You should know that. But you don't know that I've had her in counseling for years. She doesn't need to be pulled through it all again."

"She told me ages ago about the counseling."

"I see," she said, looking surprised.

"If she's had professional help, isn't she better?" Cassie challenged.

"Of course she is," Cynthia insisted, sipping her coffee, then putting the disposable cup hastily down on the Formica tabletop. "That's the point—I want her to stay that way."

"I could work around your and Jenna's direct memories of the kidnapping by using those articles Mary Drout did for the papers and by talking to others, but that wouldn't be as good—as honest."

"I don't want you to take this the wrong way, Cassie, but I wish you wouldn't use the past at all, if you must do the book. It would make your writing seem sensational, and I mean that in the tabloid way."

"But so much that has made you who you are involves what happened and how you rose above it," Cassie argued, gripping her hands in her lap. "I'd certainly have a sympathetic point of view. My family shared and understood your grief in the rock slide, and certainly in the abduction, too. Mace, especially—''

''I don't want you digging all that up, and I'm sure Mace—or your father—wouldn't, either,'' Cynthia insisted. ''You should be taking good care of your father, and this will upset him.''

''Yes, it has.''

''See there? It will upset others too, even beyond Jenna and myself. You're an English major, a journalist. Didn't you ever read Thomas Wolfe's novel, *You Can't Go Home Again?* He wrote beautifully, and no doubt truthfully, about his hometown, but they felt exposed, betrayed. They never wanted him back again.''

Cassie was amazed at how badly this was going. She had not been prepared for any of this. ''But surely you understand that I—that all of us—admire you. This will be a positive portrait. Why wouldn't you want your first official bio written by someone who knows you and cares?''

''I've been an advocate for victims' rights groups for years. Think about it!'' Cynthia insisted, leaning closer across the small table and throwing a wadded paper napkin down. ''I won't be a victim of someone else's judgment in a book—even yours, Cassie. It will be vetted by the press, it will put a spotlight on what I've worked so hard to put behind me—the pain, the loss. And I don't intend to lose again.''

''But—''

''I will remain your friend always, as will Jenna, but speaking for both of us, I can't approve of your digging around in what is over and done. It would be worse than your father opening up Deep Heart again.''

''I hear he asked you.''

"No, he informed me," Cynthia muttered. "I really must run. I'll be sure we have a moment to settle this for good at Pioneers Day this weekend, but I want you to think long and hard about all I've said. I've had to be strong for both Jenna and me. That's what I'm doing now, so please do not involve her in this, either."

As Cynthia Kirk patted her shoulder and walked away, Cassie sat there, staring at her nearly untouched breakfast. She had already thought long and hard about it. She'd talked to some people in town and had a few interviews set up, because she'd never expected this from Cynthia. But even if *Stone Lady: The Public and Private Lives of Cynthia Kirk* was now an *un*authorized biography, she was going to write it, whatever the personal cost. And she was still going to ask Jenna to help.

Jenna had no idea what she was looking for, but she was going to find it. There must be a clue somewhere to reveal who was trying to make her think Mandi was alive. And why.

At first light, on the morning after her dinner at the MacCamans', she went through all the other boxes of Mandi's things she had stored in her attic. Fighting her need to keep memories locked away, she carted downstairs her sister's collection of china and fabric cats and displayed them on her living room mantel and the deep windowsill. They looked pretty, she thought, struck by the morning light that came through the lacy curtains she had in all the windows. No thick drapes for her to shut out the outside, because that would make her feel shut in.

Despite her dread of the basement, armed with her flashlights, she went down to look at the few things stored there. Several photo albums she never looked at, but would now. A cardboard tube with Mandi's collection of *Gone with the Wind* posters. Tears came to Jenna's eyes. Mandi had watched that movie more than twenty times and read the book at least ten, memorizing lines and spouting them in an overblown Southern accent: "'Well, fiddledy-dee,'" she'd drawl, flouncing around like a young Scarlett. "'I just do believe I can make a fine gown out of these old draperies, though I may just think about that tomorrow.'"

Mandi's voice, her stunning face, her enthusiasm—all these danced through Jenna's mind as she pulled out a smaller piece of paper from among the posters. It was a panoramic photo of everyone who had gone to Washington D.C., on Mandi's senior class trip. Mace hadn't gone, but Mandi was there, standing in front of Frank Connors on the steps of the U.S. Capitol.

Jenna sighed as she rolled up the posters and the photo and returned them to the cardboard tube. She'd found nothing secretive or special, nothing even unusual. But she had to start somewhere. Whoever wanted to scare her, years after Mandi had disappeared, surely had known Mandi well or at least had been to Kirkhall years ago. Or was her harasser trying to give her hope through hints that Mandi was alive? Or...could Mandi somehow *be* alive?

In a rush now, since her construction crew was coming to erect the children's tree house early this afternoon, Jenna jumped in her van and headed into town. She hadn't been in Kirkhall for months, but she was going to look at the few things still stored there. The downstairs of the house was now used for civic functions, such as township trustee and Rotary meetings, but a few boxes were still locked upstairs.

Jenna realized just how obsessed she'd become with

her own little world when she drove under the big banner that announced Ridgeview Pioneers Day, Sat., May 6. That was this Saturday, four days away, she thought, hitting her forehead with the palm of her hand. She'd wanted to have a booth among those selling arts and crafts. Her brochures would be available, but she needed to get blowups of the tree houses, maybe even lay the floor plan of the new kids' one out on the grass with bright strings and pegs. With Mace and Cassie's return and the upheaval of the unexplained e-mail and pillow, she had completely forgotten.

When she saw several cars parked in Kirkhall's circular stone driveway, she was both annoyed and relieved. She'd have to see people she didn't have time to chat with, but at least the house wouldn't be empty. It felt full of ghosts when she faced it alone.

Kirkhall was built of buff limestone, graced with pillars that reached two stories and crowned by a roof of dark blue slate. Though its tall ceilings and windows made it seem huge it had only four bedrooms. Dad had called it great but not grand, and said it looked "cleanly classical."

Once professionally landscaped, the half-acre grounds were now cared for by volunteers, who maintained both the exterior and interior of the place in exchange for the use of the first floor for various functions, which Cynthia had arranged with the town in lieu of property taxes.

Jenna recalled her mother's suggestion that she move into the large second floor. Free rent would give her more money to invest in the new business and would, as her mother said, "keep her out of those dark, lonely woods." She could have sold off her grandmother's old house or part of the Stone Forest. But Jenna insisted on doing things her way.

She glanced up into the old oak that cradled the remnants of their childhood tree house. A pin oak, it held its brown, dead leaves most of the winter, and they rattled in the wind. But by now its new, green growth nearly hid the ramshackle tree house. Staring up at it, a thought hit her: Perhaps the person who had sent the pillow and the e-mail *didn't* know her and Mandi back then. Someone recently could have climbed up there to observe and measure the place. But no, her tormentor was someone who knew the shingles came from an old garage and the boards from Dad's lumberyard. And how many people would have known she and Mandi and their friends loved to have graham crackers and apple juice up there?

Then again, Mary Drout had done a series of articles in the *Reporter* about Mandi's life and loss, much more detailed ones than the big newspapers had carried. Jenna had never kept those copies, but perhaps she'd better find some to read again. It was possible anyone in the area could have researched Mandi's life, if they could not recall it firsthand.

As she let herself in the front door, Jenna gasped. A half dozen women stood about in hoop skirts and bonnets, as if Mandi's old *Gone with the Wind* poster had exploded to life.

"Oh!" Jenna cried, before she figured it out. "You're practicing for Pioneers Day," she added in embarrassment, as everyone stopped talking and turned her way.

"They are indeed," Mary Drout said, bouncing up from a bench by the hearth. Unlike the others, she wore a pantsuit. "And I've decided to cover the preparations, as well as the performance—a new twist after all these years, you see."

"Please, everyone, go back to your rehearsal," Jenna said. "I just need to go upstairs a moment."

Her mother kept an apartment on the second floor for the few nights she was in Ridgeview each year, though Jenna was hoping she'd stay with her this summer when she visited. It bothered Jenna that she wasn't sure whether her mom would be back for Pioneers Day or not—but Mary would probably know.

"The reenactors haven't talked my mother into wearing a costume to portray her pioneer ancestor, have they?" she asked Mary, as she leaned over the banister. She found the old woman watching her go upstairs. Mary's salt-and-pepper hair had been going white for years, and from this lofty vantage point, it looked as if she had a halo not visible from normal eye level. Yes, Jenna thought, in a way, Mary was the town's guardian angel.

"She's driving in for the day, but not making a formal speech. But for Memorial Day later in the month, she's promised us much more," Mary said, smiling.

"Good." Jenna almost asked Mary if she still had copies of the old articles about Mandi, but she didn't want word all over town. She wouldn't be a bit surprised if she could borrow those from Cassie's files.

"Jenna!" Mary called sharply when she turned away. She peered over again. "Do you have any comment on Mace and Cassie returning after all these years? Of course, I'll interview them, and maybe get some marvelous articles out of his travels and her writing career. Say, do you think Cassie would do an occasional piece for the *Reporter?*"

"I think the interviews are a good idea, Mary, so they can speak for themselves. See you later."

Jenna used the key that had once accessed the door

to the master bedroom. When they'd moved to Indianapolis, Cynthia had had it remodeled into a studio apartment, including the bedroom next door, which had been Jenna's. Now, with a new door cut through the wall, the master bedroom had been converted to a kitchen and dining area, though Cynthia usually ate out when she was in town. At least she had not made the house into some sort of shrine to Mandi, whose room was left empty and locked across the hall. Her mother had demanded that they move on from disaster—*and that's probably what I should continue to do,* she scolded herself. She should not feel trapped by her tormentor, but the whole thing infuriated her.

A few boxes of Mandi's odds and ends were still stored in what had been Cynthia's big closet. She'd refused to donate Mandi's things, worried that someone might keep them as a ghoulish souvenir. *Ghoulish,* that was the word for what someone was doing to her, Jenna fumed.

She shoved aside a hanging raincoat and stepped over random stacks of extra shoes her mother must have left. Anxious to escape from the closet, she dragged out a box marked School Stuff with Cynthia's bold penmanship.

From the first floor of Kirkhall, a recording of fiddle music began, and she heard the thump of feet. They must be practicing dancing; they usually did some country reel. Glancing at her watch, she dug through prom favors, a cheerleading team trophy, and old photos in an album embossed with the single word *Memories.* Mother must have also dumped the contents of Mandi's dressing table in here: hairclips, old lipsticks, a bottle of English Leather men's cologne with a big wooden top. It must have been Mace's; Mandi liked to wear his cologne, she'd told Jenna once, not long before she disappeared. Though her sister had been moody, sometimes she had talked and talked, and Jenna had hung on her every word...

Sudden dry sobs shook Jenna. She bent over her knees, leaning on her elbows, her face nearly to the floor. Had Mandi been silenced by their abductors when she ran and screamed in that dark cave? Had she tripped a second time and fallen down, knocking herself out? Did she get amnesia and just wander away, terrified, lost forever in that dark cave? Or was she living a new life out there, the pretty sister, taken away by their abductors who didn't want Jenna? Was Mandi now trying to get in touch with her, or did the ones who took her just want to threaten and torture those who were left behind?

Trembling, she sat up straight. Could her mother be getting weird things, too, and just hadn't said so? How could she dare to ask her? She didn't want to make her suffer again over Mandi's loss. And she did not want to give her mother any excuses for hounding her to come back to Indianapolis.

Jenna got hold of herself. She was about to shove the cologne back in the box when she heard something rattle. Lifting the old, square bottle to the light, she saw a man's gold ring with a rectangular onyx stone sitting in the remaining amber liquid. A man's class ring. A Ridgeview High ring. Mace's? She could read the year on it: 1985.

Despite the reek of the old cologne when she unscrewed the top, she stuck her face closer. How had the ring gotten in here, like a ship in a proverbial bottle? Then she saw the plastic lip of the bottle could be pried off to widen the mouth.

She looked around for something to fish out the ring.

The only hangers in this closet were her mother's padded and satin-covered ones. Frustrated, she scrabbled through the meager utensils in the kitchen drawers, but nothing looked as if it would work. Maybe she could just shake out the ring.

Taking a mixing bowl, she turned the bottle upside down and let the remaining liquid run out into it. Immediately, the strong smell of the concentrated cologne permeated the room and made her sneeze. When the bottle was empty of liquid, she shook it, but the ring just bounced around inside.

She realized then that it would have to be perfectly aligned to fall out, with its top facing downward so the slender part of the ring cleared the bottle.

Surely this was Mace's ring, Jenna thought as she tried to coax it out with one little finger. Yet the night she and Mandi were taken, Mandi had worn Mace's ring. Jenna had seen it on her in the bedroom across the hall and felt it in the darkness of the cave when Mandi fell and she helped her up.

"Darn!" she muttered, dumping the cologne from the bowl down the sink and running water after it to wash it away. Yet the smell clung to her clothes, her hair, her skin—and her heart. She used to love the smell of it. How like Mandi to have not only Mace's ring and his adoration but his cologne.

Though she had had no intention of going into Mandi's room, she wondered if she might find some regular wire hangers there. Taking the bottle with her, she dug in her jeans pocket for the right key and went across the hall to unlock the door.

Someone had dusted the floor and washed the windows in the stale-smelling room, at least. No furniture remained, nor was there anything on the walls Mandi had once so carefully decorated. They even looked re-painted. At least there was nothing to search for in here. Jenna was not staying any longer than she had to.

She hurried to the closet and yanked out a hanger. Straightening its hook, she went after the ring in the bottle with a vengeance. But her hands were still wet, and the bottle slipped and shattered on the bare wood floor of the room.

The ring skidded free, and Jenna bent to retrieve it. A tiny piece of glass cut her. Cursing, she picked it out. The small cut stung from the cologne.

She held the ring up to the window light. Usually, class rings had initials on the inside, but she could see nothing. She put the ring on her finger, where it hung loosely. Maybe Mace should have it back. Hurrying across the hall for a wet rag to wipe up the shards of glass and kill the rest of the smell, she stopped when the phone on the small kitchen counter rang.

The sound jarred her. Maybe someone downstairs had heard the crash and wondered if she was all right. This phone was on a separate line from the one on the first floor. Or maybe someone who had access to this private, unlisted number was trying to reach her mother.

She grabbed the phone. ''Hello?''

There was no one on the line. Then came the slightly scratchy sound that Jenna knew was not an echo of the country melody from downstairs. No, it was a song she hadn't heard for at least fifteen years. It was that old recording of ''Mandy.''

Jenna screamed and slammed down the phone.

6

Jenna didn't know whether to laugh or cry when she read this week's *Ridgeview Reporter.* An article about Mace's return to the family business was next to a photo of a timber wolf with the caption "Now in Area—Beware." Leave it to Mary Drout not to recognize the possible implications.

Though, no doubt, Mace would see the paper, she put her copy under a pile of nature magazines and kept straightening the place like crazy. As if she had sent him a mental message, he had called to say he'd like to stop by to see her. Jenna fingered the class ring in the pocket of her jeans. She intended to play things by ear, but she was dying to ask him if it was his.

It was after dark when she heard his truck and glanced out through the lacy curtains. She wondered if he'd know these cats on the window and mantel had been Mandi's. As far as she knew, he'd never visited her sister's bedroom, though Mandi could have told him about the collection. Yes, she recalled he'd once even given Mandi a cat, that one of the Siamese that so resembled her beloved cat Pert.

Jenna hurried to the door and opened it. He was dressed casually in a jade-colored knit shirt and black jeans. "I remembered you like these," he said, and handed her a glass apothecary jar full of M&M's.

To stem her burst of emotion, she bit her lower lip

and nodded. She *had* always liked them, but had quit eating that brand of candy when Mandi insisted the M&M stood for Mandi and Mace. Suddenly, Jenna resented the way Mandi always hovered in her thoughts, the way she'd always been so possessive about Mace, about everything. Then she felt a familiar stab of guilt for her anger, and shoved it down deep.

She accepted the jar and gave it a bounce. "You're just afraid I spend too much time in trees and can't cook or bake a thing. I thank you, but I made us dessert—strawberry pie."

"Again I'm impressed," he said, smiling. "I really am."

Their eyes held. He had recently shaved, she noted, for by this time of the day, his beard shadow used to show. She realized she had not so much as stepped out of the doorway nor invited him in. As she moved aside, he entered, glanced around, then studied her again. The color of his shirt made his eyes, fringed by thick lashes for a man, look so very green.

She gave him a little tour of the first floor of the house, which he had known as a boy when her grandmother lived here. If he recalled the cat collection was Mandi's, he didn't say so. They ended up in the kitchen, Jenna cutting pie, with Mace watching her so intently she again became sensuously aware of her every move.

"You've done a lot with the house so far," he noted. "And obviously inherited your dad's building skills."

"And not many of mother's political ones. This is decaf, by the way," she added nervously as she poured coffee, "so it won't keep you awake at night."

"If I can't sleep, it's not usually because of too much coffee. Do you have trouble sleeping?"

"Sometimes, caffeine or not," she admitted.

He looked as if he was about to say or ask something else, but instead carried the pie plates for her. She'd expected him to sit across the big table from her, but he settled himself at the corner, quite close, with their knees almost touching.

"Fabulous pie," he told her as he dug in.

"What's been your favorite food from all over the world?" she asked, enjoying his praise and proximity.

"Gorp."

"From what country is that?" she asked, unbelieving, especially when she noted the tilt of his mouth and the way one dark eyebrow lifted. "You're kidding. Gorp?"

"Seriously. I make my own. It's a caver's meat and potatoes, sustenance for climbing and rappelling. Think muesli breakfast cereal with lots of extra nuts, raisins, cranberries, other dried fruits. Easy to carry, nonfattening, high energy and delicious. I'll bring you some to balance the candy. I promise, it'll be good for tree climbers, too."

She laughed, and he grinned. Suddenly it felt so right to be close to him like this. She yearned to dump her worries about the pillow, e-mail and phone call on him, but she wasn't sure he'd want to help. It might drive him away. As she reached in her pocket for the ring, she could only pray that he would trust her.

One of Mace's goals was to get Jenna to trust him. Earlier, he'd sensed he was making her uneasy, but she seemed to be relaxing now. He really needed to clear the air about Frank Connors.

"I saw Frank yesterday when I picked up the MacCaman payroll," he told her. "He implied he's been seeing you, so am I horning in?"

She stared at him, her lips the lush color of the strawberries, though the pie had nothing to do with that. "Horning in?" she repeated, sounding puzzled. "I'm not going with him—I mean, he wanted to, but... How would you be horning in?"

"He said he felt protective of you, and it sounded as if you'd been confiding in him. You have every right to but— You're not dating him, then?"

"I have, but I'm not. I don't need him or anyone else protecting me."

"Jenna, I don't want to push you, but one thing I've learned as a caver is not to waste words. I hardly think we have to be departed-sister's-former-boyfriend and best-friend-of-sister with each other anymore. I'd like to get beyond that."

Her eyes were so wide that he could see his reflection in them as he leaned closer and tugged her hands into his. Her fingers were ice cold.

"I'd like that more than anything, but I can't quite shake the past yet," she admitted.

"You've got to. We both do."

"Mace, since you and Cassie have been back, someone's been harassing me about Mandi—someone who either knew her or...or could *be* Mandi."

His heart began to pound. He gripped her hands so hard she flinched, and he let go. "Tell me," he said. "You can trust me."

Everything felt so much more complicated since Mace arrived. She'd had no intention of telling him her fears, but now it was too late to cover up or retreat. She showed him the pillow and the printout of the e-mail, then told him about the perfect timing of the phone call when she was at Kirkhall yesterday.

"All of which means," she concluded, "it has to be someone who's here in town, watching me."

"Or someone who's not here but gets tipped off by someone watching you. You could try to get the phone company to trace the call, but..."

"But word could leak out, and I don't want the police and the media involved. I don't need investigators reopening things. I don't want that beehive kicked over again."

"Thank God. Have you asked your mother if someone's harassing her or trying blackmail or extortion?" he asked, his brow still furrowed with concentration. "In her position, she's very vulnerable. I don't know why someone would go after you, unless it was somehow to rattle her."

"I may ask her when she's here for Pioneers Day this weekend. The thing is, it will just cause another blowup because I will not go back to Indianapolis with her. I'm determined to make it here on my own."

"No one makes it alone. Everyone needs help. Jenna, whatever I can do—"

"You mean, you can't make it on your own, either. Mace MacCaman, off all these years with no family entanglements, doing solo, exotic, extreme caving?"

"I've never caved alone," he insisted, his voice hard now. "That could be suicide. If you have an accident underground someone could be kil— Sorry. What I mean is that cavers need friends, and this caveman has them. I have not been on some crazy, solitary quest over the years. I just want to make sure you don't go off on one now."

She smiled and relaxed for the first time since she'd unloaded all this on him. "'Caveman?'" she prompted, with a hint of smile.

"My nickname among my friends who are still following the call of the wild. Most of us had nicknames."

"But Caveman?" she pursued again, her voice teasing.

"Besides the fact that it sounds similar to MacCaman, I've been known to be the group's enforcer of ethics underground." His voice cracked as if he were recalling some dreadful incident, and he shook his head to throw it off. "I may walk softly but I can carry a big stick if anyone gets out of line," he added. "However, I have not pulled women by their hair into a cave like in cartoons, if that's what you're thinking."

He reached out and tugged gently at her short curls. "Actually," he said, his voice calm again, "I feel more like a zoo animal on display since I've been back in Ridgeview."

"Don't I know," she agreed, picturing the front page of the local paper again.

"Then, let's stick together through this. Friends, allies...maybe more?" His eyebrows lifted in a challenge and his green gaze seemed to pierce her.

They shook on it, but he didn't give her hand back when she tugged. She curled her fingers around his warm, tanned ones. His nails were cut close and clean, unlike some stonemen she'd known. He smelled of pine-scented aftershave, not English Leather anymore, though she couldn't really remember that he ever had. It was only Mandi she remembered wearing the scent.

"One more thing," she said, surprised that her voice was husky.

"You're inviting me to lunch tomorrow up in the tree house. I'll bring the gorp—and deli sandwiches," he said.

"Yes," she agreed as her stomach cartwheeled. He

wanted to see her again so soon! "That, and this. I wonder if this could be yours." She tugged her hands free and dug the class ring out of her pocket.

"Looks like it," he said, as she placed it in his big, square palm, "but most of the guys had this onyx. Where'd you get it?"

"It was with some of Mandi's things I was going through. It doesn't have initials inside."

"Mine didn't," he said, peering closely at it and tipping it both ways in the light. "Dad got it for me and evidently didn't order initials." She noticed he wore no jewelry other than a thick, multi-use wristwatch. He tried to slide the ring on the third finger of his left hand, but it stuck at his second knuckle.

"Doesn't fit," he said, "but I've grown and my knuckles have swollen a bit from climbing—hanging on literally by my fingernails at times." He shrugged and handed it back.

It annoyed her that she recalled the words of O.J. Simpson's wily lawyer Johnnie Cochran, spoken when O.J. had tried on the murderer's glove: *If it doesn't fit, you must acquit.* But Mace wasn't guilty, or even suspected of anything—not in her mind. He'd even admitted his knuckles had changed, so he wasn't trying to hide that the ring could well be his. And so what? She was going to trust Mace through this mess. She put the ring back in her pocket.

Their gazes met again and held. "The thing is," she said quietly, "I'm sure Mandi had your ring on that last night, on a chain around her neck, both in our house and later in the cave."

"Jenna, I can't help you there, but I can help you with the bastard who's bothering you. Call me day or night, and I'll be here if there's a problem again. Promise?''

She was suddenly afraid to promise this man anything. Because she could so easily blurt out that she wanted to promise him everything.

Jenna drove herself hard. Work helped her avoid worrying about someone out there pretending to know Mandi or to be her. And to keep from obsessing about the possibility of a relationship with Mace. She wanted that more desperately than she had wanted anything for years.

''You have an obsessive personality,'' Dr. Brennan had once told her in a counseling session. ''You must learn to let Mandi go. It's not right to resent that your mother has declared your sister legally dead. Nor should you take offense that she initially seemed more distraught that Mandi never came back than happy that you did. Just as you might delete a section of a story from a videotape or text from a desktop computer, you must delete the thoughts of that terrible night, of failing to save Mandi and of returning without her. Seize your future, build your own life as your mother has.''

''That's exactly what I'm doing,'' Jenna declared aloud now, as she tied the pieces for the porch railing of the kids' tree house to the rope sling she would use to haul it up.

She stood on the grass under the kids' tree house and surveyed the frame and floor she'd designed and built with her crew's help, now nearly twelve feet above her. Once she added this railing and completed some interior work—she was going to paint the section of tree trunk within the structure so it looked like a giraffe's neck—it would be finished. Just in time to take photos and have them blown up for her booth at Pioneers Day on the town square, she thought.

Jenna looked at her watch again. Mace would be here with lunch in about two hours. She wasn't sure if they should eat in Home Tree Home or in this new house. He was right about that bed looming large in the other.

She checked her hoisting rope, then climbed the extension ladder she was using for now. She was undecided about whether to install a rope ladder that kids could haul up after themselves, or to design and build a more permanent one. Parents probably wouldn't like a rope ladder, but if kids had a sleepover, they could pull the rope ladder up after them for better security.

Jenna hauled up the boards for the railing and stacked them on the narrow porch. Her hammer and nails were inside, and she went in to retrieve them. There, on the window seat, open and facedown as if someone had just been reading it, lay an old, well-thumbed paperback copy of *Gone with the Wind.*

Jenna backed up and gaped at it as if it were a coiled snake. "Cassie," she said aloud. "I told her she could use the other house, but she's been up here. It *has* to be Cassie."

Leaving everything as it was, she hurried down the ladder, pulled it to the ground and, despite its weight, carted it with her as she hurried toward Home Tree Home. She wanted the kids' house sealed off until she got back. As she approached the big tree house, she glanced back over her shoulder at the new house. With the trees fully leafed, it was already out of sight from here.

"Cassie!" she yelled up. Her friend's car had been parked in the driveway for over an hour. If Cassie had left this book, had she also done those other things? Did she think that was the way to get her old friend to help her write her book—by jogging her memory in the worst ways?

Cassie's head poked over the porch as she leaned her arms nonchalantly on the railing. "What's the matter? You said I could work up here. Come on u—"

"You've been in the kids' tree house, haven't you."

"I climbed up to look when I first got here, before you came out. What's the prob?"

"The *prob* is the book you left there. I need to talk to you about that, and other things."

"What the heck's the matter with you? Are you all right? Just a sec, I'll be right down."

Jenna could feel her frustration churning. "What's with the extension ladder?" Cassie asked as she came down. "And what book?"

"*Gone with the Wind,* and I—*and you*—know why."

"Jennie, I've got my own notes and a couple of books on the Indiana legislature, but that's it. *Gone with the Wind?* Didn't Mandi—"

"You said on the phone last night that you want me to help you with the book, no matter what my mother said. It would be to your advantage to rattle me, so I'd want to dig into the past."

"Honestly, rattle you how?" Cassie said, gesturing wildly. "You're starting to sound crazy."

"Come with me, and I'll explain," she demanded. "And grab that end of the ladder."

Cassie kept up a continual spate of questions and denial, but Jenna wasn't buying her innocence routine. She was going to have it out with her friend, who had admitted that Cynthia Kirk was not exactly ecstatic over the proposed biography. If Cassie was being this manipulative, there was no way Jenna was going to help her.

They put the ladder back in place, and Jenna indicated Cassie should climb up ahead of her. "What in heaven's name are you talking about?" Cassie asked, as Jenna climbed through the square hole in the floor after her.

"Right there," Jenna said, and gawked.

The window bench seat, which also served as a storage chest, was bare. Jenna jerked her head around to scan the rest of the small, single room. She yanked up the top of the seat but the storage chest was empty. The window had not been open, so the book couldn't have blown—or jumped—out. Damn. Maybe she *was* going crazy.

"Jenna?" Cassie said, coming to stand beside her.

"But I know...I swear it was just here."

She rushed out onto the narrow porch to look down at the ground, then all around, even up into the tree.

"Jenna?" Cassie said again.

"It wasn't— It couldn't be you, could it?" Jenna asked, more of herself than of her friend.

"I think you'd better start from the beginning."

"All right," she said, sinking cross-legged onto the narrow porch with her back against the wall for stability. She suddenly felt almost dizzy. Cassie sat on the edge of the deck, dangling her thin legs over on the other side of the stacked wood. "I've already shown the things to Mace," Jenna admitted, raking her hands through her hair, "but I think I need all the help I can get. And," she said, turning back to Cassie, "I promise to help you dig into the past. Someone doesn't want me to, so it's exactly what I've got to do."

Standing in the MacCaman Stone parking lot, trying to decide what he was going to do with Jenna, Mace put his key in the lock of his truck. He was in a hurry to get to her place, but he needed to pick up some sandwiches first. He had a big bag of gorp in the car, too. As he started to open the door, a man's form suddenly emerged behind him, distorted and blurred in the moving window glass. The stranger's shadow on the car grew. Instinctively, Mace spun, fists raised. For one second, he'd thought it was Clay Henshaw.

The man yelped and jumped back. "Hey, bloke, it's me!"

"Gil? Gaping Gil?" Mace said as they clapped each other on the back. Gilbert Winslow, known in caving circles as Gaping Gil, was named for Gaping Ghyll, the famous cave in Yorkshire, England. Though many hardcore, extreme cavers were loyal, they were also introverted loners. Gil was the exception, and the gaping part of his nickname reflected his big mouth, too.

Gil looked like a caver. Bearded, thin, dressed in jeans and a flannel shirt tattered from crawls, he'd stand out around here. At least right now he wasn't wearing his knee pads and the scraped-up hockey helmet with duct tape holding his carbide lamp at the correct angle.

"How'd you find me?" Mace asked.

"Bloody hell," came the answer in the familiar British accent that sounded so strange after these past few days of stone-country twang. "You're talking to a gent who can find things in the dark, miles under the earth, and get a Yank like you out of any fix you're in. You think I can't track the likes of you to a small village and a company with your name on it?"

"Did you just get here?"

"Been about for a while, just scouting. Rented an empty trailer in that caravan park, Enchanting Acres, outside the village. You're right, this area's full of caves, and I don't just mean the mapped ones. This Saturday,

I'll collect you at first dawn, and we'll pick ourselves a new blowing hole to explore straightaway."

"This weekend's out. The town's having a sort of festival—"

"Rubbish. This is Gaping Gil you're talking to here."

"I need to be there. Actually, I need to be somewhere right now, too—there's a lady..."

"Now *that* I can believe. Very nice work, indeed. But you don't mean you've given up the underworld, even for a bird?"

"Never. But with my dad's illness and some other things... No, Gil, Caveman has not given up caving, and we'll do some soon. As a matter of fact, there's a particular area I haven't been in for years that I'd like to see again. In fact, I think it might accidentally have been dynamited closed."

"But there might be another way in, and we can find it," he said with a sly grin. "You collect me if you're going there. Does this lady like to cave?"

Mace gave a rueful laugh and shook his head. Someday he would explain, but he didn't have time. "No, but she likes to climb."

"Then, you can teach her to climb down, my lad. If anyone can teach a lady, it's Caveman."

Mace watched in his rearview mirror as Gil loped to his junker of an old truck and got in. Whether underground or on the surface, Gil was something like a ghost, one which could disappear at will. He could trace or track anything, even in a black cave with one little light. No one was a more clever caver—no one but Mace himself.

Jenna was nervous waiting for him. She wanted to greet Mace with a smile, but right now she needed him for support. She deeply resented that her tormentor had invaded more than her lines of communication from the outside. He or she had actually been inside one of her precious tree houses. Her home was now the last bastion of security.

But Mace's arms were a close second. When he arrived, she had only meant to hug him back, but she ended up holding him hard.

"Hey," he said, turning his lips to her ear. "I'm going to give you one hour to stop that. Jenna, what is it?"

She told him, as they walked to Home Tree Home and went up the ladder. She'd meant to entertain him in the kids' house, but couldn't face it again right now.

"We've got to lay some sort of trap for him," Mace said when she'd explained. They sat on the porch bench, eighteen feet off the ground, the food and pop cans between them.

"You think it's a man?"

"A figure of speech. And I don't mean a literal trap, like for a wild animal. We'd as soon catch one of those wolves."

"I'd rather live with them than the games someone's playing. Before, I kept telling myself it was someone distant, but now, with that book appearing, then disappearing..."

"Jenna," he said, as they finally unwrapped their sandwiches, "there's an extra bedroom at our place where you could stay. That way, since both Cassie and I know and are going to help you—"

"No. Thanks, but no. I'm not leaving here. It's obviously just harassment, not something dangerous."

"Not yet," he added ominously. "I'm tempted to start spending nights on your couch downstairs."

For a moment she couldn't answer, as all sorts of scenarios tumbled through her mind, but she managed to say, "Things aren't happening at night, Mace. Everything's been done in broad daylight."

"Which shows he—or she—is bold. I'd like to take the bastard on. I knocked a guy around pretty bad once. He not only scooped booty, but he defaced a virgin passage. I shouldn't have gotten violent but I just lost it. It wasn't my damn cavern, but I felt so protective of it, just as you do here."

"Scooped booty? In a virgin passage?" she echoed.

"He went ahead into an untouched subterranean area someone else had found and had the right to enter first—it's a tradition, honored among cavers. It's the worst sort of violation from a caver. Jenna, tell you what I'll do. I'll stop by whenever I can and look around, even at night. I can call you on your cell phone if you want to know when, so you won't blow my head off with that shotgun you mentioned."

"To tell the truth, I've never used it. One thing I did not get from my dad is his love of hunting or guns."

He nodded. She watched his profile as he looked past the railing, through the foliage, toward the ground. "You're thinking how you and your dad used to hunt on some of this land," she said.

He nodded and reached for her hand, then rested their clasped hands on his lower thigh. "Did you know," he whispered, "you can actually see the cemetery from up here? See—when the leaves shift in the wind."

"I know. I partly chose this tree for that. It's quite a clear view in the late fall and winter."

He slid their food back farther and shifted his big body to turn toward her. "We have so much that binds us, Jenna. I love this land of yours, too, and not just because Dad and I used to shoot here, way back before we began to snipe at each other. When I was small, I used to think the stone animals your granddad carved were way cool. I wish…'' he added and sighed.

''That you—we—could go back again, before everything fell apart?''

''No, I wish that people we loved could just be buried here in the Stone Forest and not the one over there with the fences, roads and manufactured monuments.''

He nodded toward the cemetery again, but she just stared at him. ''This forest, where I was found that night,'' she said, her voice breaking, ''feels more like a place where I was born to start over, not a place to remember death.''

''I didn't mean to get you more upset,'' he said, reaching for his uneaten sandwich as if to close their intimate conversation. But he dropped it back in its sack again. ''Jenna, I'm not very good at helping, even when that's what I want to do.''

As if in slow motion, he reached for her and tilted her toward him. Their shoulders bumped, their hips slid together. She wasn't certain if he turned her face to him or if she did that, but his eyes devoured her as their noses touched, then rubbed.

Mace's mouth took hers, gently at first, then possessively. She put her free hand behind his head to hold him there; he tipped his head to deepen the kiss. Frustrations, fears—everything slipped away from her but this need for this man. The breeze made the sunlight bounce through the treetops, but Jenna was already soaring high above them.

Late that night, as she lay in bed, Jenna heard a wolf howl. The hair stood up on the back of her neck. Yet, because she had been warned, it startled her more than it scared her. It was raining, too, a soft sound that blended and muted the howls.

Excited that wild nature had come nearly to her doorstep, she decided to get up to try to spot the animal. She kneeled in her bedroom window and tried to discern the direction from which the sounds had come. It had sounded close, but she saw nothing. Perhaps the fringe of tree branches hid him from this angle. The night-light and hall light she'd left on were making it hard for her to see out; her own reflection was superimposed in the glass.

She stuffed her feet in her slippers, tugged on her terry-cloth robe and, carrying two flashlights, padded downstairs into darkness. Kneeling again, this time at one of the windows overlooking the front porch, she moved a few cat figurines aside and unfastened the lock. She edged the window open just an inch and waited.

Nothing now, though the damp earth made everything smell lush and wonderfully fertile. Her beloved trees bowed and thrashed. Spring in all its wet grandeur, she thought, feeling so at peace, feral visitor or not.

Then came the mournful wail again, both terrible and beautiful, so wild, so perfectly punctuated by the tattoo of the rain on the porch roof. She was proud of herself for not feeling fear, even staring out into the endless night. It gave her hope that she could discover whoever was trying to torment her about Mandi—unless her nemesis was simply a random sadist.

But then she heard a high-pitched human cough. Close! Very close, maybe on the porch. A man or a woman? Had Mace come by without warning, to be sure she was safe?

"Who's there?" she cried, her mouth pressed to the inch of open window. "Mace?"

When no one answered, she tried to peer sideways. In a sudden hush of wind and rain, the porch creaked as it did when someone came up or down the first step. But she saw no one.

Jenna banged the window closed and dove for the porch light. It illuminated only the slick ebony night pierced by a pair of gleaming eyes that blinked and then disappeared.

7

The next morning, Jenna drove into Russ Pierce's gravel driveway and parked. His place on the other side of town was small. What had evidently once been the garage was now converted to an extra room, so his black station wagon sat outside. His bright yellow bumper sticker said, Eat More Possum. Jenna just rolled her eyes as she got out.

Like many area residents, Russ's yard boasted a collection of various-sized waterwarts—water-carved chunks of limestone hauled back from quarries and creek beds. The prized ones had natural openings to let light through, and Russ had several with holes at least as big as cabbages. But unlike other locals, he seemed to feel no need for grass, flowers or plants. His front yard was the bare reddish soil of the area that was so hard to get out in the wash.

Jenna had been extremely surprised to receive his early morning call, explaining he wanted to build a tree house as soon as possible for the twelve-year-old kids he coached on his Little League team. She thought it was a great idea, but her advertising said, *Don't live earthbound,* and she'd never seen Russ as anything but down-to-earth.

She noted as she approached the front door that his drapes were drawn shut; at one window, old-fashioned venetian blinds no one used anymore were down. She shuddered at the idea of being so closed-in.

This had been his parents' house, and she wondered if he'd changed anything since they'd moved to Florida. There was no sign of Russ anywhere. He'd said to come early before he went in to work, to see if he had a spot for a good-size tree house. Could he have overslept? She had so much to do to prepare her display for Pioneers Day tomorrow that, if he didn't answer, she was just going to leave. Still, she was thrilled to get a job so close to home—and for a kids' tree house, to boot.

Lately, Jenna was aware just how important it had become for her to create an escape for children. She supposed it was part of her healing, her soul-searching self-therapy. She regretted how long she'd delayed going into designs for kids, since they, above all others, inherently treasured the wonder of tree houses.

She went up onto the concrete porch with its plastic lawn furniture. It was the cheap, webbed kind she detested, the sort that had been in the cave when she and Mandi were abducted. Half the porches in Ridgeview seemed to have it. Just as she lifted her fist to knock, the door jerked opened. Startled, she gasped and jumped back.

"Saw you coming," Russ explained, grinning at her, though she had no idea how he'd accomplished that through the shrouded windows. "Come on in." As he swung the door wide, the smell of coffee assailed her. He was dressed casually in jeans and a Chicago White Sox sweatshirt.

"Why don't I just walk around to meet you," she countered, not wanting to enter the enclosed space, "and you can show me which trees you're considering. It looks like you have a pretty nice stand of tall ones out back by the creek.''

A look of hurt—or anger?—flashed across his narrow face. She noted something she'd never paid attention to before: even in good light, even when his expression changed, Russ seldom blinked. It made her feel self-conscious, especially because his thick glasses hugely magnified his eyes.

''Besides,'' she added hastily, ''I've got to get a few things out of the van. And don't think I've come here to hit a baseball. I use a bat to test the strength of the trees.'' She forced a smile, and he seemed to accept that.

''Sure,'' he said. ''Let's go hunt us up a good tree.''

A glimpse into his house behind him had revealed a dim but neatly kept room, empty but for an entertainment center wall unit. On it sat a computer workstation with the screen lit, so he'd obviously been up a while. If he'd been staring at the screen, he must have heard her car and then looked out to see her. Probably he kept the drapes closed in order to see the screen better. And his unbroken gaze was probably the result of too much staring at the screen.

He met her out back with two mugs of steaming coffee.

''Thanks,'' she said, tucking her sample photographs under one arm and grasping the mug in her free hand. He took the baseball bat from her, and made a few smooth practice swings like a kid showing off, one-handed. Instinctively, she stepped back. ''So, do you have your Little Leaguers here a lot?'' she asked.

''Occasional picnics,'' he said, fanning the air between them. ''I even hit balls to them in the field across the road. I want them to have fun now, and great memories of their childhoods later. Can't say I did. Bet you understand that better'n about anyone else."

"Yes and no. I had some very happy times, despite the obvious terrible ones."

As they sipped their coffee, their eyes met and held. Though a weak, watery blue, his gaze bored into hers. She suddenly wondered if the confirmed bachelor was interested in her as a woman. That was the last thing she needed, especially from Russ Pierce.

"So, any particular style of tree house you had in mind?" she asked, putting her mug down on a stump and taking her bat back from him. She had to tug it free of his grip as they strolled toward the creek.

"Of the ones you mentioned on the phone, I been thinking the one you call a Treepee might be good. Those kids are like a bunch of wild Indians at times, but don't tell anybody I said so. Gotta be politically correct in my government job these days, even in good old Ridgeview."

She forced a smile and went a bit closer to the creek to look up into the tree canopy. She felt him staring at her, not at the trees. He was giving her the creeps.

A memory struck her, and her hair prickled on the nape of her neck as surely as it had when she'd heard the wolf howls last night.

"He gives me the absolute creeps, Jen," Mandi had said once, not long before she was lost. *"That nerdy Pierce looks at me through those Coke-bottle glasses like he has X-ray vision to see through my clothes."*

"Like Superman."

"That twit. Hardly. I used to feel sorry for him 'cause his dad drinks and his mom's always running out on them, but I'm going to have Mace or Frank deck him if I see him one more time, just hanging around..."

''So tell me—'' Russ's voice came so close behind her she jumped. ''What makes a good tree house tree? More than just size and lots of branches, right?''

''Right,'' she said, stepping away and tapping several trunks. ''Roots matter, too. They can be diseased or have exposed root crowns. But I've seen several good possible ones here, so if you're sure you want to proceed—''

''Told you I do.''

''Then, next time I come back I'll check what's under the bark. I imagine you need to get in to work about now.''

''Told them I'd be late. There's real advantages to being in charge.''

''Oh, right. You know, Russ,'' she went on, still looking up into the foliage, ''you can't expect this tree house to just appear overnight. My crew or I will probably have to prune some branches, cut out deadwood and cable some limbs together. The Treepee design needs an umbrella foundation, where beams fan out from the trunk like umbrella ribs,'' she went on, gesturing, ''but it's perfect for that Indian teepee look.''

''Sounds good to me,'' he said, smiling almost smugly. ''I'd be glad to help, too, 'specially if there are any math formulas needed when you're fixing to draw the design—or anytime you need help with something like that.''

''I remember, that's your thing,'' she said. ''Oh, there's something else I didn't mention on the phone. With kids, I don't like to build too high. You don't have to be way up to capture the feeling of height and soaring.''

''Sure,'' he said, flinging the rest of his coffee on the ground. ''Gotcha.''

''Now that I see it can be built here, I'll be back

another time to really look around, pick a host tree, draw a few preliminary sketches and give you a ballpark estimate."

"That's a good one, 'ballpark estimate,'" he said, grinning as if she'd made the wildest joke. "Hey, that reminds me, my team's playing a demo game after the festival tomorrow. Why don't you come on over to the old high-school diamond and meet the kids, even if you're a little busy with your own stuff or friends."

"That's a great idea," she told him. "I'd love to get the boys' input—things like whether they'd like a hatch entrance. Maybe we can actually have them help hammer nails later, when it's still on ground. If they know we're taking their ideas into consideration, it will mean more to them."

"I'd like that. A few kids come from tough situations, and I'd like to do all I can to give them something great here."

He sounded so proud each time he mentioned his team. She felt guilty at being uneasy with Russ, a man she—and the entire town—had known for years. And one who wanted nothing but the best for kids, no doubt in place of the family he'd never have himself. She'd just been too on edge lately, and that was hardly his fault.

"I'll try to help you do that, Russ," she said, and put out her hand to shake on their deal. "See you and the Treepee Indians tomorrow then."

Volunteering to help Jenna with her booth to promote Out On A Limb Tree Houses was paying off for Cassie, too. Most of Ridgeview and the surrounding area's denizens had passed or dropped by, which gave Cassie a great chance to put bugs in certain ears about her book.

To a select few, she implied or said outright that she'd love to hear any good anecdotes they had about their former state senator and current lieutenant governor, especially tales from way back when. She even found one woman who had been helped by Cynthia's early founding of Right-A-Wrong, a victim's rights advocacy group that advised and counseled accident survivors. If only people would come up with as many recollections about Cynthia as they did recipes for Cassie to gain weight, it would be an absolutely fabulous day. As one oldtimer put it, she "looked a mite puny and she wasn't even feeling poorly like her daddy."

"You *are* still going to help me with my writing project, aren't you?" Cassie asked Jennie during a lull. "I know finding that book in the tree house upset you, but I didn't leave it there."

"You're asking me to pit myself against my mother more than I already have?" Jennie countered, straightening the pile of brochures without looking at her friend. "She tried to censor your book, but you're plunging ahead and still want my help."

"It's going to be a great book, an uplifting, inspiring story that will do her a lot of good, not bad," Cassie insisted.

"Well, she's wrong about one thing," Jennie muttered as the mingled smell from the popcorn wagon and pizza booth wafted past them on the breeze. "I am not too delicate to handle the past. I'm facing it, looking into it myself—with your and Mace's help, so I guess I owe you. I'm sure she'll find out I'm helping you, but whatever happens, I don't want you telling her someone's harassing me. I'll tell her myself if I can."

"It's a deal, then," Cassie said. "We research the past together. You find what you want and nail the jerk who's bugging you, I get my stuff, and she doesn't stop either of us—nor will it hurt her, I swear it."

Cassie got up from the table and drifted off, as Mary Drout—with her cameraman this time—stopped to interview Jennie about her display. It looked pretty good, Cassie thought. From a maple tree on the town square at the end of the craft tables, they had hung three large black-and-white blowups of the tree houses that were already built in the Stone Forest. On the far side of the table, they had laid out on the grass, using bright yarn and pegs, the floor plan of the children's tree house where Jennie had found the copy of *Gone with the Wind.* After that windy storm last night, Cassie thought, shaking her head, her friend was just lucky that her *tree houses* weren't suddenly missing, like the book had been when she'd dragged Cassie up there to see it.

"Hi, there." A woman's husky voice behind her made Cassie spin around. "You're the author, right?"

Despite the years she'd lived away, Cassie was surprised to see someone over fifty she didn't know. This had been like old home week for her with anyone who was at least forty-something.

"Yes, that's right. How did you know?" Cassie asked, smiling and nodding.

"I overheard Mary Drout say so, though I wasn't eavesdropping. I used to live over the county line, but I left the state years ago. I'm only back for the summer because my daughter had twins and she needs the help, but I just had to come to this today—you know, for old time's sake."

The woman spoke in long, breathless sentences. She had what Cassie's dad called "a whiskey voice," but considering that she smelled of tobacco, it could have been a smoking voice, too. Yet she looked grandmotherly indeed, with white, newly permed, frizzy hair and blotched skin that had seen too much sun.

"I'm Cassandra MacCaman. And you are..."

"Brenda Sage. So, you're doing a book about Lieutenant Governor Kirk."

"It's barely started yet, but I should have known Mary would pick up on it," Cassie admitted, realizing that all of Ridgeview would soon know—and that Cynthia Kirk would hear Cassie wasn't letting it go. Cassie had seen Cynthia here today, hobnobbing with the mayor and township trustees over by the display of old quilts, and Jenna was excited that her mother was having dinner at her house before heading back tomorrow to the state capital. Hopefully, Cassie thought, Cynthia would not have time today to berate her again for daring to go ahead with what was now an unauthorized biography.

"So, did you know Cynthia Kirk years ago?" Cassie asked the woman, who had suddenly gone reticent and was playing almost coyly with her clunky charm bracelet that evidently bore grandchildren's profiles. Cassie wondered if Brenda Sage was waiting to be offered money for her information.

"Not really," Brenda drawled.

"Then, do you have an anecdote that would be considered hearsay?"

"No, I was an eyewitness."

"To what, exactly?" Cassie asked, trying not to sound annoyed.

"The thing is, I used to see her—to watch her all the time. For a while I thought of her as some kind of Joan of Arc, you know, chosen to suffer but also to give of herself, to lead. I really admired her."

Joan of Arc, Cassie thought. Now, that was a comparison she'd never thought of, although she knew a few folks in town who thought Cynthia Kirk was a candidate for sainthood. "But then," the woman said, wetting her pink lips and glancing around nervously, "I realized she was just like the rest of us, with weaknesses and temptations she gave in to."

Cassie's heart began to beat harder. "In what way?" she managed to say, in a calm, journalist's voice.

"She used to come in real late at night to the Limey Roadhouse."

"That old place over on County Line Road near Bloomington?"

Limey's was a redneck joint if there ever was one. At least, that's the way the place was years ago when the high-school kids used to buy six-packs of beer out the back door from a guy they tipped really well. Teens were willing to drive the extra twenty miles so no one recognized them. Other than that—and the kids never went in—no one from Ridgeview frequented the place, since several bars and taverns were closer.

Brenda nodded. "That's where I waited tables years ago. She'd always meet a man—left with him in his car, too, then picked hers up lots later. I saw that more'n once. Of course, I wouldn't want to be quoted on that."

"But when was this?" Cassie asked. "I mean, before the rock slide disaster or aft—"

The woman looked over her shoulder at something or someone and shook her head in warning. Cynthia Kirk stood nearby at Jenna's table with an entourage surrounding her, including Mary Drout and her photographer. Just then, Cynthia glanced over at Cassie, waggled her fingers in a wave, and smiled so sweetly that Cassie could have fallen over with shock. But when she looked back to ask Brenda Sage who the man with Cynthia had been years ago, Brenda had disappeared into the crowd.

"Jenna," a familiar voice said, and she turned to see a smiling Frank Connors leaning, stiff-armed, on the end of her display table. "How's our business going?"

"*Our* business?" she said. It annoyed her that Frank always referred to *Out On A Limb* that way just because she'd taken out a modest loan from his bank. But she had to get hold of herself. She was just strung out from so little sleep lately, and was fighting a headache.

"All right, all right," he drawled, balling up a fist and leaning closer to playfully punch her shoulder. "*Your* visionary dream, *your* business. I haven't seen you much lately. Have you been out of town to see new clients again?"

"Actually, I've been keeping close to home. I may build a kids' design for Russ Pierce for his Little League teams to visit."

"Pierce, huh?" Frank said with a grimace and a sniff. "Sometimes I think I could turn the entire bank's affairs over to him, since he always seems to know about them. If I want to keep things private, I need to use FedEx or UPS. In high school, the only thing I thought he had going for him was that he could run like the wind—"

"And had a computer mind for numbers," she put in.

"Yeah. But now, 'Neither snow nor sleet nor gloom of night can stay our illustrious postman from his appointed tasks.' Or something like that," he finished lamely.

"Since we're quoting today, he always 'marched to a different drummer,'" Jenna admitted. "But you've got to admit that stone country is full of individuals."

Frank nodded. "Some would say eccentrics. Weirdos." Though they had managed a lighthearted conversation, Jenna felt as if it wasn't what he wanted to talk about at all. The silver-blue knit shirt Frank wore over his chinos really brought out the icy blue of his narrow eyes. His nose and cheeks had already begun to turn pink in the spring sun today. He'd evidently been wearing the sunglasses now perched on top of his head, because he was starting to get that raccoon look around the eyes. They looked puffy, so maybe he wasn't sleeping well, either. When he reached up to pull his glasses on again, she noticed black-and-blue bruises on his forearms.

"Looks like you had a fall," she observed in the awkward silence that followed their chatter.

"I scraped myself on the back porch, trying to get my scared dog in during that windstorm last night," he muttered, sounding angry with himself. "It's nothing. So, you glad Mace is back?" he asked, sunglasses back on.

Aha, she thought, the real topic of the day. "Of course," she said. "And happy Cassie's come home, too. It's a blessing for their dad, considering what he's facing."

"And, no doubt, the Godfather thinks it's a blessing for MacCaman Stone, though scuttlebutt says Clay Henshaw's not too thrilled about the black sheep's return. You heard they're going to reopen Deep Heart?"

"I heard."

"And?" he prompted.

"And there's no reason not to after all these years, though it came as a shock. The memorial for the rock slide is here—" she nodded toward the monument on the town square "—and in all our hearts."

"Right. Sure," he said, sounding surprised. "Jenna, I'd really like to see you again and give building a relationship another shot. If I came on too hard, too fast, or if you thought I was trying to use the fact the bank held your loan— Hell, I don't want to say all these things in the middle of this circus today. I'm going to call you, okay?''

He waved and hurried off, as if to ensure she didn't have time to answer. She was almost tempted to go after him and ask him not to call, but new people were drifting toward her, past the wood-carving and tole work tables. Jenna sat up straighter. It was her mother, walking in the midst of a small crowd, some of whom she knew.

''I just might have you build a tree house for my Samantha,'' Garth Brennan called to Jenna as he strolled closer. He had emerged from the little swarm of people that stopped one table away from her. ''I really love this layout and the photo of the one you've already done,'' he added, nodding toward a blowup photo behind her.

''You'll have to bring her to see it in person,'' Jenna told him, excited at the prospect of getting to partially repay him for all the help he'd given her family over the years. ''I'd love to design one for her. How's she doing?''

''Ah, since you asked, the proud father just happens to have a recent photo,'' Garth said, beaming. ''I would have brought both her and Claire today, but they've been under the weather lately. You know, Sammy brings some bug home from school and we all get it.''

Jenna took the well-worn photo Garth handed her from his billfold with a flourish. If it was a new one, she thought, it was already dog-eared from having been taken out and shown numerous times. Samantha Brennan had a heart-shaped face and huge hazel eyes. Her straight, brown hair was pulled back from her pretty face in a ponytail.

''She's darling,'' Jenna told him, studying it. ''Only the prettiest kids can wear their hair straight back and still look that good.''

She realized she was also describing Mandi, who had occasionally tried to tame her bounteous, curly hair. Garth hesitated as if he were waiting for more, or—damn him—reading her thoughts. No way was she going to be convinced to have him counseling her again.

"Obviously, she looks like her mother," he said after a pause, still smiling. From behind him, Mary Drout, who was Samantha's great-aunt, snatched the photo and began to show it to others.

Suddenly, Jenna's headache began to pound. Frank's visit had jump-started it again. It had begun earlier, perched between her eyes, when she stood with Mace to watch the brief parade. She'd become almost dizzy as the participants moved past: costumed pioneer reenactors sitting on bales of straw in several pickup trucks; kids on decorated bikes; a quarter horse equestrian unit; the consolidated high-school band. At the end came a single crepe paper-decorated float, carrying the teenage Pioneers Day queen who was waving her arm off. Mandi had been the queen one year, but she'd smiled, nodded, and waved regally, as if she were Princess Diana.

Now Jenna massaged the flesh between her eyebrows. After the wolf's visit last night, she had been awake for hours. Finally, she had convinced herself that the sound she had thought was a human cough must have been a tree limb snapping in the wind. And that creak of the step could have been simply the old house cracking its bones under what architects called the "wind load." She was only too grateful that the three tree houses had stood firm.

The squeals of kids on the few simple amusement park rides, the shouts from the vendors, and the women's chatter at the craft fair and tent events seemed to heighten her pain. Jenna was just about to try to pull her mother away to get a soft drink and find out what time she was coming to dinner when Mace and a skinny, bearded guy she didn't recognize strode toward her across the green. She hardly heard Garth's parting words as he moved on to join her mother's entourage: "Let me know if there's anything I can do, Jenna, anything at all."

"Mace," Jenna said, smiling as he grinned at her. "I didn't know you were here."

"I checked on Dad, but he kicked me out. He said he wasn't up to the 'the damn hoopla' today."

Cassie evidently heard and came over. "Should I run home? You sure he's okay? Mace, you didn't have an argument over reopening Deep Heart, did you?" she asked, her voice accusatory. "I could tell one was brewing."

"No, Cass. He just runs himself too hard, and he's wiped out on weekends, that's all. Jenna, Cassie, I'd like you to meet an old buddy of mine. Gil Winslow, my sister Cassie and my good friend, Jenna Kirk."

"The tree-house lady," Gil said, nodding. "I've heard about you."

"Gil's a caver friend," Mace put in hastily. "We've been a lot of places together. He's in the area for a while to check out the great local limestone caverns."

Handshakes, further introductions and small talk ensued. Jenna wondered if Mace had sent for Gil, intending to go back to caving full-time. She'd ask later. Suddenly, everyone seemed to be talking at once. Gil's English accent soon blurred with the local lingo. Hoping to make a graceful escape to nurse her headache, she was just about to invite Cassie and the cavers to dinner tomorrow, when she saw one of Clay Henshaw's boys trip himself up in the yarn she had laid out on the ground. As plastic pegs flew, he inadvertently yanked out most of the tree-house outline, while his two older brothers whooped and hollered. She saw that the culprit wore a Ridgeview Stonemen Little League shirt, and remembered she'd told Russ she would watch some of the game later.

"Hey, hold still a minute, so I can rescue you and the rest of this yarn," Jenna yelled to them as she ran over.

"Oh, sorry," the youngest said. "Din't know it was your stuff, Ms. Kirk. We been all over your forest and din't mean to hurt nothing."

"It's okay. Let's see, what are your names again?" she asked as she rewound the yarn in huge loops between her hand and elbow.

"Jeb—that's me. He's Pete, and he's Bill," the oldest said, pointing.

Pete was the ballplayer. He was a cute blonde with freckles and a fake decal tattoo of a fighter jet on his left upper arm. "You're on Mr. Pierce's team?" she asked him.

"*Coach* Pierce's," he corrected solemnly as if she'd made a grave error. "Sure. He's our boss, and we're gonna win today, 'cause we can do anything we try really hard to do if we believe in ourselves."

Jenna noted that their dad, Clay Henshaw, was sitting on the stone base of the rock slide memorial eating ice cream and just watching. She almost called to him that there was no problem. But was he staring at his kids or at Mace, who was walking toward her?

She waved to Clay, sent the boys on their way and turned back to her friends. Gil was scrutinizing the blow-ups of her three tree houses. "What do you think, Gil?" she asked as she and Mace rejoined them. "Those are my favorite caves, only they're aboveground, not under. I just climb them, crawl in and—"

''But what's this in the shadows right here?'' Gil interrupted, squinting at the middle photo. He pointed, not at the tree house but at a thin bush under it, part of the distant, natural frame.

''The forest is full of old stone sculptures,'' Cassie explained to Gil, not looking at the photo but away, as if searching for someone. ''*That* you have to see to believe.''

But Jenna took a closer look. The spot Mace's friend was pointing out was not near a cluster of sculptures, though the carved frogs and toadstools were not far back. She bent nearer her own photo, feeling foolish that she hadn't spotted the form before. But she'd been so busy and distracted.

From the foggy gray—this area was slightly blurred so she could focus on the child's tree house—a lighter silhouette emerged. A dimly outlined figure, not tall, sporting a ruff or mane. Surely she hadn't captured a watching wolf in her picture!

''Here. Stand back right here,'' Gil insisted, making a frame with his open hands and shifting so that the natural outdoor light didn't glance so brightly off the glossy finish.

Jenna saw it then. A small, thin person, evidently just standing and staring up at the tree house. A child? Yes, a young girl—one with full, curly hair. But how could someone have stood there without Jenna seeing her when she shot the photo?

''Jenna, what is it?'' Mace asked. His fingers clamped around her arm. ''You look faint. Are you okay?''

''I...yes, sure. I'm just getting a headache from squinting.''

''I'll keep an eye on things here,'' Cassie piped up, finally bending closer to the photo, too, ''and you go take a nice break. It's just some kid, I think. Probably someone was in the forest looking at the sculptures, that's all."

But Jenna knew that was not all, though she let Mace guide her away from the crowded square to the van which she'd parked close to unload everything. She leaned against her van.

"What?" he said, standing right in front of her.

"Didn't you see it?"

"Yes, but what—"

"It looks just like Mandi, a younger Mandi, staring at me."

"Jenna," he drawled in a warning tone, "come on now—"

"No," she said, digging her keys from her jeans, "you come on with me, if you want. I'm going home right now to see that exact spot and figure out what's going on! I don't believe in ghosts or hauntings, but I'm getting mad as hell about all this."

Without even a glance at Cassie and Gil, Mace pried the keys from her fierce grip, put her in the passenger side and got in to drive.

8

Mace could see Jenna was increasingly distraught. He was grateful he was the one driving as he made the three sharp turns around the Mother Lode Quarry, just outside town.

"We'll find an explanation," she told him for the second time, as he turned her van up the crushed stone driveway through the fringe of the Stone Forest. Hands gripped in her lap, she frowned out into the sun-dappled woods. He wondered whether soon she'd need not only his advice, but his protection.

"I wish I'd brought that blown-up photo with me!" she cried. "I'll run into the house and get the original three-by-five, but it won't help as much."

He grabbed her arm when she tried to open the door before he completely stopped the van. "Jenna, you've got to stay steady through this. I don't want you to get hurt. There's probably a rational explana—"

"I need my keys," she interrupted as if she hadn't heard him. She leaned toward him to yank them out of the ignition the instant he turned it off.

He waited impatiently as she tore into the house. The big wind and rainstorm last night had left puddles and littered the ground with limbs and leaves. When Jenna didn't return immediately, he started in after her. But just then, she ran out with a stack of photos splayed in her hands like playing cards.

"There must be others taken from that angle," she said, shoving some of the pictures at him. "I took a bunch."

"These are too small to tell," he told her, studying the ones he held.

"So I see. If I hadn't had the one blown up, we'd never have seen it—the person—which means the someone is not *trying* to be seen. Or..." Her voice trailed off.

"Or what?" he asked as they went out into the Stone Forest, heading for the vantage point from which she'd taken the pictures. The earth smelled fresh and wet; if they brushed too close to a tree or bush, they got flecked with water. He tried to hold some foliage back for her, but she seemed oblivious to getting sprayed.

"Or," she said grimly, "someone knew I was going to get the pics blown up, but planned to be gone by then. Whoever is doing this is not stupid—or they just know me and my family very well."

"And the harassment's escalating."

"Tell me about it. I was considering hiring someone from Indianapolis to see if my house is bugged, but I don't think any stranger's been inside. I'd feel it if that had happened. Besides, I never said aloud in either the house or the van that I was planning to get the blowups made. And I'll be damned if I'll call in the county sheriff so the word gets out around here. That's probably just what my harasser wants—to feed off things getting in the papers again."

"Could the crank callers who bothered your mother after Mandi disappeared be to blame? Someone local who's getting sick kicks out of shaking you up since you've been back, especially since Cynthia's usually out of the area now."

"I've thought of that—" she said, her voice breaking.

"Let's go at this from another direction. Did anyone know you were planning to get the photos enlarged? Jenna?" he prompted when she hesitated.

"Cassie knew."

"You don't think it's her?"

"Hardly, though I did jump to that conclusion once already. But who knows who she told?"

"Actually, she mentioned it to me and Dad at the dinner table," he admitted, seizing her arm to swing her around to face him. "But I swear to you, it's not us."

"Mace, I *know* it isn't," she assured him. "You have a few things of your own to worry about. Right now the MacCamans are my best supporters."

"I know I said I lusted for this piece of land, but not at the expense of all this to drive you off."

"For Pete's sake, forget the true confessions. And no one's driving me off. But, as I said, who knows who else Cassie told—or who overheard her. I did call the photo lab in Bloomington to ask if they could blow up the photos in one day, but they were all strangers as far as I know. Or i-it's," she stammered, "simply that someone's been watching my every move, saw me taking the photos and perversely decided to get in them."

"Or it's pure accident that you caught some kid standing there watching you."

"So you think it's a child, too? It's sure not Clay Henshaw's boys, though they said they've been in the forest."

As she craned her neck to look around, she snagged her toe on a root. Mace caught her and steadied her before they went on. "Maybe I should try to be here more so I can catch whoever might be watching you."

"Isn't that all we need?" she retorted, her voice bitter.

"You and the wolves hiding in the forest at night. Or if you followed me around town, we'd get the gossips reporting Mace MacCaman is stalking his old girlfriend's sister, even if it is years after the kidnapping."

She stopped abruptly. When he halted and turned to her, she hurled herself into his arms. Surprised by the sudden move yet touched and triumphant, he hugged her hard.

"Do you think I'm losing it?" she asked, her voice muffled against his shoulder. "I immediately saw Mandi in that silhouette on the blowup, like looking at a Rorschach ink-blot test, one that proves I'm going crazy."

"Jenna, stop it! I don't know what I think about that photo, and you don't either, but you're not going crazy." He tried to soothe her. "Come on, sweetheart, let's go check out the spot so you can put your mind at rest. We're almost there."

She pulled away slightly and looked up at him. "You think you know the spot?" she asked, her tone suddenly wary.

"It has to be at a certain angle and distance from the kids' tree house, that's all."

She nodded, and they walked the rest of the way in silence. When they stood near the tree house, both of them began to look down instead of up. Mace was mostly looking for wolf tracks, since he too had heard the animal's howls in the rain last night. Jenna, he was sure, was watching for the print of a human sort of wolf.

Jenna thought she knew the spot, but it took them a lot of shifting around to discern exactly where she had stood to take the photo, and then more shuffling through grass and last year's sodden, packed leaves to try to see where the figure must have stood.

"That's a good one," she heard Mace mutter from behind her.

"What?"

"The person—if it *was* a person and not just a trick of shadows and light—must have been standing between Heaven and Hell."

Her stomach cartwheeled, but she saw exactly what he meant. Over the years, as her grandfather had carved various stone figures, animals and plants, he had grouped them by scenes. Live-looking limestone rabbits and flowers inhabited what Jenna, from childhood, had called Rabbit Run. Farther back in Fairy Land, elves cavorted around knee-high toadstools. A single stag watched over fawns and does in Deer Park. Child-size stone furniture, with cats curled up on chairs, was closer to the back of the house, in what was termed The Living Room.

But here, clearly visible from where she'd built two of her prototype tree houses, was the most unique and detailed section of stone carvings. Looking toward the distant cemetery, as if guarding its approach, two majestic angels spread their wings over a cluster of cherubs. Grandma had called the angels Mandi and Jenna, and dubbed the grouping Heaven. Literally a stone's throw away, seven grinning gargoyles crouched, their faces and forms sprouted from various-size waterwarts. They weren't exactly Satan's demons, but someone had named that section Hell.

As kids, they'd made grotesque and funny faces here. This was once the favorite photo site for visitors, who used to be common but had dwindled over the years. Town talk had once suggested that the Stone Forest would make a unique public park. Several influential folks, including Frank Connors, had pushed for that, but then backed off when Jenna had returned.

One thought scared Jenna now. When they were little, the angelic-looking Mandi had loved to jump out at her from behind these gargoyle rocks, making horrid faces and howling like that wolf last night. No one had known that but her and Mandi. And now, that silhouette in her picture had appeared near here, as if Mandi—or her spirit—still played on these grounds.

"Jenna?" She started at Mace's voice. Gargoyle heads laughed and leered at her from behind him. "Don't you think it must have been right here?"

"Yes," she agreed, coming to stand beside him in the spotted shade. "With those bushes behind and these hanging limbs around, the figure must have been about here. Some kid *might* have just wandered in—but out here, without an adult?" she asked in disbelief, challenging her own theory.

"We'll have to recheck the blowup, but maybe it was an adult on her knees. Or, if we want to get crazier, on *his* knees with something wrapped around his head."

"Look at this dark, mottled shade," she insisted, craning her neck again to look around. "It was about this time of day I took the shots. Could that thick mane of hair have been this foliage or a trick of the light?"

"You go stand where you took it, and I'll stay here," he suggested.

As shaken as she still felt, it was good to be doing something concrete about this, Jenna told herself as she strode away from him. She did not know how to proceed against her invisible tormentor except by probing the past, by herself and with Cassie. Odds were, she thought, that it was just some kook being cruel. Still, it seemed to be someone who knew her.

"Okay, kind of hunker down there," she ordered, when she thought they were well aligned. "The ground's still too wet to kneel. Now wrap your arms around your head to simulate that hair."

"Well?" he asked, as she made finger frames from where she stood, peering intently at him. "Is that enough?"

"I still can't tell. Do you see anything on the ground, like footprints?" she asked as she walked back to him.

"Beaten-down grass and wet moss don't lead to good footprint preservation, Sherlock," he said, straightening at last.

"Mace, I'm serious. And scared."

He hauled her into his embrace again. She went willingly, holding him, feeling a thrill each time he touched her.

"I know. I was trying to lighten things up, not make light of them. And I *am* going to come by sometimes at night, like I said before."

"But so far everything has happened in broad daylight."

"Have you thought about getting a dog?"

"A watchdog?" she mused aloud as they held hands and walked back toward the house together. "I've always had cats. Well, they were usually Mandi's and mine, until that precious Siamese of hers."

"Pert," he said, his voice taking on a dark tone. "I wonder whatever happened to poor Pert."

"She never turned up again after the day I was found. And she was such a baby, too, a real spoiled house pet. Mother said she somehow got out and just never came back. I used to think someone had kidnapped—catnapped—Pert, too. I had a dream once that Mandi wasn't dead and Pert went to live with her nearby...."

She pulled her hand away from Mace's and leaned against a tree. Her voice trembling, she choked out, "I wanted to let it all go—bury it, bury her—but now I can't. Now I have to resurrect her, to look for more clues about who...would do all this."

Mace tried to hold her again, but she shook her head wildly. Instead of embracing her, he held her hard by her shoulders at arm's length.

"You're right. You've got to let her go, to bury her here and now. Then you can pursue all of this more objectively. You can protect yourself. If we want to build a real relationship together, you've got to go forward, not back. Let Cassie worry about that. Mandi's starting to obsess you—"

"*Starting* to?" she mocked, her voice rising. "How could she not, from the very start of my life? The beautiful, the perfect, Miss Mandi—and more so when she was gone and it was somehow my fault."

He shook her once to halt her hysteria. "It isn't your fault, none of it. And I agree that you—we, together—have got to find out who's doing this, but then you've got to put it all away."

"You sound like my psychiatrist Dr. Brennan, or my mother. That's what they've said for years, and where has it gotten me?" she challenged, struggling to pull free.

"It's gotten you to start to build your dream here," he insisted, letting her go but blocking her in against the tree trunk with both hands. "It's gotten you to become independent of your mother—not that I blame her for trying to hang on to you. It's gotten you to turn into a beautiful, strong—"

"I'm not."

"—and totally desirable woman who stands in no one's shadow. And it's gotten you me, as a friend. Maybe even more than that."

He sounded out of breath, as if he'd run for miles. This time they met halfway in a mutual, fierce embrace. He clamped her to him. She encircled his neck with her hand, pulling his mouth to hers. As her breasts flattened against his hard chest, they breathed in unison. The kiss went on and on, harder and deeper. Dizzy, she leaned her hips against his hard thighs for support.

And if anyone was watching—even Mandi's ghost—Jenna was staggered by a maze of emotions she'd never fathomed, and defied them to try to make her regret it.

"Cassie, I was hoping I'd get a moment to speak with you alone," a voice called from behind her.

Cassie turned from taking Jenna's blowups down. It had been over an hour since Jenna and Mace had left and things were winding down here, so she and Gil were packing up. Cassie thought she had recognized the voice, and she was right. She was only surprised that her visitor wasn't looking for Jenna.

"Mrs. Kirk," Cassie said, walking over to her while Gil went on working. "You said you'd be busy today, and I saw you were."

"But not too busy to settle things between us. And I'm never too busy to spend a moment with Jenna's best friend. I'm afraid I had too many things on my mind at the restaurant the other morning to be very attentive, and may have overreacted. My life may be an open book, but that doesn't mean I enjoy others reading it. However, I've given your proposal some thought, and I think we can work together on the project."

Cassie hoped her jaw didn't hit the ground too hard. "That's great. It will make a world of difference to have your help and your blessing."

"Hmm, that's one way of putting it. Look, Cassie,

before someone comes over to interrupt us, I just want to say I'm so grateful you're back in Jenna's life."

"Mace is back, too."

"Of course, though I'm sure he'll be busy learning the ropes at MacCaman, and overseeing the opening of Deep Heart."

As if it had called to them, Cynthia and Cassie darted glances toward the rock slide monument. "In short," Cynthia plunged on, "Jenna's all I have, and I tend to be overprotective of her. But I'm pledging my help—when my schedule permits, of course—so please keep me completely apprised of how the work is going. And, since you'll be my eyes and ears here with Jenna, let me know if there's anything she needs, too, won't you?"

To Cassie's surprise, Cynthia reached out to give her a brisk, light hug. It was, Cassie thought, a far cry from their last meeting.

"Sure," she agreed, stepping back from what she was certain must be a freshly applied cloud of Chanel perfume. "I'll definitely keep in touch," she promised.

"And I with you. Speaking of which," Cynthia said as she fished a ring of keys out of her cavernous purse, "I'm going to stop by to see your father en route to Jenna's for dinner. It's been weeks. Now, don't you worry," she added, evidently when she thought Cassie was going to protest. "I've heard he's not seeing guests and wears himself out at MacCaman during the week. And if he's napping, I'll just leave a note."

Cynthia gave that little finger-waggle again, and set off briskly across the town square. At least, Cassie thought, noting how elegant she looked, even in slacks, a blouse and flats, the Stone Lady of her book has changed her mind about it. Cassie might eventually even get up enough courage to slide in a question about whether or not Cynthia used to stop by the Limey Roadhouse. She wished that Brenda Sage had not suddenly vanished today. She hardly knew how to track her down, unless she could do that through a visit to the roadhouse.

"Why not strike while the iron's hot," Cassie muttered.

"What's that?" Gil asked, looking up from stacking the big photos.

"Oh, just talking to myself," she told him, not wanting to admit she'd forgotten he was here. "Since these giant pics barely fit in my car, I think I'm going to stow this stuff at Kirkhall and go get a beer somewhere out of this bustling town."

"That sounds very nice, indeed."

"Come along, then. It's been years since I've seen the place I'm thinking of, but it used to be off-limits and not the best of neighborhoods. I can use an escort."

"Bloody hell, it sounds like a walk in the park for a caver. I'm game."

"So am I," Cassie whispered to herself, as she turned to stare again at the ghostly figure in Jennie's photo. She shrouded it with the tablecloth. "So am I."

"I heard something," Jenna said, bouncing up from the couch in her living room where she and Mace had been talking over cups of coffee.

He half stood to glance out the large window that overlooked the front porch. "Your mother's finally here," he told her. "That was her car door. I'll leave you two alone. But," he added pointedly, pulling her to her feet and gripping her shoulders, "you *will* call me, day or night, if anything seems funny here."

"I'm grateful for your support, Mace."

"I'll bring your van back later, after I get Cassie or

Gil to drive my car home,'' he told her, starting for the door. He dropped a quick kiss on her mouth, as Cynthia knocked. ''But it will be before dark. I'll just put the keys between the screen door and front door, so I don't disturb you. I know how important parent time can be.''

''I know you do,'' she said as she hurried to open the door for her mother.

''I only saw one car out front,'' Cynthia said, obviously surprised to see them together. ''Mace, your father's awake and Cassie's not home, in case you want someone with him.''

''I was just leaving.'' From afar at Pioneers Day, Jenna had seen her mother and Mace speak for the first time in years. She suddenly wondered what they'd said. ''It's nice of you to stop in and see him, Mrs. Kirk,'' he added as he edged toward the door.

''When everything first fell apart,'' Cynthia said, returning Mace's steady gaze, ''I don't know what I would have done without Rod MacCaman. And the town would have gone under without his rebuilding MacCaman Stone. I'm glad you've come home to help him.''

Mace made his goodbyes, and Jenna was glad her mother didn't quiz her about why his car wasn't here. ''So,'' her mom said as they went out to the kitchen, where Jenna began to pull out food she'd prepared early this morning, ''did you have a good day selling tree houses?''

''I have tentative orders for three, and two sites to inspect as possibles,'' she said, pulling off the tinfoil and putting the pan of lasagna in the oven. ''And Russ Pierce wants one for his kids.''

''His baseball boys, you mean? It's probably for himself,'' her mother insisted with a little snort.

''Oh, no!'' Jenna cried, hitting her forehead with one

hand. "I told him I'd stop by to watch their exhibition game and meet the boys, but I forgot."

"Then, I'd say you're getting a bit too involved with Mace MacCaman. And I don't think this family needs to go through that again."

Deciding not to respond, Jenna poured two goblets of wine while Cynthia washed her hands. She almost told her mother what had happened to distract her this afternoon, but she just couldn't upset her. "I'll call him later to apologize—to Russ, that is."

"Good luck. He's an arrested adolescent, if you ask me, so you've probably hurt his feelings. He used to get all bent out of shape when Mandi would have nothing to do with him, which just shows he's always lived on his own Fantasy Island. Now Jenna, last time I was here," she went on in a rush, drying her hands, "I know I sounded as if I disparaged your business, and I want you to know that's not the case. It's simply that I sometimes panic when you are off on your own. If I don't know where you are and what you're doing, I occasionally experience something like an anxiety attack."

"I understand, Mother, really. We've both had to learn—far too often—to let go."

"Exactly," she said, throwing down the towel and taking the glass of wine. She put one arm around Jenna, and they clinked glasses. "To the new us, apart but ever together," she proposed a toast.

"You don't get any crank calls anymore, do you?" Jenna pursued, though she knew it was best to just enjoy this tiny, temporary victory. "I mean about politics and since you're a public figure now," she added hastily.

Cynthia frowned into her goblet as if she were reading tea leaves. "No, thank God. That's all I'd need right now. Those crank calls when Mandi was lost were horrid. The authorities never found out who did that to us. It may have been more than one person. It's a good thing I didn't know, or I might have added the desire to kill to my hatred and fury, the state I was in then."

Jenna decided she was not going to upset her mother by telling her what was going on. She'd handle this with Mace's help.

After dinner, as dusk set in, the Kirk women climbed into Home Tree Home to watch the sunset fade from the sky. Jenna was thrilled, for her mother was showing an appreciation of her work that she seldom had before.

Shoulders touching, they leaned their elbows on the railing and watched the clouds catch the pinks and purples. "I never meant to shut you out or try to make you toe the line," her mother whispered.

The change of topics shocked Jenna, for after their initial, heartfelt exchange, they'd kept their conversation light at dinner.

"Mother, I underst—"

"No, just wait. You see, my brilliant, talented father had done that to me—shut me out to make me behave the way he wanted. I don't mean to turn around and do something to you that I always detested. I was good at talking, at people skills, but my father's dreams for me included inheriting his artistic brilliance, and being a loner to foster that brilliance. Hell, I couldn't even make a good clay ashtray for a Father's Day gift at Girl Scouts."

"If he could see you now, he'd be proud."

Her mother shrugged so hard she bounced Jenna slightly away. "I doubt it. He'd probably order me to shuck the chance for the vice presidency and hang out in this forest instead, chiseling away at Bambi and Thumper and cherubs and gremlins or whatever."

"Gargoyles."

"Right. Your dad would have been proud of you, Jenna, building things, like he did—good with your hands. You took after him, just like Mandi did me."

"Yes," Jenna said after a pause. "She even looked like you."

"I felt I lost a piece of myself when she was gone," her mother went on as if she hadn't heard. "That I had to make up for her being gone, keep busy, keep doing good things to help others...."

Jenna put her hand over her mother's on the railing. Her mother didn't budge. She felt stiff and cold.

"Mother, I know I could never make that up to you. Never replace—"

"I realize you don't need counseling anymore, Jenna, but sometimes I do. I'm still seeing Dr. Brennan off and on. Sometime, it would be good if you'd go with me. You see, I feel as if I could say some things—things I need to say—while you're there."

Jenna nodded, but her words caught in her throat. "Since you put it that way, all right."

"Good," she said with a single sniff. She nodded and turned her hand palm-up to give Jenna's a squeeze. "Meanwhile, I'm glad you have a lot of new orders for these castles in the air of yours. Believe me, it helps to keep busy, one day at a time."

They stood, gazing out through the foliage in the direction of the cemetery as the last remnants of sunset fled to leave only shades of gray behind. "Let's get down before it's too dark," her mother said, her voice much stronger as she looked closely at her watch. "Without Vince driving me, I've got to head back."

"I'd love to have you stay all night. You could leave early in the morning," Jenna suggested as she followed Cynthia down the ladder.

"No can do, darling. Besides, the last thing I need waking me up in the middle of the night is wolf howls. I'm going to just kiss you goodbye and be on my way."

Jenna walked her back to her car and waved as she drove out. Mace had dropped off her van. Cradling her car keys, which Mace had left as promised, Jenna stood on the porch to watch her mother drive down the long, curving driveway. The car reached partway, then stopped. She must have changed her mind, Jenna thought, or have forgotten something.

But she didn't drive back. Jenna watched through the tree trunks as the light popped on in her mother's car. It looked from here as if she was brushing her hair, maybe even applying lipstick or powder. For a drive back to Indianapolis?

Then she heard the car engine rev again. The twin taillights reminded Jenna of wolf's eyes as the dark forest devoured the car.

9

"This isn't the place I remember," Cassie said as she turned into the parking lot. A lighted sign identified the building as The Historic Limey Roadhouse, Est. 1940. Gil leaned forward to stare at the repainted facade through the front windshield of her car.

"It's certainly not the way you described it, but with some of the city suburbs creeping out this way, what do you expect?" he asked. "More than one bloke's neighborhood pub's gone the way of the British empire. And I've seen too many visitors ruin more than one good virgin cave in my time."

Hardly listening to him, Cassie got out and gawked. No pickups or old clunkers huddled in the parking lot, the way she remembered. Several BMWs, a Saab, and a couple of sporty convertibles with their tops down sat between newly painted parking lines that included four disabled slots and a prominent wheelchair ramp. Wooden slat shutters instead of neon beer signs adorned the windows. And the tasteful ads she could see as she peeked inside did not shout Budweiser! or Marlboro! but politely presented imported beers like Tuborg and Amstel and touted a smoke-free environment. A young, college-age couple with Indiana University logos on their jackets came out as she and Gil headed in.

"Oh, jeez," she muttered, thinking she'd never get a

lead here on either Brenda Sage or Cynthia Kirk in days gone by. This was going to be a wild-goose chase.

Inside, the dark and dingy atmosphere Mace and his buddies used to talk about, and that she'd sneaked into a few times, had been obliterated by indirect ceiling lights and ecru paint. A large-screen TV over the bar was tuned to a soccer game, which Gil immediately gravitated toward.

"Be right back," she told him when she saw one of the two female bartenders head for the back hall where a sign read Rest Rooms. "Order us something."

The hall leading to the rest rooms displayed photos of the Bloomington campus, including one glorifying Indiana's unofficial religion of I.U. basketball. On the sidelines, in front of berserk fans, longtime tough-guy coach Bobby Knight was screaming and pointing. His eyes were wild and the veins in his neck and forehead stood out. She shuddered. Despite the fact that her dad didn't scream but whispered, it reminded her all too much of his tirades at her or Mace, back when they were kids. Maybe, she thought, she should not be mourning the loss of the old days.

She went into the small ladies' room and bided her time until the bartender, a pale, bleached blonde thirty-something, with lots of blue mascara above and below her eyes, came out of the stall.

"Hi," Cassie said, as she washed her hands in unison with the woman at the twin basins. "You know, I had friends who used to come in here years ago before everything was remodeled."

"We get everything from yuppies to gen-Xers now," the bartender said, reapplying fire-engine-red lipstick she produced from her slacks pocket. "And of course, students. Not many baby boomers anymore—not that you're that old."

"My friends are," Cassie said, smiling at the woman, whose metallic name tag said Sally, in the mirror. "And they mentioned a waitress who was here quite a while ago, named Brenda Sage."

"Never knew her," she said.

Cassie wasn't surprised; this had been a real long shot. Still, she was disappointed.

"But," Sally said, straightening her gold chain necklace under the collar of her white blouse, "she was in a coupla weeks ago. I got a great memory for names."

"Oh, good. I wish I did. So, you talked to her?"

"She hated what they've done with the place. Some do, some don't, but I can't argue with the tips."

"Did Brenda mention where she is now? I think it's somewhere near here, staying with her daughter, who just had twins," Cassie continued in her leading voice.

"Over in Oolitic. I remember that 'cause I got a cousin there."

"Are the owners still the same as years ago?" Cassie added hastily when she saw Sally was going to go back to work. "I'm looking for someone who might remember what it used to be like around here—I'm a writer and I may do a story on the changes," she added when Sally skewered her with a long look.

"Not far's I know. The previous owner passed a coupla years ago. Two women own it now, and they like things just the way they are, without somebody lobbying for the old loud and rowdy days. Everyone's pretty polite around here, like, you know, politically correct."

The door swung shut behind her. Political correctness would probably be a key element in her book on Cynthia Kirk, but the loud and rowdy days would have been a lot more fun to write about. Still, Cassie felt she'd gotten somewhere. She wasn't going to drive to Oolitic tonight. But maybe being able to trace Brenda was a sign she should pursue the lead. She went out to join Gil, who was muttering about someone switching the big TV from soccer to baseball.

"No bar nuts, no fish and chips, just burgers, salads, veggie pizzas and pita sandwiches," he groused, as she took the other seat at a small table he'd commandeered for them. Two beers in tall glasses sweated onto scalloped napkins. "Look at this, will you?" he went on, thrusting the contents of a small glass bowl at her. "Little goldfish crackers to eat, and not a dart game in sight."

"What's this world coming to?" Cassie agreed, and she meant it. Even if she turned up proof that Cynthia Kirk used to frequent the original Limey Roadhouse to meet a man, few of these habitués who might be her future readers would think a thing of it. Yet it was worth pursuing. She'd have to do a bang-up job of describing how different things had been around here once upon a time.

And she was also going to have to find out which once-upon-a-time she was researching and writing about. Surely Cynthia Kirk never sneaked away at night to meet a man before the rock slide, when her husband was living. Even if Jenna's dad had worked nights, which Cassie doubted, Cynthia couldn't just leave her young girls. After she was widowed, she'd hardly let Mandi and Jenna out of her sight, especially at night, unless maybe when she was doing her Right-A-Wrong victims' advocacy work or attending a township trustee meeting. She'd just have to ask Jenna, without telling her why yet.

For her friend's sake, perhaps she should let it go, but the possibility of such a chink in Cynthia's glittering armor howled to her journalist hound-dog blood. Wow, she thought, talk about a mixed metaphor. But, determined to see if the scent would get stronger, she wasn't about to abandon this trail.

"Jenna!" Mace called up to her as she worked on finishing touches of the kids' tree house interior on Sunday afternoon.

She hurried outside and peered over. Since she'd pulled the access ladder up after her—she was much more careful since the disturbances had occurred—he couldn't have climbed it if he'd wanted to. He stood in jeans and black T-shirt, shading his eyes to look up at her.

"Is everything all right?" she asked.

"Sure. I just decided to stop by to see if you could say the same."

"I'm fine. Just thinking over my next move while I work. I'll put the ladder down for you."

"Put it down, then come down. I'd like you to go somewhere with me."

"Where? What's open around Ridgeview on a Sunday except the pizza parlor?" she teased, trying to sound lighthearted. She'd been working hard to pull herself out of her depression and dread.

"What's open is Deep Heart. I want to face the place before tomorrow, when I'll need to start overseeing the movement of equipment there. It would really help me if you'd come along."

She gazed down at him, wanting to shout at him to go away. Face Deep Heart after all these years? But she needed to confront her traumas and search through their rubble, too, all of it. Maybe Deep Heart Quarry was a good place to start. Besides, Mace needed her, wanted her with him.

"I'll be right down."

Mace parked his truck behind a huge stand of poison sumac bushes near the entrance to the quarry, then got out and came around to open Jenna's door. In shaky hands, she gripped the little bouquet of pansies she'd picked from the bedding plants she was going to put in her yard tomorrow.

"You okay about this?" Mace asked. He took her arm to help her out.

"Yes," she managed to say.

They walked along a path off the road, following the trace of old railroad spur that was once used to haul the monolithic blocks of stone from here. Now grass grew between the rotting ties like unshaved whiskers. This time limestone would be taken from the site to the mill by truck. Silently, holding hands, they approached the lip of the quarry where the disastrous Fourth of July picnic had been so long ago. They gazed below at the huge hole in the earth, partly clean-cut and partly littered by the big blocks of the fatal avalanche.

"Sometimes I still hear and feel it," she whispered. "But I don't have those awful flashbacks anymore."

"Me, neither. Just a bad dream sometimes. Jenna, if it were up to me, I'd keep it closed, but it's good for MacCaman Stone and the local workers," he told her passionately, in what sounded like a rehearsed speech or maybe a repetition of what his father had said. "It will give the whole town a lift if we've got more than one active quarry. And I thought it might make you feel better to know that the stone's being used for a church in St. Louis."

Jenna nodded, listening to him and letting her gaze wander the thick rock walls. "It's not the time to fight your father or upset him," she said. "A church—that's nice."

She was surprised to feel strangely detached, not at all as she had thought she'd react. But maybe it was her way of keeping control of chaos, as Dr. Brennan would have put it.

They clambered down and around the edge to the area where the slide had begun, so she could leave her flowers. She saw chalk marks on the walls and string stretched out on uncut stone between stakes.

"Your men have already been here," she noted.

"It's strange to think of them as 'my men,' but I am going to be riding herd on the site operations. Clay Henshaw will be working with me, so these are his survey marks. And since I won't be at the office much, I'm going to give you my cell phone number in case something goes wr—you need me."

Atop the tumble of giant blocks that had so changed their lives, she found a shallow, cup-size pockmark filled with rainwater to use as a vase for the pansies. No need for them to die as a sort of sacrifice here. No need for anyone else to die.

"You want to go back around the other way?" he asked as they stood on the windy heights together.

"Down and around?" she said, gazing into the quarry below them. "I'd rather not. It looks…kind of closed in."

"I was thinking that taking that path back might be a good first step to help you in facing something else."

"You think the cave where Mandi and I were held could be near Deep Heart?" she cried, turning to him.

"What I meant was that you've got to come to terms with your claustrophobia. It's part of conquering what happened."

"I know. You'd think all the counseling I've had over the years would help me overcome it, but we never really addressed that. Dr. Brennan said I should just learn to live with it."

"And you agreed with that?"

"I told him I didn't want to face it, let's put it that way."

"Jenna, I'm no psychiatrist, but I think you could overcome it by just taking tiny steps. I've read about how they desensitize agoraphobics and people afraid to fly. Maybe a walk down there in broad daylight with me, where you only go through a couple of short, tunnel-like areas, is just what you need."

"I don't know. I could go back the other way and meet you. That obviously doesn't look like much to a caver, but for me..." She stopped talking and just sighed.

"No problem. I'll go back with you. Come on."

She was sorry she had disappointed him and herself. But why had he set her up like this? She wanted more than anything to trust him, and his intentions.

"Wait," he said, tugging her back as they started to make their first turn around the edge of the quarry. "Who's that over there? Can you read what their truck says?"

She looked to where he was pointing. A large, white, enclosed truck with a painted logo and numbers on the side had pulled up to the quarry, much closer than they had parked.

"I see a satellite dish on top," she said, shading her eyes. "Oh, it's a TV station from Indianapolis. I recognize their channel number and their 'Always Breaking News' slogan."

They watched as the two-man, one-woman crew got out with a camera and started shooting. Jenna was sure that she recognized the anchorwoman with the bouncy black hair. Unfortunately, the crew had spotted them, too. The crew shouted and came toward them, the camera held aloft on one man's shoulder with tape evidently rolling.

"They're trespassing and would probably sue if they got injured," Mace muttered. "But I'll take that over having to do an interview here. They called Dad for a story about the reopening, but he told them no, that this was strictly business, not bleeding-heart time."

"Hey," the anchorwoman called, waving madly at them as she closed the gap. "Excuse me, but I'd like a word with you!"

Jenna saw that the cameraman was still shooting. With the zoom lenses they had today... "They evidently don't recognize us," Jenna said. "Let's go around the other way and lose them."

"But you said you couldn't."

"I'll try. If I'm going to open up the past, I'm going to do it privately, and that doesn't include on the six o'clock news. They'd soon be rehashing not only the rock slide but the other—Mandi and me. And that's all my mother would need now, too."

"Let's go."

Taking care not to slide out of control, they edged down the slant of uncut rock Mace had pointed out before. They were out of view of the TV crew already. Always Breaking News would have to come a good distance to catch even a glimpse of them. Jenna and Mace could only hope to lose the crew in this limestone labyrinth of tumbled blocks and that the intruders would not go back to Mace's truck to wait for them like vultures.

Mace led the way as they began to cut through angular, twisting passageways formed by fallen blocks or the lifting of them in the recover effort. Most of the enclosed parts were short runs, with sunlight or at least daylight visible at the end.

This wasn't too bad, she kept telling herself. It was just like passing under thick trees in a shade-spotted forest. Trying to ignore the high walls that seemed to lean toward them, Jenna kept her eyes on Mace or the quarry floor. She tried not to bump into the blocks they ran past or through, but she saw him touch many of them, almost as if he felt his way along. Though she'd gotten the idea he'd avoided this place, he seemed to know the way out.

Panting, they stopped between two blocks leaning in and touching tops to make a triangle. "You know the way?" she gasped.

"More or less. Come on. We'll climb out the other access road that leads away from them, then double around."

But ahead of them loomed a long, darker passage made by massive stone walls. What if the rocks shifted or shook before they could run out the other side?

"That looks like a dead end," she protested, and stopped.

"No, it has two wide twists before we're to the other access road," he said, taking her elbow in a firm grasp. "This is perfectly safe, and we can run through it fast."

She felt both trapped and betrayed. Now she'd have

to retrace her steps and face those newspeople and explain why they ran.

"Jenna, come on," he said, tugging at her arm.

"I can't. I couldn't breathe in there."

They heard one of the news crew shout. The woman's high-pitched voice echoed off the quarry walls, perhaps not far behind them.

"You can," Mace insisted. "We can."

He came at her so fast, she thought he was going to throw her down, but instead he bent low and bumped his shoulder into her midriff. Before she knew what hit her, he had her over his shoulder in a fireman's carry and was striding through the tunnel.

"Mace!" she cried, then just closed her eyes and held tight to him, wrapping her arms around his waist, upside down.

As her belly bounced against his shoulder, she fought the onslaught of nausea and nightmare. Being carried into that cave... Had it been like this? She and Mandi must have been drugged or unconscious. There was so much she didn't remember—that she had buried, the police had said. Perhaps this would jog her memory, but she just wanted out. The ropes and thick tape wrapped around her again, the sleeping bag... The dark stone walls pressed in, suffocating her and Mandi under their black weight, like Dad and the others under tons of rumbling, settling stone.

Suddenly Mace sat her down, propping her back against a tree trunk. They were out of the stones and the quarry. She gasped for air.

"I—did I faint?"

"Not with that iron grip you had on me the whole way out."

He was sweating and breathing hard, but not half as

hard as she. Dazedly, she blinked up at foliage and clear blue sky.

"I'm sorry," he said, kneeling and brushing her hair back from her perspiring face, "but we needed to ditch them, and you needed to go through there, even if you didn't want to."

"Is that right, Doctor?" she countered, but she felt a strange sense of accomplishment. And she was deeply moved by his tender touch just a few moments ago.

"Don't forget," he told her as he pulled her erect and they hurried back to his truck, "you don't have to go through tough things alone. Anything happens, you call me."

Jenna nodded. She knew one thing for certain, though. Even that taste of impromptu, aboveground caving had been enough to last a lifetime.

The next morning, Jenna felt like she had a new lease on life. She had slept soundly for once. No wolf howls awakened her, and nothing strange had happened yesterday or last night. She'd received two orders for tree houses, in addition to the one for Russ's. She and Mace were getting closer, and her mother's visit had made her feel they were patching things up. Dressed in her nightgown, Jenna had cleaned house last night, so it wouldn't look totaled all week. That, too, had given her a lift and made her feel more in control of her life again. Today, even though the skies threatened rain—"rainy days and Mondays," the old Karen Carpenter song lilted through her head—she felt better than she had in weeks.

After making a few business calls, she went out to plant the pansies she'd bought at a nursery last week. She loved the flowers, with their varied colors and impish faces. They'd flourish in her window boxes, where she could enjoy them outside as well as in. It was starting to sprinkle, but she'd plant them and let nature water them.

Jenna put the plastic tray of pansies down under the first window box, but dropped her trowel. When she bent to retrieve it, she saw the footprints.

She took a step back and scanned the area before looking again. Strange footprints, definitely not her own. Oddly close to her house, facing toward it. But made with bare feet. Had someone small and barefoot been staring in this window?

Careful not to disturb her finding, she stood on tiptoe to look inside herself. The entire living room was visible. Even with her drapes closed, as they had been last night while she cleaned in her nightgown, the weave of the drapery material was wide, so she never felt closed in.

But someone had been looking in. Looking in at her.

She darted to the other windows. Near three of the four others she found the same weird footprints, clear in the damp, reddish soil. Small, narrow, bare feet. A child's? And in several of the prints, it was obvious the person had leaned forward on his—or her—toes to peer in better. On one of the sills, she even thought she saw the smudge of a dirty handprint, faint as the silhouette of the girl in the forest.

Her stomach churned. Someone had been spying on her inside her own home, for who knew how long!

With shaky knees, ignoring the mist of rain, she leaned back against the house and covered both eyes with her hands. She had to think, not just feel. React, not just become immobilized.

Because of the rain Friday night, she reasoned, looking at the prints again, these had to have been made either on Saturday or last night.

"Damn!"

She tore into the house to get her camera. Her first instinct was to call Mace as he had asked, but she hated to bother him at work. It was his first busy morning in charge at the quarry. And time was of the essence: it was starting to rain harder, so the prints might get washed away. She decided to cover them carefully to preserve them, though she'd take exact measurements and photos, too. Besides, what would she tell Mace, or the police, for that matter, if she summoned them? Kids were welcome in the forest, at her invitation. She'd call Mace later this afternoon, and he could stop by on the way home, she decided, returning outside.

She bent close in the rain, snapping pictures of all the prints and shuddering to think she might have been watched, especially in that nightgown last night. She'd have to buy sturdier drapes; it was ridiculous to feel closed in by them.

Yet how odd, she agonized as she rushed back inside and wiped her camera off, that the feet that made the prints had been bare. It wasn't that warm. Who would go barefoot in a forest at night other than some woodsprite or ghost?

She gripped the kitchen counter to steady herself as she pictured the blurred image of that child in the forest, floating forward from the gargoyle garden to peer in at her.

"No," she cried. Again, though she wanted to lock herself in the house, she forced herself to action. She'd run this film into town for the one-hour developing right now. And retrieve that blowup and the others from Kirkhall, where Cassie said she'd stashed them. Then she'd have everything ready when she phoned Mace late this afternoon.

* * *

But it was Mace who called her at 3:30 p.m.

"Jenna, I'm in the hospital in Indianapolis—with Dad," he said. She could hear a P.A. system paging someone in the background. "Cassie's here, too. He was really feeling bad, dehydrated, I think, so we called his doctor and got him admitted to ICU. Just for a couple of days, I hope."

"How's he doing?"

"Better already, the tough old tyrant. Despite ordering that the nurses quit poking him with needles, he's on IVs and new meds. How are you doing?"

"I've been busy," she said, choosing her words carefully. "Actually, I found some footprints outside and took photos of them I want you to look at, but there's no hurry. You just take care of your dad."

"Footprints where?" he asked as if he hadn't heard her advice. "You went back out between Heaven and Hell where the figure seemed to be?"

"No, closer to the house. I'll show you when I see you."

Though she wanted to beg him to stop by before it got dark, she didn't. Besides, the rain was over and the sun was out, and she refused to let anyone or anything scare her this badly in her own home.

As darkness descended that night, it began to rain again, a gentle, passing shower that Jenna knew would obliterate what was left of the footprints. She stayed completely dressed, kept the lights inside low and both the front and back porchlights on. The curtains—which she was going to replace with lined drapes tomorrow, even though she could not afford them right now—were pulled open so that she could see out just as readily as someone could see in. That brazen move might just work to deter a peeping Tom, she reasoned. Maybe she would have to get a watchdog. After all, Mace had his hands full with family and work, and she could hardly expect him to constantly look in on her, even though he'd said he wanted to.

She finished dinner—a salad of leftovers—though she had no appetite. Nervously, she paced from window to window, even as she dried the dishes, glancing out as night closed in. She supposed she could try to bait a trap for someone, but how, when she didn't know what they wanted?

The rain drummed on the porch roof, a friendly but lonely sound. Jenna turned on a country radio station and sat at the dining room table to work on sketches for the Treepee tree house for Russ and gathering materials for another client. She'd tried to phone Russ on and off this evening to apologize for not making his team's exhibition game yesterday, but he wasn't in. Maybe if she did go see Dr. Brennan with her mother again, she could bring up the idea of a tree house for his daughter and have that one to design, too.

She glanced occasionally at the blowup of the kids' tree house she'd retrieved from Kirkhall. It leaned against her dining room wall between the two windows. She'd looked at it from every direction and illuminated it with varied light sources from different angles. She was still certain there was a figure there, and she intended—

She jerked rigid and strained to listen. A distinctive, scratching sound from the kitchen. But not from the back door; Mace never used that, anyway. Furthermore, he hadn't said he'd stop by, because he didn't know how late he'd be, although Jenna had been hoping he would.

He'd explained that Cassie might stay at the hospital, but he'd be coming home to sleep and then heading back to Deep Heart tomorrow, at his father's request. He'd do anything right now to help his dad keep calm.

Jenna was anything but calm.

She rose slowly and stood in the doorway between the dining room and kitchen, looking and listening. She knew no branches reached that window. Surely it was too high for the wolf to reach, and she hadn't heard the howl for two days.

The noise came again—*scratch, scratch*—against the window glass, though she saw nothing.

She shook her head at her jumbled fears as she turned out the kitchen light and leaned close to peer out her back window over the sink. The story of "Little Red Riding Hood" used to scare her as a child, especially the part about the wolf getting into grandmother's house and sleeping in her bed. But it wasn't the wolf outside that scared her—it was whoever had left those human prints.

The ring of the phone rang jarred her, and she spun to answer it. But she stopped, frozen, her hand outstretched toward it. What if it was that song again?

Then through the door to the dining room, next to the picture with the staring figure in the forest, she saw a face blurred against the window glass before the person turned away and disappeared.

Not Mace.

Someone blond.

Someone looking in, then running. Had she really seen that?

Jenna screamed, then seized hold of herself to answer the phone.

"Mace?"

"I was worried when you didn't answer. I'm on my cell phone, about five minutes away, and didn't want to startle you by just pulling into—"

"She's here. Get here fast!"

Though she could hear Mace's voice shouting on the phone, she dropped it, killed her dining and living room lights and darted to her front windows. Through the drizzle, she saw someone in a flowing gown with long hair running toward the driveway. Jenna darted for the front closet, grabbed her dad's shotgun and ran outside.

10

The figure running in the rain was barefoot. Those prints outside her windows...Mandi had always loved to go barefoot....

This can't be happening, Jenna thought as she raced out of the house to the edge of the porch and lifted the shotgun to her shoulder. But she did not shoot, and probably would not hit the woman if she tried. Besides, if she did, it might kill her. Kill Mandi.

"No!" she told herself as she leaped off the porch and tore down the limestone road. It could not be Mandi.

"Stop! Stop!" she screamed, but she no longer saw the figure on the curved driveway. The stranger must have ducked into the forest to hide or was running through the trees.

Jenna knew she should go back into her house, close and lock the door, and call Mace back. But when he came, would he look around and find nothing?

Jenna wanted to end this now. She wanted answers. She was not crazy. Someone was doing this to her and damn if she wasn't going to find out who and why.

Gripping the gun tightly, with her finger curled around the trigger guard, Jenna crossed her driveway and moved into the fringe of the forest. The rain was letting up but everything was dripping wet. Boughs bent under the weight of the water. Foliage, looking as if it should be guarding some haunted house, sagged and drooped. She held her breath and listened.

Someone was walking in the woods. The crunching sound was distinct, rhythmic. Definitely larger than a wolf. And two-footed.

Jenna gripped the gun so hard her hands cramped. Letting out a huge breath, she sucked another in and held it again.

She hunkered down behind a bush, certain that now the footfalls were coming closer, when she'd been so sure that the woman was moving away. Finally, she was going to see who this was, who was trying to make her think that Mandi was back.

She moved her finger from the guard to the trigger itself. She was shaking uncontrollably. A form emerged, a gray silhouette among the other grays. It was not a woman, but a man, a man walking fast.

"Mace?" she cried, as he emerged from the gloom. As she came out from behind the bush, she startled him. He dropped his cell phone and the large limb he carried.

"Jenna, thank God, you're safe. Give me that!" he cried, lunging to take the shotgun from her. "Why are you out here?"

"I was just going to ask you the same."

"You panicked me. I thought I'd park partway up the drive and come through the trees, in case I could sneak up on whomever you'd spotted. Don't tell me you're chasing him?" he asked, retrieving and pocketing his cell phone.

"It's a her. I saw her, I swear I did, with flowing light hair and some sort of gown blowing when she ran. She looked in and turned away just before I could really see her face."

But his face said it all. He wasn't sure he believed

her. She wondered if she could believe herself. A distant roar made both of them jump.

"Just a car on the road," he said, glancing that way.

"Yes, but it could be her, if she parked there instead of in the driveway. Let's follow her in your truck!"

They ran to it and jumped in. Before he turned the key in the ignition, a vehicle on the road roared across the bottom of the driveway. "That's her—it's got to be her, going that fast!" Jenna cried.

By the time they skidded off the crushed stone drive onto the slick surface of Cutter Camp Road, the taillights of the other vehicle were pinpoints of red heading north.

"At least it's late, so there won't be traffic," Mace muttered. "Fasten your seat belt."

He leaned forward, trying to see through the mist on the windshield as his wipers whipped it clear, only to have it cloud again. "We're closing the gap," he said.

"Maybe she's slowed down. She might not know we're back here if she didn't see your truck. If so, she thinks she's home free. Look, she's turning onto Chestnut toward town. She took that turn so wide the car skidded."

"There must be water on the road. Hold on."

A wave sprayed the air as they made the turn. Mace stomped on the brake pedal twice, then accelerated again. "It's a dark car, black or blue—an old one," he said.

She nodded. Her heart nearly thundered out of her chest at the thought that she might soon see who was driving....

Their headlights were close enough to illuminate it now. A black station wagon.

"See, the driver has big hair!" Jenna cried, leaning

forward. "Light-colored hair. I can see its silhouette, just like in the blowup of the tree house."

"She's seen us."

"How can you tell?"

"She's speeding up again, heading toward that sharp left by the quarry."

"Look, there's a bright yellow bumper sticker on the back fender."

Jenna gasped. She knew where she'd seen that black station wagon, the bumper sticker—and what it said.

"Mace, that's Russ Pierce's car!" she cried.

The vehicle ahead of them smashed through the fluorescent dead end sign that marked the entrance to the short old access road that led to the deep Mother Lode beyond. The car crested the railing and embankment that hid the quarry from the road, and soared up and over into blackness.

For an eternity, only Jenna's scream and Mace's curse seared the air. Mace hit his brakes and swerved into the space on the narrow berm where the safety railings gaped like broken teeth. The jarring crash from below seemed to bounce, to echo.

"Oh, no. No!" Jenna shouted.

Mace gripped her arm. "I need the cell phone. It must have skidded onto the floor."

She found it, and he punched in 911, even as he got out. He seemed so calm, stoic. In the beam of his own headlights, he clambered up the slippery grass slope to gaze into the quarry, then half walked, half slid back down to the truck.

"That's what I said," she overheard him say, still talking into the phone. She forced herself out of the truck. She leaned against it, shaking so hard her teeth chattered. "The southwest corner of Chestnut, the first turn around Mother Lode. The car's at the bottom, so the regular rescue vehicles won't be much help. No, it's not on fire. Mace MacCaman. Yes, I saw it happen."

"It couldn't have been Russ in there," she protested when he punched off and pocketed the cell phone. "I saw a woman."

"We may have been chasing the wrong person."

"I swear, the silhouette I saw in Russ's car was the same one that flashed by my dining room window and ran. It resembled that figure in the blown-up photo."

"Jenna, listen to me," he said, and pulled her toward him. He tipped her chin up so she had to look directly into his eyes, hooded even in the stark shadows made by the truck's headlights. "Russ or anybody else around here knows about the sharp angles around Mother Lode. The only thing I can think of is that his brakes got waterlogged in that turn onto Chestnut."

"Either that, or maybe his glasses slipped off. His eyes were so bad he wouldn't be able to see exactly where the turn was. Something like that has to explain it," she said, nodding as her mind began to clear. "I didn't see his brake lights go on. But you said the driver sped up because we were chasing—"

"No guilt trip over this," he said almost harshly, and gave her a single shake.

"But what if it was Russ spying on me, dressed as a woman—as Mandi?"

"I guess making that public would smear his name, as well as dredge up losing Mandi all over again." He turned his head slightly, and his eyes glinted. With tears? She watched his mouth move as he went on. "I'd hate to see all that rehashed by the sharks in the media. Mary Drout would start circling again, and we'd have that TV crew we saw at Deep Heart camped outside your mother's office, especially since she's state and even national news with that convention committee lately."

"All right, I get your point," she agreed. "Anyway, I still can't believe Russ could have staged all that's happened. And we'll never know if he was responsible for everything if he's dead...."

"He's dead. No one could survive that."

"How sad if his legacy was as perverted peeping Tom, after all his work with his Little Leaguers and as Ridgeview's postmaster. He's had a good reputation for his job all these years. He's helped a lot of kids who seem to adore him."

It took nearly twenty minutes for the paramedics and volunteer fire trucks to arrive with sirens screeching. Even on this deserted stretch of road at midnight, they soon drew a crowd, including Mary Drout. As Jenna and Mace stood in the glare of pulsing emergency lights, answering the sheriff's questions, neither of them mentioned that anyone had been trying to terrorize her nor that they had been chasing the wrecked car. If her harasser had been Russ, Jenna told herself, at least one good thing came from this tragedy: her nightmare had died with him.

"You're probably exhausted and sick to death of being interviewed," Mary Drout said to Jenna as they sat at Jenna's dining room table the next afternoon. "All those questions from the county sheriff. Did you get any sleep at all, dear?"

"A little."

"Well, I certainly appreciate your giving the *Ridgeview Record* your take on this tragedy. Poor thing," Mary murmured, reaching over her cup of coffee to pat Jenna's arm. "As if you haven't been through enough over the years. This won't take long. Just a few comments to go with those Mace gave me."

Jenna recounted the story she and Mace had hastily decided on. After Mace had stayed late at the hospital with his dad, he stopped to pick up Jenna and they headed into town to the Ridgeview Pizza Parlor, the only place open in town at that time of night. They saw a speeding car take the turn at Cutter Creek and Chestnut, skidding through water, then saw it crash through the barrier to Mother Lode. Mace called 911. They thought they recognized the station wagon. Jenna explained she'd seen it just three days ago when Russ ordered a tree house for his Little Leaguers. She suggested that Mary ask Clay Henshaw's boy Pete for a quote about Russ as a longtime coach.

"Though I'll not speak ill of the dead," Mary said, as she put her pad and pen back in her big purse, "Russel Pierce was an odd one from the start. But he rose above how wild his parents were, I'll give him that."

"Odd in what way?" Jenna pursued.

"A bit of a loner, never dated, that sort of thing, you see. Oh, I don't mean the boy was gay or anything, though I'd thought more than once he had too much of a fixation with hanging out with his Little Leaguers, like he never quite grew up. I recall he used to have these huge crushes on girls, though—including your sister. He was under close scrutiny after Mandi disappeared, you know."

Jenna had not known, but then Mary Drout was the queen of gossip around here. Jenna only nodded and frowned at the dining room wall where the blowup of the figure had been. She'd put it under the bed in the small bedroom for now. She'd been horrified when Mace finally drove her home last night to find her front door still stood open—but they'd looked around carefully inside and nothing was amiss.

"You know," Mary mused aloud, tapping her pen against her chin, "it *is* strange that Russ died speeding. I never saw him go much over a rural route postman speed—you know, slow starts and stops. Jenna, may I use your phone a moment?"

"Oh, sure, Mary. Right on the kitchen wall there," she said, pointing.

"I never did take to newfangled, electronic doohickeys," Mary explained as she rose from the table. "Cell phones, laptops, and PalmPilots, indeed. I have a theory you can get brain cancer from all of it. No, the good old telephone, my steno pad and pen have always done the job for me. I eventually have to keyboard my notes into a computer, but that's it."

While Mary used the phone, Jenna cleared their coffee cups. She tried to tell herself again that it was best Russ be laid to rest with accolades and not unproven accusations. It would serve nothing to accuse him of voyeurism by explaining why they were chasing him.

"That's really strange," Jenna heard Mary say into the phone. "To tell you the truth, I don't know whether I should print all of that or not. Now, you call me after the autopsy."

"An autopsy?" Jenna asked when Mary hung up, even though that made it obvious she'd been eavesdropping. "For a one-vehicle car wreck victim?"

"I'm afraid they need to know if he had alcohol or any other foreign substance in his blood, that sort of thing. Besides, don't forget that Russ was a federal government employee, to whom Ridgeview's mail has been entrusted for years."

"Maybe it's standard procedure, then," Jenna said.

''The sheriff phoned Russ's parents in Tampa, and they'll be here for the funeral. Nice of them,'' Mary muttered sarcastically, ''since they copped out of his life when he was growing up. But you know what's *really* bizarre about all this?''

Jenna's stomach twisted. Guilt sat hard on her about not telling the authorities everything. ''What's that?''

''The sheriff says Russ wore untied shoes with no socks. But inside his shoes, his bare feet were covered with mud, as if he had been walking barefoot in that rain we had last night. Well, of course, there's no way to trace where he was walking, since that soil's everywhere around limestone country. Oh, yes, and he wore a beige raincoat with a pointed hood, an old one that might even have been his mother's.''

''A woman's light raincoat with a hood and muddy feet,'' Jenna repeated.

''That's right. I told you that boy never was quite right. But I am going to report on the results of the autopsy they've already done on that old station wagon of his,'' she whispered as she fished out pad and pen from her purse again. ''You and Mace guessed right about his brakes. The sheriff says he must have lost them when he made that turn and not realized they were gone.''

''I was thinking maybe his eyesight wasn't good, either, especially at night, and he just miscalculated the turn. And if his brakes were gone...''

''The sheriff's garage mechanic said that the impact of the fall completely severed his brake fluid line in a clean cut. That's what I mean about an auto autopsy, and I'm going to write it up exactly that way.''

Seeming pleased with herself, Mary made a few notes, then headed for the front door, still talking. ''They're going to check with the garage that did his work—not that he kept the car up, evidently. At least his gas tank was on empty, so that saved him from a conflagration where we'd have ashes and not a body to bury. Saddest thing that's happened in this town in—well, in years," she finished, looking embarrassed by what she'd said as she turned back to Jenna on the porch.

Mary patted Jenna's shoulder. "Details, details," she said. "In newspaper work, like in life, it's all in getting the details right."

Jenna watched Mary as she drove away and turned out onto Cutter's Camp, just as she and Mace had last night. Though she grieved Russ's loss, Jenna had to admit she felt great relief, too. She couldn't wait to call Mace and tell him that Russ *had* been the one peeking in her window. He must have been the mastermind behind Mandi's apparent return from the past—or the dead.

After all, Russ had delivered the package containing the heart-shaped pillow that started all this. Mary had said he'd more or less followed Mandi around years ago. Maybe he'd done it sneakily even back then, spying on her. She'd seen a computer in his house through which he could have e-mailed her an order for a kids' tree house, based on the one she'd had as a kid. Perhaps Russ had seen with his own eyes the apple juice and graham crackers, and even how Dad had built their childhood tree house out of odds and ends from his lumberyard. Or maybe Mandi had mentioned those things to him. It's all in getting the details right, as Mary had said.

And Russ had acted so strangely when Jenna had gone to his place to talk about building a tree house—ordered, no doubt, so he could keep an even closer eye on her. Town folk all agreed Russ knew everyone's business—perhaps, Jenna concluded, Mandi's and hers most of all.

In wanting to believe Mandi was still alive, he'd tried to resurrect her. Or, if he had once stalked Mandi, he could have transferred his warped feelings to her younger sister.

"Free at last, free at last," she whispered, and ran for the phone to call Mace. But before she could dial his number, it rang. For the first time since the strange phone call when she was at Kirkhall, Jenna answered without trepidation.

"Jenna Kirk here."

"Jenna, I got your call."

It was her mother. Jenna had left her a long message, just in case any of the local publicity about her daughter's eyewitness report of Russ's crash spilled over onto her.

"I just thought you should know before it hit the papers or TV," Jenna explained.

"Are you all right?"

"Yes, fine. Mace and I are both fine."

"The whole thing's dreadful. And isn't it a little much that you and Mace were running out for pizzas near midnight?"

Jenna went on the offensive before she could stop herself. "Meaning, I should be following some high-school curfew hours, or calling you for permission if I go out at night to—"

"Jenna! Meaning, I can't believe you are apparently dating Mace MacCaman."

"We're good friends right now, so you can leave it at that. But times changes, and people change."

"They do, indeed. And I'm glad to see you making your own decisions, really I am. It's—it's partly my finding the courage to accept your independence, which

I would like us to talk about with Dr. Brennan together sometimes. You said you would.''

''I haven't changed my mind, as long as it's not some searching probe of me again. I'm really ready to move on with my life.''

''How would next Thursday afternoon about three o'clock be? I'll meet you at Dr. Brennan's office, then we can have an early dinner before you head back—though, of course, you're welcome to spend the night. I'm sure Russ's funeral won't be until Friday or Saturday, with the autopsy and all, and you'll no doubt want to attend.''

''I hadn't thought that far ahead, but yes, I'll go to the funeral. But how did you know about the autopsy already?''

''Jenna, I've seen freak accidents before and know how these things work, that's all.''

''Yes. All right, Thursday at three.''

She had begun to dial Mace's number again, but heard a car pull up in front. It didn't sound like his truck, but maybe he was here. She hung up and hurried to look out her screen door. How good it felt to leave the storm door open, not to feel she must shut herself in. She wouldn't even have to buy those new draperies now.

It was Frank Connors, getting out of his low-slung, hunter-green sports car. ''I've heard about banker's hours,'' she said, stepping out to meet him. Jenna knew she should ask him in, but couldn't quite bring herself to do it. Indicating a padded wicker porch chair, she took the one opposite him.

''I just wanted to see how you were doing and tell you that if you need any help, let me know,'' he began.

''I appreciate that.''

''But I don't think you appreciate the implications of

what's happened. Jenna, I was in Indianapolis seeing my kids last night and only heard about Russ's death on the radio driving back to Ridgeview early this morning, but I've got to warn you. It sounds like *déjà vu* all over again, as some jokester used to say."

"What do you mean?" she asked warily, gripping the arms of her chair and sitting up even straighter.

"I mean, people knowing about you and Mace getting involved with each other, the way he and Mandi did."

"That has nothing to do with—"

"Just listen without arguing for a minute. I'll bet Russ watched both of you like some lovelorn puppy. That's a blast from the past, too, or haven't you heard he used to stalk Mandi?"

Jenna was startled but tried to hide her surprise. Did everyone know that but her? "I heard," she said. But surely, whatever Frank knew about Russ's following Mandi, he couldn't know that Russ had been stalking her.

"At Pioneers Day, I saw him watching you, practically with his tongue hanging out," Frank explained, scooting forward in his chair so that their knees almost touched. "And the reason I know about Russ having the hots for your sister is that she asked me once to make him lay off."

"And you did?" she asked. She'd known Frank and Mace had been friends once, but why would Mandi go to Frank for protection instead of to Mace?

"I did," he admitted, frowning at her. "Not that I'm proud of it, but I was a pretty cocky, angry kid then. I half dangled him over the edge of Green Eye and threatened him."

"But...why you?"

"And not Mace, you mean?" He leaned back again

as if he were suddenly enjoying this. ''Because Mace had one hell of a trigger temper. I knew it, and Mandi did, too. He's not the Godfather's son and heir for nothing. Mandi didn't want Russ in our—her way, but she didn't want him beat up, either, so I used a more subtle method.''

''Of psychological terror,'' Jenna put in, her voice accusing. ''Which you think, of course, was kinder to someone like him?''

''Don't you?'' he countered. He amazed her by rising and going down the steps, when she was certain he'd press his advantage or expect to be asked in.

''Jenna, for your own good,'' he said, turning back with his hand on the open car door, ''I'll pick you up right here for Russ's funeral, whatever day they finally schedule it. There will be enough talk in town. You really don't need to be seen attending with Mace MacCaman.''

''Or you'll dangle me over Green Eye until I see the error of my ways?'' she challenged, her mind racing. Psychological terror is exactly what someone had been using on her. But all that was over now, she told herself. It must have been Russ Pierce, and now he was gone.

''I'll call you later about what time I'll pick you up,'' he said as he bent his big body to get into the car.

The only reason she didn't hurl a pot of pansies at him was that she was still determined to go back to facing her past, and Frank was a part of that. He had obviously been closer to Mandi than she'd ever realized. Had Mace known that? Maybe she *would* go to the funeral with Frank. Suddenly, she felt he could help to jog her memory about those dreadful days when someone kidnapped her and Mandi.

* * *

"You been keeping up with that Kennedy nephew murder case?" Clay Henshaw asked Mace as they leaned wearily against a derrick overlooking Deep Heart. They were taking a short break after overseeing the transfer of cutting and hauling equipment to this site where the actual work would begin tomorrow.

"Not really. What about it?"

"I'm sure the tabloids are all over it, too," Clay said, taking off his hard hat and pulling a newspaper article out of it. Just the article, Mace noted, not an entire newspaper like most men might read on their break. Mace felt his heart speed up. Ever since he'd been back in Ridgeview, Clay had been subtly harassing him, and he could smell another veiled accusation coming.

"Because of the Kennedy name?"

"Sure. It always rivets everyone when a wealthy, important family has a scandal."

"I think I'll see you later, before we have unprofessional words," Mace warned. "I'd hate for one of us to have to tell the boss that this partnership at Deep Heart isn't going to work out."

"You know, I never took you for one who'd run to Daddy with a complaint. But you haven't even let me answer your question yet," Clay said, shoving away from the derrick and turning to face Mace head-on. He stabbed a blunt finger at the article, but looked at Mace. "The big thing here is that a neighborhood girl was killed back in seventy-five when she and the accused were both in high school. He was questioned but cleared at the time. He's gone scot-free all these years, and the only question is whether he'll be tried as an adult or as a juvenile. There's going to be a hearing soon to see if he should stand trial. His lawyer's saying he didn't do it, but someone's stepped forward to testify he did. Of course, sometimes the law changes when it involves a big family name."

"You have a strange way of surviving around here," Mace told him, "considering you've been my father's fair-haired boy for years and probably want to stay on at MacCaman's." He fought the urge to take a defensive tone or stance, but knew he succeeded at neither. He hoped he wouldn't lose his temper. Ever since he'd beat up the bastard who had ruined that virgin cave site two years ago, he had vowed not to let his frustration and anger get the best of his self-control again.

Though he almost hated to turn his back on the guy, he walked away from Clay and whipped out his cell phone to call Jenna. Let Clay wonder if he was phoning his father. He could only hope Jenna was having a better day than he was, preparing these monster machines to start ripping stone out of Deep Heart.

11

"So you don't mind if I use a tape recorder for this interview?" Cassie asked Jenna the next day. Like carefree kids, they swung their legs over the edge of Home Tree Home after having lunch together. Their sandwich sacks and pop cans, as well as Cassie's tape recorder, filled the small space between them.

"Okay by me—*if* I can have a copy of it for my project, too," Jenna countered, leaning back on her hands and stretching luxuriously. She'd slept well again last night and was quite sure she was—literally—out of the woods, no longer being stalked and scared. And that freed her up to focus on finding out who had abducted Mandi years ago.

She sat up straight again. Perhaps Russ hadn't merely transferred his fixation for Mandi to her. If he'd had something to do with her sister's disappearance, he could have been trying to keep Jenna off balance so that she'd have no time to pursue the past. Or perhaps he'd thought he could even get her to leave town, leave the places Mandi still apparently haunted.

"I'll share the tapes," Cassie interrupted her agonizing, "but I don't need any rival books out there." She made a little face and grinned.

"If I ever write a book, it will be strictly about tree houses, so don't worry," Jenna promised. "Now that I can be objective again, I'm more determined than ever to turn over rocks to see if I can find out who took Mandi and me."

"Then, you don't think it was Russ?"

"He's my top suspect, but I'm not letting this go until I know."

"Then, we're in this together all the way," Cassie said, and they hooked little fingers together in a secret handshake the way they had years ago. She was so blessed, Jenna thought, to have Cassie and Mace to trust.

Later that day Jenna listened to the tape she and Cassie had made. She concentrated on the recording as she worked in her office, sketching a tree-house proposal to surprise Dr. Brennan with later this week. She was trying to psychoanalyze two things which stood out in Cassie's questions. After all, she was going to have to start by trying to remember things—clues—she might have repressed. She was starting to sound like Dr. Brennan, Jenna thought, except for the fact he always urged her to go on with life and not let the past obsess her.

She ran the tape back a bit to listen to the first section that interested her. It was not only for her own answers. Cassie's questions seemed revealing, too, though Jenna wasn't yet sure how.

Cassie: I hope you don't mind my taking you back to the night you and Mandi disappeared.

Jenna: You can try. I'm pretty good on details before I got hit or drugged that night, but I'm really foggy after.

Cassie: Understandable. So, just as background, Jennie, did your mother ever go out on business at night or did she just stick to calling people from home, as you mentioned in your deposition to the police years ago?

Jenna: You've been combing through that old stuff? That reminds me, if you have that series of articles Mary Drout did back then, I'd like to borrow them.

Cassie: Sure. So, did your mother ever go out at night? I was thinking, perhaps the man who seized Mandi thought you two were home alone.

Jenna: Yes, she went out on occasion. There were regular township trustee meetings, maybe for a rare Right-A-Wrong evening event, too. But until Mandi was in high school, she paid our part-time maid to stay with us.

Cassie: That would be Lily Thompson, who moved away from here years ago and whom I can't track.

Jenna: No kidding? You tried to track her? Talk about leaving no stone unturned.

Cassie: Was it only after your dad died that your mother did this? Or before—and did your dad ever work nights?

Jenna: What does that have to do with the night Mandi and I were taken?

Cassie: I'm just trying to establish a long-term family pattern for whether or not an adult was in the house at night.

Jenna: Okay. But my dad had been gone for years by then, so what does it matter if he ever worked nights?

Cassie: It just always helps me to go way back and begin at the beginning, that's all. The perpetrator might have been watching the family for years....

Though they'd gone on with the interview, Jenna now thought that whole section of taped talk had some sort of subtext she could not quite decipher. She'd have to pin Cassie down on that. But it was another part of the tape that really bothered her. In retrospect, it seemed to have nothing to do with a book on her mother's past. That was the trouble with being interviewed by a friend who had known you from childhood. The personal kept getting confused with the professional.

Cassie: Since Mandi was so popular at school, she probably broke a lot of boys' hearts.

Jenna: True, but not intentionally. You and I both know she loved Mace, and he loved her. Are you referring to Russ Pierce having a secret crush on her that must have gotten out of control? I won't pass judgment on Russ for that. After all, I cared deeply and secretly for Mace then—no, that's off the record, Cassie. I forget sometimes it's not just me talking to my best friend here.

Cassie: Okay, okay. No, I was referring to Frank Connors. I'm going to ask Mace about this, too, when he has time to answer some questions, but I'm wondering if you had any knowledge of why best buds Frank and Mace had a fight and stopped speaking.

Jenna: For one thing, when Mace quit the football team, Frank probably thought he let him down. A lot of people did.

Cassie: But that meant the coveted position was wide open to Frank, just for the taking. And take it he did.

Jenna: You're implying they had a falling out over Mandi? But she loved Mace.

Cassie: Jenna, did you ever think that you saw Mandi through rose-colored glasses? I know you loved her and have built her up in your thoughts and heart even more over the years she's been gone, but she could well have reveled in attention from more than one man. It's *your* faithful love of Mace you're judging her by, not the way she was.

Jenna: You don't know how I felt about her or what she was really like. You may have blabbed it to Mace how I felt about him, but I don't need you blabbing how you think I felt about my sister, when you weren't there day and night to really know! I loved my sister, and I wanted to be more like her!

Cassie: Okay, sorry. That clears that up. Let's stop here and pick it up another day.

Jenna slumped over her drawing of a Peter Pan tree house for Dr. Brennan's little daughter. If it wasn't to help her mother, she wouldn't be seeing him on Thursday. Who needed a shrink when she had a best friend like Cassie MacCaman, hot on the trail not only of her biographical subject, but of every Ridgeview resident's psychological past?

As Jenna went into Dr. Brennan's office building on Thursday afternoon, she was still dismayed at how shaken she had sounded when Cassie questioned Mandi's behavior on that tape. If her friend hadn't been so busy with her dad—Cassie and Mace were taking him home from the hospital today—Jenna would have nailed her on it. Granted, Mandi had been a bit self-centered at times, but what young woman with her looks and magnetic personality wouldn't have been?

Dr. Brennan's office looked much the same, with carpets and walls in muted blues. Jenna smiled when she saw the drapes were open and all the table lamps were on, as well as the ceiling lighting. He'd always done that for her visits, helping to get her through her toughest times. Thank God, those were behind her now, though Mace was right—she should work on the claustrophobia, too.

"Jenna, so lovely to see you again." Anne, his longtime, grandmotherly receptionist, smiled at her from her desk in the corner of the deserted outer office. "Come on back."

"You don't mean my mother's actually on time?" Jenna asked as she went through the door to the short hall to Garth Brennan's inner sanctum.

"Not quite yet, but you're to go on in," Anne said, and closed the waiting room door behind her.

Although the doctor's office door was ajar, Jenna knocked. "Jenna, enter," he called to her, looking up. Though her nose told her the doctor still never smoked in here, he was tamping tobacco into his pipe with his ubiquitous golf tee.

"I came in early to show you these," she told him as they shook hands. She handed him the lavender manila folder with her Out On A Limb logo on the front. "Preliminary sketches for a Peter Pan tree house for your Samantha," she explained. "I owe you so much, I'd do much of the work *gratis*."

"Jenna, these are great!" he told her, skimming the drawings as he came out from behind his desk. "Her sixth birthday's in August. Maybe we could shoot for that."

"Next time you come to visit her great-aunt Mary, bring Samantha along and let her see the tree house in the Stone Forest, so we can get an idea of what she really likes."

"Great, will do. I read that you had been planning to do a kids' tree house for Russ Pierce. It's in the last paragraph of the article about him, with the quotes from his baseball team. Is there anything I can do to help you through seeing Russ die so—well, so suddenly and violently?"

"I didn't really see him die, thank God," she said, as they took two of the deep, upholstered chairs he'd arranged in a little circle. "But I can imagine how dreadful it was for him—the long plunge into the dark, the final crash." She shuddered and hugged herself.

A long silence followed, which years ago she would have filled by blurting out to him what really happened with Russ Pierce. Though he pocketed his unlit pipe, the sweet smell of tobacco emanated from him. "But," she added hastily, "it hasn't triggered flashbacks again to losing Dad or Mandi, if that's what you're wondering."

"Good. Jenna, you recall we talked a lot about your survivor's syndrome."

"Similar to traumatic stress or shock syndrome of soldiers, you always said, it's characterized by deep guilt that one person survives while others—often friends—are dead."

"Exactly."

"I'm beyond that now, Dr. Brennan. I completely agree with your earlier counseling that being abducted with Mandi and escaping without her is not my fault. I'm going on with my life, as you have always urged."

But, she thought, staring into his calm, patient, dove-gray eyes, I'm doing that by probing the past and I don't need your help anymore. Her thoughts were so clear to her that, for one moment, she almost thought she'd said those words aloud.

He kept fiddling with his golf tee as he explained. "I'm only bringing that up because I'm afraid your mother's under great stress and that facing possible future success—yes, I know about the probable vice-presidential nomination—may be a problem. She's still suffering from survivor's syndrome. The more success she achieves, the more she may feel guilt and hate herself, since neither her husband nor Mandi are here to enjoy it. And now, with your increasing independence, when she needs your support desperately..."

"I didn't know. She's seemed so strong and purposefully busy—even more so lately."

He nodded. "She's riding high and fast, but I fear that's when a fall can come."

Russ's black station wagon soaring up and out into the blackness of night flashed through her mind. She shook her head slightly to clear the vision.

"Dr. Brennan, if Mother does get the nomination, you know what legal vetting and press scrutiny candidates go through. I'll admit I've worried about that. Everything will be hauled out again in the media. I remember one vice-presidential candidate created a big scandal when it was discovered he'd been treated for depression or something. And they took him off the ticket."

"Thomas Eagleton, I believe, but that was back in the seventies."

"Even today, it can cause ripples if it's revealed that a candidate's spouse has been treated for mental disorders. Remember Kitty Dukakis? Or even Vice President Gore's wife, Tipper, who's been treated for depression," she argued.

"But times have changed, Jenna. I believe that the

sympathy for your mother's losses will be so strong when her entire story comes out that people will see her as absolutely heroic, a victor before she's even elected. I would wager that public opinion polls would show that her 'baggage,' as the politicos call it, only strengthens her appeal as a candidate.''

Jenna felt goose bumps. Public opinion polls, baggage and politicos. It all seemed so cold and calculating to have to think that way.

''So,'' Dr. Brennan said, as Jenna glanced nervously at her watch, wishing her mother were here, ''how does it feel to be close again to Cassandra and Mason MacCaman from the old days? No problems, I take it, with reforging ties with them? Your mother says Cassandra's doing a biography of her, and I'd wager that may be partly what has set her off on this new soul-searching—that and the looming nomination.''

''Don't you think we should wait for her to answer those questions herself? As for Cassie and Mace, it's worked out well. Mace can use a good friend, with his father dying, and I'm going to help Cassie with background for the book.''

''Good,'' he said, getting up and going to his desk. ''Anne,'' he said, punching his intercom button, ''page the lieutenant governor to see if she's hit a schedule snag. My aunt told me,'' he said, looking back at Jenna, ''that Rod MacCaman's dying, but that it hasn't exactly made him want to live his last days in peace with anyone. But, I take it he's going to be opening new quarries to his last breath, probably opening old wounds, too.''

A buzzer on his desk sounded and he picked up his phone. ''That's too bad, but good, too. Thank you, Anne.''

''Mother's all right, isn't she?'' She'd refused to be

counseled by Dr. Brennan again, and now she'd just spent all this time having a heart-to-heart with him.

"She got caught in an emergency meeting—with several of Hal Westbrook's top advisors," he said, lifting his eyebrows and grinning at the mention of the probable Republican presidential candidate's name. "*Ad astra per ardua!*" he declared.

"Sorry, but my Latin isn't..."

"'To the heights, to the stars, through whatever difficulties,'" he translated. To her amazement, Dr. Brennan, who so seldom showed emotion, looked and sounded ecstatic. "Listen, Jenna, as long as she can't make it, and we've got a half hour left, is there anything I can do for you, just as a friend?" he asked, sitting down by her again.

"I think I'm beyond being counseled, even by a friend," she told him. "But if you want that children's tree house described a bit more, I'll stay. Then I'm heading home, as I have a lot to do before the funeral tomorrow."

"Ah," he said. He leaned over to take her sketches from the end table. "Now there's someone who could have used my help. I wouldn't doubt that Russ Pierce stopped his social development about the time his parents emotionally deserted him. Then they simply moved south without him later."

"Did you know he used to stalk Mandi?"

To her surprise, he didn't so much as blink. "Your mother told me years ago. She—and evidently the FBI, after much questioning of the boy—concluded he was harmless. Don't you agree?"

"I think I didn't really know him. Maybe no one did," Jenna said.

"And why is that?" he pursued.

"No more sad talk today," she insisted. "Look, this Peter Pan tree house can be built to emphasize the pirate theme, or the fairy theme."

"Hmm," he said, still playing with his golf tee, tipping it end over end as he turned to studying her sketches instead of her. "If it was for me, I'd say the pirate, but I think Samantha would be much more into fairies. All right, explain it all to me so I can discuss it with my wife, and then we'll decide. At home—or in dealing with your mother—I'm hardly the one in charge."

Although Jenna's father's funeral had been devastating, it had also been beautiful and comforting. Russel Charles Pierce's funeral, on the other hand, was the worst she had ever attended.

His mother and father—whom most people in town were hardly speaking to, since they'd been such public misfits and dreadful parents—had insisted the funeral be held in a rural church located nearly in the next county, which no one, including Russ, had attended. There was an itinerant preacher whom no one knew and who hadn't known Russ. The little clapboard church, however, was packed on the hot day and reeked of the blue-dyed carnations on the open casket.

And that was not the worst abomination here, Jenna thought, as she took her place in a crowded pew, wedged in between Mary Drout and Frank. Russ's parents had arranged for a pre-service viewing, but Russ certainly didn't look a bit like himself after that fall. Even the local funeral director's ministrations hadn't helped. For one thing, Russ's trademark thick glasses, which he'd never been without, were missing. It might as well have been a stranger they mourned, as the minister finally closed the casket and began the funeral service.

"Absolutely ghastly and appalling," Mary whispered to Jenna as she fanned herself with her notepad. "I swear, the Pierces have just come home to get what they can out of that house and the land their boy's been paying for all these years so they could keep their old carcasses in the sunny south. And did you see the abysmal interview they did with that Indianapolis television station yesterday?"

Jenna hadn't, but she'd heard about it. The Pierces had threatened to sue the county for not putting up a better barrier by the quarry. Yes, Jenna thought, Madge and George Pierce were doing a great job of winning friends and influencing people here.

But what bothered Jenna most was that the Indianapolis papers and TV stations had sent reporters to cover this. She'd seen them featuring the young Little League boys attending the funeral, who were so overwhelmed they kept crying. Jenna had spotted the same bouncy brunette reporter outside who had chased her and Mace in the quarry.

She squirmed in her seat when they sat down after the prayer. What bothered her the most, she decided, was that Mace was evidently furious with her for coming here today with Frank. She'd explained to him that she needed to talk to Frank about his memories of the day Mandi was taken. Besides, Mace had to drive in from Deep Heart, so picking her up would have been out of his way. He'd slammed down the receiver, and she could feel his glare even now, without looking.

But she did look. He sat with Cassie, who was also apparently taking notes, though of what, Jenna had no idea. Yes, Mace was staring at her again, seething.

She shifted on the hard wooden pew, ever so slightly, farther away from Frank. She clenched her thighs and felt her belly flutter. She'd not meant to upset Mace; she'd expected him to understand. Even from across the crowd, he emanated a dark, magnetic appeal. His green eyes narrowed; his nostrils flared slightly as he pressed his lips together in a straight line. As the energy arcing from him made her pulse pound, she felt as if he'd reached out to seize and stroke her. A rivulet of sweat trickled down the hollow of her back. From him she felt an intensity that almost burned her, but she only wanted to run headlong into that conflagration.

The soft *whisk-whisk* of Mary's notepad fanned some air to cool Jenna's flushed face. She shook her head to get hold of herself. After all, this was church; this was a funeral. She rose with everyone and reached for her own hymn book, despite the fact Frank held his out to share with her.

"'Rock of ages, cleft for me.'" They sang the old hymn, beloved in stone country.

"'Let me hide myself in Thee...
While I draw this fleeting breath,
When mine eyelids close in death...
Rock of ages, cleft for me,
Let me hide myself in Thee!'"

The sonorous "amen" echoed in the little church. Jenna blinked back tears, not for Russ's loss, but because that had been the hymn they sang at her dad's funeral. Suddenly, despite the rows of windows with sunlight streaming through them, she felt utterly closed in and trapped. Before everyone sat again, she edged out of the pew and hurried down the side aisle and out the front door with Frank behind her.

"Do you feel sick?" he whispered. They stepped outside where the hearse and a rented car waited, though not for a trip to a local cemetery. Russ was being cremated in Indianapolis before his parents flew back to Florida; that had also riled the community, where burials were tradition. His parents were going to scatter his ashes in Florida, something else that made no sense since Russ had hated the place and had only been there twice. But then, *nothing* made sense to Jenna right now.

"I'm not physically sick, just sick of that sham of a service his parents are staging," she told Frank, walking around to the side of the church that sheltered a pioneer graveyard within a stone fence. Tombstones tilted this way and that in the turf. She leaned back against the fence and frowned across the rugged, hilly countryside.

"I can understand," Frank said, leaning gingerly beside her, his shoulder barely touching hers, his hand between them almost touching her hip.

"I doubt it."

"I realize you're thinking of your dad and Mandi."

She turned to face him. "You don't know what I'm thinking. But...how well did you really know Mandi, Frank?"

His eyes darted away, then back. "Everyone knew her."

"Cop-out answer. You were the best friend of her steady."

"Mace and I stopped being best friends right after he quit the football team."

"I didn't think that was what split you up."

"Hell, you make Mace and me sound like the couple,'' he muttered. ''A couple of hot-headed kids is what we were.''

''But were you both hot over Mandi?''

He pushed away from the wall but spun to face her, trapping her with his hands on either side of her. ''What does it matter now? It's all water over the damn. It's you I'm hot for.''

''Let's just stay with Mandi for now,'' she said, lifting both palms as if to hold him off. ''I'm just trying to understand her better, that's all.''

''She was sleeping with Mace, if that's what you're asking.''

''It's not what I'm asking. And—I guess I knew that, though she didn't exactly say so and I never let myself think that, at least back then. I was so naive and blind,'' she added, almost to herself.

''And now you're determined to follow in her footsteps?'' he challenged, his voice rising. ''Or have you already?''

As he leaned closer to kiss her, she tried to shove his shoulders back, then hit him in the throat when he didn't budge. ''You obviously need a hand here,'' another voice said. *Mace.* Mace was out here, and everyone was streaming out the front door.

''Jenna, you said you needed to talk to Frank. Are you done now?'' Mace said, not taking his eyes off Frank as the two men seemed to square off. Surely they wouldn't come to blows—not here, not over her. But the blow that did hit her was a blinding but clear knowledge: Mace and Frank had fought over Mandi. That's why they'd become estranged. And Mandi had obviously chosen Mace.

Hadn't she?

"I believe I've said enough to him, since he doesn't seem to be able to converse in a civil fashion."

"Then, I'll drive you back," Mace insisted, gesturing to her.

"The hell you will!" Frank countered, shoving Mace's arm.

"Listen, you two," Cassie cut in, appearing suddenly like an avenging angel. "I'll drive her back, okay? Jenna?"

"Sounds good to me," Jenna said. "Here I thought poor Russ never grew up—but maybe it's all of us."

She went with Cassie, head held high but her eyes filled with tears. When she got in her friend's car, she blew her nose. "It was like stepping back in time," Jenna tried to explain, "but like I was suddenly Mandi and not me."

"You want to run that by me again?"

"Maybe Mandi was playing them against each other. You were trying to suggest that with your questions on the tape, weren't you? Oh, Cassie, I keep telling myself I loved her, but I think I hated her, too. I always wanted to be like her, but now I don't. And I can't help still loving Mace, and now I've screwed everything up. I just don't understand men—women either, half the time."

"Welcome to the club. So you want to go right home, or you want to take a little ride with me over to Oolitic? They've still got the best old-fashioned soda fountain, since you're time-traveling today. Besides, I need to stop in to see a woman there about a story I'm doing."

"Good. Just drive," Jenna ordered, blowing her nose again.

"One piece of advice I can give you," Cassie said as they rolled down their windows and let the warm May air ruffle their hair. "It's best to just do without men, except for those with terminal cancer who really need you, even if they are still mean bastards who think they're tough as nails.'' Her voice almost broke and she sniffed hard.

''My mother used to watch some miniseries about the emperor Claudius,'' Jenna said. ''You know, on Masterpiece Theatre. It was all about how no one could trust anyone else in ancient Rome. But the worst traitors were friends and family—betrayals, poisonings, you name it.''

''Ick.''

''Yeah, well, she used to quote a line from it, and used to say it was her motto in politics. But it just seems so right today—with Russ and all. 'Trust no one, my friend.' I'd hate to think the world's really like that, wouldn't you?''

''It's not for us, no way,'' Cassie declared as she swiped at her tears with her hand. Jenna handed her a tissue. ''Listen, you won't mind waiting in the car while I pop in to see this woman for a sec, will you? I finally tracked down where she lives, but don't have her phone number. Then we'll hit the soda fountain and both overdose on hot fudge.''

''Sounds good to me. Anything to get some pounds on you, though I've been bingeing on those M&M's Mace brought me.''

''Trust no man, my friend, even one bearing chocolate.''

They got a good laugh out of that, but Jenna still felt like crying.

12

"So, what exactly are we looking for?" Gil asked Mace on the day after Russ's funeral, as they walked from Deep Heart toward a rocky, unused pasture. They both had bright blue Perlon cord ropes looped over their shoulders. "I can't believe there would be an undiscovered cave entrance in this area," Gil went on. "But I'll humor you, since I've been over the moon caving around here, while you've had your nose to the company and family grindstone."

"We're looking for a cave entrance that might have been partly obscured by rubble," Mace said, deciding he'd come clean with Gil about the "what" if not the "why" quite yet.

"In others words, we're hot on the trail of sinks or blowholes? Piece of cake, bloke. But I can't believe ridgewalkers like you and your father haven't found all of them around here by now. And why waste a perfectly good Saturday fooling around aboveground when we could be underground in some great local caves?"

"I'm looking for a back or side entrance to a cave that might have had its 'front door' covered by a blast," Mace explained further. "After the fatal rock slide in Ridgeview, the government dynamited hanging rock around here on and off for years, to prevent such a disaster from happening again. I've been thinking about it and figure they might have inadvertently covered caverns that were accessible, say, ten or fifteen years ago. So we'd need to find another way in."

"Favorite caves you yearn to find again?" Gil asked, squinting into the sun.

"Not exactly. Anyhow, with our caving noses, I thought maybe we could uncover and enter them again. At least they'd be untouched by the amateurs like the university students you've been caving with lately. They might be," he added, his voice snagging, "almost as they were last left."

Mace felt guilty not totally leveling with Gil, but he didn't need to have anyone know he was looking for the cave where Mandi and Jenna had been held fifteen years ago. He'd studied Cassie's old newspaper articles and skimmed both the official deposition Jenna gave and Mary Drout's series of pieces, focusing on Jenna's somewhat foggy, drug-induced reminiscence of the abduction and its aftermath. Mace was determined to find Mandi and put her to rest once and for all.

Gaping Gil was rattling on as they ridgewalked—caver's terminology for following limestone outcroppings to look for cave entrances. Ridgewalking was one of the few really great childhood memories Mace had of time with his dad, and he was surprised that Gil recalled his sharing that. Rod MacCaman had been looking for possible new quarry sites, while Mace had rambled through rocks hoping to find a hole that sucked or blew air. To Mace, caves had seemed like living, breathing beings, hidden in the earth. Later, he learned they were only trying to balance their inner atmosphere with the constantly changing air pressures above. Yet he could still hear himself calling out, *"Look, Dad, here's another giant's mouth!"*

"Look at that!" Gil called out, pointing and yanking

Mace from his memories. They clambered over a ledge to get closer to what he'd spotted. "Cave ho, right-o," Gil chanted as if to congratulate himself.

"It looks like a possibility," Mace admitted, clapping him on the back. Before them, partly obscured by tall weeds, lay a rock-edged one-yard hole. They had both worn their army surplus fatigues and flannel shirts in case they found something to crawl into. For a long trek underground, which they didn't have time for today, they'd wear state-of-the-art fluorescent coveralls of ballistic nylon over wet suits; razor-sharp rocks could tear clothes and skin. But it looked like one of them could wriggle in here safely.

"Let's move what breakdown we can and get in a ways," Gil said, his voice excited. They only needed to move a few pieces of rubble; Gil was so skinny and wiry he could crawl through seven-inch openings, though Mace needed more. The cave blew warmer and wetter in their sweating faces as they leaned over it.

"Let's go back to our trucks and get gear," Gil suggested.

"Or I can just go down on this rope. Since I've been cave-deprived since I've been back here, you said I'd go in first."

"You drive a hard bargain, especially if this leads to a virgin cave, but I'll let you give it a go. We can anchor you right here, and there's enough natural light for a first rappel. But, bloody hell, if you spot some verticals, you're out of there and we'll go get our gear. Tie your own knots, then, as you're the master of the bowlines and prusiks—I'll give you that much, Caveman."

Their banter ebbed as their anticipation grew. "I can almost hear the ghosts down there," Gil said, gleefully rubbing his hands.

They stuck their heads deeper into the four-foot-diameter hole they'd made and strained to listen. Air movement or distant subterranean rushing water created strange whisperings that always seemed just out of reach. Mace thrived on caving, but since Mandi had disappeared, the sounds had bothered him. It was as if someone was trapped within, always hiding just around the next corner. He tried to concentrate instead on avoiding the other "haunted" beings of the world's caves. Hodags, as cavers called the imaginary gremlins of the netherworld, were always blamed for errors or glitches underground: a blown-out carbide lamp, dropped flashlight, or even shoelaces coming untied in the worst moments.

Mace tied a bowline and let himself carefully over the edge, playing out the rope to drop effortlessly to the lowest ledge they could see. No need for a harness or ascenders for this short distance. He could easily chimney his way out of here with no rope at all.

"Get out of my light, Gaping Gil!" he shouted up.

There was, he told himself as he looked around, both good news and bad. This was obviously a dead bottom pit with hardly any vertical passages to explore. On the other hand, the air and moisture meant it linked somehow to a larger network of unseen caverns nearby, and that was exactly what he was looking for.

Jenna had gone into the house to pour herself some herbal iced tea when she heard the knock on the front door. Hoping it was Mace, who hadn't called since the argument at Russ's funeral yesterday, she poured a second glass of it as a peace offering and hurried into the living room, calling, "Coming!"

Little Pete Henshaw stood at her screen door, shading

his eyes to see in. She knew the Henshaw boys and their friends were sometimes in the forest, but none had ever stopped by.

"Hi, Pete," she said. "Are you with your dad or the other guys?"

"Just me," he said solemnly, taking off his backward baseball cap. "But the team sent me. On business."

"I see. Come on in, then, unless you'd like to go have some pop in the tree house?"

"In here would be okay. I don't want to drop the money climbing up there. But I like your tree houses. We all do."

Not certain who "we" were or why he'd brought money, she let him in and went to get him a can of pop. She came back in to find him scrutinizing the collection of cats on the windowsill.

"You must have been buying these a long time," he said, peering closely at the Siamese that Mace had bought Mandi so long ago. She realized then why Pete especially touched her heart. He was just the age Mace had been when she'd first known him, when he was literally the boy next door, before Dad built Kirkhall, and they moved away from the old neighborhood.

"Those were my sister's once," Jenna said, but her voice snagged in her throat.

"And she gave them to you?"

"When she went away, yes."

"So you might have to give them back when she comes here again," he said solemnly, still not looking at her. Jenna was about to explain that Mandi was dead, when Pete spoke again. "I like this one best," he said, still eyeing the figurine that so resembled Mandi's beloved Pert. "Cats with blue eyes are kind of cool."

"It sounds to me as if you came here on business,"

Jenna said to steer him to another topic. "Did you say the guys sent you?"

"Right." He turned back to her and perching on the edge of his chair. "To see if you'll still make us a tree house like Coach Pierce was going to get for us, even though he died. We can name it after him. We don't know what it costs but I collected fourteen dollars. If we need more, we can charge for games and stuff when we get a new coach. I guess my dad might do it for a while, when he's not so busy opening up Deep Heart again and keeping an eye on Mr. MacCaman's son."

She wondered if there was some trouble at the stone company. Mace hadn't mentioned it. But her heart went out to Pete. "The only thing is," she told him as he swigged his pop, "I was going to build that tree house on Coach Pierce's land, and now that's gone."

"The guys were thinking," he said, his face serious, "it could be a 'morial to the coach. You know, like that one on the town square to the other people who died in a quarry. You got lots of trees around here and those neat statues of stuff, too. Couldn't we rent one of your trees for our tree house, or something? Like I said, I can get you more money. My dad says he's going to be rich someday."

"I'll tell you what, Pete. If you can get me some dads to help us build it, we can put it on my land, and it won't cost too much more than what you have. We'll ask at my dad's old lumberyard for donations of wood and shingles. I can work on that."

"Great!" he said, breaking into a gap-toothed grin. "Do I have to sign a paper or something?"

"Let's just shake hands on it," she said, and they did.

Cassie: This is Cassie MacCaman interviewing Jenna Kirk, tape number two. It is Saturday afternoon, May 13, 2000. Jennie, we're going to focus on your memories from the night you were released from the abduction and found wandering in the forest outside your grandmother's home. All set?

Jenna: As you know, the abductor or abductors had knocked me around a little when I—we—tried to escape, and I was drugged, but I will try to recall what I can. I should have done this years ago, but after the police and FBI questioning, it was suggested I just bury it and go on.

Cassie: Suggested by…

Jenna: My mother and my psychiatrist—well, he was more like a family counselor. He talked through a lot of things with both Mother and me.

Cassie: That would be Dr. Garth Brennan?

Jenna: You're not going to try to talk to him, for heaven's sake?

Cassie: Been there, done that. He said no—professional privilege, patient information and all that. So anything you can recall will be helpful.

Jenna: I think I became unconscious in the cave after Mandi and I tried to escape in the dark and the men came back—yes, two men. She ran and I tried to tackle the first guy, but he shoved me on my face on the cave floor and put a knee in my back. I either fainted or else he might have given me a shot again.

Cassie: Again. So he'd drugged you before with an injection?

Jenna: Yes. Not only when I was first seized, but when I screamed, "What do you want?" and tipped my chair over. That was how I learned Mandi was there. I—I felt her legs when I slid down to the cave floor.

Cassie: You're sure you were on a cave floor? Not in a cellar or something like that?

Jenna: Cassie, if you've read the interviews I did, you know that, and I haven't changed my mind. A cave. I saw it later when I got my blindfold off. I saw it and smelled it and heard it.

Cassie: Okay, just rechecking. But you heard it?

Jenna: Echoes, funny echoes, murmuring. Even when we weren't whispering, it seemed to whisper, too. But we're getting way off my being brought back here—to the Stone Forest, I mean.

Cassie: That's okay. All your memories of events are important.

Jenna: For a book about my mother? By the way, did you ever go back and talk to that Brenda Sage, since no one was home when we drove there?

Cassie: Questions, questions. I'm the interviewer here, remember. But no, I haven't gotten hold of her yet and don't know her number, so I've dropped her a postcard asking her to name a time and place.

Jenna: She knew my mother once? Is that it?

Cassie: Right. And like I said, the first half of the book is about how she was shaped by key events—her father's expectations, then losing her husband and daughter. I'm convinced that surviving all that has made her what she is today. But let's get back on track. What do you recall about being returned to the Stone Forest after being held in the cave?

Jenna: I think I remember being put out of a car down by the entrance to the cemetery, because I remember crawling past gravestones to get back into the forest. Then it all changed to seeing gargoyles, as if I were...crawling out of hell. That's when I got to my feet and started toward the house. I was yelling for my grandmother, and she came out of the house, looking like she'd seen a ghost.

Cassie: What happened next?

Jenna: She started crying and saying "Praise the Lord!" and she took me inside and called my mother, who came with the police. Mother kept screaming at me, "Where's Mandi? Where's Mandi? Did you leave Mandi?" Grandma Darva held me tight almost all night, while they searched the forest, even with dogs. But my scent stopped at the cemetery road, and they couldn't get any farther, couldn't find Mandi, and all I could tell them was that I'd heard her scream echo before I blacked out....

Cassie: It's all right, Jen—

Jenna: It isn't all right! Everyone says that, but it's never been all right! Even Mother said we had to declare her dead, if just to stop the crank calls and the hopeless waiting. But I couldn't bear to think she was dead. I *never* wanted her to be dead, not when she was better than me, not when Mother loved her so much, and not so I could have Mace. Never!

It was late Sunday morning when Jenna noted that the figurine that looked like Pert was missing.

"Oh no," she said as her heart fell. It was obvious what had happened to it. Pete must have put it in his backpack when she went to get him some cookies to take with him. Her first instinct was to drive immediately to the Henshaws' and demand it back, but she'd probably do better for herself and Pete if she asked him for it privately, and gave him a little lecture. He'd said the team had a game at one today, so she'd have to wait until later.

She was about to take her laptop up into Home Tree Home to get some correspondence done, when she heard a truck. Mace? She wanted so badly to make up with him, and wished he'd called yesterday. She peeked out her window. A truck, but not Mace's. It was his friend Gil Winslow.

Jenna went out to meet him. "Hope you don't mind my just popping in," he told her. Gil wore frayed, patched jeans, a flannel shirt over a T-shirt and heavy-duty boots as if he'd just emerged from the underground. She loved his lilting British accent. "Mace has said so much about the carvings and Tarzan houses at your place here," he told her, "so I had to come see for myself."

"Tarzan houses. He would say that. I'd be happy to show you around."

"Smashing. I don't mean to be a bother."

She assured him he wasn't, poured them two cups of coffee to take with them and locked her door. She had thought she'd gotten past having to worry about unwanted visitors since Russ died, but she guessed the whole episode had left her a little wary. She walked Gil through the various sculpture groupings her grandfather had made.

"I've never seen anything better," he told her, often stopping to admire them, "except God's handiwork underground."

"Stalactites and stalagmites?"

"Right-o. You wouldn't believe the carvings we cavers find. And He bides His time, too," he said, smiling.

"It's estimated it takes one hundred years to grow one cubic inch of limestone. There's everything from delicate bursts of what we call soda straws, to carved columns two stories high, limestone draperies that frame stone waterfalls, and entire cathedrals underground." His gaze was distant, his voice awestruck. "You'd find it all beautiful and moving beyond belief."

"Mace told you I'm claustrophobic, didn't he?"

"Got to admit he did." He looked like she'd caught him in some dire deed.

"Then, despite what you just described, I have to tell you I can't fathom caving. I'd love to see photos but...Gil, can you please explain why men like you and Mace are so drawn to caves? It isn't just the raw, untouched beauty, is it?"

They perched on stone toadstools in the Fairy Land section. "I've lectured on the lure of caving a time or two, but never can explain it," he told her, "so I'll have to give you the pat answer for starters. Some cave for science, some for sport, and some for unknown reasons."

"Like the call of the wild?" she suggested, when he paused.

"For Mace, maybe it's escape," he said, looking out over the sun-splashed forest. "Or then again, sometimes it's as if he's looking for something just beyond the next turn. Cavers are a strange lot."

"How so?" she said, leaning forward.

"I thank you for asking, rather than just taking a look at me and nodding, Jenna Kirk," he said with a little smile. "Truth is, they tend to be introverted, close-mouthed—but for me—and even hostile."

"Toward..."

"Hostile toward themselves, for some reason, but not

necessarily aggressive. Let an angry man loose in some of those priceless formations I described, and you've got a bloody disaster. Indiana Jones action heroes don't make good cavers. You've heard the motto of all good cavers, haven't you?"

"Not really. Mace and one other local guy are the only cavers I've known—till now—and Mace has only been back in my life three weeks after the past fifteen years. What's the motto?"

"'Take nothing but pictures. Leave nothing but footprints. Kill nothing but time.'"

"Sounds like it would make a good poster."

"I imagine it has. But you know, I've heard Mace's motto more than once, and it's a better one."

"Tell me," she said, when he stared off into the distance again.

"The man's hardly a poet, but he says, 'There's another world directly beneath our feet, waiting in the dark.' That's what's pulling cavers, if the truth be known. In caving, there's a double challenge. They discover a cave—and they explore and fight back against their own inner dark places."

Jenna shuddered and wrapped her arms around herself to stop the sudden chill.

"Sorry," he said. "Didn't mean to get too deep." He grinned at his own pun, then sobered again.

"You know, Gil," she said, "I would like to get over my claustrophobia, I really would. But I think I have enough trouble just negotiating this world—and myself—in broad daylight."

He laughed, a rich sound. "I can see another reason he came back here when he said once that he never would."

"I'd like to think so," Jenna admitted, "but it was

his dad's illness and saving MacCaman Stone that brought him back."

"Right," Gil said as he rose and started back toward his car, muttering so low she could hardly hear him. "And saving himself."

"Jenna, it's Mace."

She gripped her cell phone tightly. Since Gil had gone, she'd been working in Home Tree Home. Glancing at her watch, she was surprised to see it was mid-afternoon.

"Mace, hi. I was hoping to get to talk to you, to apologize for my part in the fiasco after Russ's funeral."

"We were both on edge. How about cooling off with a swim at Green Eye and then talking. Can you leave the house? You haven't had any trouble since Russ died, have you?"

"No, it must have been him. Do you want to come over?"

"Get on your swimsuit, and I'll meet you at Green Eye. The water will be cold, but we can handle it."

Jenna hurried back to the house and changed into a swimsuit, but not without agonizing over which one to wear. She settled on her more conservative, older one-piece. No good trying to look like Miss America at a stone quarry. She recalled that Mace and Frank used to go skinny-dipping there. She'd actually stumbled on them once, years ago, and had spied on them, though from such a distance that she couldn't see much. Buck naked, they'd cannonballed off the rocks. She'd written all about it in her secret diary, but she'd never told a soul, and long ago she'd given that little book the heave-ho.

Mace was already sitting on the tilted monolith, where

kids used to sun themselves. She saw no towel, but he'd laid out an old plaid blanket on the hard bed of limestone. No sunglasses, but then Gil didn't wear them, either, so maybe that was a caver thing.

He watched her approach, his face all in stark planes and angles in the afternoon sun, his eyes shaded. He made her so aware of her body, of the way she moved and even breathed. She threw her towel down beside him.

"I didn't mean to get hot under the collar yesterday," he said, arms linked over his bent legs. "I was mad at Frank, not you."

"And I didn't mean to upset you by going with him. To the funeral, that is."

As she sat down on the blanket, he flopped back, put his hands behind his head and stared up at the sky. "Maybe it's just as well that everyone didn't see us together," he said, "since we were in that car together late at night, and that's been in all the papers."

"You think there's something wrong with us being together?"

"No," he said, turning his head to look at her. "The hell with them. I'm just thinking of you."

"I happen to be a big girl now, Mace."

He sat up again, and his voice got rougher. "I see that."

He studied her so intently she felt as if he'd stroked her skin. "Jenna, the real reason I didn't call yesterday...the reason that I fight coming to see you—"

"You do?"

"—is that I can't seem to keep my thoughts and my hands off you. Hell, I've only been back three weeks. We've been apart for years, and we've got some baggage—"

"Do you think Mandi's standing between us—the memory of her?" she demanded, leaning closer to him.

He reached for her, ruffling the blanket between them as he pulled her closer. "Only if we let her."

"Then, let's not. Let's...

He moved like lightning. Somehow she was sprawled out on him, over him, then under him. Blanket or not, she knocked the back of her head on the rock as he took her mouth with his. The kiss soon spiraled out of control, wild and crazy, with hands moving and grasping. She was dizzy, her emotions, too, went flying everywhere, bouncing inside her, careening to him and then back.

His hot breath was in her ear, down her throat, along her collarbone. How warm his skin was in the sun, scalding her, despite the breeze. He gripped her waist and moved his open free hand down the curve of her hip to the outside of her thigh. Though he pinned her down against the solid rock, she was suddenly certain the rock was shaking.

He trailed kisses down her throat to the curve of her neck, then between her breasts. She raked her fingers through his short crisp hair, pulling his head down, closer, harder, kneading his powerful back muscles...needing him.

A kid's cry echoed off the quarry walls. For one instant, Jenna pictured the child she'd seen, who looked so like Mandi, staring at her in the forest. Had she emerged now to protest Jenna and Mace's being together? She tensed and pulled back before she realized how crazy the thought was.

Out-of-breath, looking dazed, Mace lifted his mouth from hers. "Damn."

"Visitors? Clay Henshaw's kids?" Jenna asked, turning and shading her eyes.

He frowned, then shook his head as a child's shout bounced past them again. Sitting up and shading their eyes, they could see a group of six youngsters with two adults, carting a picnic basket and cooler. They had evidently approached from the old access road where Mace had parked, but they were coming around this way.

"I've got to cool off, anyway," Mace muttered, though he looked furious. "The equivalent of a cold shower's badly needed before I really lose my head."

He pecked a kiss on her lips, ruffled her hair, stood and knifed into the green water. Annoyed at herself that the vision of that child still haunted her, Jenna stood and jumped in an explosion of foam not far from where he'd gone in. They both popped to the surface at the same time. He came at her, taking huge strokes, cupping her bottom underwater to pull her close for a wet kiss before he released her again.

"You're it," he told her.

"I'm not playing tag in this c-c-cold water."

"No, I mean you're *It,* the one I want, the one I'm going to chase, the one who's going to need me. So consider this fair warning."

She grinned at him like an idiot. If he only knew how long and how desperately she had wanted to be his. She blinked moisture away, unsure if it was quarry water or tears of joy.

That night, Jenna heard the wolf howl. That *was* the wolf, wasn't it? She hadn't heard it for ten days.

But it was windy outside, so maybe she'd imagined it, she told herself as she stood at the top of the stairs, straining to hear. It had been windy the other night she'd heard it, too. But why had it sounded now as if it were *in* the house?

She donned her terry-cloth robe, took two flashlights and went downstairs into the pitch-black living room. She thought about getting her shotgun, then recalled that it was still in the trunk of Mace's truck, where they'd tossed it the night they chased Russ. The sound came again, almost like a baby's cry. Perhaps it *was* just the wind howling.

Using her flashlight beams, she went from window to window until she was out in the kitchen.

"Waaa. Waaa!"

Close, but where? In the cellar?

She put her ear to the door she kept locked and listened. Yes, the sound—not a wolf's howl she was sure now—came from the cellar. No way she was going down there. But the weird wail sounded like something was in distress.

Jenna strained to listen. Again the cry. She undid the dead-bolt lock and opened the door just far enough to click on the single light. No sound, no movement from down the steps. She'd best lock the door and wait until dawn. Not much light filtered down there through the narrow windows. But was the sound from down there or not?

When she heard it again, muted, she grabbed the railing and descended two steps. Bending, she peered down. The ceiling light wanly illuminated the main room. Her grandmother had kept her washer and dryer here. Jenna had hers in the kitchen, and only used the place for storage of extra wood and, in bad weather, her dad's tools. If she went into any of the three side rooms, one of which used to be the coal cellar, her flashlights would be her only illumination.

She thought of Gil's admission that Mace had said she was a claustrophobic. She did want to get over that;

it was only since the kidnapping that she had been haunted by enclosed or dark places. She'd never go caving, but her own cellar was surely one thing she could face and conquer.

Jenna took a step down, then another. Gripping the railing, she played both flashlights, held in one hand, into each dim corner of the main room, on the old shelves, through the piled wood and power tools. She sensed something nearby, just waiting to leap at her. Her heart pounded; she began to sweat and shake.

"Waaa!"

Jenna shrieked but didn't run. Angry, unearthly, that cry. It echoed differently down here, as if it had been in stereo before but was now more focused.

It sounded high now, near the ceiling. Before she even directed the flashlights up into the window well and saw the feral face with gleaming eyes she knew what it was. A cat, huddled in the window well. A stray cat, wanting shelter, a home.

A blue-eyed Siamese, just like Mandi's long-lost Pert.

13

"What do you want the ad to say?" Mary Drout asked Jenna, pen poised above her steno pad in the *Ridgeview Reporter* office early the next morning. Mary stood behind the wooden counter that separated her desk and files from the tiny reception area. "Female seal point Siamese cat found," Jenna dictated.

"Place found?"

"In the Stone Forest."

"Really?" Mary looked over the top of her reading glasses. "Usually such an expensive breed isn't tossed out like a mutt or unwanted kitten, or even left outside in case it runs away. Any collar of identifying tags?"

"None. Just in case people can't picture what a seal point is, you might put in that she's beige with dark brown ears and paws. Her eyes are sky blue."

"She'd be a lovely one to just keep, though I suppose you'd rather have a watchdog out there."

"Why do you say that?" Jenna demanded. Mace had said the same thing. She tried to tamp down her rising unease. Of course, finding a cat that looked just like Mandi's Pert—who was surely dead by now—could be a coincidence. But her troubles with Russ had made her wary.

"Why?" Mary countered, frowning. "Because you're a woman living alone out there, and your stone carvings can attract unwanted visitors, that's why, my girl."

"Sorry. I didn't mean to snap at you. I've recently been told that Russ Pierce stalked my sister years ago. The police and FBI once suspected him of—well, harassing her, at the least."

"But he had a rock-solid alibi on the night you two were taken," she said, tapping her pen on her paper.

"I was just wondering if anyone else looked culpable at the time. It's only been lately I've started to think about this, and I know you're the expert on anything and everything that's Ridgeview history."

Though they were alone in the little office, Mary glanced around as if someone might overhear. "Everyone knows they looked closely at Mace, of course, though I'm sure he was as innocent as Russ. Aren't you?" she challenged, leaning over the countertop.

"Of course. I don't suspect him of anything but suffering still over Mandi's loss, as we all do. But was anyone else investigated besides Mace and Russ?"

"Really, Jenna, do you want to drag all this out again? Why do this to yourself or to your mother at this point? You've made such a good start back here, and your business seems to be building. Why, I'm going to do a feature on you and Russ's baseball team building a tree house in his memory, and that will be excellent publicity for you."

"And asking if anyone else was at all implicated threatens your story or my publicity? Mary, I thought if anyone knew—and cared—it would be you." Jenna knew full well she was manipulating Mary, but the old shrew had been blatantly doing the same to her.

"I was just trying to spare you, because what I have to say isn't going to help," she said, doodling a maze on the margins of her notepad.

"I don't want to be spared. I want answers."

"All right, then. Yes, the FBI did suspect another man. But I never could discover who—privileged information that didn't pan out somehow. So I never printed it because that would have been hearsay, and I don't write what I don't know."

"Then, how did you know there was a third male suspect?"

"Jenna, dear," Mary said, scribbling through her doodling, "there were hundreds of suspects. Everyone in town who ever said 'boo' to Mandi or your mother was scrutinized. But there was a third person who looked like a strong lead—and then it came to nothing, evidently. I learned about it by simply overhearing something said, if you must know, not by my usual tried-and-true reporting methods. And never mind trying to get the backstory on the third man, because I tried years ago and your friend Cassie tried recently. The FBI agent who oversaw the investigation fifteen years ago is dead, and the files are sealed."

"Sealed? Could my mother get them unsealed?"

"You'd best ask her. But why would she want to open a can of worms when she's dining on caviar lately, excuse the mixed metaphor. I'm telling you, you'd better just worry about finding this valuable Siamese a home and leave the research work to me and Cassie. If either of us turns up a thing, you know we'd both share it with you."

Jenna paid for the ad and thanked Mary. She'd bet anything that the other man who was the third focus of investigators was bank president and venerated township trustee Frank Connors. She'd try to pin Cassie down, though she didn't want her to think she was second-guessing her or checking up on her. As wrenching as Cassie's taped interviews could get, the soul-searching seemed to be helping in a way that Dr. Brennan's counseling never had.

For one thing, instead of freaking out when she found the cat, Jenna simply told herself that it could not possibly be a setup by someone trying to send her off the edge again. Russ was dead, and nothing had happened since.

As she left the office of the *Ridgeview Reporter,* the jingle of the bell on the door made her jump. She hadn't slept much last night, trying to calm the cat. Unless it was just the wind outside or she'd scented the wolf, someone had really upset the poor thing.

Jenna hurried around to the back door of her van and slid it open. Slightly astigmatic like most of her breed, the Siamese peered warily up at her through the slats of the crate Jenna had built for her last night. She might just ask the vet for a tranquilizer to put in the cat's milk. Maybe she could use one herself.

"It's okay, Pretty Girl," she crooned to the svelte animal, and stroked its sleek fur through the slats. "We're going to get you checked out at the vet, and then we'll go home again. I'm trying to find your family, but I'll take care of you till we do, I promise."

Still restless and spooked, the cat jerked when she touched it. "I knew a cat just like you once, Pretty Girl, and I used to wish she was mine. Now everything's going to be just fine."

Cassandra MacCaman, interviewing Jenna Kirk, tape number three.

Cassie: Did finding a cat that looks like Mandi's Pert bring back a lot of memories?

Jenna: Sure, but most of them happy.

Cassie: You said that Pert was always strictly

Mandi's, whereas you'd shared the earlier cats. Did that make you feel left out or angry with your sister?

Jenna: Pert was a one-person pet, but that wasn't just the cat's preference. Mandi was into collecting *everything* privately by then.

Cassie: I remember. Including boys.

Jenna: Looking back, I guess that's right. She had Mace's ring, and Russ following her around. I'm pretty sure that Frank Connors liked her, too—better not put that in the book, though, unless you talk to him first.

Cassie: I already have. He said he was crazy about her. He actually gave her his ring, too, though I guess she never wore it.

Jenna: You're kidding? I—I can't believe she'd take Frank's when she had Mace's.

Cassie: Well, you just said she was into collecting things.

Jenna: You know, I found a ring in her things not long ago. I'll have to see if it was Frank's, because I was sure she was wearing Mace's that last night.

Cassie: Or vice versa. So you've been sorting through her things. I noticed you put the cats and pillows out.

Jenna: Back to Frank for a sec. If he was closer to her than anyone knew then, did the authorities ever consider him a suspect?

Cassie: Not that I can turn up. I'll eventually ask him, but I didn't want to upset him in my first interview. I think, though, the connection to Frank—if there was one—would have been the crank calls your mother received after Mandi had been gone a while.

Jenna: Frank made them?

Cassie: I'm not accusing him of that. But I did uncover that he'd made "dirty" phone calls to a later girlfriend, and she reported him. Jennie, are you listening?

Jenna: Of course. That's a leap, though. I think Frank, like Mace, is the type of man who doesn't mind direct confrontation. And to use phone calls…

Cassie: You've seemed so strong lately, and I told you I'd share things I think you should know. I've recently turned up that one of the so-called crank calls your mother received—this one was about two weeks after the abduction, according to what the FBI agent who oversaw the phone taps at Kirkhall recalled—was about you.

Jenna: About me? How?

Cassie: The call was completely discounted. The male on the line accused your mother of being too busy and ambitious to spend time with her daughters, and said that you and Mandi had staged the kidnapping for attention.

Jenna: What?

Cassie: And then he claimed the plan backfired when Mandi evidently fell or was killed in the cave. Jennie, I knew this would upset you. Want me to stop the tape?

Jenna: You know, nothing shocks me anymore. People are so sick. I'm tempted to ask Mother about that call, but she's stressed out lately and doesn't need the past pulling on her, too. But was there anything else about that call? A man, you say?

Cassie: The only agent I could locate who

worked the case recalled that the guy spoke with a western, cowboy-type accent, which he thought was really phony.

Jenna: But since one of the two guys holding us wore western boots, maybe that's not so far-fetched. I mean, the call was, but—Cassie, what did I say?

Cassie: Western boots. Like what?

Jenna: Mandi's the one who saw them and mentioned it to me. I don't know—just western boots, cowboy-type boots, I guess she meant.

Cassie: That wasn't in your deposition. Why didn't you tell anyone before?

Jenna: I didn't think of it. We weren't talking about it. Why?

Cassie: It's nothing. But I want you to go with me tonight to talk to that woman I missed the other day when we were in Oolitic. She's meeting me at the old Limey Roadhouse tonight. She wouldn't tell me what I wanted to know on the phone.

Jenna: But who is she? You look pale and shaky all of a sudden.

Cassie: I'm fine, but I'm the one who's had enough of this for now.

That afternoon, Jenna walked through the Stone Forest and down Cutter Camp Road to wait for the school bus that would drop Pete Henshaw off at his house. She'd seen the bus go by, morning and night, so she knew the approximate time it would arrive.

The Henshaws lived in the old Gray homestead, and had done wonders with the house, barn and land. It was obvious to everyone that Clay had been moving up over the years at MacCaman Stone. The house had been remodeled and enlarged, they had a swimming pool, and the venerable barn now housed several of the sixties and seventies vintage cars that Clay liked to work on. The stand of oaks just beyond the barn was where Jenna was hoping to find a spot for the Little League team's tree house. She had first thought she'd put it on her land, but Clay had insisted it be built in his woodlot.

The bright yellow bus came trundling along on time and let Pete out with his brothers. He grinned and waved to Jenna, seemingly glad to see her. The two others ran up the long driveway to their house, laughing and hitting each other, while she came across the road to talk to Pete.

"You got those tree-house drawings yet?" he asked.

"Not quite yet. I've lost something and thought maybe you could help me find it."

"Sure," he said, folding his arms over his chest. "What is it?"

"Remember that cat statue of mine you liked the best? It's missing, and I really need it back."

"But I don't know where it is," he said, shaking his head. "If I did, I'd give it back, 'cause Dad said your sister that went away is really dead."

Jenna nodded and swallowed hard. "So you can see why finding it is extra important to me. Besides, someone dropped a cat off at my house that looks just like the statue."

"Who did that?" he said, suddenly looking suspicious. "Our whole family likes cats but we haven't lost one."

"I didn't see the person. The poor cat was crying in a windstorm right outside my basement window, and I didn't want the wolf to find it, so I took it in. You don't know anyone who lost a cat who looks like that statue—a Siamese cat—do you?"

"No, but I can ask around at school."

She opened her mouth to try another tack, but just closed it. It had to be Pete who took that figurine. It had to be him...but what if it wasn't?

"You okay, Ms. Kirk?" he asked. "Honest, I'd like to help you."

"Tell you what, Pete. Just promise me that you will try to get information on both my cats. And if someone you know has the figurine, please just bring it back—no questions asked, okay?"

"Sure. You want me to walk you home or something?"

"No, you'd better get in so your mom won't worry. And tell your parents I'll be over as soon as I can to check out their trees, like we talked about."

"Great!" he said, smiling that darling gap-toothed grin again. "But be careful across the road where that slippery stuff's all over the grass."

"What stuff?" she asked, crossing the road and looking down at where he pointed. "I don't see anything."

"No, back farther," he said, jogging across the road, things in his backpack bouncing rhythmically. "In that place behind the bushes that's like a little parking lot—see?" he said, and led her into a spot hidden from the road. Jenna gaped. It was obvious from the smashed-down grass that someone had been parking here recently and perhaps frequently.

"Oh, I see," she said, trying not to panic. She'd forgotten the spot. Some folks left cars here to walk back to Green Eye, and it had been a make-out spot years ago with the high-school kids. Then she saw the reddish, gummy stuff he was pointing at. It clung to the grass, matting blades together in clumps.

"Ick," she said. "What's that?"

"Brake fluid," Pete told her, importantly. "I know 'cause my dad works with it all the time with his old cars in our barn. But why so much of it is spilled there, I don't know. It's like someone parking there got his line broke."

Jenna stood as still as a statue but her mind was racing. It hadn't rained since the night Russ died. And this area was greatly covered with the thick foliage of big trees. The material was viscous, so maybe it would not have run off.

She might not have her cat figurine back, she thought, but Pete could have given her something much more important. If Russ Pierce had been parking here to spy on her, had someone deliberately cut his brake-fluid line?

Cassie knew this little fishing expedition could be worthless—or else it would give her a sharp enough hook to catch a big fish for her book. If it panned out that Cynthia Kirk had been meeting some secret lover here years ago—and exactly how many years ago was a crucial point—it was no doubt going to be the grand finale of any possible, amicable working relationship between the lieutenant governor of the great Hoosier state and her biographer.

"I can't believe they've changed the place this much, like you said," Jenna told her as they got out of Cassie's car in the crowded parking lot that evening. "Or that it's so packed."

"And on a Monday night," Cassie observed as she hit the automatic door locks. "I can't, either."

They only got as far as the door before they figured it out. Final Party Before Finals, a hand-printed sign read, and listed the names of two fraternities and two sororities.

"Oh, great," Cassie muttered. "Brenda Sage picks this place this night."

"She didn't know," Jenna said. "It's probably just Greek to her."

"Very funny." Cassie held the door for both of them. Damn, she hoped Jennie wouldn't hold this against her. *Know the truth and it shall set you free.* To stop burdening herself with guilt, Jenna had to accept that her sister had been much less than perfect and that her mother was a control freak. Jenna was making progress, but she had to get more distance from both of the other Kirk women to save herself.

And, Cassie thought, she herself had a mystery to solve now. Those western boots...

"The white-haired woman waving to us—is that Brenda Sage?" Jenna asked, interrupting Cassie's agonizing.

"Bingo," Cassie said, and started in that direction, but it was tough going. Guys and girls, talking loudly, stood in clumps, making a barrier between them and the bar.

"You needed a witness?" Brenda asked Cassie, nodding toward Jenna the moment they worked their way to her. Someone from the crowd plopped two beer on the bar, without their even asking, but both of them kept their eyes on Brenda.

"Just a friend," Cassie said, taking a sip of foamy beer.

"I recognize her," Brenda said as if Jennie wasn't even standing there. "I said just you."

"Hey," Sally, the blond bartender, called out with a wave, obviously recognizing Cassie from their brief encounter. "I see you finally found your friend!"

Cassie only nodded. Brenda was putting bills on the bar and getting up to head for the door. "I don't like everyone knowing the source," she muttered—at least, that's what Cassie thought she read on her lips in the rising noise.

"She's not here for her mother," Cassie said, shoving through the crowd after her. She pulled Brenda's arm to tug her back to face her. They stood near the door but still had to shout.

"I'm only gonna tell *you,*" Brenda said. "You're doing the book, I figured you could handle it. But she's been through a lot."

"Handle it? Please. I think what you have to say can help both of us."

Jenna came up behind them and handed Cassie her drink. "I'll be glad to wait for you while you two talk, Cassie. No problem," Jenna said, though she looked both ticked off and curious.

Cassie tried to apologize. "This is my fault. I'll just spend a couple of minutes with Brenda and be right out. Here are the car keys."

"No, I'll wait in here—just be over there," Jenna said. Gratefully, Cassie watched her edge her way across the packed room.

Jenna settled in a corner, leaning against the wall and sipping her beer, but she made certain she could see Cassie and Brenda. Something was really off about this. It was too cloak-and-dagger. She wondered if Brenda Sage, however grandmotherly she looked, was trying to sell Cassie information, or if she was some sort of a groupie who just wanted her name in the book. She watched Cassie talk and fling gestures, evidently still trying to convince Brenda Sage to divulge whatever.

It was getting warm in here, and the shifting crowd was making Jenna feel dizzy. She debated stepping outside for a minute, but she didn't want to leave Cassie.

Suddenly she couldn't see Brenda at all. Then, there she was, leaving. When Cassie just sat down at a table—no, slumped against it—Jenna realized that Brenda must have given her shocking news.

Jenna tried to shove her way toward her friend. The room was buzzing like that nest of bees she'd disturbed in a tree last year. And her head was twisting around, spinning as if she still hung from her harness, swatting at them as they tried to sting her.

Her legs went weak and watery, but she had to get to Cassie. Suddenly she fell to her knees, dropping the rest of her beer, and began to crawl on all fours through the towering trees.

Cemetery stones went by as she crept toward her grandmother's house, toward safety. Then she knew that she was close because she saw the gargoyles' grinning faces bending over her. Didn't they know she was only lying on a sun-warmed rock with Mace? She wanted him to kiss her again, to hold her, to love her. So happy. If only they could get rid of Mandi, they could be so happy…

Jenna wanted to write about all of this in her diary, but then Cassie might grab it and read it when they were trying to get their homework done. Maybe Jenna would write a whole book about how much she loved Mace. And about how angry she was at her mother for loving Mandi more.

"Wha—a-a-a-t's wro-o-o-ng?" a voice from deep in a cave asked. *"Are you s-i-i-ick?"*

Someone was leaning over her, but he wasn't Mace. Where was Mace? She was spinning far and fast on that rock with Mace at Green Eye again. He was kissing her. He said she was *it....*

She tried to concentrate on what the gargoyles were saying as they leaned over her, shouting to each other.

"Two women sick. Get the squad. Someone call 911! The redhead's unconscious, and this one's delirious. Anyone know these women?"

"Jenna! Cassie!" came a deep voice Jenna was sure she knew. Mace. Mace was kissing her on the rock...no, they had both jumped in the cold quarry and were swirling down and around. She was so cold now, where was the sun?

"What the hell happened here?"

"I don't know. They both fell over. We called the squad."

"Jenna! Cassie!" Mace kept calling. Jenna knew her brain was trying to shut out all the lights and leave her in the dark, but she wouldn't let it. She fought so hard....

Nightmare after nightmare washed over her like waves, like breakers breaking her. Back in the black cave with Mandi. Two men. *Let's get out of here.*

"Jenna, you're in the E.R. at Bloomington Hospital. This is Dr. Jack Cole. Can you hear me? You've been drugged. Did you take something intentionally?"

She fought to form words. "Just beer...someone... gave us. Feed...my cat. Feed Pert."

"Someone will feed your cat. Was there any strange taste to the beer? Did you see someone slip you something?"

She fought to make sense of the man's questions. Slipped something? She had slipped on the floor, the cave floor and felt Mandi's legs when she fell. Tied. She was tied.

"No! No-oo-oo!" she screamed and tried to break free.

"Nurse, we're going to need restraints! She'll pull her IVs out!"

Hands on her, holding her down. Blackness all around. But then she opened her eyes. Three strange faces, a man and two women. All wearing pale green like the first spring leaves.

"My mother?"

"Your mother's been called. She's coming. And your friend who brought you in is with his sister."

"Cassie. Is Cassie all right?"

"Jenna, you and Ms. MacCaman have evidently been slipped some Liquid Ecstasy in your drinks."

"It wasn't—ecstasy. Huge bees buzzing and a cave..."

"It's a hallucinogen, called GHB, often referred to as the date-rape drug."

Again, Jenna tried to force her brain to seize his words. "Cassie?" she asked.

"Her brother's with her, but he said he'd be back here as soon as he could. Cassie has not regained consciousness. Since she's so much smaller than you, she may have ingested more for her body weight...."

Jenna was sure she slept then. At least there was no duct tape or sleeping bag to hold her in, only a sheet and blanket and wires and tubes. And Mace, sitting by her bed.

"M—Mace."

He jumped to his feet and bent over her bed as if he'd

climb in, too. "Jenna. Thank God, you're conscious. What happened?"

"Nothing. I just went with Cassie to the Limey Roadhouse."

She wasn't sure what she wanted to say next. "I love you," she told him before she could stop herself. "I have always loved you even if you loved her."

She saw tears in his eyes. "Jenna," he said, taking her hand in both of his, "I knew you were at the Roadhouse only because I heard you tell Cassie what time she should pick you up on her answering machine at the house. She didn't erase it. I thought it must still be a dive and rushed over there. But—why did you two go there?"

"Was there a woman in the crowd? Brenda Sage?"

"Who? Who's she?" Mace demanded, leaning closer over her bed and holding her hand harder now.

"Someone Cassie wanted to meet about—about the book. You'll have to ask her."

"I can't ask her, for who knows how long!" he blurted. "She ingested so much of that damn stuff someone slipped you, she's comatose."

Jenna's head cleared as it had not before. Had Brenda arranged this so she didn't have to tell Cassie something, or had she told Cassie and then tried to make sure she didn't tell anyone else? Jenna had assumed it was something about the book, something about her mother. But why did Cassie want her to hear it? And who had given them the beer?

"Jenna, do you know where to find that woman?" Mace demanded, just as Cynthia Kirk appeared in the door behind him.

Jenna didn't answer, and her mother swept in to shoulder him slightly aside and hug her.

Jenna did know where to find that woman, and she was going after Brenda Sage in Oolitic as soon as she could. But not with Mace and not with her mother, she vowed as she returned her mother's hug weakly. Cassie had stumbled on something scary and dangerous. But whatever the risks, Jenna was picking up where her friend had left off.

14

Jenna kept rubbing her wrists after they took out her IVs the next morning.

''I can't believe you two were crashing some fraternity party at the Limey Roadhouse!'' her mother said, pacing back and forth across the foot of the hospital bed. She'd arranged for Jenna to be moved to a private room. ''What in the world were you thinking?''

For one minute, Jenna almost told her that going to the Roadhouse had been Cassie's idea. But she didn't want to blame her friend, nor could she explain what Cassie was so desperate to find out. And she didn't want her mother any more upset by this than she obviously already was, not until Jenna looked into it herself. ''Mother, the Roadhouse is completely different from the old days.''

''Thank heavens. I hear it used to be a hangout for roughnecks from every quarry area but Ridgeview's. The clientele may have changed, but look what happened to you, anyway. All right, then,'' she added, flinging up her hands when it became evident Jenna was going to argue more, ''you made a mistake going in there. Now you've both just got to get better, get past this and go on.''

''That's always been your motto,'' Jenna accused, surprised at her vehemence. ''But if Cassie's comatose, she and her family aren't getting over this and going on.

I think it's a mistake to handle any tragedy that way. It takes soul-searching and examining exactly what happened and why."

Her mother stopped and turned; her stare pierced Jenna's. "I'm not saying the police shouldn't investigate or the perpetrators shouldn't be prosecuted and punished. But you mean I haven't handled Mandi's loss the way you'd like, don't you? Or your father's, for that matter? I had to survive, to do it my way."

"I know, and people handle things differently," Jenna admitted, feeling so exhausted she just wanted to back off for now. "I just hope this won't cause you any crazy publicity."

"Dream on," she said, blotting at tears, though Jenna hadn't seen her crying. Her voice was much softer. "I've already given two press statements, and you know how they'll identify you somewhere in the article. 'The surviving daughter of the 1975 abduction of both daughters, which—'"

"I'm sorry. I just hope the police can talk to enough of the university students at the Roadhouse to figure out who slipped us the GHB and why. It was probably some random, stupid act—someone's warped idea of fun during the 'final party before finals.'"

Her voice broke and trailed off. She realized she did not truly believe it was some random act, any more than the cat's appearance in her window well had been. Yet Russ was dead, and she had wanted to believe so desperately that he was behind her harassment.

Cynthia perched on the edge of the chair by the bed and leaned close to take Jenna's hand. "The important thing is that you are all right, and Cassie's going to be. She's *got* to be."

"I've been driving the nurses nuts asking about her,

but they said she's no different,'' Jenna told her. ''Comatose. And they don't know how long she'll be like that, because the idiot who dumped that stuff in the drinks didn't adjust the dosage for her size,'' she choked out before she began to cry, too. Her mother sat on the bed, and they held each other.

''She'll be all right, surely she will,'' her mother crooned as if Jenna were still a child. Her mother's support was the only good thing to come out of this catastrophe, Jenna thought. Poor Mace and Rod had to deal with Cassie's coma on top of Rod's cancer.

''I'm going to go see Cassie before they release me today,'' Jenna vowed. ''I was having such horrible hallucinations, I can't imagine what she's going through.''

''I think you should come home with me,'' Cynthia said, setting Jenna gently back and watching her closely. ''It won't do any good to see her.''

''Of course it will,'' Jenna insisted. ''I don't think you and Dr. Brennan are right about just forging ahead all the time, no matter what. Some people would argue that those who don't study the past are condemned to repeat it.''

''And considering our past, what is that supposed to mean?'' Cynthia cried, seizing Jenna's wrists. ''If I'd stayed mired in the past, I'd be crazy or dead by now. Studying the past—our past—can bring nothing but grief. I'm telling you, for your own good, keep going forward, not back!''

In the end, her mother insisted on accompanying her to see Cassie when Jenna was released several hours later. Both Rod and Mace huddled at her bedside. Mace rose to hug Jenna, and Rod, frail as he looked, rose and walked Jenna's mother out into the hall.

"No change?" Jenna asked Mace as they gazed down at Cassie. Her red hair seemed faded, her face white as the hospital sheets, and she looked so small, so lost, even in that narrow bed.

"She has what they call a level thirteen mild brain injury. She barely moves."

Jenna nodded as she took in the vast array of machines than surrounded her friend. A tube went into Cassie's mouth. She was linked to a ventilator that breathed for her. Hissing and sighing rhythmically, monitors displayed lighted graphs or readouts.

"They'll test her neurological responses again tomorrow morning," Mace explained. "We'll get her the best long-term care in a Brain Trauma Unit when we move her to Indianapolis after she's stabilized, then maybe into a Brain Recovery Program."

"Long-term. Did they say how long she could be...like this?"

"It could be a while. It's a waiting game, so they basically just feed and medicate her against infection while she gets weaned off the ventilator and undergoes all sorts of stimulation to help her emerge from these—these depths of unconsciousness. They suggested we talk to her, play her music, use scent stimulation, that kind of thing. I've been—trying." His voice broke.

"I'll help. I want to help." She put her arms around his waist and pressed her head to his shoulder.

"It would be good for her to hear your voice."

"We can take turns, but I want to tell her something now," Jenna insisted, and stepped from the security of his embrace to lean over the bed. Sudden dizziness assailed her; she had to put both hands on the mattress to avoid toppling onto Cassie.

"Cassie, it's Jennie," she whispered, her mouth close

to her friend's ear. "Don't worry about a thing, because I'll find out what happened. I'm glad you left a lot of your research in Home Tree Home when we made that last tape, because I'm going to go through it. You might have uncovered something that made someone want to stop you. I'll find out if it's Brenda Sage."

Mace's voice, close behind her, made her jump.

"Do you think her eyelids fluttered, like she tried to wake up?" he asked, seizing Jenna's elbow. "They said she might do things like yawn or stretch, but she hadn't moved until just now. What did you tell her?"

"I told her I'd take care of everything."

The cat was ravenous and even more nervous when Gil Winslow dropped Jenna off at her house. Her mother was still in a snit that Jenna hadn't agreed to go home with her. Gil volunteered to come inside, but Jenna sent him on his way with thanks. He'd also volunteered to sit at Cassie's bedside and help talk to her until she recovered.

"I'm so sorry I didn't leave more food, but you had enough water, didn't you?" Jenna asked Pretty Girl in her most calming tone as she poured more food in her dish. "At least the vet gave you a clean bill of health."

As famished as the cat must be, she didn't eat, but pressed herself tightly to Jenna's legs, rubbing her ankles and purring madly. "Come on, Girl, calm down," Jenna urged, petting her so the cat arched her back. "You're going to trip me, and I'm not that steady on my feet right now, anyway."

Finally, she carried the cat around in one arm as she fixed canned soup and crackers. As she forced herself to eat, Pretty Girl kept up a nervous pacing under the table.

"You're as bad as my mother! Sit down or go to sleep! That's what I'm going to do."

Outside her windows, daylight fled. Jenna lay on the sofa with her eyes closed, planning what she must do next. Finally, Pretty Girl jumped up and pressed against her hip, head cocked, ears alert, as if waiting for something or someone.

Exhausted, Jenna dozed until Mace phoned at 5:00 a.m. to say that Cassie was the same and to see how Jenna was doing. He hadn't eaten all day and was going to take his dad home, sleep the night there, then go back to the hospital at dawn. His dad would go into MacCaman Stone for half a day, and Clay Henshaw would have to oversee the cutting at Deep Heart.

"That will please Clay to no end," Mace muttered.

"What's the problem between you two?"

"I've been in his way since I came back. He has big plans for MacCaman Stone, and this MacCaman's not part of them. But Henshaw's not the one I want to talk about. This obviously isn't the time to go into detail about us—you and me...."

A long pause.

"I want to help, Mace, with Cassie and with anything."

"You said you loved me," he whispered. She heard a sharp sniff. Could Mace be crying? "But I know you had that damn hallucinogen in you then, so I won't hold you to it."

"I want you to hold me to it. I want you to hold me, period."

"Will do. Definitely. Get a good night's sleep. And call me on my cell phone if you have any problems."

At least that phone call waked her up a bit; she still felt drugged, though the nightmares were gone, thank

God. The cat had bolted off the sofa when the phone rang, but came back now, looking up at her, ears perked as if listening for something.

"You're not helping, Girl," Jenna told her. "Calm down and get a life—at least, one of your nine lives."

And then, looking beyond Pretty Girl as she petted her, Jenna saw it. The Siamese figurine was back, just where she'd put it. She shook her head. Pete could not have brought it back and gotten it inside—nor would he have placed it so perfectly where it was before it vanished. Besides, she'd actually begun to believe that he hadn't taken it.

Trembling, she got up and went to it, picked it up gingerly and then turned it over. Just as it had always been, including the Made in England inscription, the hole in its flat base. But from that hole emanated the strangest, sweetest smell.

Jenna sniffed closer and almost gagged. It smelled just like the concentrated cologne in that bottle, English Leather, that Mandi had said she took from Mace and liked to wear.

Jenna spun to survey the room. Had the statue been here when Gil brought her home, or had someone placed it here as she slept? Could someone still be in the house? The cat kept jerking alert at any sound, ones Jenna heard and ones she didn't. Surely this was not just another hallucination.

As exhausted as she was, she armed herself with her grandmother's old wooden rolling pin and searched each first-floor room, looking for anything else out of place, including Mandi's pillow collection, which Jenna had scattered around. Nothing seemed amiss. Everything was fine, she told herself.

Except that she was going crazy. She was absolutely

certain that the cat figure had been gone and reappeared. And then there was Pretty Girl. Her arrival definitely did not seem like chance or coincidence now. She should never have named her Pretty Girl. When Mandi was little, everyone had said that to her: "Pretty girl—you're such a pretty girl." So Mandi's first word was a baby-talk mispronunciation of that—Pert, her first name for herself.

Jenna glanced at the cat, which had followed her and was staring, unblinking. "Stop looking at me like that!"

But the Siamese trailed along as Jenna checked the locks on the outside and cellar doors and the window latches, then went upstairs.

Someone must have been in this house, Jenna reasoned. He or she had broken through her last bastion of security from all that had happened. The package, the e-mail, the phone call, the photo outside, the book in the tree house—none had affected her *in here.* But now she felt invaded and violated.

And Russ Pierce must not have been to blame at all.

"No," she argued with herself as she turned on lights upstairs, "it had to be Russ."

Jenna leaned against the wall for support as another fear ripped through her. *Who drugged Cassie and me?* That event echoed what had happened to her and Mandi the night they were taken. The doctor had patiently explained that GHB, or gamma hydroxybutyrate, was a depressant that affected the central nervous system. It was a fairly new drug, he'd said. But, Jenna reasoned, that didn't mean the person who used it on them hadn't also used something similar on her and Mandi years ago. Could their abductors be back? But why would they try to make her think Mandi was alive? Or that Mandi was trying to contact her? Whatever was going on, she would not just wait for something worse to happen.

Jenna rushed into the small room where she had the blowup of the photo of the child under the bed. She was certain it would be gone.

No, it was there, though that hazy silhouette of the curly-haired child seemed more clear and dominant than ever. Jenna rummaged through the chest of drawers where she'd hidden the e-mail requesting the same tree house that she and Mandi had shared as children. Still there, untouched. Good, because these might be either clues to track the bastard or evidence when she caught him. Going to the police right now seemed insane. Not only did she not want the publicity for herself or her mother, but what would she tell them? That a book and a cat statue came and went? That someone had sent her a package and an e-mail, ordering a tree house? The police were already looking into her being drugged.

She tried to calm herself, but Pretty Girl jumped up on the single chair in the room and peered out between the lacy drapes into the depths of the darkening forest. The motion of the paw was so human, so deliberate....

Jenna tore into her own bedroom. She wanted extra flashlights right now. What if the lights went out?

She stopped dead still inside her bedroom door. Her bed looked as if someone had taken a nap in it. The bedspread was wrinkled in the shape of a human body. But worse, there lay the pillow that Russ Pierce had personally delivered to begin this nightmare.

Jenna staggered back against the wall. That pillow had been downstairs, still in its box. She'd never added it to Mandi's collection, which was scattered only in the living room. A guttural, keening cry came from her lips, more haunting than any wail from the Siamese.

As if mesmerized, Jenna walked closer to the indented bed, the pillow. *Absence makes the heart grow fonder,* it read. And snagged in its stitching were two long, blond, curly hairs.

Cassie knew she was deep, deep inside a dream. Fearful, crying faces came and went, mostly her own. She was wearing western boots and trying to take them off. She had to get rid of them, bury them. If only she could put them in the grave with Mandi.

But now it was Christmas morning, and she and Mace were opening presents. Dad was there, and Mother was smiling and laughing. The lights of the Christmas tree shone in her eyes so bright, as Santa Claus in his light green suit said, "Her pupils are still dilated."

Mother said, "I love your daddy so much, even when he gets in his moods." It was wonderful to see Mother smiling again. Jennie had a mother, but Cassie didn't anymore, and that was so sad. And Mother had a present for her, too: a beautiful book of stories. But when Cassie turned to thank her for the book, it wasn't Mother's face anymore, but Jennie's mother's.

Cassie wanted to push Santa Claus away when he kept tapping parts of her arms and legs. "Reflexes nonresponsive," Santa said. She wanted to push away her fear of who might have buried Mandi, but she just couldn't. Just couldn't.

By ten o'clock the next day, Jenna had been in action for hours. She'd forced herself to eat breakfast to keep up her strength, then she'd driven to Bloomington Hospital and sat with Cassie for an hour. The nurse had said she was too early for visiting hours, but let her stay to talk to her unconscious friend, anyway.

"The kidnapper's back, at least one of them. I'm sure of it," Jenna told Cassie in a whisper, leaning close. "Mandi can't be back, no matter what he wants me to think. If Mandi was still alive, she wouldn't pull some haunting. Not unless she blames me for leaving her, for coming back without her—" Jenna's voice broke, and she fought back sobs. "So here's what I'm going to do to protect myself until I can put all of the pieces together." She forced herself to go on. "I'm getting my door locks re-keyed this afternoon, though I had to pay an extra fee to have it done without waiting. And no one, not even Mace or my mother, is getting a copy of the keys."

Cassie seemed to frown but then just yawned. Jenna's first impulse was to run for the nurse, to rejoice that she was waking up, but Mace had warned her that this meant nothing. She bent closer, listening to Cassie's breathing, praying she'd hear, that she'd open her eyes and be *there* instead of looking so vacant, even when her eyes were half-open slits. It reminded Jenna of that cat, staring at her all the time without really responding.

"Then I'm going to buy myself a gun," she confided, talking even faster. "Mace still has my dad's shotgun in his truck, but I need something small and quick, not that big honker thing. I hate guns but I can't afford not to have one. I'm going now, Cassie, but I'll be back as soon as I can." She bent to lay her cheek briefly against her friend's. "Oh yeah," she added, "and I've got to find a way to check if there are hidden bugs or cameras in my house, too, like something secreted in a pillow. I was tempted last night to just rip Mandi's entire collection of them apart, but there has to be another way."

By noon, Jenna had filled out all the papers to buy herself a five-shot 38-caliber special snub-nosed revolver. It was seven inches long and fit perfectly into her purse. She'd had a short demonstration and arranged for lessons to learn to aim and fire it. But after the computer background check came back on her, she took the gun with her. Loaded.

Next, she stopped by a store just outside town called Techno-Spy. She wanted to have her house, van and tree houses debugged by an expert, and the gun-store owner had said to try here.

She was surprised to see a woman behind the counter, then scolded herself for expecting a man. Actually, it made her feel more comfortable to talk to a woman about this. The fact that the clerk was currently with another customer suited Jenna just fine as she studied the various small-camera devices used for surveillance, some as small as a matchbook.

"Those can be concealed in every possible device," the attractive saleswoman told her as the other customer left the store. A tall, thin brunette with a slash of silver hair, she was dressed entirely in black. With her powerful physique, she looked like a physical fitness expert.

"Such as?" Jenna asked, thinking of the cat figurine.

"Clocks, lamps, teddy bears, statues, exit signs, pagers, phones, plants, framed pictures—you name it."

"A pillow?"

"Sure, if the camera is aimed correctly and its lens is exposed. The audio devices I have over here can go in about anything."

"This reminds me of espionage movies or CIA-type stuff."

"People use them to guard against theft or to keep an eye on their baby-sitters," she explained. "See this wireless video camera here?" she asked, indicating yet another glass case. "Absolute state-of-the-art."

"It's about the size of a sugar cube!"

"That sugar cube can transmit more than 100 yards to a computer monitor or VCR. The cost for the whole shebang right now is about a thousand dollars and up. But what can I do for you?"

"First of all, you said there are legitimate uses for these. But there must be plenty of illegitimate ones."

"Not bought in this store!" she countered. "You're not a state inspector, are you?"

"No. I'm here to see about getting my property debugged of possible cameras or listening devices."

"Husband trouble?" the woman asked, lifting both sleek eyebrows. "I could tell you a tale of woe about that."

"No husband. I just need it done."

"You've come to the right place. The freelance guy who does that used to work for the feds. Top of the line, though he's pretty pricey per hour. He's used to working for lawyers and CEOs, I'm afraid," she added with a small shrug, "but he's the best in the area, probably in the state."

"All right. Meanwhile, at least now I've got an idea of what to look for on my own, too. By the way, he's not afraid of heights, is he? I've got three tree houses."

"No kidding? No, this guy's not afraid of anything."

"I wish I could say the same, but all this stuff is pretty sobering." Jenna clutched her purse closer so she could feel her new revolver in it.

"Tell me about it. My ex-husband took both photos and video of me in our own home—bathroom, bedroom—then put them on the Web, all without my knowing. That's when I got rid of him and bought this place with the settlement—he was a criminal lawyer, no less. There're a lot of wackos out there, and some of them are really dangerous, especially the ones you think you can trust.''

After the man came to re-key her locks, Jenna called Mace to check again on Cassie, then headed for little Oolitic. If Brenda Sage was still there, Jenna was going to demand that Brenda tell her exactly what she'd told Cassie before she passed out.

She had to drive around quite a while to find the right street. She'd been so upset by the argument between Mace and Frank after Russ's funeral that day—and Cassie had been driving—that she didn't pay much attention. She should have looked through Cassie's notes left in Home Tree Home, which were now safely locked in Jenna's newly fortified house. But she'd pore over those later.

On the second street that paralleled the main drag, Jenna finally recognized Brenda's house by the towering pin oaks that crowded the small front yard. An elderly neighbor man raking out his front flower bed was already watching her, so she called to him. ''I'm looking for Brenda Sage's house.''

''That's the Comptons' place,'' he said, still raking. ''Brenda's Emma Compton's mother. She's visiting, what with new twins come and all. Think she's heading home soon, if not gone already.''

Clutching her purse, Jenna almost went back to the van to hide the gun inside. No reason to take a weapon into a house with new twins. Besides, Brenda had not only *looked* like a grandmother but was one, and that made Jenna feel a little better about facing her.

She thanked the man, marched up the short crushed limestone walk and knocked. The young woman who opened the door looked exhausted, but definitely resembled Brenda.

"Hi," Jenna said, smiling and trying to sound cheery. "Mrs. Compton? Sorry to bother you when I'm sure you have your hands full, but I'd like to talk to your mother, Brenda."

"You a reporter?"

"No. Have reporters been here?"

"Luckily not. If you're selling something, she don't want to be bothered." When Jenna shook her head and stood her ground, Mrs. Compton added, "All right. She's hanging the wash out back, but you can go around."

Jenna walked around the small house. She heard the wind flapping clothes before she got a glimpse of Brenda, in jeans and a blouse, facing away to lift sheets to a laden clothesline.

"Excuse me, Mrs. Sage?"

She spun, wide eyed, her mouth bristling wooden clothespins like fangs. She spit them out into her hand and dropped them in a canvas bag, which also hung on the line.

"How is she?" Brenda asked, frowning and speaking so fast her words ran together. "I read the paper. I'm sorry you both got sick after I left, but I didn't have a thing to do with it."

"She's still in a coma. Why didn't you come forward?"

"Because I got *nothing* to do with any of it."

"But you do have something to do with why Cassie took me there to hear what you had to say. Mrs. Sage, please tell me what information you gave Cassie. I'm sure you have nothing to do with the attack on us, but I have to know."

"*She's* the one tracked me down," Brenda insisted, wiping her open hands repeatedly against her jeans. "Sometimes it's best to let sleeping dogs lie." With that, as if Jenna were dismissed, she whirled back to pinning sheets on the line.

"I won't hold it against you if you tell me, no matter what it is," Jenna said. "But I will hold it against you if you won't tell me, because I believe what you know could help me to find who drugged us. Also, if you help me, I'll keep reporters completely out of this," she added, assuming that Brenda and her daughter had worried about that.

In the wind, with Brenda facing away, Jenna had to lean closer to catch her next words: "Look, I don't want any part of this, of mixing in powerful people's lives, okay?"

"Powerful people, such as my family or Cassie's?"

"You said it, not me."

"You see, if you don't tell me, Mrs. Sage, I'm going to have to assume all kinds of things. I'll believe you're much more involved than perhaps you really are and—"

"All right!" she said, turning again. She let the half-hung wet sheet bump heavily into Jenna, but she wasn't budging.

"It was for her book on *your* mother, and I just thought she could use it to show that *paragons* of virtue can have feet of clay, just like the rest of us. I'd always looked up to her—Cynthia Kirk—" she plunged on, wiping the back of her hand under her nose "—and here I'd just been caught by my husband for cheating on him."

"I'm sorry, but I can't follow you. What did you tell Cassie that she'd want me to hear—that she could use in her book?"

"That all those years when I worked at the Roadhouse—when it was the *old* Roadhouse—I kept my eyes open. And she used to come in, dressed real casual with her hair pulled back, to eat, drink and dance with Rod MacCaman."

Jenna gasped, but Brenda plunged on. "Not so many folks knew who she was then, and I didn't know him, till I saw his picture in the paper once. I played along like I didn't know them 'cause their tips were good and they were fun to watch. And then they'd always leave together in his car, and she'd come back hours later for hers. Oh, this was from the late seventies, can't recall the exact year, but after I got divorced in '77. She came in quite a while, till she—you and your sister—had that tragedy, and I read she moved to Indianapolis when she first got elected, so don't know what happened with them after that, of course...and nobody cares anymore if someone had an affair, anyway, but with her..."

Brenda Sage's words rolled on, punctuated by the boom of flapping sheets. But the roaring sound in Jenna's ears was the shock of knowledge. It took her but a moment to realize what the woman had told Cassie just before the drug took effect. Jenna had watched Cassie fling her arms. She'd seen and sensed her surprise from across that crowd at the Roadhouse.

Quite simply, completely unknown to those who loved them and town busybodies like Mary Drout or Russ Pierce, Cynthia Kirk and Rod MacCaman had been meeting secretly and carrying on an affair, evidently for years. But did it begin before or after the so-called freak quarry rock slide killed both their mates?

15

Stunned, Jenna filled the van with gas in Oolitic and headed north toward Indianapolis. She had no idea where her mother was, in her busy schedule this late afternoon, but she had to find her and ask exactly when her secret love affair with Rod MacCaman had begun. It was not the secrecy she objected to. Her mother had a right to her own life, however much a long-term secret affair might have affected her political life. But she had to hear her mother say—no, swear—that the loss of her father and Mace's mother had come before the affair.

Because, otherwise, the unthinkable would haunt Jenna forever. More than once growing up, she had overheard people wonder how fireworks could have set off a rock slide in Rod MacCaman's quarry. He knew his business. He would have spotted an unstable situation. That's what she—as well as Mace and Cassie—had ignored for years. But Rod couldn't have created a catastrophe to eliminate two, also killing three others. And if he had, surely her mother knew nothing of it.

At her next thought, Jenna jerked the steering wheel and nearly went off the road. Why did her mother never want to look back? Just because parts of her life had been so painful, and she was blazing her own way to the stars? Or did she have something unspeakable to hide?

Shaken, Jenna pulled over at a deserted roadside picnic area to call her mother's secretary. Leaving the van idling, she got out, and sat on a limestone table. She pulled her cell phone out of her bags and punched in her mother's office number at the state house in Indianapolis.

She recognized the voice of the office receptionist. "Hi, Tracy," she managed to say, then cleared her throat. "It's Jenna, trying to track my mother. I'd really like to see her today. Do you know what time she'll be going home later, or if she's working late?"

"Where are you, Jenna? She's in Bloomington this afternoon."

"Visiting the hospital?"

"No, at the Monroe County Courthouse. Hmm, just a sec, I'm looking to see exactly where you'd find her there. She has a meeting with some financial backers in room 204, the county treasurer's office, about support for Hal Westbrook's presidential nomination."

In other words, Jenna thought, she's lining up support for herself as Westbrook's vice-presidential candidate.

"Jenna, are you still there?"

"Yes, Tracy. Thanks a lot. I'll try to see her there before she heads back to Indianapolis."

"I'll try to let her know you're coming, but the meeting should be under way. Anyway, it will be lovely for you to surprise her, especially after that close call you had."

"I think I just will surprise her," Jenna said, gripping her cell phone so hard her fingers went numb.

Mace alternated between talking to Cassie and playing radio music for her. It was a station he liked, so he figured she would, too. Strange that golden oldies songs were the ones that he, Cassie, Jenna—and Mandi—had grown up on. The station had even played that Barry Manilow song "Mandy," which he still had on an old cassette tape. He had once liked the song, but now it depressed the hell out of him. He kept hearing that line in his head about the man sending his lover away.

But real life hadn't been that way. When he'd found out his Mandi had been doing a lot more with Frank than flirting and that she'd had Frank rough up poor Russ Pierce after she'd led him on, too, Mace was the one who had finally decided to call it quits. He'd planned to tell her when they sneaked out to meet after Jenna's sixteenth birthday party, before everything veered from his control. Since then, he'd buried the truth. Even now he fought to keep the nightmare from replaying in his brain, right along with that damn song.

"Okay, you golden oldie lovers out there in Hoosier land," the deejay was saying, "here come the famous birthdays for today, May sixteenth." Mace focused on watching Cassie to see if she'd react to new voices, to old songs. Other than yawns, she wasn't budging. He studied her flaccid features as the deejay rambled on: "Famous folks born on this day include actors Henry Fonda, and Pierce Brosnan, good old 007, the newest James Bond. Also musicians Liberace and Janet Jackson. I'll be getting to important historic events on this day in just a minute, so hang on during these commercials. Someone's gotta pay the piper, know what I mean?"

Mace clicked off the radio with a sick feeling. Tomorrow was May seventeenth. If Mandi had lived, it would have been her thirty-second birthday.

He started at a knock on the open door behind him. "Hey, bloke, I figured you could use some help." Mace almost didn't recognize Gil, who poked his head around the door, then sauntered in. He'd had his beard and hair trimmed and wore clean jeans and an untorn shirt. He held his baseball cap in his hands for once.

"Thanks for coming by. I think Cassie can use a new voice."

"Run out of gab, have you, Caveman?"

"Just turned off the radio, but yeah, I'm pretty sick of hearing myself talk."

"I wanted to tell you something that might cheer you. Yesterday I took my mangy university cavers back near the site you and I were ridgewalking. We may have found another passage into that cave you've been looking for, though I didn't let them in it. Now if you can just find some spare time from all the family obligations and your quarry work..."

Mace's pulse began to pound. If anyone could smell out a cave, even one that had its main entrance covered with dynamite-blasted, tumbled rocks, it was Gaping Gil.

"How about right now?" Mace asked. "My dad called to say that Clay Henshaw's bringing him here to spend some time with Cassie. I don't want to see Henshaw, anyway. There's not much daylight left, but let's go see this new blowhole. If you've found the entrance to the cave I think you have, I owe you big time."

"I think," Gil said, narrowing his eyes suspiciously, "you'd better tell me straightaway what's so bloody special about this cave."

Rush-hour traffic clogged the roads, but fortunately it was coming out of Bloomington, not going in. Jenna easily found a parking meter on Walnut and walked up the two flights of steps toward the historical courthouse. The limestone edifice, with its solid but graceful dome, columns and statues, dominated the downtown. The clock under the dome said five-thirty. She hoped she hadn't missed her mother.

The cool, cavernous interior of the three-story rotunda echoed her footsteps. Workers scurried past on their way out; the closing of various doors resounded distantly. She'd always liked this building because it never seemed to close her in. Even what she'd always thought of as the basement, below this floor, seemed airy, with the large, banister-framed opening in its ceiling so the rotunda could be glimpsed upward. Jenna heard whispers below and looked over the railing, but saw no one. The dim vastness now looked and sounded deserted.

She climbed the stairs to get to the second-floor rooms, set around a circular hall and stone balustrade. Again distant voices buzzed, then diminished. Perhaps her mother's meeting wasn't over. Jenna hoped to get her alone, here or in the van. Once she did, she wasn't going to let a moment pass before confronting her. A sign over a door showed her what she was looking for. Treasurer's Office, Room 204.

"Hi, Jenna," a man's deep voice said from behind her.

She spun to face Vince Sabatka, her mother's driver, leaning against a shadowed column.

"Oh, you startled me. Then, she's still here. I need to see her."

"So Tracy said. The meeting's over, but she's waiting for you."

"Good. She's alone?"

"What am I, chopped liver?" he said with a tight smile.

Jenna wasn't in the mood to be teased. "I haven't seen you around for a while," she told him as he opened the door for her. Vince was dressed impeccably as ever, today in a navy blue, double-breasted suit. He always looked like an ad for men's hair spray, with every silvered strand in place, or maybe some sort of tanning booth with his perpetual healthy color.

"Oh, I'm around," he said, but she was hardly listening to him anymore. In the doorway beyond the outer, cluttered office, her mother stood, drinking from a plastic water bottle she always carried. She swiped at some of the water as it dribbled down her chin.

"Tracy told me you were coming when I checked in with her," her mother said, plopping the bottle on the first desk as she hurried to Jenna. Vince closed the door to leave them alone. This entire office complex looked deserted. "What's the matter, darling?" her mother asked. "Did you find out something about who drugged you and Cassie?"

"That's not what I want to talk about."

"Come on into this meeting room. It's small but better than this," she said, indicating the office with one hand as she drew Jenna through the doorway. A polished oak table was lined with a dozen chairs. Notepads and used water glasses sat at each place. Jenna actually preferred the spacious outer office, but she did want a private place.

"There's coffee or tea left here from the meeting," her mother went on. "Let me pour you something. Tea? You don't look very good yet, and you shouldn't be out running around, right now when—"

"Mother, I'm just going to spit this out and get it over," Jenna cried, still standing and gripping a chair back. "I've just learned something that really upsets me about you and Rod MacCaman. The miracle is not just that you kept it from me and Rod's kids so long but that our busybody town never—"

Her mother dropped the cup she'd just reached for and visibly swayed. Jenna lunged for her, pushing her toward the table while trying to pull back a chair for her.

"No—don't! Just say it!" Her mother demanded, but her voice was weak and her eyes wild and wide. Then, to Jenna's amazement, her mother went from rag doll to stone statue, poised, regal, just waiting. When Jenna gaped at her, her mother walked to the open door and shut it firmly. Arms crossed over her breasts, she turned back to Jenna. Her concern that her mother would faint vanished in the face of her own renewed fury.

"Unless my source was lying, Mother, I understand you and Rod MacCaman had a lengthy affair. Clandestine meetings at the Roadhouse, for one thing, with your disappearing with him for hours afterward. Well? Are you going to deny it?"

"Keep your voice down. Are you going to play judge and jury?"

"The deceit's your business, on your conscience. All I want to know is when it began. Were you seeing him before Dad's death? Cassie quizzed me on whether Dad worked nights, whether you went out at night. I should have known she was onto something."

"Oh, my darling, I'm so sorry you could ever think such a thing," her mother said, when Jenna had braced herself for an explosion. To her amazement, her mother looked almost relieved. She held to that hope, because that would mean she had not cheated on her father.

"How can you even ask *when?*" her mother went on, her voice controlled, even soothing now. "Of course it was after your father died. I just didn't want you to think that you—you and Mandi—weren't enough of a comfort for me after we lost him. I never could have told you years ago, because you were both too young to understand and perhaps forgive. And then, after a time, it was too late and pointless for true confessions.''

She sat in a chair and pulled the next one out for Jenna. Relieved and exhausted, Jenna collapsed in it. Her mother bent toward her, holding her hands, but Jenna still leaned stiffly away.

''Then, if you swear that,'' Jenna whispered, ''you don't have to tell me more.''

''I want to tell you. I want you to understand. It all began when Rod and I worked on the rock slide memorial together. We were both devastated by our losses. He partly blamed himself, since it was his quarry. I guess I tried to reassure and comfort him that it wasn't his fault.''

Jenna sat still, barely breathing. She certainly understood sharing tragedy, wanting to comfort. At that moment, she longed for Mace with a physical ache.

''We knew,'' her mother went on, ''that it was too soon for our relationship to be understood and accepted and that some of the old biddies in town or even Rod's competition, since his business was still in dire straits financially then, would use it against us. After all, we were the so-called martyrs who had lost our mates and who had collected all those local donations for the rock slide memorial. Though it wasn't so long ago, the moral climate was quite different then, and I was climbing the ladder of public service. You know,'' she said, looking away, ''we feared they might think the same thing you did—that we were together before the slide or had somehow caused it. Jenna, it's during those early months without your father that I learned to be really strong, that I learned to keep busy and not just shrivel up and die without him.''

''Why didn't you ever marry Rod?''

"I wanted to pursue my career, and he hardly wanted or needed a wife in the statehouse, not Rod MacCaman. Nor did I think I could become a stone country wife again, especially not with a take-charge man like Rod. I needed to control my own life, and he couldn't understand or accept that."

"So you just ended it?"

She shrugged. "If I ever thought so, I lied to myself. It was Rod who called me on my cell phone that day I came to tell you about the possibility of the VP nomination. He was telling me his cancer was worse. I—I almost lost it there in front of you. Though we are not as—as intense as we once were, we still love each other. When I heard his disease was...terminal, I almost convinced him to get married. But it would have been foolish."

"I remember that day at the Stone Forest, when Vince drove you and you got that call."

"I went immediately to see Rod," her mother admitted, standing and walking down the length of the table to look outside. "I still see him sometimes. He's my supporter, my oldest friend. Just as with you and Mace, Rod knew me when I was a child. He knew I wasn't happy then and said years ago that I should just say to hell with the past and move on.

"So," she went on, spinning around to lean in the deep window ledge facing Jenna, "are you going to tell Mace, or does he already know? It's not something I need in that book Cassie was doing on me, but I guess I'd better get used to all the truth coming out about me if I'm going to play with the big boys in the national political arena. And that's exactly what I intend to do."

Suddenly, no matter what her mother had done, Jenna

wanted to protect her. "I wish I had your courage, Mother."

"Nonsense. You do. You've always proved you do, both years ago when you and Mandi were kidnapped and lately. Now, just tell me you will at least try to understand what I've told you. I know how much you loved your father. Believe me, so did I."

Jenna stood. Their eyes met and held. Jenna nodded.

"Then, that's something for us to build an even better relationship on. Look, it's early," her mother said, glancing at her watch, "so why don't we leave your van wherever it is and let Vince drive us to get something to eat and then to see Cassie."

"Yes, I'd like that. See, looking back can sometimes help to make one stronger." In that moment, she almost blurted out everything that had been happening to make her think the kidnappers were back.

"Hmm," her mother said, walking slowly closer. "I recall that quote from Nietzsche—that which doesn't kill you makes you stronger. Jenna, I know you think sometimes I loved Mandi more—that she was somehow more lovable. You feared that maybe I blamed you for coming home that night without her. I admit I've tried to hang on to you, and that I can become a basket case if I think you're unguarded or in danger or hurt. All I can tell you is that I love you and am very proud of you. I can only hope and pray you will not turn away or—"

Jenna moved first. They hugged hard. No way was she telling her mother anything now that would upset her even more.

Before she went back to the hospital the next morning, the phone rang. Jenna jumped for it, thinking it was word about Cassie's condition. It was Garth Brennan.

"Jenna, is there anything I can do?" he offered. Though he admitted he'd talked to her mother, he encouraged Jenna to fill him in on exactly what had happened at the Roadhouse. "I imagine it was pure chance that you two got the spiked drinks," he said. "They were probably intended as a very bad joke for some coeds. College kids today can be not only irresponsible but destructive."

"I hope their bad joke sends someone to jail."

"Exactly. I understand your mother is pressing the authorities to see they do a full investigation. But my question is, would you like to come by the office or can I come to you? After your other tragedies, I want to be sure you get through this."

"I assure you I will. What's that old saying from some movie? 'I'm mad as hell and won't take it anymore.'"

"But such anger can be self-destructive."

Suddenly furious at him, she almost slammed the phone down. He was trying to manipulate her into a counseling session—exactly what she had refused from him before. And she'd bet her tree houses that her mother had put him up to that, too.

"I really need to run, Dr. Brennan, but I will call if I need your help."

"Oh, sure. Just one more quick thing then. I'm sorry to say that your offer of a tree house for Samantha will have to be put on hold, probably indefinitely. I knew she was slightly acrophobic, but she's being very ornery about this. She insists she doesn't want a playhouse if it isn't on the ground."

Jenna had a good nerve to counsel him to tell poor Samantha to just grit her teeth and stay afraid of heights her whole life. But she said instead, "Why don't you bring her out here next time you visit your aunt Mary? I'd love to show her the houses from ground level, of course, or maybe she could see the one I'm building behind Clay Henshaw's place for Russ Pierce's Little League baseball team. If you could bring her out this evening, I'm giving a talk and demonstration there. I'd love to help her work her way out of that before it's a full-blown phobia, like I've got,'' she ended, trying to keep her anger at him out of her voice.

''Oh, that won't be necessary.''

''Yes, it is. Don't try to make light of it or cajole her out of it. She needs to face it and deal with it. And anyone who tells her different is dead wrong.''

With that, she slammed the receiver into its cradle so hard the kitchen wall shuddered.

''I know you've been through a lot with Cassandra's coma these past two days, just like Rod and Mace have,'' Clay Henshaw told Jenna the next evening on his woodlot. Clay's wife Sara kept nodding at almost everything he said. ''So we could put this off until another time,'' he added.

Though she didn't want to say so, Jenna had intentionally crammed this day full: May 17th was Mandi's birthday and it would do Jenna no good to have spare time to brood about that. So she'd accepted the Henshaws' invitation to host her and the Little League team for hot dogs and s'mores, cooked over their backyard grill. The boys were going to watch Jenna rope rig the oak she'd selected for their tree house, so she'd had the boys practicing knots before the cookout.

''The kids have been disappointed more than once lately,'' Clay added, as the three adults talked under the oak, ''so I'm sure they'd understand.''

"That's exactly why I don't want them disappointed today," Jenna insisted as she continued to check the climber's knot in her safety line. "I hope to take them through each step of building their tree house, even letting them help when possible." In the distance came the cries and shouts from the kids' impromptu baseball game. "Anyhow, after spending most of today at the hospital with Cassie, it's good for me to be out with my trees."

"Poor Rod MacCaman's too sick to be dealing with Cassie's coma," Sara put in. She was a quiet, slender woman.

"Not to mention," Clay said, shaking his head, "having to face leaving behind the company he saved and loves. And you love what you're doing, Jenna. I can relate to that."

"Clay loves his work," Sara said.

"Then, things are going well for re-quarrying Deep Heart?" Jenna asked as she snapped her tree-climbing saddle to the ropes and tested its grasp.

She was hurrying now, hoping to have the basic rigging in place within an hour so she could catch Frank at Kirkhall after his weekly township trustees meeting. They would not be alone if she timed it just right, and it would be literally on her home turf.

Making her house secure again with re-keyed locks and a security sweep, which had turned up nothing, had gotten her sidetracked earlier today. But she was back on the trail of a person she was certain knew her abductor, or was her abductor. To pursue that, she needed to talk to Frank. As for her and Mace, they kept passing like ships in the night, taking turns sitting with Cassie. Though she missed time with him terribly, she tried to tell herself it was just as well. She feared that the moment she first saw him alone, she would blurt out what she'd learned about their parents—and that didn't really matter now, did it—?

"Yeah, other than Rod being so ill, things are going great at MacCaman Stone." Clay interrupted her thoughts, as Sara proudly linked her arm through his and nodded again.

"I'm glad to hear that," Jenna assured him, but she noted the discrepancy between what Clay said and what Mace had told her.

"Guess I'd better go corral the wild horses," Clay said. "Pete! Pete," he yelled as he loped away, windmilling his arm. "Pick up those bats and balls and get on over here!"

"You really do love trees," Sara observed to Jenna when they were alone. "And there you are with so many of them in your Stone Forest. Just think of all the limestone that's probably under there, too. You could make a fortune selling the area for quarrying to the MacCaman interests someday."

Jenna felt as if she'd been slapped. Selling the forest for the stone under it would mean ripping up all that lay above—not only the wondrous trees, but the fantastical stone carvings and her home. But the MacCamans did own the land surrounding hers, even touching hers. Sara seemed like a dim bulb, but was she actually clever enough to deliberately drop something on Jenna like that? Had she just let something slip or laid some groundwork for Clay or Mace?

"I'd never sell," she told Sara, more stridently than she'd meant to.

"Oh, I know that. I guess everyone does. I was just

what-iffing,'' she said, and the moment passed, buried in the loud, tumbling avalanche of sixteen screeching boys.

''You found exactly what I've been thinking about for years,'' Mace told Gil as they emerged from the narrow opening in the earth.

The blowhole was hidden in the cleft between two tilted rocks, beyond an old slag pile, about a quarter of a mile from Deep Heart. Poison sumac bushes and two silver maples all but obscured it. Mace was so excited he could have danced out of the vertical shaft—or cried his way out. What if, after all these years, he'd found the cave?

''I theorized there would be another way in,'' he told Gil, clapping him on the back as they hauled their ropes up after them, ''but you put legs on the theory.''

''My own legs, you bloke. But when are you going to find enough time to really go down there with me? You want me to get my mangy student pack to scope it out?''

''No!'' he shouted before he got hold of himself. ''I mean, I'd rather you didn't. I can't trust a bunch of newbies. I'll find time for us to check it out together soon, I swear I will. And then, if that works out—''

His voice caught in his throat.

''Then what?'' Gil asked, as they stowed the gear in backpacks to hike back to the truck. ''What, exactly, are we looking for in the cave? I get it that we're looking for a cave that you loved years ago, but what aren't you telling me?''

''I will tell you that I'd like to take Jenna down with me.''

Gil hooted and slapped himself dramatically on the chest, pretending he was trying to catch his breath.

"Dream on, Caveman MacCaman. Are you daft? Jenna Kirk, with her claustrophobia? That will be a cold day in hell!"

"It just may be," Mace muttered.

The sight of Kirkhall, with its downstairs lighted golden in the growing dusk, moved Jenna deeply. She parked down the street and stood beyond the bushes watching and waiting, just as her and Mandi's kidnappers must have on that spring night so long ago, she thought. Years later, could someone aside from Russ have spied on her in the Stone Forest? Could it have been Frank? It had been her own birthday that night, but today was Mandi's. She was more than ready for the day to be over, along with the confrontation she was facing now.

Jenna was waiting for Frank, hoping to see him alone but before everyone else cleared out from the regular Wednesday night trustee meeting. Gingerly, she dipped her hand into her purse and felt the cold metal of her pistol. Beneath that, she snapped open the coin purse on her billfold to be sure the class ring was there. Yes, still reeking of the English Leather cologne it had been steeped in for years.

Moving around to the side of the house, she stood under the old tree house. The meeting was breaking up. People were rising, shifting across the set of tall windows in what used to be the living room. Mary Drout was there, no doubt taking notes on her steno pad. Frank, tall and blond, was easy to spot. He wore his hair long enough that those two blond hairs snagged in the pillow could have been his.

Her stomach knotted in dread at this meeting. Jenna pulled out the class ring so she wouldn't have to fish it out later. She put it on her index finger but even there it was still slightly too large.

A few folks came out to get in their cars in the curved drive and pulled away. Mary emerged chattering. Her shrill voice carried over the others. "Like some Shakespearean tragedy," she was saying.

"Shakespeare?" a man's voice said. "More like a soap opera."

"Since Rod MacCaman's involved, it's more like *The Godfather,* parts V and VI," another woman's voice carried to Jenna. "Did you ever read that quote by the author of *The Godfather,* Mario Puzo, Mary? 'Nothing is interesting but trouble,' he said. If that's the case, the MacCamans are the most interesting family I've ever seen, at least not counting the Kirks...."

Blessedly, their voices faded. Though such gossip still hurt her, Jenna was not going to be deterred.

She moved quickly when another group came out. If she didn't find Frank now, he'd be the only one left in the house, and she didn't want to face him alone. Could he have gone out another way?

She went in the front door and saw him instantly, down the long hall, through the entire length of the house. He was staring out the kitchen door, the same one she'd let Mandi out that last night before impulsively following her. Hearing voices in the meeting room to her left, she felt braver. She walked toward Frank.

The ceiling light was on in the kitchen, and Jenna could see without going in that a coffee urn and picked-over plate of cookies were on the table, so surely someone was coming to clean up.

"Frank," she said, "I'd like to talk to you."

He jolted and spun to face her. "Don't sneak up on me like that."

''Sorry. I guess your thoughts were far away.''

''But I'm glad to see you, Jenna. How's Cassie?''

''The same, unfortunately. But she just needs time.''

''And are you the same and need time? When we talked after Russ's funeral, you were pretty upset, but at least you didn't go off alone with Mace, either. Cassie rescued you when it should have been me. If you want to talk, let's go out in the backyard or take a walk around the old neighborhood.''

It had never been Frank's old neighborhood, and she resented his claiming it. ''I'd rather just stay here,'' she told him.

''Fine with me, if you can stand the ghosts.''

Her gaze slammed into his, but he didn't blink or flinch.

''What?'' he said, coming toward her. ''You don't believe in ghosts?''

''I believe in the kind I let haunt me, not the kind that others try to scare me with.'' She watched him closely for some shift of his eyes or telltale tic. Nothing. ''Let's just sit in the den, then,'' she suggested. ''I mean, the other meeting room.''

She thought she could smell faint English Leather cologne on him but she must be mistaken. Surely, it was from the class ring on her own finger. She was starting to perspire, and the scent was suffocating, though he didn't seem to notice.

They went in a room that was now used for various craft clubs. A large quilting loom dominated the area, while stacked bolts of bright cottons lined the walls on Peg-Board shelves. The ceiling light washed the room in wan light; they sat in the front window seat where she and Mandi had spent many a rainy day reading with Pert curled up near Mandi's feet.

"Let's go get some food or a drink somewhere," Frank urged, nervously raking his hand through his hair. When he disturbed the way it was combed, Jenna noted it had a slight curl to it. And, yes, it was approximately the hue of the blond hairs she'd found stuck in the *Absence makes the heart grow fonder* pillow.

"Let's just stay put," she countered. "Frank, I found a Ridgeview High Class of '85 ring in some of Mandi's things recently and wanted to return it to you. It is yours, isn't it?" She tried to keep her voice steady as she thrust her open hand with the ring between them.

"A ring Mandi had? You're talking to the wrong guy, aren't you?"

"She wore Mace's ring the night she was lost. I saw it. I think this one's yours."

He shook his head so hard his hair bounced. "Mine was garnet, not onyx, with my initials on it, though I've lost it since. What's the point? Are you trying to accuse me of something?"

"I just want to know the truth about you and Mandi."

"Then, you should look up all the old police interrogation records, because I'm not rehashing it!" he said, his voice rising. "I never laid a hand on her, and I had an alibi the night she was taken. I was absolutely cleared."

"As Mary Drout says, everyone in town had an alibi. Everyone was cleared."

"You've been digging all this up again?" he demanded, blanching. "If you want to live here, what good is it going to do?" He threw himself back against the edge of the window seat, glaring at her.

Jenna was certain the ring was Frank's and that he had lied to her. But that was hardly enough to make her believe he'd abducted Mandi. Would the fact that he was angry with Mandi for staying with Mace be a motive? Adolescent angst aside, she couldn't accept that.

"I had a feeling you were the third man the police really looked at," she said calmly.

"Then you know I was the third man cleared of any involvement, at least in her abduction—and yours."

"So you were involved with her otherwise. Emotionally? Physically?"

"You sure you want to hear all this? I'm telling you, honey, you'd be better off to let her stay wherever she ended up."

His foot bounced against his crossed leg so hard his voice jerked. He was obviously close to losing control. He never called her "honey," and it sounded like an insult, not an endearment. She noted too that his hands had balled to fists, but she wasn't giving up on this.

"Yes, I want to hear it! Mandi might have always wanted things kept pretty," Jenna said, surprised at her own bitter tone, "but I can't afford that right now. She was seeing you as well as Mace before she died, wasn't she? *Wasn't she?*"

"Yeah, but 'seeing me' is sure a euphemism for the way she operated. You want to hear this? Okay. Every time she went all the way with me she told me she was leaving Mace—but she was probably telling him the same thing. I was so damn mad at that gorgeous girl being so ugly inside—"

"Frank! Ugly? Not Mand—"

"Shut up! You wanted to hear this, so you're gonna hear it. She led me on, though I'm sure I was a willing mark—" His voice cracked as if he were a teenager again. "Mace and I actually fought over her, but she liked having both of us with our tongues hanging out, not to mention that poor, damn sap Russ Pierce. Give me that ring back, then, if you're so sure it's mine,'' he said, grabbing her wrist and trying to pry her fingers open.

''Let me go!'' she cried, yanking free. ''I knew it was yours—and now I know you lied about it. What else have you lied about? Here, take it, then.'' She took it off and slapped it in his open palm, scratching him when she pulled away.

''Oh, I'll take it all right and maybe much more. I'll be seeing you, honey.''

His handsome face contorted in a mask of rage before he quickly covered it with a mere frown. Lifting her arms defensively, she braced herself, certain he would lunge at her.

She was grateful when he stormed out, instead. He slammed the front door so hard that Kirkhall seemed to shake to its stone foundations. Though she was still trembling, Jenna produced a flashlight from her purse and searched where he'd been sitting until she found a single blond hair. She carefully tucked it in a handkerchief right beside her gun.

16

With her home and tree houses more secure and professionally inspected for electronic bugs, Jenna felt safer and calmer. Still, after she returned home one evening from having dinner with her mother and seeing Cassie, she checked all her doors and windows, and made certain the cellar door was bolted. She even planned to buy new opaque draperies tomorrow and perhaps have Mace help her move her bed downstairs for a while. She'd hear noises better that way, and didn't want to feel trapped upstairs. Pretty Girl had turned out to be as good as a guard dog, running to any door or window if she heard an unusual sound. And she evidently heard one right now.

Jenna had been concentrating on reading through Cassie's notes at the dining room table; she heard nothing unusual. But from a dead sleep on the chair next to her, Pretty Girl stirred, then leaped to her feet. Like an Irish setter on point, the cat froze with ears perked, one paw in midstep. Then Jenna heard it, too: a pickup truck engine and tires crunching the limestone driveway.

"It's okay, Girl. Maybe it's Mace."

Jenna glanced at the clock: nine-thirty. Her heart beat faster as she turned off the living room lights and peered out through the front window. The porch light shone on a white truck as it pulled up in front. She saw Mac-

Caman Stone emblazoned in red on its front door. That wasn't his usual truck, but it could still be Mace.

She opened both dead-bolt locks and fumbled with her new key for the re-keyed lock. She and Mace had both spent time with Cassie today, but she'd missed him—missed him in more ways than one.

Two men were in the truck. Had Mace come over with Gil? But that meant Gil was driving, because Mace was getting out on the passenger side.

Looking again, she gasped. No, it wasn't Mace. It was Rod MacCaman. When he stepped down so tentatively, she could tell it was an older man, a weak man. Yet for one moment she had thought she recognized the broad set of shoulders and assured tilt of the head as Mace's.

When she saw it was indeed Rod, her insides cartwheeled. Rod MacCaman never came calling. Something dreadful had happened with Cassie, and he'd come to break the news to her. Or could something have befallen Mace?

She banged open the door and rushed out. Clay Henshaw was the driver, but she ignored him.

"Is Cassie all right?" she cried, stopping at the edge of the porch and grabbing the railing.

"Cassie?" Rod MacCaman had always whispered in a raspy deep voice, but now she could barely hear him. She stared at him to read his lips.

"Nothing new," he said. "I just wanted to thank you for hanging in with her—with all of us. Clay, you won't mind waiting a few minutes for me, will you?"

"No problem, sir."

"Clay's welcome to come in," Jenna said, before she sensed that, for some reason, Rod didn't want him to.

"Tell you what," Clay said. "I'll just run home and

tuck the boys in with Sara and be right back—fifteen minutes or so?''

It was a question for his boss. Jenna might as well not have been there, making any suggestions or extending invitations.

''Good thought,'' Rod said, dismissing Clay with a jerky wave of his hand. Rod came slowly up her steps, as Clay got back in the truck and backed out.

Jenna held the door for Rod. ''You didn't have to come here to thank me for anything,'' she assured him. He was dressed casually in navy slacks and a pale blue shirt, with a large chunk of turquoise holding a string tie, something Jenna supposed Cassie had brought him from out west. Jenna's eyes filled with tears as she tried to explain. ''Cassie's as dear to me as—''

''As your sister,'' he interrupted, his voice husky with emotion, too. ''Maybe she's been your sister these past years, even when you've been apart.''

She almost quoted, ''Absence makes the heart grow fonder,'' but couldn't bear to say it.

Rod MacCaman didn't sit in the comfortable, deeply upholstered chair she indicated but on a straight-backed one. ''Easier to get in and out of if your carcass is going to hell,'' he muttered. ''Sit down and quit fussing about me, and don't bother offering me something to drink. I'm just into pills and meds lately. Jenna, I didn't really come here to thank you for helping with Cassie but for being grown-up about your mother and my—hell, our long-term relationship.''

Jenna sat across from him, leaning forward, her hands clasped on her knees. Pretty Girl watched them from her perch among the fake cats of Mandi's old collection.

''So she told you I knew,'' Jenna said. ''Then she

must have told you how I found out—that Cassie learned it first."

"I'll explain things to Cassie when she…when she's better. And I'm going to tell Mace as soon as I can, so I'd rather you don't lay it on him."

"I wasn't going to. I suppose he will be upset if he finds out I've been keeping it from him, but I only needed to clarify something with my mother."

"Jenna, I swear to God, neither your mother nor I had one damn thing to do with that rock slide. There's no way I could have staged that, rigged that—not without the experts who investigated knowing. I just want to level with you, girl, about that. Sure, the government blasters came around later to close off some old caves, but I never did anything like that."

"I believe you, Mr. MacCaman. I just wanted her to tell me," Jenna tried to explain, "that your feelings for each other came after she was widowed."

"Hers did and mine, too. Hell, I wasn't capable of even loving my wife then and certainly not someone else. I've got to admit I was only passionate then about saving my family business from going the way of so many stone companies in the new age of steel and glass. I wish I'd paid more attention to Cassie and Mace's mother, done some of the things she wanted—travel, pay attention to her flower gardens…"

His voice and gaze drifted off, but he sat up straighter and lifted his chin. The cutthroat businessman people called the Godfather still emanated strength. Though his children and Jenna had seen him as hot-tempered and brusque, her mother had loved him for years, and he had sired Mace and Cassie.

"Got to get going," he said, breaking the spell. "I talked to Mace on my cell phone coupla minutes ago, by the way, and he said he was coming here to see you tonight. He went caving with that Brit buddy of his in the middle of all this mess. Said it relaxed him.'' Rod snorted and shook his head. ''Wish all these years he'd been as gung-ho for the quarry caves aboveground as the ones under it.''

He started for the door and Jenna hurried to open it for him, though Clay had not driven back yet. ''My mother says you are still her touchstone and supporter,'' she said, wanting to offer him something in parting.

''Touchstone, that's a good one,'' he said. He turned back to her on the porch, rotating his whole body and not just his head. His smile was more of a grimace, perhaps because some pain racked him. ''Jenna, your mother's one of the two greatest, strongest women I've ever known. She's made mistakes, sure, but she's made up for them. And, if you're wondering, yeah, I know what ladder she's intent on climbing next. I don't want her hurt ever again, but she's stubborn about it. She wants to be the first female VP, and you know what the next stepping-stone is beyond that.''

Jenna nodded numbly. She knew, but she hadn't let herself think that far ahead. Gazing into the distance, she saw headlights turn off Cutter's Camp and head back along the road, a beacon lighting the crushed limestone under the black trees.

Clay returning, or Mace here already? It was Clay in the truck.

Just when she thought Rod would go down the steps, he turned back yet again. ''You're much more like her than you know,'' he whispered gruffly, with a frown that crunched his brow to obscure his eyes. For one moment she thought he was going to kiss her goodbye. Instead, he weakly lifted his fist to her jaw and gave her a little tap with his knuckles. ''Maybe you and Mace can build a tree house together someday,'' he said softly as he turned away.

Cassie tried to swim upward toward the surface, but she kept sinking back into the thick water of Green Eye. The other kids splashed overhead but their shouts were muted.

''I think we'll be able to wean her off that ventilator soon,'' a woman said. It must have been Jenna or Mandi, but at least now she knew that she had a scuba tank on. That must be what was helping her to breath in this heavy water.

But was Mandi still alive? She remembered that last night she'd seen her, at Jenna's sweet sixteen birthday party at Kirkhall. No matter how much Mandi pretended not to care, it had ticked her off to see Mace kiss Jenna on the lips. Even though Cassie had seen Mandi go after other guys—even telling Mace when she did—Mandi was like a fisherman. She didn't want to let anyone on her hook get away.

That was really funny, Cassie thought. She would have laughed if she weren't underwater. No way she wanted to drown. But it wasn't funny when she thought of that last night she saw Mandi. After the party, she heard Dad and Mace arguing, though at first she could only hear what Mace was shouting, not what Dad was whispering. She shouldn't have done it, but she went down the hall and listened outside Mace's bedroom door so she could hear her father, too.

''I don't want you sneaking out at night. You think I don't know what you're doing?'' Her father's raspy voice floated to her.

''Like father, like son?'' Mace challenged. ''You

think I don't know you've got some whore somewhere you sneak out to see and—''

Cassie jumped at the sound of a smack and a grunt. Since Mace had a hair-trigger temper, she feared he'd actually hit Dad, but she knew better. As usual, it was the other way around. ''Don't you ever talk to your father that way again!''

''It's fine with me if we don't talk at all.'' Mace went back to shouting. ''You can punch me all you want, I guess, but I won't punch some curfew time card around here.''

''It's Mandi Kirk, isn't it,'' Dad demanded. ''You get her pregnant and I'll kill you. Cynthia Kirk doesn't need that kind of setback when—''

''Oh, great. Glad you're only thinking about sweet, innocent little Mandi and her knockout babe of a mother, not your own son.''

''I am worrying about my own son!'' their dad had roared. Cassie was shocked he'd raised his voice and that the sound carried underwater so well. She wanted to stop the movie scenes, rolling on like breakers, but they kept going.

''You stay in this room tonight, or I'm done with you for good, you hear me, Mace?''

''It would be good for you to get rid of me, wouldn't it?''

''No, it would be good for me if you'd act like saving MacCaman Stone meant something to you. I'm locking this door, and I'm going to go call Mrs. Kirk and suggest to her that you two really don't need to be going steady or even see each other anymore.''

''For once, we agree. But I don't need my daddy taking care of it,'' Mace mocked. ''Everyone's so willing to worship at the altar of Saint Mandi. And, by the way, if she does get pregnant, you're going to have to question Frank Connors, too, and maybe Russ Pierce, and who knows who else in town."

"Then, that's another reason to stay clear of her. I'll see you in the morning. By then, Mandi's mother and I are going to make sure you two are history."

Cassie swam away from Mace's door as fast as she could, when her father stalked out and locked him in. But when he went into his own room and closed the door, she came out into the hall again and strained to listen. His voice was so muted behind his door that she couldn't hear his words now, but she guessed he was on the phone already. Poor Mace and Mandi. This was starting to remind her of *Romeo and Juliet,* which she'd picked to write about for her English paper. But Cassie believed in love, especially forbidden love, which she was going to write about herself someday. Maybe she'd let Mace out. She knew he'd sneaked out other times to meet with Mandi.

"Mace," she whispered at the keyhole. The hissing sound that helped her breathe underwater sighed in her ears.

"You see?" a man said. "We can't get her off the ventilator yet. Leave her door open, and I'll check back in a few minutes. But note it on her records that she's very agitated, possibly moving from coma level I to II. I think I'll test her responses again."

"Mace!" she whispered at his door, but got no response. She knocked quietly.

She unlocked the door with the key Dad had left in it. Mace always slept like he was in a coma, but he could not have fallen asleep already. She swung the door open, not certain what she'd see. Yes, Mace was already asleep on his bed, under the covers. Strange, because usually after a fight with their father, he'd stalk around and rage for hours.

"Mace?"

She tiptoed in and closed the door. At least she'd assure him she was on his side. She couldn't wait to get away from their dad and out of this stupid town when she graduated, just like Mace was going to do.

Cassie reached out to touch her brother's shoulder, then gasped. It was only pillows molded to look like his body. Pillows and some wadded-up clothes. Then she saw his window was open.

Amazed and perversely pleased at his escape, she went over to the window and leaned out into the warm, sweet night. He'd removed the screen; if it were light outside, she would be able to look way down the stone ridges to the deep ravine that ran behind the back of their house. But night sat in the rocks below, as black as pitch.

But there, below her, she could barely see something moving. Yes! Picking his way brazenly along a narrow ledge not far beneath her, forty feet above the rock-strewn stream, was Mace, making his great escape for the night.

She started to laugh, then got angry that someone—it must be her father—kept tapping on her knee to make her leg move, then lifted her arms. Someone touched her eyelids to open them and stare into her soul with a light.

It must be the police questioning her again. They were questioning everyone, but kept focusing on Mace.

"Mace was in his room all night," she told them to keep her brother safe. Besides, he would never have hurt Mandi, or Jenna, either. Dad told them the same and so did Mace.

"Did she speak?" a woman's voice asked.

"I think she may have asked for her brother. His name is Mace, isn't it?"

Cassie tried to tell them again that Mace could not possibly have kidnapped or killed Mandi. She wanted them to know she'd spend the rest of her life trying to prove that, but she was so tired of swimming, and the deep waters of Green Eye swallowed her again.

It was after ten that night when Jenna heard another truck, and this time it was Mace. She went out to meet him on the porch, then hurried down the steps and hugged him.

His kiss convinced her that he had missed her, too. They didn't even go inside, but stood, partly propped against the porch railing, holding each other in a long kiss that began breathy and turned breathless.

"Come in," she told him, and they moved inside without breaking the embrace. He closed the door but pressed her to it, his hands hard on her back and waist, as he took her mouth again.

"You make me lose my head," he finally murmured against her ear. "I didn't mean to make an entry quite like this."

"It's a great way to start."

"Yeah, but where do we go from here?"

She almost laughed when she recalled she'd been planning to ask him to help move her bed downstairs. If she said that now, she'd have no willpower at all.

His lips caressed her temple, then trailed wet kisses down the slant of her cheekbone and her arched throat to the hollow where her pulse beat so hard. He took a deep breath. They leaned together, thighs, hips. She felt his need for her. Her breasts pressed to his chest; her head fit perfectly under his chin as she heard and felt his heart beat, too.

"Jenna, Jenna, what would I do without you?" he whispered in a voice so husky it could have been his father's.

"You don't have to do without me. But how's Cassie?"

"The same when I left. Dad saw her last."

"Have you seen him? This evening, I mean?"

He looked down at her and gave her a bit of space. "No. Gil and I have been looking for the entrance to a particular cave and think we may have found it."

"A particular cave? At this time of night?" she asked warily, stepping back from his hands at last. At the mention of caves, her heart kicked back into the frenzied rhythm his mere presence had incited.

"First of all, there's no day and night in a cave, so it doesn't really matter when you go down. It's another world down there..." His voice trailed off and his expression turned sweetly wistful, even on that rugged face. "Let's sit down a second so I can explain," he said as he pulled her onto the couch beside him.

But at that moment, Pretty Girl jumped up on the arm of the couch. Mace jolted back to his feet. "What in hell—?"

"It's a stray cat someone dropped off here. With things so crazy with what happened to me and Cassie, I forgot to tell you."

"It's a dead ringer for Mandi's Pert!"

"You think I don't know that? But no one's claimed her yet, and I can't just toss her out in the forest with one or more wolves loose. I'm advertising in the *Record* to see who it belongs to. Since the paper came out today, I've been hoping the owner might call."

She explained to him that she'd had all her locks re-keyed and the place debugged, along with both tree houses. But she didn't explain about the gun in her purse on the dining room table, or that she was going to take shooting lessons as soon as she could. "I hope you won't mind the cat being around," she concluded, petting her, as Mace finally sat down again. "She'll just paw at the door and yowl if I lock her in somewhere."

"The cat's the least reminder, compared to all of these artifacts," he said, his voice hard, as he indicated the china and glass cat and pillow collections. "But listen to me, Jenna," he said, pulling her hand free from stroking the cat, "because I've got a way to get beyond all this, hopefully to lay Mandi to rest, once and for all. For years I've had a theory about where you two were kept when you were taken, a theory distilled from caving."

"Go ahead," she ventured, but she felt they'd started down some slippery slope together.

"Ever since the rock slide, you know certain caves have been intentionally dynamited closed around here."

"So?" she challenged, her mind skipping ahead to where he might be going with this. Perhaps the cave where she and Mandi were taken had been inadvertently closed off. If they found it, could there still be evidence in it? Clues that would point to the criminals or to Mandi's fate?

"Mace, the rock slide was seven years before our abduction," she protested gently.

"But, like I said, they closed cave mouths that could have rock slides from above or within. And they continued that practice on and off for years, even after you were taken. I've checked both county and state records on the Net and made some phone calls from work. The cave where you two were kept had to be somewhere in the area—''

''As you well know, there are hundreds of caves around here!''

''Just listen. Hear me out,'' he pleaded, his expression both eager and wary. ''The fact that so many caves were searched—at least at the openings and their peripheries—but nothing was found must mean it was a cave that was either officially or unofficially dynamited closed after you were held there. Maybe shortly after. It narrows the search.''

''Or whoever was originally searching the caves didn't go deep enough in, or turned down the wrong passage or something. There are holes in your theory.''

''You're fighting me on this already, when you haven't even heard me out.''

''All right. But you mean whoever sealed that particular cave could either have been working under orders, or they did it on their own and hoped it just looked like another in a long line of closings.''

''It's possible. But remember the fact that caves honeycomb this immediate area. Though one entrance might be closed under tons of rubble, the cave where you were held could still be accessed through another entrance if it's part of the web of caverns.''

''Web is right. More like a maze,'' she said, putting her face in her hands, then raking her hair back. ''I really don't need all this today. You know it's her birthday.''

''I know, but we've got to face this.'' He leaned closer to her again, one arm around her waist. ''For someone who knows how limestone caves form, for someone who's explored and mapped them all over the world, it's not impossible to find that lost cave even now. I came back intending to try, but with Cassie, and Dad, and the business, it hasn't worked out yet. Now, with Gil's help, I've got a lead, one I'm going to check out soon."

She squared her shoulders and turned to face him. "You actually believe you could find where we were held? And that if the cave were found, you could find evidence—remnants—of her, if she died there?"

Jenna jumped up and walked away. She fought hard to keep that cave nightmare from crushing her. Mandi's scream echoed again in the depths of her being.

"You really believe you could find that cave?" Jenna repeated, turning back to face him. He'd come after her; he was close again, his hands on her shoulders. She wanted to throw herself into his arms for strength and courage, but she held back.

"Yes. And if I find it, I'd need you to go there with me."

"Never! Impossible. What if there's another rock slide?"

"I won't lie to you. It's extremely rare, but rock slides can occur within caves. That aspect of it scares me, too."

"You see? You admit it's crazy."

"I admit you're going to make yourself crazy, and I am, too, if we don't get answers. Jenna, maybe I could locate some clue to her fate there. But yes, I'd need you there to ID the place, maybe to help find Mandi."

"ID the place? Mace, I was blindfolded."

"Not all the time, were you? Cassie said you recall a lot about the cave and glimpsed it briefly when the kidnappers returned."

She pushed past him, almost stepping on the cat. Pretty Girl darted back to her favorite perch among the lifeless cats on the ledge, threading her way delicately among them. Her eyes were huge, mesmerizing, as she turned to stare at them. Jenna tore her gaze away and back to Mace.

"This is just another attempt you're making to convince me to conquer my claustrophobia," she accused, folding her arms. "Nice try, but there is just no way I could ever go into a cave—and especially not that cave."

"With me at your side? Gil would go, too."

"You two cooked this up together!" she accused, hands on her hips. Panic pounded through her as he rose to get right in her face. "First of all, your proposal is outrageous," she insisted. "Even if Mandi were still—still there, it's obscene to think of searching for her after all this time."

"I thought you wanted this settled. Closure, as the pop culture shrinks would say. You said you wanted to face things, to look back in order to free yourself to be able to look ahead. I need to know some things so we can go on, you and me, whether separate or together. And I need to have my name cleared around this damn town, once and for all!"

"Then, you and Gil go right ahead when you're not trying to help your dad or Cassie or MacCaman Stone! I've got my own business to build, and I've promised to help my mother when she—when she runs for whatever office again."

She knew she was going on the attack when she should be grateful. But the mere thought of what he proposed was suffocating her.

"Jenna, you've got to learn to trust me. Gil and I are good, and we'd take care of you." From his pants pocket, he produced a paper and unfolded it. On it, he or Gil had sketched a crude map.

When the phone rang, she silently blessed the interruption. Her gaze snagged Mace's as his eyebrows lifted. Surely it was nothing bad about Cassie, but the call *could* come here, since Mace's dad knew he was stopping by.

"Maybe it's just a phone order for a tree house, or someone claiming the cat," she said. But as she hurried to the kitchen, he stayed close behind her. She grabbed the receiver.

"Jenna here."

"Happy birthday to you," a woman's voice sang. *"Happy birthday to you."*

"Who is this?" Jenna cried, holding the phone slightly away from her mouth and ear. "If you're selling someth—"

But her own voice trailed off as she listened, her eyes wide.

"What is it?" Mace mouthed to her, coming closer. She barely saw him, hardly heard him. It was...dear God, it was Mandi's voice—and on her birthday.

"Happy birthday, dear Mandi..."

Jenna realized she must have looked stricken, because Mace grabbed the phone.

"Happy birthday to you."

"Who is this?" Mace demanded, but he, too, blanched. He dropped the map and grabbed Jenna's wrist in a hard hold.

She could hear the words, the melody over the phone he held, more muted now but so very clear. The other things she'd been sent or that had happened, even that other phone call—anyone could have done that. But she'd swear that this was Mandi. She'd know that voice, talking or singing or shouting—or screaming—until the day she died.

And she could tell by the look on Mace's face that he would, too.

17

After the phone call, they sat shaken, holding hands on the couch.

"You need to get caller ID," Mace muttered. His ruddy skin color had paled; his usually assured motions and voice had turned jerky and jumpy.

"I'm tired of someone trying to terrify me—and of buying things to prevent it," she said, tugging her hands free and flopping back with her bent arm lifted over her eyes. "At this rate, I'll go broke before I'm broken."

"At least you can laugh about it."

"Mace," she said, twisting toward him, "I'm ready to do nothing but cry."

"No, you're not," he insisted, caressing her cheek with the back of his fingers. "You're stronger than you think. You know, as real as it—she—sounded, that could have been a recording of Mandi's voice."

"Even so, it *was* her voice."

"I know." He shook his head; his eyes darted past her to scan the room. "I can't believe someone could imitate her that well."

"But did a recording like that ever exist?" Jenna asked, sitting up straight. "One where she sang 'Happy Birthday' to herself?"

"Not that I know of. Ask your mother."

"She doesn't know any of this. I've refused to go running to her, and still do."

"You've kept a lot of it from me."

"I know," she admitted, feeling guilty that she had not yet mentioned their parents' affair. "I thought I could handle it alone at first. Besides, you haven't exactly been aboveboard with me."

"Meaning what?" he demanded, his voice ominous as he turned her to him again. His grip hurt her shoulders.

"Meaning," she countered, pulling back until he freed her, "I've picked up from the Henshaws that MacCaman Stone would like to get its—your—hands on my land."

"I told you that before."

"No, you told me *you'd* love to have it, not that the Stone Forest is being considered a prime site for a new quarry!"

"It isn't! Yes, it would be a great adjunct to our holdings, and yes, Green Eye abuts your land, which, if it's not riddled by caves, probably has a prime limestone bed under it—"

"Which means a fortune, right? Mace, I'm never selling."

"Let's get one thing straight. MacCaman Stone may lust for your land, but I love you."

She could only stare at him, speechless. He'd said "love." Never had she heard that from him. Never had she dared to hope she would.

"Let's not argue," he rushed on, hardly realizing he was ruining the precious moment. "I think you're still floundering for an excuse not to go caving with Gil and me."

"Oh, I'm definitely *not* going caving with Gil and you, or anyone, anytime," she insisted, crossing her arms. "I have enough trouble hanging up my clothes in anything smaller than a walk-in closet."

He turned sideways on the couch, facing her with one arm behind her. "But if you really want to escape the past, confronting and conquering your claustrophobia could jog your memory. If you could recall anything else about your abduction, it might help nail the bastards who hurt you and Mandi. And Gil and I will find a good way into the cave and check things out first."

"If I could conquer a cave and find information about what happened to Mandi, my life would be...very different," she said with a huge sigh.

"Then, think about my offer. I would never let anything bad happen to you. And, Jenna, there's a raw, untamed beauty to be found underground, one that can match your Stone Forest—I swear it."

His eyes burned with a passion she would give anything to share. She had felt like that toward him as long as she'd known him. Mandi used to be in the way. Perhaps, unless Jenna went with him to find what had happened to her, her sister always would be—

"I hate to sound like his nurse," Mace interrupted her agonizing as he rose, "but I've got to be sure Dad took his meds. He hates the whole idea of being sick and weak. Sometimes I wouldn't put it past him to just stop using what's keeping him alive. But I could come back," he added, turning to her. "After that phone call, maybe I should stay the night."

"You need to be with him." But Jenna cringed inwardly at the thought of what his father was planning to confess. Mace had always idealized his mother and, she thought, had been secretly pleased that the father he had battled so long had never fallen for another woman. "I'll be fine,'' she added when he hesitated. ''If I can't sleep, I'll just keep going through Cassie's notes.''

''Cassie's notes?'' His head jerked around. ''Is that what's all over your table? She left them with you?''

She followed him into the dining room. He took one glance and began to gather them.

''Mace, she left them in the tree house,'' she protested, gently taking his arm. ''We were working on things together.''

''But until she regains consciousness, we'd better guard all this. I think she'll share with you and your mother whatever she wanted to at the appropriate time.''

She was surprised and hurt that he swept the entire spread of books, tapes and journals from the table. Cassie was his sister, but she'd said Mace hadn't had time to sit down with her yet for her research.

''I'll lock up this stuff at our house until she's better,'' he promised, as he propped the whole unruly pile under one arm. ''You've got enough to worry about. Why don't you come stay with Dad and me?''

''I am not leaving my home and the cat. And don't you trust me with Cassie's work?''

''Of course I do, but I don't trust whoever's been trying to shake you up. Besides, Cassie did research for me to check into caves being blasted shut, so we've been working together, too.''

''Helping you find the cave? She never told me that.''

''I asked her not to, but maybe she made some notes in here that mention something additional about the dynamiting.''

''What else did you ask her not to tell me? What else aren't *you* telling me? You're asking me to go down in some maze of caves with you to look for my sister's remains, yet you don't trust me to look through your sister's things?"

"It isn't that, sweetheart," he said, and dropped a quick kiss on her lips. "Just trust *me* on this. I'll call you tomorrow, okay?"

It was not okay, but she was exhausted from arguing with him. She held the door open, then locked it firmly behind him.

After taking the phone off the hook, she got her gun from her purse and turned off all the lights but the outside ones. She lay down on the couch fully clothed. With a flashlight in her hand and the cat pressed to her hip, she dozed and jerked awake until a rainy dawn grayed the windows and she finally slept.

The next day Jenna got a late start and felt enervated in whatever she did. She dragged herself to see Cassie, whose slight improvement was the only thing that cheered her. She worked for several hours after a late lunch, sketching diagrams of the Little League team's tree house and returning calls. Though a chilly drizzle still fell, at about four in the afternoon she picked some pansies, locked the house behind her and walked to the cemetery just beyond the edge of her property.

Despite its proximity, she seldom visited the place anymore. When the drizzle subtly shifted to mist, she closed her umbrella and raised her face to the gray heavens. The graveyard haunted her, not for the lurking sadness here, but because this was where she'd been brought for release—without Mandi. It had been the location of her deliverance, but the memorial of her guilt, too.

Her father wasn't really here, anyway—not an entire body—since the rock slide had been so devastating. He had only been identified through dental records—just a few intact teeth—since DNA testing was in its infancy then.

A thought hit her so hard she jerked the umbrella handle. She had two blond hairs that had been caught in the pillow on her bed, as if someone had been sleeping there. And she had the sample of Frank's hair from two days ago. She'd read how long it took to do DNA testing, but maybe she could make Frank believe that her mother could speed up the identification of the blond intruder through matched hairs.

If she could bluff Frank, he might either give himself away or say something to clear himself. It was a much better plan than telling Mace she suspected Frank, because they'd probably have a worse scrap than they did after Russ's funeral. She hated herself for thinking of lying to Frank. She was starting to stoop as low as whoever was taunting her, but she was getting desperate. Yet she didn't plan for one minute to actually have her mother get the DNA testing done for her. Things had been going well between them lately; she had no intention of hurting or upsetting her.

Despite the damp grass, she knelt at her dad's grave and arranged the pansies on the flat tombstone around the incised letters of his name and dates. She prayed, trying to remember happy times, but her heart was heavy. Rising, she took three blue pansies with her and walked toward Mace's mother's grave.

But she is in her grave and, oh, the difference to me, the Wordsworth quote on Susan MacCaman's tombstone read.

The tears Jenna held back burned her eyes. She had been so certain Mandi, too, was in her grave somewhere, and it had made all the difference in Jenna's life. But someone wanted her to believe Mandi was still alive. To scare Jenna away from her land? To make her—and Cassie—back off from their investigation? To drive her crazy? If only Mandi could be in a real grave, a hallowed grave in this cemetery. Mace's outrageous idea of searching for clues and a corpse in a cave was starting to make sense. Gil and Mace had caved safely all over the world, so surely they'd take good care of her if she went with them.

"No," she told herself as the rain pattered harder and she opened her umbrella again, "I am not going caving. Could not go caving, not even with the Lord Himself."

Jenna walked quickly toward the Stone Forest, cutting crosswise through the neat rows of tombstones. As the rain pelted harder and she huddled under her little umbrella, a memory flashed through her brain so strong it made her stop.

She knew that as she slowly emerged from her drugged state she had been driven in the back of a truck into this cemetery the night she was released. But now she was certain she'd been covered with a heavy plastic tarp—something she had never recalled before, never told the police or anyone. Years ago, Dr. Brennan had suggested he try to hypnotize her to see what she remembered, but it had turned out she was one of the rare persons not susceptible to a hypnotic trance. Yet suddenly, Jenna was sure a brief rainstorm must have passed that night, because she recalled the pelting sound of the drops on the tarp, just as on this umbrella.

For once, she concentrated on the memory instead of trying to stop it. The tarp had been ripped away, and she'd been helped down from the truckbed. She could not stand, so they—two men with ski-mask hoods—held her up and pulled off her wide tape gag and blindfold.

Over there—right over there on that crushed limestone road that cut across the cemetery.

They'd half laid her across a tombstone, facedown when they saw she couldn't sit up on her own. Had they whispered something? Had they told her to go home?

Western cowboy boots on one of them—dark, tooled leather. Dazedly, she'd watched them walk away, drive away. She'd stared at their truck, a white truck. No headlights, just red taillights that left her in the dark again.

Was she recalling things clearly now, or were these memories drug-induced hallucinations? Even more frightening, could her kidnappers have returned after fifteen years to use a drug on her and Cassie instead of on her and Mandi?

Hair prickled along the nape of her neck. Her stomach churned. And not just because she recalled being dumped here. She was suddenly certain she was being watched.

She spun around to survey the cemetery and the fringe of forest. No one was visible, but whoever it was could be huddled behind a tombstone or lurking among the trees. Gripping her umbrella handle so tight her fingers went numb, she closed it to use as a weapon before she recalled she had her gun in her jacket pocket. With one hand on it to keep if from bouncing, she jogged into her forest, carefully scanning the path ahead.

The wolf's distant howl brought her up short; she drew her gun. Dropping her umbrella near the grinning gargoyles, she held the cold metal pistol in both hands to steady it. Slowly, she rotated in a complete circle. Her index finger trembled as it caressed the trigger.

She saw nothing, heard nothing but forest sounds and rain dripping off leaves and branches. Her increasing paranoia had to end. Yet she could not bear to go into a cave to face and conquer her worst fears. Gil and Mace would have to go without her and just tell her what they found.

Though it was not dark yet, she sprinted for her house.

Late that night, five stories underground on hands and knees, Mace and Gil navigated a narrowing section of limestone cave they'd just dubbed The Velcro Crawl. Single-file, Mace led this time, with Gil close on his heels. They traveled fairly lightly, since this was to be just an all-night reconnaissance expedition. This passageway, which hopefully linked larger caverns, was a spacious yard high, so at least they didn't need to slither along on their bellies.

Without their knee pads and heavy gloves, as well as their ballistic nylon coveralls, the sharp rock would have shredded their skin. As it was, the rough ceiling scraped and snagged their backpacks, but they didn't want to drag them along on cords that could be cut. The earlier part of the cave had not been like this; they hoped it would end soon.

Entering at dusk, they'd already navigated the three-story vertical shaft drop, then walked a seventy-foot downward slant that housed hundreds of bats just heading out for their night foraging. It was the stream of bats spiraling into the sky that had originally tipped off Gil to the presence of an alternative cavern entrance here.

Mace was praying this would be the eureka cave for him, the one that turned southwest and eventually slanted upward toward the dynamited entrance that could have once provided easy access to the cave where Jenna and Mandi were kept years ago. He'd finally entrusted his theory to Gil, who had agreed it might pan out. But his friend had adamantly argued that Jenna would never be a part of it—unless they could unblock tens of thousands of tons of dynamited rock and march her in through a sunlit, open entrance.

But now, darkness and light meant nothing in the depths of the earth, and Mace was running on pure adrenaline. He had been ever since Cassie and Jenna were drugged; he'd tried to keep an eye on both of them, as well as watching his dad and Clay Henshaw. He hoped like hell that he and Gil could check this virgin passage out by dawn, so he could get to work in the quarry in time to watch Clay with the MacCaman workers.

"Maybe we should have dubbed this The Slicer," Gil said, grunting with exertion. They both were breathing hard, alternating a duck waddle with a baby crawl through here.

"Or The Meat Grinder."

Just before this section, they had roughly mapped a large chamber they'd named The Atrium. Their surface maps had suggested this maze of caves was tied to the cavern system under Deep Heart, and The Atrium was shaped like a chamber of the heart called by that name. There, they'd easily managed to walk and leap across medium-size boulders over an underground river swollen by the light rains on the surface. They'd used climbing ascenders to go up a vertical twenty-foot wall that accessed this knife-surface crawl.

"I still say you're daft if you think Jenna will come down here with us, Caveman," Gil gasped as they finally glimpsed the end of the narrow passage. "Not if you level with her about all this."

"The woman's skilled at climbs and drops," Mace argued. "I've seen her rappel the side of Green Eye just for fun. She's great with ropes, harnesses and ascenders."

"If she's aboveground, under an open sky."

"It all depends on what we find beyond," Mace said, as they belly-slid from the crawl into a large chamber. Because their carbide helmet lights illuminated only a few yards beyond, they retrieved their high-powered flashlights from their packs.

Shoulder to shoulder, as they'd stood so many times in distant, exotic caverns, they stared in awe at this pristine place.

Gil gasped. "You know what this looks like?"

"I know," Mace whispered. "Amazing. She'll come to see this."

"If she believes us."

They gaped at the unique formations in this chamber that had probably never been seen by humans before—although occasional Native American bones or artifacts turned up in Indiana's caves. Here, even before their meager lights bounced off the massive stone pillars and dramatic limestone foliage, experience told them it had to be a large room.

"Fresh moving air from beyond," Gil whispered. "There's a lot more cave over that way. And those ghost voices..."

"Just the echoing murmur of that river we crossed or one beyond," Mace insisted.

"Or those little gremlin hodags waiting for us to take a wrong turn."

"Surely you don't want to turn back," Mace challenged.

"You know I don't. Besides, you're going to need a corroborating witness, as it's sure not going to be Jenna Kirk."

Gil knelt to take his crude map out of his pack and started to sketch what they could see of this chamber. "But you know, bloke, that fresh air current's going to lead us. Bloody hell, it might even take us straightaway toward where the entrance used to be, even if it's been dynamited closed. There's always leaks and gaps when men try to close off in one quick blast what a cave took eons to build."

"I know."

"So there. Buck up. Maybe we'll find something."

"I want to find it and get rid of it once and for all," Mace admitted, surprised at the vehemence in his voice. His words echoed strangely off the creviced walls and shadowed stone structures along the ceiling. "But come hell or high water, I'm bringing Jenna down here to see it first."

As daylight fled that evening, Jenna, with her cell phone and gun in her fanny pack, rechecked all three tree houses and their surrounding limbs and foliage for a possible camera or listening device. She'd not only studied them in the Techno-Spy shop, but carefully observed the security expert when he searched her house.

She began to breathe a bit easier. Surely there was nothing suspicious here, but that didn't mean she was going to let down her guard.

Yet she couldn't keep herself from sitting on the lofty perch of Home Tree Home to watch the colors of sunset stain the sky pink and lavender. It was a stunning, romantic view. She felt disappointed that, other than a quick call at noon to see how she was doing and ask about her visit to see Cassie, Mace hadn't called.

Before she locked the place for the night—she'd installed padlocks on all her tree houses—Jenna went back into its single room. The big bed looked so inviting. It was such a sweet-smelling, gentle evening that, ordinarily, she would have loved to spend the night. She imagined all sorts of aromas on the breeze, of grass, flowers and foliage, of rich garden loam and rustling trees.

Suddenly relaxed and exhausted, she sank on the bed and flopped back, her arms thrown over her head in luxurious abandon. With the tips of her toes, she nudged off her shoes and let them thud to the floor. Wriggling her toes, she rolled over catty-corner on the mattress, thinking of Mace again. Of Mace here, in this intimate, private place with her. Of Mace next to her, rolling toward her, taking her in his arms—

"I told you I'd see you again, honey."

She gasped and jerked upright. *Frank.* Frank, his big blond head bent to get in the door, his outstretched arms blocking escape. She hadn't heard him climb the ladder or walk the deck.

Standing to face him, she silently cursed herself for being in her stocking feet. She'd never run well like this—not that there was anywhere to go, thirty feet above the ground.

"This place is by invitation only, Frank. Let's go down if you want to talk."

He swaggered two steps in and stopped. He could not have been watching her for long, but it was long enough to know when she disappeared inside. Was he the one making the calls, the clever threats?

"I don't want to go down," he said with a tight smile. His words were slightly slurred. "I kind of like it up here."

"Yeah," she said, trying to sound nonchalant and steady, "it's great up here. But I have a feeling you've been drinking and heights can be double dangerous then. Go on back down, and I'll follow."

To her rising dismay, she did smell liquor on him, even at this distance of six feet. He ignored her commands as if she hadn't even spoken. She wanted to go for her phone or gun in the fanny pack she was still wearing, but didn't yet dare to let him know she had either. Suddenly, her plan to rattle him with the suggestion that she was comparing his DNA to that of the hair found in her house—on her bed—seemed completely crazy.

"Nice place. *Really* nice bed," Frank said, spreading his legs and hooking his thumbs in his belt. A dark, deliberate fire burned in his eyes that really scared her. She fought to keep calm.

"I have friends coming, and I need to be at my house to meet them," she said, trying to stare him down. "Otherwise, they'll come out here looking for me."

"Really? Is that why you were going to take a nap here?"

"How long have you been watching me?"

"Long enough to know you're not quite as deceitful as your slut of a sister, but you're working on it—with Mace MacCaman as the common factor."

"I was under the impression *you* wanted to be a common factor with Mandi and me."

He laughed sharply and took two more steps into the small room. If she could just draw him in farther, she might be able to dart around him. Even shoeless, she could make it down the rappeling rope faster than he could handle the ladder.

"I've got news for you, honey," he said, holding out both arms as if to embrace her. Carefully, slowly, she edged around the corner of the bed. Her fanny pack felt heavy with her phone and gun. Could she get to either in time if he tried to grab her?

"What news?" she countered, when he stepped to the window and glanced out and down. She wondered if he believed her lie about people coming. "Something about Mandi, years ago—or lately?" Her pulse was pounding so hard she began to shake. What if Frank and a friend had abducted Mandi and her, or what if he were her present harasser? Or both?

"Naw, I want to talk about you," he said, coming even closer. "You and me, not her, though I thought I'd taken Mandi away from him—"

"You took Mandi?"

"Not the way you think. Got her away from Mace, but she still wanted him. Wanted to use me to make him go to college with her instead of somewhere else. But I hate to break it to you that I didn't really want you, Jenna. Just wanted you to fall for me, to belong to me, in case Mace came back. And now he has. But you're trying to use him against me—turn him against me again, just like Mandi did."

"Frank, I'm not Mace's, and I'm not trying to turn him against you. Now please, just go back down the ladder and let's forget all th—"

"None of us have forgotten her or what happened, have we," he said, smirking. "You know, you Kirk girls owe me a lot, so how about a little repayment for the loan for all these pretty treetop places?" he said, and swung his arms wider as he lurched at her.

Jenna ducked and threw herself across the bed, rolling over it so fast she fell to the floor on her knees. There was no time to get her shoes, not time for anything but running.

She scrambled for the door while he cursed her. With

his size and the booze in him, she was quicker, darting outside, going for the climbing rope she kept tied to the west side of the porch.

It was gone. He must have pulled it up or cut it off.

Jenna lunged for the ladder as he came out the door after her. He grabbed her in a backward bear hug, but she bit his arm. He yelped and fastened his fingers in her hair to yank her head back. Pain seared her scalp. Afraid he might try to throw her over the railing, she braced her feet and grabbed him.

When he turned her to him and bent her back in his arms, she kneed him as hard as she could. He doubled over long enough to free her. Jenna scrambled for the ladder, trying to hold to it and descend quickly. Partway down, she let go and dropped to the ground. She was grateful he wasn't on the ladder behind her. But he threw her rappel rope over the railing on the other side of the tree and came down it, arm over arm.

Doubting her chances to escape in her stocking feet against someone so in shape, Jenna made a split-second decision to go for the gun and phone before she tried to run. She fumbled to turn her fanny pack around. Before she could get it out, he shifted his position to block her access to the house.

"Come on," he said, his face contorted in a sneer, his voice dark and menacing. "Let's go on back up and play house—tree house. You owe me for both of you clever little girls screwing up my life. You know, all women are users—and now it's my turn."

Giving herself time to draw the gun, she backed away, unfortunately not toward the house but toward Green Eye. When he rushed her, she darted away. Surely she could outrun a drunk man, circle around to the house or even the street. Maybe she could get to the Henshaws' place across the road.

If not, she might have to shoot him.

She managed to dig out her phone first because it was on top, but she couldn't punch in numbers as she ran. He was staying close, so close.

She scrabbled to get the gun in her hand, but her panicked glance back revealed he'd closed her lead. The mammoth blocks of Green Eye loomed ahead in the growing dusk. She knew this place so well, but so did Frank and he was keeping up, gaining on her.

She considered darting around the corner of the quarry to lose herself in the woods on the other side, but she preferred to make a stand in the open. Racing up a slant of stone to try to gain an advantage, she pulled the gun and pointed it at him. He skidded to a halt ten feet below her.

"Stop it, Frank, or I'll shoot you."

"Just calm down, would you? Hey, let's go skinny-dipping here, just like the good old days."

"I'm coming down off this block, and you're going to back off while I make a phone call."

He snorted a laugh. "Can't you just see the headlines?" he said, his voice mocking. "'Daughter of the Illustrious Cynthia Kirk, Rising Star in the Political Constellations, Shoots and Kills Hometown Tanker, Township Trustee, Father of Two.' Then in small print," he went on as he framed an invisible newspaper with his spread hands, "'Years ago, same daughter was kidnapped, then returned alone while—'"

"I mean it, Frank," she cried, but he'd cut to the core of her fears. "Just stay off my land and leave me alone! You've been bothering me for weeks, and I won't have any more of it!"

"Doing *what* for weeks?" he demanded, looking truly puzzled. "Bothering you? Hell, you won't even go out with me, unless you call that poor SOB Russ Pierce's funeral a date. You know, Jenna, it was right here that I once dangled him over the edge and told him if he didn't leave Mandi alone, I'd drown him."

"And you've tried to use scare tactics with me!" she accused. "Little gifts, phone calls, the e-mail, and then breaking and entering!"

"What in the hell are you babbling about? All I'd like to do is beat out your lover Mace for once to—"

"He's not my lover. Now back up, because I'm coming off this block with this gun cocked and trained on you."

Grinning, he thrust both hands high into the air as if he were under arrest. "Better keep that gun real close, then," he taunted, as he finally took a few steps back. "Sleep with it under your pillow. Take it with you into the shower, because you—and your slut of a sister—both have outstanding debts with me, and I plan to collect. If you tell the authorities anything about this, I'll deny it. Or maybe I'll give the press and good old Mary Drout my side of the story, no matter how much it hurts your mommy in her bid for the heights of the political heavens. Tell Mace if you want to, because I'd like to take him on again. Now just put the gun away, because I'm leaving—not even going back on your land, see?"

He jumped down from the rock and started away. She kept the pistol trained on him. It was a good thing, because he stopped and turned back.

"Jenna," he said, suddenly sounding dead sober, "if you're still looking for candidates for the guys who took your sister and you, just ask Mace. He was out that night. I saw him. If I had admitted that in my deposition, I'd have given away that I was going to meet her and that I had been for a couple of weeks. Mace was mad enough at her for cheating on him with me to kill her. The guy has a short fuse when crossed, or haven't you seen that up close and personal yet? I repeat, see you again, honey,'' he threw over his shoulder as he walked away. She watched until the MacCaman forest beyond Green Eye swallowed him.

She stood, stunned. She realized suddenly where he must have parked. He was heading directly toward the hidden spot across from the Henshaws' place where she'd seen tire tracks and the brake fluid spill that might have caused Russ's death.

Keeping her gun in her trembling hand, Jenna hurried back into her side of the forest, but Frank's sudden, sober accusation of Mace kept sounding in her ears.

18

"Mace isn't here, Jenna," Rod MacCaman whispered over the phone when she called his house that night. "Him and that hippie Brit friend of his went caving."

"Caving? Tonight?"

"'It's always just as dark down there,' he said. I told him about my relationship with your mother. I thought he took it pretty well, but I couldn't stop him from this harebrained idea of going caving. You know anything about that?"

"Only that he has a theory he can find the cave where Mandi and I were kept prisoner."

A long pause followed.

"Mr. MacCaman, are you there?"

"I wish to hell he—all of you—could let her rest in peace, like your mother's done. Nothing good comes from rehashing everything. But I'm glad you called," he said, "'cause Cassie's doctor phoned to say she's stirring and seems to be trying to talk. I was just going to call Clay Henshaw to drive me in, so—"

"Don't call Clay. I'd be glad to take you. Thank God, she's better!"

"Remains to be seen, they warned. But I can't bother you this late at night."

"Please. I'd just go in on my own."

"All right, then. If you don't mind playing escort and chauffeur to a weak, dying man..."

We're all dying, Jenna thought, and she shuddered with the chills which had racked her since Frank had accused Mace tonight.

"I'll be right there," she told him.

When she got the microphone out of her throat, she felt better. People kept talking about prepping her. Lights blazed in her eyes. She was going to be on television, giving an interview about her book, about the stone woman in her book.

"Look," a woman's voice said. "The second we got the trach tube out, she started moving her lips. Her hands, too."

"She's been comatose for four days, but we're finally seeing some improvement," a man's voice said. "I've called her father and he's coming in."

Her father must be in the audience. Cassie hoped, for once, he'd be proud of her. But she was worried she wasn't dressed well enough, in a solid-colored suit, of course, because stripes or patterns were bad on TV. She should have prepped harder for this interview. She had more work to do on it and on the patterns in her life.

"Her stats are improving. She's up the scale to moderate."

She tried to tell the TV host about her book, but her mouth was not working with her brain. It must have been shock from the rock slide or from losing Mandi that had done this to her.

"I'm going to check her eye reflexes again."

The lights in the studio were so bright in her eyes. The cameraman came too close. Someone was asking all sorts of questions, talking, talking. She had to talk, too, because she wanted everyone to read the truth about the powerful woman who had climbed out of the rock pile that was Ridgeview.

"Cassie, it's me, Jenna. I'm here with your dad, and we're grateful you're starting to wake up."

Rod, tired at the effort he'd made to come here, was sitting in the chair by the bed already, while Jenna leaned over Cassie and took her hand. Cassie's doctor, stethoscope draped around his neck, stood at the foot of the bed. Though Jenna gestured for Rod to step closer to the bed, he hung back a bit.

"I know you," Cassie whispered, looking at Jenna, her voice almost as raspy as her father's. Her eyelids flickered but did not remain open. She looked so small and frail.

"Yes, it's Jenna!" she told her, pressing Cassie's hand. When she winced, Jenna let go. At least her friend was feeling things now. Tears in her eyes, Jenna smiled at Rod and the doctor, who nodded for her to go on.

"Jen-na...was Mandi swimming with us?" Cassie whispered.

Jenna gasped. Her shocked gaze collided with Rod's. He shook his head and looked away as tears sprang to his eyes and disappointment crushed his features.

Jenna had planned to ease his heart by letting him see Cassie's progress, then drive him back, see that he took his meds and went to bed. Then she'd sit up at the MacCamans', waiting for Mace to return from his crazy caving expedition. She needed to confront him about what Frank had said and tell him once and for all that she wasn't going caving. But Cassie's confusion rattled them both. What if that date rape drug had damaged her brain? Perhaps that fear was too much for Rod, for he shuffled toward the door.

"Cassie, we don't want to tire you. You just take it easy and get better," Jenna said, though her throat constricted as if she was about to sob. "Your father's here. We both want you to get better."

As she bent close to kiss Cassie's cheek, her friend's eyes flew open. "My father," she whispered so softly that Jenna was sure no one else could hear. "There's something—about my father and your mother." Her eyes widened and focused. Jenna hoped everything would not come back to her right away, for she didn't want her friend upset over what she must have learned about their parents as she was being drugged.

"Doctor?" Jenna said and turned to gesture him closer. "Her eyes look clearer. She's really starting to recall things." Out of the corner of her eye, Jenna noted Rod stepped to the foot of the bed.

The doctor put his hand on Cassie's wrist as if to take her pulse, but he kept glancing between his patient and the readouts on the monitors.

"I'm Dr. Glasson, Cassie. I know you're very weak, but can you tell me what year it is?"

"I—I'm not sure."

"What year you were born, Cassie?"

"I thought I was back in high school, but I think I'm about thirty."

"Can you tell me who is president of the country?"

"I think I know if I can just remember."

Jenna's heart fell but Cassie no doubt simply needed time and treatment. Yet, she scolded herself, she had just been grateful that Cassie didn't recall everything.

"But I can tell you," Cassie whispered, and they all leaned closer to hear, "who is going to be president sooner or later. You know who, Jennie, and Dad does, too."

At that moment, Jenna thought, Rod MacCaman somehow managed to look pleased. But he also looked panicked.

It had been a living nightmare, but now there was a ray of hope, Jenna thought as she stretched out on the long leather couch in the MacCamans' living room. Rod had told her to take Cassie's bed, but she couldn't bear to. Whatever difficulty Cassie seemed to have with recalling dates, she was now recognizing people—even recalling abstract details about Jenna's mother who had not been there. Excitement that Cassie was so much better buoyed her up. Mace would be ecstatic.

Yet with great trepidation, she was waiting for him. If he kept insisting she go caving with him, they'd have another battle royal. Worse, she needed to face him about what Frank had accused him of. And that could lead not only to another fight between those two former best friends, but to a deep divide between her and Mace. He'd never told her, the investigators, or anyone that he'd been outside on the night of her and Mandi's abduction. Actually, with his father's—and Cassie's—corroboration, he'd said the opposite. Though Jenna had never believe he could be guilty of more than lying to protect himself, just as Frank had, could she really trust the only man she'd ever loved?

She got off the too-soft couch and paced the large living room along the western windows overlooking the ravine. The sky was clearing, and rain clouds scudded before a three-quarter moon that shed cold light.

She stared out over the deck where she had stood in a Three Musketeers 'one for all and all for one' embrace with Mace and Cassie after they'd returned to Ridgeview. It had just been a few weeks ago, but it seemed an eternity of turmoil and terror. She unlocked the sliding glass door and stepped out into the blowing, rustling night. Gazing down into the dark ravine reminded her of the view from a tree house. Unlike at her own place, she didn't feel watched or nervous. Anyone hiding an audio bug or camera in a cliff-clinging tree here would have to be a mountain climber. It was thirty feet down to the stream she could hear gurgling over rocks below.

But as she turned to go back in, she was sure she saw Rod MacCaman's form. He was standing in his window on the farthest curve of the house, the bedroom wing, silhouetted by a dim light. She almost waved, but wondered if he would rather be alone. She could understand his having trouble sleeping, with his pain and the fate he was facing. Or perhaps he couldn't rest until Mace was home safely.

Realizing she desperately needed sleep, she forced herself back inside and finally drifted off into half dreams, waking each time the house creaked or the wind moaned.

Jenna woke to find daylight flooding the room and Mace, evidently just showered with his hair still damp, putting breakfast for two on the dining room table. He wore jeans and an open-necked polo shirt but was barefoot.

She was instantly alert and alarmed. "When did you get here? What time is it?" she asked as she sat up.

"It's nearly seven," he said, putting a milk carton on the table. "Dad filled me in on Cassie's progress and what she knows and doesn't. We called the hospital, but she's still sleeping. They've sedated her. Dad's gone into work, but he's going to the hospital from there later this morning. I told him I'd relieve him after I check the progress at Deep Heart today. But first you and I are going on an early morning field trip to see a cave entrance—from the outside, so don't worry about going in."

"Why? Where?" she demanded, getting up and trying to stretch the soreness from her limbs. "I've got a lot to tell you—to ask you—first."

He smacked a box of cereal on the table and turned to face her. "Just trust me for once, will you? The time for talking and asking is over. Whatever you have to say, everything's going to come down to this—you trust me or you don't. You love me or you don't."

"You don't think I can love you without trusting you?" she countered, raking her hand through her wild hair as she hurried to the table. She sat down across from him, glad for the distance, because if she didn't have this space between them she was going to throw herself into his arms, no matter what Frank had said.

"Not the kind of lifetime commitment I want, no," he insisted, sitting across from her but leaning forward with his elbows on the table.

"All right. I want that, too. But there's nothing wrong with explanations before people leap. Frank paid me a surprise visit last evening, and—"

"Are you all right?"

"More or less. He says you were out the night someone took Mandi and me. He saw you because he was outside, too. He didn't tell the authorities because he was trying to protect himself."

"I've always considered Frank a suspect. Mandi was using him, and he finally figured it out. But I never could come up with who might have helped him."

She smacked her palms flat on the table. "Didn't you

hear me? Because you were out that night and lied about it, Frank's always considered *you* a suspect."

"So we're back to trust," he said, bouncing up to lean stiff-armed on the table, nearly hovering over her. "I've tried for years not to speak ill of the dead, partly to protect you."

"Protect me how?"

"You had an idealized view of your big sister. Believe me, I understand that, because she had me fooled for a long time, too. I'm sure it was natural little-sister adoration of an outwardly beautiful person, but when you felt guilty over coming back without her, it evidently got worse—total Mandi worship."

"That's not true!" Jenna cried, and stood up so fast her chair fell back and hit the wall. "I've come to see her more realistically since I've returned to Ridgeview," she said, her voice quiet now as she retrieved and righted her chair. "My talks and interviews with Cassie helped with that. Your sister did much more to help me than a professional psychiatrist."

"All right, all right," he muttered, holding up both hands either to surrender the point or hold her off. He straightened, lowering his arms to his sides. "Now hear this, because I'm only going to say it once and wouldn't have to say it at all if you trusted and loved me."

"Mace, I—"

"Just listen! I did *not* have anything to do with Mandi's and your kidnapping. Yeah, I was out that night and mad as hell at her because I'd just found out she'd been meeting Frank on nights when she wasn't meeting me. Russ Pierce told me. I guess he finally got disillusioned with the golden goddess, too, even though Frank had evidently roughed him up and threatened him."

"Russ told you about Mandi and Frank? When?"

"Right after your birthday party, so I hardly had time to plan an abduction, even if I had been warped enough to think that would teach her a lesson. When I went out to my truck right after the party at Kirkhall, there was Russ, sort of loitering, though I didn't realize at the time he'd been stalking Mandi. Damn, I'd been sneaking out to see her—I admit that. But I had no idea she was running the same seduction scam with Frank. He and I had gone from friend to foe before that. We were so hotheaded, both of us, we'd fought and killed the best friendship I'd ever had."

He shook his head as if to clear it. His steady gaze met and held hers again.

"And Russ that night..." she said. "You don't think he still lurked around in the bushes, do you?"

"So he and some buddy, like maybe that lousy father of his, could abduct Mandi? I don't think so. I drove him home, went home myself, had a big argument with my dad, and went out my back bedroom window."

"Into that steep, rocky ravine?" she challenged, pointing.

He shrugged. "Piece of cake. I always went out that way."

"Frank—Gil, too—claim you have a temper," Jenna said. "You fought with Frank, and Gil said you beat up a guy who scooped a virgin cave."

"Gil talks too damn much," he said, slumping in his chair, exhausted and drawn. The morning window light etched the ridge of his nose and the creases on his rugged face deeper, as if he were carved from stone.

"But yeah," he went on, "I carry my own regret and guilt around. Maybe that's why you and I have such a magnetic connection," he added, looking up at her with those intense green eyes. The little crow's-feet at the corners made her think he would smile, but his mouth only tightened.

"Enough soul-searching—back to cave-searching," he muttered, mostly to himself. "Will you come with me to see the rubble at the mouth of the cave I found, or are you giving up on tracking what happened to you and Mandi—giving up on me? Now that Cassie's coming out of her coma, you two can start your own investigation again," he went on, his voice mildly mocking, "and hope it doesn't get both of you hurt, or worse, again."

He rubbed his eyes with thumb and fingers. "One good thing's come out of this, at least. Your mother can't criticize our relationship, considering her track record with my dad. I followed him once, years ago, when he drove to the Limey Roadhouse to meet her. I was still so immature and angry about my own mother's death that I fought him tooth and nail on everything—even quit the football team to spite him—but I never let on to him, or Mandi, that I knew about his affair."

"And never told me, even years after."

He stopped rubbing his eyes and stared at her. "Did you tell me when *you* found out?"

"Your father asked me not to. He wanted to tell you."

"Yeah, well, he did—briefly—before his busy schedule made him rush out to work again."

She almost stood up for his dad. After all, if Mace hadn't been caving in the middle of a family crisis, his father would no doubt have made a special effort to explain to him, as he had to her.

Mace turned his head away, but not before she saw the glint of tears in his eyes. She stepped behind him and put her arms around his shoulders, leaning against his chair back. To her amazement, he tipped his head back so it rested between her breasts as he stared up at her. She could see each dark lash fringing his eyes, glazed with tears that did not fall. But they gilded his irises, the color of green water with flecks of hazel. In the silence, his intense stare devoured her fears and challenged her to trust him.

"Yes," she said, "I'll go with you to see a cave from the outside. You think you've found *the* cave, don't you. But it was dark, and I was drugged, going and coming. Don't expect me to actually recognize it."

He nodded and stood slowly. "We can't let this haunting go on. We have to start somewhere and pray that something might trigger a memory in you, before—"

"Before what? Did you and Gil get in the cave? What was there?"

"One step at a time. Together," he said, pulling her into a crushing embrace. She nodded and hugged him back hard.

Dew clung to the grass and weeds just outside town. A knee-high shelf of fog hovered over a rocky field. Beyond loomed one of the tumbles of boulders and crushed rock that remained from when the government had dynamited, in a quest to keep other rock slides from occurring. Mace parked down the limestone road and pointed out the mouth of the cave, now sealed with thirty feet of rubble.

"I know it's going to remind you some of the Deep Heart rock slide, but I want to show it to you, anyway," he said as they got out of his truck together.

"I'm okay. It's not as big as the Deep Heart slide."

"And this one's man-made," he added.

He took her hand and drew her closer, even as he

produced a piece of paper from his shirt pocket. "Gil and I drew rough maps of both above and belowground in this area. We located a stream up here that plunges underground and which we've seen down there. We've matched any landmarks or geoforms we could."

"You went underground here?"

"Not here, a good mile-and-a-half away as the crow flies. But we're positive we ended up here, just on the other side of this massive rubble that's blocked the cave mouth."

"Are you sure there's not some shorter way in, maybe through these stones?"

"No, but it would take us weeks to find a convoluted entry here through the rubble, if there is one. Gil's going to check it out after he gets some sleep."

"Which you haven't had."

"I can't sleep when I'm onto something like this. You haven't exactly been getting your eight hours of beauty rest for weeks, either."

"Thanks very much," she said, shoving her hair back from her eyes.

"That's not what I meant. This has to end, that's all, no matter what it takes. Do you agree?"

"Mace, I can't go in that cave with you. But short of that, I'll help in any way I can. I cannot help my claustrophobia. I—I wish I could." But her hypocrisy mocked her. Two days ago she'd told Garth Brennan that little Samantha needed to face and deal with her fear of heights.

It annoyed her now that Mace pretended he didn't hear her refusal or excuse as he laid out the map on a rock. "It took us four hours in and four hours out, Jenna. Eight hours of your life to view the cave where I think you two were held."

"But how can you think that? Hundreds of cave chambers honeycomb the land here!"

"Exactly, so I need you there to verify it. But wait until you see this underground version of your Stone Forest," he said, jabbing his index finger on an early portion of the cave they'd sketched. "It's a huge room—honestly, except for two areas, maybe three, it's spacious down there."

She folded her arms to cup her elbows with her hands, and walked away from him. Trying to block out the rubble, she stared at the hillside, at the road, at the field across the way.

"I don't recall anything before I regained consciousness in the cave," she told him as he walked over with the map in his hand. He thrust it before her face again.

"Then, that's where you have to go with me. However dark it was part of the time you were held, you might recognize things in there. You might figure out what happened to Mandi or even who caused it."

"But you were inside, and you didn't."

"You were there then and I wasn't. Stop running from your fears aboveground. Go under with me."

Gil Winslow showed up at Jenna's door just as she was preparing to leave for the Henshaws' that evening.

"Has he sent you here to try to convince me, too?" she asked as she handed him a beer from her fridge.

"My favorite bloke Mace? Not at all. He says he's done all he can to bloody well convince you, so it's up to you. But I did think I'd go along with you for your demonstration at the Henshaws' he mentioned. I'm always looking for new rope techniques, and Mace says you're great with ropes."

"As if I could teach either of you something about

that,'' she muttered, as he helped her haul her gear out and she locked the door behind them.

''Then, let's just say I want to see Clay Henshaw up close, to figure out if the guy's as hostile as Mace thinks he is.''

''No excuses needed, and I'm glad to have your company. You'll love these kids. Besides, they can use help with their grapevines and bowlines.''

Though Jenna was relieved to have something to do tonight, she wasn't looking forward to all of it. However hospitable Clay and Sara seemed, she sensed strained feelings toward her. She felt she was continually breaking the ice with them; maybe Gil could help thaw them out.

When they arrived to a noisy welcome, Jenna saw the crowd didn't include just the Henshaw kids and the baseball team, but Mary Drout, pen poised and camera clicking.

''This will make a poignant follow-up to the story on Russel's sad demise,'' she assured Jenna. ''And I'd love to do a feature on your views of England,'' she told Gil with a half bow, as if he were some visiting British peer. ''I've always loved English rose gardens.''

''Me, too,'' Gil told her. ''Especially through a long-distance lens.'' He tipped his baseball cap and went jauntily off to talk to the beleaguered-looking Sara Henshaw, while Clay yelled at the kids to sit down and shut up.

Mary pursed her lips at what she probably considered a snub, though she didn't say so. She turned hastily back to Jenna. ''One angle I'd use in this story—and think of the good publicity for you, dear—is that the boys are actually helping to assuage their grief over losing their coach by helping you with the memorial tree house.''

"Speaking of which, I guess I won't be building a tree house for your great-niece Samantha. I didn't know she was afraid of heights."

"Hmm, neither did I," Mary muttered, flipping notebook pages. "By the way, I have a new picture of her somewhere. It's very Alice-in-Wonderlandish. I've hated those where she had her pretty hair scraped back like some plain-Jane, especially with the beautiful curls she has—ah, here."

The photo Mary thrust at Jenna was day-and-night from the one Garth had shown her at Pioneers Day. Naturally curly tresses—though, these days, of course, it could have been a perm—haloed a pretty face.

"She's really growing up," Jenna marveled. "And that bounteous, beautiful mop reminds me of—"

"Of Mandi as a child? I wanted you to see it, anyway. Life goes on, doesn't it. Well, best get on with your demonstration before these boys tie everyone up in knots." She laughed at her own lame joke as she put the picture back in the pad.

Though Gil looked as if he were holding his own, Jenna got everyone settled with coaxing, which worked better than Clay's shouting. He always bellowed at the boys, and she wondered if he reared his own three sons that way. If so, perhaps that was the way he dealt with the quarrymen under him, too. No wonder Mace was uneasy with him, for quiet command was more his way, at least as far as she knew.

Since she'd checked and double-checked her rope rigging in the tall oak just yesterday, Jenna began by demonstrating how to get into a seat harness for ascending without a ladder.

"Believe it or not, this is sometimes called a diaper sling," she told them, and they giggled as she figured they would. ‘‘I’m now going to attached this Perlon cord to make a safety loop for the sling.’’ She did so quickly, using the knots she’d already taught them. ‘‘Okay, now everyone hold up the prusik knots you learned last time and be sure your loops will slide along the rope. That’s exactly what I’m using here.’’

‘‘It uses friction to grab and keep you from falling!’’ Pete Henshaw put in, parroting her words from the first lesson.

‘‘That’s right. Now, these are my Gibbs ascenders, and I’m going to show you how they let me climb up in a tree to rig ropes to hoist up supplies.’’

‘‘You already told us about that!’’ another boy told her helpfully.

‘‘I know, but now I’m going to show you how it all works. I’m going to need your help to pound nails here on the ground. Then we’ll get some help from Mr. Henshaw—and maybe Mr. Winslow, but this will work better than ladders for me to get started.’’

‘‘Mr. Winslow talks kind of funny,’’ a voice put in from the back row.

Jenna laughed. She felt sure of herself and strong again. It was great to be outside, ready to climb—building a tree house, especially one for kids.

‘‘But you see,’’ she told the boys, ‘‘Mr. Winslow probably thinks *we* talk funny.’’

‘‘He said we can call him Gaping Gil.’’

‘‘Quiet and listen to Ms. Kirk!’’ Clay roared. ‘‘And you call him Mr. Winslow and act polite or you’re gonna hear from me!’’

Jenna paused a moment, then went on calmly. ‘‘Now, I attach these loops to my feet…’’ She tried to explain her double-bungee Gibbs system, but she knew a demonstration was needed. She carefully attached the so-called chicken loops around each ankle so she could not accidentally shed the slings around the soles of her boots as she went up her rope.

"You see," she told them as she started to climb it, lifting one leg above the other while the devise winched her up one step at a time, "your legs do most of the work, so you can have your hands free. But you must keep your weight close to the rope and watch your balance."

They squealed with excitement and some applauded as she rope-walked upward into the tree. Though the boys would not be allowed to do this, she wanted them to see all the possibilities and problems of working high in trees so they'd appreciate the fun, the challenge, and the dangers, too.

"I see I have everyone's attention now," she said as she rotated on the rope about twenty feet up.

"Don't talk *down* to them, now," Clay yelled and guffawed at his joke, which none of the kids caught.

Snapping pictures, Mary Drout was standing almost directly under her, although Jenna had told the boys never to do that. Gil, who had extricated himself from the kids again, stood leaning against a nearby tree, hands under his armpits, grinning.

And then she felt the slightest jerk.

Gibbs ascenders almost never slipped. She looked up to be sure the tree limb itself still looked solid; yesterday, she'd checked and rechecked it, her gear and the ropes thoroughly. But that was yesterday.

Her main rope jerked again, harder. She'd best go down and re-rig. But then, craning her neck to look up, she saw her problem: where the master rope looped over the big limb, it was cut and fast unraveling.

"Jenna—rope!" Gil shouted.

She started down, but each movement of her legs yanked the remaining strands above. Desperate to keep balanced now, she did not look back up but she could sense it fraying, loosening. Perlon rope was the best; it never did this....

"Get back, get back!" Clay's voice sounded in her ears from so far below. Mary or Sara screamed. Kids' cries, chaos.

Jenna rotated on the rope as she tried to control her descent, to hang on, to get down. She knew she should try to lift her feet out of the loops, but their purpose was to hold firm, and she had no time. She was going to fall, snared off balance like this—

The rope snapped, and she dropped. She managed to keep her feet under her, but she couldn't free them to help break her fall. Gil partly caught her, but she still slammed to the ground. It jarred every bone and rattled the core of her pride and sense of safety. Stunned, she just lay there.

"No, don't touch her!" Gil ordered, as Clay and Mary rushed to help. "Give her a minute. Jenna, you all right?" he asked. He knelt to yank the ascenders and chicken loops from her legs as she sprawled on her back.

"You—you broke the worst of it."

"But," Mary cried, leaning over her, with the camera, "is anything broken?"

"Just my pride," Jenna whispered, mostly to herself as, once again, Gil warded the woman off.

Clay shouted at the kids to stay back. Slowly, Jenna sat up. She moved and flexed her limbs. "Just shaken up—a shock," she whispered to Gil. "But I checked all those ropes."

"Oh, great, just great," he muttered. "After this, you'll never go caving with us."

With his help, Jenna got gingerly to her feet. She was sure someone must have cleverly, carefully, weakened that highest rope since yesterday. She walked over and saw that it had indeed been slightly sliced, just enough to let it unravel under her movement and weight. Clay would be the obvious culprit, but she'd been wrong before, and besides, others knew she was working here.

"You're wrong, Gil," she told him, her voice still shaky. "I'm not waiting for the next thing to scare me or hit me. Maybe the answers are in that cave. I'll go with you and Mace, the sooner the better."

19

"Jenna, are you all right?" Mace demanded. As he stepped in her door, he hugged her as if she were fragile. "From what Gil told me, I'd better take you in to get X-rayed." His intense gaze looked her over as if he could see broken bones or strained muscles through clothes and skin.

"I'm fine—at least, in that way," she assured him as they stepped inside with their arms around each other. "And since I'm going to have a black-and-blue bottom and other aches and pains tomorrow, I figured I might as well go caving."

"So Gil said." His eyes lit, but his expression was wary. "I'm not going to ask you if you're sure, because I don't want you wavering."

"Then, don't ask why, either. It's for more reasons than you—or maybe I—know."

"Dad phoned to say Cassie's continuing to improve. But she has absolutely no memory, he says, of walking into the Limey Roadhouse with you. The last thing she recalls is a funeral, but she had a nightmare it was hers."

Jenna shuddered, but no matter what foreboding racked her, she was not turning back on this. She had learned her fear of closed places when she was kept prisoner in a cave. She was determined she could unlearn it, and at the same time settle what happened to Mandi.

And then she might know who'd been trying to terrorize her.

"Since tomorrow's Saturday," Mace was saying, his voice excited, "we'll use it to get our gear together and prep for our initial vertical descent. We'll go down very early Sunday morning. I figure with the three of us, five hours in, a couple of hours there, then five hours out. We'll grab sleep before we go and only rest on the way. Can we use your house for our base camp? We can prepare and sleep here to get a really early start."

"Good idea. I'm tired of looking over my shoulder—or up into trees for the next catastrophe. If this is the best way to fight back, I'm taking it. Gil told you I didn't just fall, that my rope was cut, didn't he?"

Mace nodded and pulled her gently but firmly into his arms again. "We'll check every inch of all our ropes, every cam, carabiner, rivet and pin. I swear I'll take care of you down there."

She looked deep into his eyes and decided to believe him.

"Finally, I'm going to get to eat gorp the only place it should be eaten," Jenna teased Mace and Gil. She was trying to keep from thinking too much about what she was doing. Besides, it was fun and exciting to be planning a trip with them, even if it was hundreds of feet underground. Or so she kept telling herself.

After a visit to Cassie—without telling their parents about what they were planning—they had commandeered Jenna's kitchen to lay things out. Ropes, webbing, helmets and headlamps, food, backpacks and scattered gear littered the floor and stretched down the counters. The two men seemed euphoric, while Jenna—and pacing, nervous Pretty Girl—were totally on edge.

The strange clutter and swift movements had driven the cat into the dining room, where she sat on the nearest chair, pushed under the table. She watched Jenna, evidently in disgust that she was part of such folly. Jenna went to pet and reassure her.

"I have to do it. I've got to learn some things about my past and my future," she whispered. But the Siamese just whipped her tail, jumped down and moved to the chair directly across the table, as if her mistress were too stupid to bother with.

When Jenna peered under at the annoyed cat, she saw a thin notebook wedged between seat and chairback where Pretty Girl now perched. Jenna went quickly around the table to see what she'd dropped. But the softbound notebook was not hers. *Memories,* it was labeled in Cassie's distinctive handwriting. Jenna fanned through it, thinking it might be her friend's notes from an interview with her mother for the biography. But it seemed to be Cassie's notes about her own past.

Rather than give it to Mace to put with his sister's other things he'd taken from the table, she slid it into the single drawer of her corner cupboard. She'd glance at it later and give it personally to Cassie.

Gil's voice from the kitchen startled her. "Bloody hell, Jenna, you're not taking *all* these batteries?"

She hurried back to them. "I certainly am. And I'd feel better taking double. Other than that, I'll defer to you two extreme cavers for advice on my gear."

She saw Mace nod almost imperceptibly to Gil, who shrugged. "Fine," Gil said. "You know why I think you'll like caving? It demands all your attention, so your troubles just blow away down there. It's another world."

"Right," Mace muttered as he filled his carbide headlamp. "One that's always fifty degrees and may be wet."

He and Gil had batteries for their flashlights, but relied more on the old-fashioned carbide helmet lights. Though they lasted only about four hours before needing to be refilled and could be doused by water, cavers could use them for other necessities such as heating food and warming hands.

"Fifty degrees or not, I'm going to feel like a mummy with all these layers," she protested. Like the men, she'd be wearing fluorescent nylon ballistic coveralls over a wet suit—both loaned by Gil—and a tight flannel shirt over that. All clothing had to fit snugly so that nothing could snag or grab. Thick leather gloves would be needed for a rough crawl they'd described, but at least there would be good clearance, they'd claimed.

Jenna's belly clenched at the mere mention of a place that needed any sort of a crawl. As ever, when she pictured herself in an enclosed place, her heart began to race, she broke out in a cold sweat, and thought for a moment she couldn't breathe, even in her kitchen with a warm breeze blowing in the windows. But she wanted her life back, and if these two could go caving and emerge alive time after time, she could, too.

She and Mace had had only one disagreement so far. Jenna wanted to use her garden knee pads since knee protection was a must, but Mace had vetoed them. He claimed they'd be hard to walk in, and he'd supplied her with an extra pair of wrestlers' pads from a sporting goods store.

"Thanks for sharing the tricks of your trade with me," she'd said. When Gil went out to his truck for something, Mace knelt before her chair to demonstrate how best to strap them on.

Their gazes met and locked at close range as she leaned forward to watch and help. "Not that I wouldn't really like to wrestle with you," Mace said, his voice husky. He ran his hands up the outside of her legs to her hips, cupping her sore bottom, but she didn't protest or flinch. "As for showing you the tricks of the trade, anytime."

She actually laughed, the sound so throaty it surprised her. "I believe you said something about keeping this professional," she said, but leaned farther forward to give him a long, deep kiss.

"Yeah," Mace whispered. "Down there, we'll be all business, but after we get this settled, we—"

Gil had clattered back in with a bang of the door. "I knew I'd brought an extra water bottle," he said.

Their intimate moment passed back into preparations as Jenna checked their first-aid kit for everything from bandages to aspirin, then re-laced her tree-climbing boots. They were the equivalent of their paratrooper boots with the necessary solid but flexible soles. Layers of socks would make certain there would be no blisters. She understood the reason for most things they put in, and asked about anything that seemed strange.

She was falling into a pattern of finally, completely relying on Mace for her safety and sanity. That really was, she thought, the only way she'd ever survive putting that first foot over the edge into a dark, closed-in cave.

"See," Gil said as they approached the vertical drop cave entrance at four o'clock a.m. on Sunday morning, "we're going to rely on your old friends to get us down into the cave."

She didn't know what he meant until she saw they

intended to rig their ropes using two trees as anchors. "Hold these until I'm ready for them," Mace said, handing her the leather pads that would keep the ropes from being abraded or cut against the limestone as they descended.

As the memory of her recent fall flashed through her mind, Jenna thrust back her shoulders and stood straighter. Her body ached all over and her fears plagued her, but she was going to do this. Instead of going up, she was simply going down. And once she'd gone each step of the way in and out, she'd be cured of her debilitating phobia and, perhaps, know what happened to Mandi.

Using two tall, sturdy trees and several cross ropes, the men rigged a descent for a rappel-drop into the cave. They seemed to be taking forever, though she wanted them to be sure and safe. Waiting eternally, Jenna tried to shut down her thoughts, feelings, fears. She concentrated on Mace and Gil's fluid teamwork while she held a lantern. They'd been down that dark hole before, she assured herself. They knew what they were doing.

But when they took the pads from her, keeping her lantern trained on their work, she turned on her helmet light and looked down into the hole. The beam snagged on darting bats that zigzagged out and up. She even felt some fly by her, but she had no fear of them. It was their home she dreaded.

They rigged and cross-checked their own gear and a belay rope for a body rappel. Jenna was totally familiar with equipment and techniques for this. As long as someone didn't come along to cut these ropes—and Gil had hired two university cavers to be certain no one did—she'd be fine, just fine, she told herself.

"Where are those guys?" Mace asked Gil.

Finally, backpacks and supplies in hand, the two cavers who would make sure they got out safely appeared. Introductions and handshakes were exchanged all around. Jenna was ashamed her grip was so cold and shaky.

"All set?" Mace said, gripping her upper arm. "Gil, go ahead."

"We're inward bound!" Gil said with glee.

Inward bound, Jenna thought. That she was, in more ways than one.

They had decided that Gil would always lead off, with Jenna next, then Mace. They'd carefully gone over the lingo of safety with her. "On-rappel," Gil said and stepped backward over the edge. Jenna's insides plummeted with him as he disappeared down the ragged, four-foot-wide opening that widened just below.

She knew then that she could not do this. Absolutely could not. Mace would eventually forgive her. He would tell her what they found, and she could help him figure out things from there.

But when Gil's voice echoed up—"Off rope!"—she amazed herself by stepping to the edge of the black abyss. No, not completely black anymore, for a gray pinpoint of Gil's headlamp shone below. Unlike the surefooted Gil, she was linked to Mace with a belay, an extra rope that protected a climber in case of a fall.

"Belay on?" she asked, her voice tremulous.

"Belay on!" Mace told her and squeezed her shoulder again.

"On-rappel," she called to Gil. She glanced at Mace, who nodded, even smiled.

She stepped off the edge.

Jenna tried to tell herself this was just like coming down a big tree trunk, or maybe like dangling over the edge of Green Eye at night. But the hole devoured her; her little helmet light seemed nothing in its maw.

However much her muscles ached, she rappeled well enough, her feet bouncing off the rock, the outward, then inward sway and swing of her body almost mesmerizing. The rope buzzed through her rappel rack and gloves. When Gil talked her down the rest of the three-story drop, she put pressure on her brake bar to slow her descent.

''Good girl!'' he told her, and helped her unhook.

''Off-belay! Off-rope!'' she shouted up to Mace. Though her journey to what felt like the center of the earth had just begun, she felt triumphant to have come even this far.

She kept looking up at Mace's descent, because she didn't feel so closed in with his light coming toward them, not with the sprinkle of stars she could see high above. But too soon the three of them began to walk into a steeply down-slanted tunnel the men had dubbed Nursery Roost.

''It's like a bat incubator—a smelly one,'' she observed as the stench of guano assailed them. Bats, big and small, whizzed past her without so much as brushing her. ''Great radar. I hope you two are as good.''

They seemed to sense her increasing panic, for they kept up a string of lighthearted talk with her. This wasn't so bad, she tried to convince herself. There was indeed plenty of room in here. She'd just imagine she was walking in the cavernous county courthouse. Besides, she's rather have a bat behind each pillar than her mother's Vince Sabatka lurking.

Time seemed to roll on, and she lost track of it. Only putting one foot carefully before the other, only keeping up with Gil and knowing Mace was right behind kept her from going crazy.

"Mace and I had a caver friend named Batman," Gil was saying. His voice echoed eternally down here in the silence.

"*Had* a friend? What happened to him?"

"Nothing that we know of," Mace put in hastily. "We just haven't seen him for a while. We're almost into The Atrium that made us name this stretch of caverns. Be prepared for the Boulder Walk."

She understood why they named everything. Not only was it a discoverer's right to do so, but it imposed some semblance of order and control on a wild, untouched place like this. Yet she knew control down here was strictly an illusion, like the forms that seemed to emerge from the shadows to snatch at her.

In the sudden silence, she blurted, "I hear voices!"

"Just a stream up ahead," Mace assured her.

"Water or wind," Gil added. "Some call it ghost talk."

Jenna hated that terminology. But she did feel better when the ceiling opened up above them, arching into space. And seeing the burbling stream that had caused the whispers helped, too; it was just like a rock-strewn, small river on the surface—except that they were now nearly five stories under where the stream had once sparkled in the sun.

Jenna saw where other passageways occasionally snaked off in various directions. Using their compass more than their exploration skills, Mace and Gil had earlier discounted them. "Dead ends and tight places can suddenly open up to passages when you're ready to give up," Mace had told her about caving. She prayed fervently that there would be no tight places and no dead ends on this trip.

They rested briefly, ate granola bars and drank water before they started across the so-called Boulder Walk that followed the creek. It traversed the entire section of this chamber they called The Atrium for its shape and proximity to Deep Heart. She didn't say so, but if this was the atrium of the thick limestone layers of rock, this stream was the lifeblood that coursed through it. Fortunately, they were across the tumbled rocks before Jenna reasoned out where they had come from. The lofty ceiling must have been made by a rockfall where boulders became mammoth raindrops.

They rested briefly again at the other end of the tumbled trail, this time not eating or drinking. But she got desperate for human talk again.

''What about that stream for a water supply?'' she asked.

''It has the best filters in the world,'' Gil answered her before Mace could, ''but we don't make a practice of drinking it. This far underground's not a good place for surprises. Might as well eat that popcorn there.''

She looked where he pointed and shone his light. Limestone popcorn seemed to cling to the wall where some giant hand had thrown it. They'd passed other unique formations called speleothems down here, but they'd been pushing on and she hadn't asked about them. It was as easy to get out of breath down here as out of control.

''There're better formations beyond,'' Mace said as they set out again. ''First challenge just ahead,'' he added from behind her, as if it were a mere afterthought. ''The Velcro Crawl, and we'll have to climb about twenty feet to get to it.''

* * *

By "climb," Jenna saw that Mace meant without ropes. The slope upward was less than forty-five degrees, which wasn't steep enough, Gil explained, to necessitate classic rock climbing skills.

"It will come naturally to someone used to scrambling through trees," Mace told her, and threw an arm around her shoulders. "You do whatever feels right—climb or jam."

She managed to nod as she eyed the twenty-foot, rugged slope. Mace set up two extra flashlights to bathe the surface in light, which she knew neither of them needed.

"Jam," she said, recalling their earlier talks about caving techniques. "In other words, hanging on for dear life in any toe- or handhold I can manage. I guess I've done that in trees for years. No problem."

Gil and Mace high-fived her. Gil went up so skillfully that she'd almost believe it was a flat surface. He leaned back over, she thought to give her even more light, but he ended up calling out suggestions for handholds to her as she went up. For the first time since she'd been underground, she became so intent on what she was doing—and on doing it well—that she almost forgot her fear. The result was a clean, pure rush of adrenaline and exuberance in her accomplishment.

Until, standing on the shelf of rock as Mace scrambled up to join them, she saw what lay ahead.

The jagged-edged hole the men had dubbed the Velcro Crawl seemed to be lined with tiny teeth; its top came only to her waist when she was standing. Plunging into utter blackness, it looked like it led nowhere but oblivion. As she stared at it, the circumference seemed to shrink, to suffocate her. Pressing herself to the wall so her legs wouldn't buckle, she began to hyperventilate.

They both turned to her. "I can't—can't go through that," she insisted.

"It's just like the small entrance to a kids' tree house," Mace said. "You're shorter and smaller than either of us, and you'll crawl right through. And, like a tree house, it soon opens up on the other side to a big room we've named The Stone Forest. It's fantastic. Wait until you see it."

"I'll wait here for you."

"No way," Mace insisted. "You can do this with no problem. Go ahead, Gil, and we'll be right behind."

Gil bent over and started through, though she saw he soon dropped to all fours to go on.

"I can't," she said again.

"You mean you won't. Then, I guess it's time for tough love, sweetheart." He got right in her face, his eyes blazing. "You're going through, Jenna, and coming out the other side. You need to, and I know you want to. And you can."

She almost told him he was crazy. Love. Tough love. *Sweetheart,* he'd said. The only man she'd ever wanted was waiting for her to go with him.

Somehow she found the strength to push away from the wall and crouch. Every muscle she'd strained in her fall from the tree suddenly seemed to pull and knot and scream at her.

"Sling your backpack to the side like Gil did so it doesn't snag on the ceiling," Mace said, and helped her position it. "You'll have more room against the wall. I'll be right behind you, and there's plenty of light."

"You have no idea what 'plenty' of light is," she said, but she started in. He dared to pat her fanny as she began to crawl.

She was furious to see that the passage was not a

straight shot. It dipped and curved, but she could still hear Gil moving ahead of her. This was endless! They had tricked her. It was like being buried alive, like what had happened to her father. No, she could not go on.

She began to pant in great gasps. Sweat and tears blinded her eyes. But she made the next turn, on hands and knees now. Her backpack snagged, no matter what Mace had said. He had no idea what he was doing down here. One slight turn, then another, and she saw Gil again, looking back in at her, his helmet light in her eyes.

"You go, girl!" he called.

She almost laughed, except she was pretty sure she would cry, instead. He took the weight of her pack and helped her out of the jagged tunnel. And what she glimpsed in the single flashlight he'd put on a flat rock almost made the horror worthwhile. This new room, large and lofty, was a fairyland of limestone foliage supported by thick stalagmite pillars like towering trees.

"The Stone Forest, see?" Mace said as he emerged behind them, out of breath himself. She realized that she must have led him through at breakneck speed.

"I see. But this is a far cry from where Mandi and I were held. I would have remembered all this."

"No, it's still beyond," Mace said.

"I should have looked at your map more carefully, but I couldn't bear to. Can I study it now?"

"Later. It's jammed under a lot of stuff in my pack."

She thought that was strange, but she had no choice but to keep trusting both of them. Boldly, she walked into the vast room, training her own largest flashlight on the magnificent surroundings. And then, for the first time, she felt the familiar but eerie air movement that she recalled so clearly from being in that—this?—cave with Mandi and their abductors.

She sucked in a sharp breath. "What?" Mace said, coming up behind her.

"That strange breeze. It feels familiar. But when I was held captive, it must have been coming from the opposite direction."

"Because the cave mouth was not yet dynamited shut," Mace suggested, "or because its source is ahead. We have to pass it to get to the part where you were held."

"Let's go," she said, amazed at herself. "We're this far, so let's get this over. Besides, I always did like a walk in the woods."

Gil grinned, and Mace looked so proud of her that for one split second, before she recalled where they were and why, she was almost glad she had come.

Cassie was astounded to awaken and have the world make some sense. But that didn't keep her from being surprised to see Cynthia Kirk standing at the foot of her hospital bed, holding a framed oil painting of a desert setting at dawn.

"I got it in a Native arts shop, and I hope you like it," she said. "Jenna told me how much you loved living out west, and this will be restful for your eyes and thoughts. And then, it's a kind of mental game to try to see all the little details. See, here's a tiny Navajo hogan down here, and there's a pony up on this bluff. It's just full of surprises."

"It's lovely."

"I know how terrible everything's been for you." Cynthia propped the painting against the foot of the bed with its frame leaning against Cassie's feet. She came closer to take Cassie's hand. "By the way, has Jenna been by lately? She's not answering her phone or e-mail, and I worry about her."

"I saw her...ah, yesterday, I think it was. What is today?"

"Sunday, May 21st, early afternoon. I wanted to see Jenna before I go on a rather impromptu trip for a week—actually, a fact-finding one for Hal Westbrook. You do remember who he is?"

Cassie began to recall things in a rush. That Jenna had longed to spend weekends with her mother, but the lieutenant governor was often too busy. And it came back that someone had told her that her own father and Cynthia Kirk had managed a secret, long-term affair, and in nosy Ridgeview, no less.

Cassie almost smiled at that last thought, but her face felt so stiff she thought her skin might crack. "Hal Westbrook," she said, "is the man you're hoping will be a presidential nominee so he can ask you to be the other name on his ticket."

"You're better than your doctors realize," Cynthia said, dropping Cassie's hand. "Did Jenna tell you that, or your father?"

"My own deduction. I must be better if I'm thinking like that again," she said, scooting a bit more upright.

"Do you recall the book you're writing about me?" Cynthia asked, crossing her arms and leaning one hip against the mattress.

"I do. Can I quote you that on this date you admitted to me that you hope to be the first female vice president?"

"If you don't tell another soul for eight days," Cynthia said with a glance at the door. "I plan to make the announcement I'm being considered at the Ridgeview Memorial Day festivities. So after that, you may tell the entire world. I'd love to see press speculation on it before the convention to give me even more clout during it."

Cassie's eyes met Cynthia's regal stare. Suddenly, the mere vice presidency seemed far beneath her. She might as well be president—or queen.

When Cynthia left, instead of just crashing back to sleep for once, Cassie mulled over what had been said. At least her autobiography of the woman was evidently still authorized. But where had Jenna disappeared to? She'd better call Mace to see if he knew.

But as she reached for the bedside phone, her foot bumped the western painting. Another thought—a memory—bombarded her, as so many had in her fight to climb out of the depths of her hallucinations.

Years ago, when she was packing to leave for college, she'd been scrounging in the basement for something sturdy to pack things in. She'd stumbled across a metal, under-the-bed trunk, shoved way back in the corner with other things in front of it. Because the house had been partly hewn from the cliff, this section of the basement was not concrete but rough, raw stone.

She'd recognized the metal trunk as Mace's, and opened it to see if she could take out whatever was there. It was only a pair of cowboy boots she'd never seen him in. She had no idea where he'd gotten them. Tooled leather, dusty, scuffed—how had she missed him wearing them?

No way to ask Mace, for he'd left home two years before and had not been back. But since he'd gone out west to cave and work and try to go to school, why hadn't he taken these with him? she'd wondered then. Missing him as she did, before he'd gotten back in regular contact with her, she'd taken the trunk and the boots to college with her. She'd had them when she too moved out west, but they'd been such a mess that she'd discarded them long ago and never thought to mention it to Mace or anyone.

And then Jenna had blurted out that one of her abductors had worn western boots. But so what? It meant nothing. Still, she'd better talk to Mace, to let him clear all this up. But she couldn't recall her own home phone number and began to panic about losing her mind again.

"Nurse!" she cried, and pushed the button that summoned them. They were always around waking her and poking and prodding when she wanted to sleep, so where were they now when she just needed a simple phone number?

"Nurse!"

"Next stop, Santa's Chimney," Gil said jauntily as they left the subterranean stone forest behind.

"After that crawl, nothing's going to scare me," Jenna said, trying to keep herself pumped up.

"No boasting underground," Gil threw back over his shoulder. "The hodags don't like it and will take their revenge."

"Didn't I tell you to keep it light?" Mace challenged him. "They don't call you Gaping Gil for nothing."

Jenna was enjoying being a part of their banter. Besides trying to keep up with their caver talk, each new turn down here was a challenge. It did tend to shrink one's troubles aboveground, though she'd managed to bring her two main tribulations with her: the trials of her claustrophobia and losing Mandi.

The vertical tube the men had named Santa's Chimney was a fifteen-foot, narrow climb to a slightly higher level—about as tall as a one-story building, Jenna judged.

''There's a place to rest your rear about halfway up,'' Gil assured her. ''You just brace your back against the smoothest wall and scoot up in a kind of crab-walk.''

''And if you fall, it's no longer a piece of cake but crab chowder,'' Jenna muttered, but the technique itself didn't scare her. She'd sidled up more than one tree crotch to fasten bolts or support cables. Once again, what rattled her was the tightness of the rock, but she could see the end in sight when Gil leaned back down from his quick ascent to bathe the rockface in the twin beams of his carbide light and flashlight.

Her back and feet pressed to opposite walls, up she went, with Mace standing under her in case she fell. Her heart thudded so hard she thought the solid limestone walls reverberated. She prayed she wouldn't slip right down from her own sweat. Every sore spot on her body from her fall two days ago shrieked at her. But she had such tight tension going that she didn't even stop in the obvious resting spot Gil had mentioned. Soon, he helped to haul her out atop the chimney.

Her light fell on more boulders up ahead. ''What did you name this room of our maze?'' she asked when Mace's head appeared up the chimney.

''The ceiling collapsed in here years ago, maybe a reaction from the dynamite blast outside,'' Gil said before Mace could get a word in. ''I wanted to just call this cavern Damn Boulders—you know, like Boulder Dam—but Mace insisted on Tombstone.''

20

"*Tombstone* is one of my favorite western movies," Mace explained. "These boulders aren't as bad as they look to get through, though. There's a sort of shelf on that side we walked on—see, elevated over there, on the far wall."

Both men played their lights where he pointed.

"It looks narrow," she said.

"Yup, pardner," Gil said in a lame attempt at a cowboy accent. "But you're a wee lass."

"They don't say 'wee lass' in the American west, English!" Mace said, clapping him on the back. "It would probably be more like 'little lady.'"

"They'd say 'wee lass' if the speaker was a tenderfoot from the British Isles!" Gil insisted, and another tense moment was diffused by their banter. But Jenna was right: the ledge path was very narrow, with a fifteen-foot fall to the tombstone-shaped boulders beneath.

She told herself it was like walking a big tree limb and concentrated fiercely on staying balanced several steps behind Gil. The air current blew stronger here, and the ghost voices, as Gil had described them, began again from up ahead, as if calling to them. Occasional drops of water plopped on her helmet to make a dull dripping; a few puddles underfoot made the going slightly slippery.

"This is still better than taking more time threading

through those stones down there,'' Gil said. ''There's a little jump down here, so let me go first and help you d—''

Gil turned, twisted slightly, then slid several feet to where he meant to jump.

''Bloody hell! My ankle!''

From behind her, Mace's hand came to pin her to the rock wall. ''Don't trip over him,'' Mace said. ''I can't get by you to help, so you'll have to get down past him. Be careful!''

She stooped, then slid, missing Gil and getting out of Mace's way.

''Not a bone break?'' he asked his friend. Feeling helpless, Jenna just shone her light for them.

''A sprain, I think,'' Gil said between clenched teeth. ''Let's see if I can walk on it. Aagh!''

''We'll have to go back through the boulders,'' Jenna said, ''so we can both help support him. Gil, can you make it through the Velcro Crawl?''

''You—we—aren't going back yet,'' Gil said as he sat on a rock, cradling his ankle. ''Too close to paydirt.''

''He's right,'' Mace said, not looking at her, as he helped Gil ease his foot from his boot. ''We have only one more crawl and we're there. Gil can wait here for us—one hour, two at the max—then we'll get him out together.''

Jenna took the first-aid kit from Mace's pack, but her brain worked faster than her fingers as she fished out a tube of instant ice gel and an elastic bandage. She didn't want to go on. She'd proved she could cave. And yet, that next room seemed to lure her with its voices, the air currents. If indeed it was the place of her and Mandi's imprisonment, she needed to know everything that had happened in there.

"All right," she heard herself say. "If it's coming up next."

She caught a lightning-fast exchange of glances between the two men. "It'll swell like a stuffed sausage soon enough," Gil muttered, "but I can tend myself while you two go on. Jenna, you'll do fine. I pray you'll find some answers."

She could only nod her thanks for his encouragement. Wiping her sweaty hands on her flannel shirt, she looked in the direction Gil had glanced. She could see little but gray-and-black shadows and depths. She rechecked her four flashlights and extra batteries. Her heart began to bang against her ribs with a new frenzy that had nothing to do with caving or claustrophobia. Finally, maybe, she was going to figure out what had really happened to Mandi and who was to blame.

"There's about a twenty-foot crawl that accesses the room just inside the dynamited rock slide outside," Mace told her when they'd walked ten minutes beyond where they'd left Gil.

"Twenty feet doesn't sound bad," she said boldly. "Is it about as wide as the Velcro one?"

"A little smaller. This one's no problem, either."

"Where is it?"

"There," he said, shining his light.

"No, that's just a hole in the wall!" she protested.

He could not be serious. It was another attempt at caver humor. It wasn't much bigger than a small sewer pipe.

"Mace, I can't crawl through that, and you most certainly can't, either! No way!"

"Gil and I did it going and coming just three days ago, and you're smaller than either of us. The walls are smooth as silk compared to the Velcro Crawl. Here, you don't exactly crawl, you kind of slither. You've seen pictures of Marines in training who scramble under barbed wire on their elbows."

"Right. And under enemy fire. That's what I feel like here. You never mentioned anything like this. Is that why you've been hiding the map?"

"We're going to be a great couple, especially at fighting," he muttered, shaking his head. "Jenna, I'm going in there, and I hope you'll come, too. Because you need to see that cave just a few feet away. You need to face the things you're afraid of and—"

She shrugged her pack off her back and slammed it to the cave floor. "Am I going first or last? And couldn't Gil at least crawl with that ankle? We need him."

"We need each other. And pick up that pack. You're going to be dragging it right behind you on a cord."

"I'll get stuck."

"You know how the Europeans do small crawls? In the buff, so nothing snags. You want to try that?"

"You're demented! But I'll try it if you promise me one thing."

"Which is?"

"If I say I can't do it after I've started in, you'll back up and pull me out."

"All right. Deal. Let's go."

Jenna shed her flannel shirt because the nylon ballistic material underneath seemed sleek and almost slippery. She let Mace tie her pack to one ankle with a cord.

"You and Gil lied to me," she insisted. "A rough crawl but good clearance, you claimed. What else have you lied about?"

"Not about loving you. Let's go."

"Great try at changing the subject. Tell me what you

two named this limestone straw,'' she demanded, growing furious at him, wanting to blame him for her cresting frenzy.

''You don't want to know.''

''I do, too.''

''The Birth Canal,'' he admitted. ''Now listen to me. Push with your toes, elbows, anything. It's not as bad as it looks.''

At the last moment, in case her headlamp went off or out, she insisted on pushing a flashlight ahead of her. He seemed to know not to protest.

Fitting her frame into the rock tube, she could not believe it had come to this. Could a hobbled Gil pry them loose or would the university students come to save them if they both got stuck in here? Why did she trust this man? She should have told everyone she knew she was coming caving—left it on her mother's answering machine, at least. Even told Cassie, who, thank God, finally seemed to be on the road to recovery.

She concentrated on thrusting herself forward. Elbows, toes for propulsion, as he had said. She almost felt the limestone groping her. It scraped her breasts and grabbed at her buttocks. The rock squeezed her thighs and yanked at her helmet if she held her head up. Soon she pictured herself as burrowing through a narrow squeeze in tree limbs and thick foliage, and that helped.

''You're doing great,'' Mace grunted from behind her, but his voice seemed so distant. He must be in the tube now, too. At least he was with her.

Straining, she managed a slight turn, though she had to lie on her side and suck in her stomach to avoid a single protruding rock. This was absolute insanity. How could human beings do this for fun?

The next moment, she felt as if the rock would collapse against her. Again, she thought of her father and Mace's mother under all that falling rock. Dear God in heaven, she was stuck. Her shoulders began to heave; she sucked in huge breaths. She began to pray, hoping God could hear her from the depths of this hell. She was wedged, trapped. She would die here.

Tears burned her eyes, and she sniffed hard.

"Jenna?" came a muffled voice from behind.

"Stuck!"

"Wriggle a little. Let one shoulder drop back. Exhale."

"I can't. Back up. You said you'd back up and pull me out if I got stuck."

"It's ten times harder to go back instead of forward. Try what I said. You've got to go on!"

You've got to go on. His words echoed in her brain. That's what Dr. Brennan had urged so many times after Mandi's loss. Her mother had said that, too. They'd both been wrong. She had needed time to grieve, even to blame herself for leaving Mandi so that she could forgive herself before she could recover. But now it was true: she had to go on.

Jenna rolled her flashlight as far ahead as she could. She'd crawl to that light, pretending it was sun and freedom. Exhaling, breathing shallowly, she let one shoulder drop back. She felt again how sore she was from her fall, how much her muscles ached. But she shoved on, inching through this spot.

As she moved again, she realized the blowing air was no longer in her face. Obviously, that had been the case since she'd entered this crawl but she'd been too scared to notice. Had her wedged body just stopped its current, or had the direction somehow shifted? It now seemed to blow in the same direction as when she and Mandi were in the cave.

She made it to her flashlight and tossed it a few more feet. Was Mace behind her? Why wasn't he urging her on?

"Mace?"

"You're doing great. Go!"

She told herself she was doing this to put her deepest nightmares about leaving Mandi behind her. And for Mace, who believed in her and needed his name cleared in Ridgeview, once and for all. For Gil, too, poor guy, the ultimate caver who had seemed so indestructible and suffered a freak accident that didn't look like it could hurt his leg.

She stopped her grueling efforts and sucked in fresher air. Had he *really* hurt his leg? Surely, the two of them hadn't conspired to let only Mace go into this cave with her to settle things privately about Mandi. She shook her head to free herself from such thoughts, and shoved on.

"It's widening!" she cried.

"We're almost there!"

When she went another few feet, she sensed not to heave her flashlight again. Her head popped out into openness; she was free. She'd conquered the Birth Canal! She sucked in a full breath of air for the first time in ages. Half falling, half crawling, she emerged into a vast space that was filled with a breeze and those whispering cave voices again. Clambering to her feet, she shone both headlamp and flashlight into the hole to see Mace come through.

His face was contorted in a grimace instead of the grin she'd expected. He shoved his big shoulders free, wriggled out and stood.

"This chamber is massive," Jenna whispered, awestruck as they surveyed the cavern together. The four lights they held between them didn't illuminate ceiling or walls, only rugged floor in a shadowy circle around them.

"Not compared to some I've seen," he said. "The Golden Gate Bridge will fit into the Big Room at Carlsbad Caverns. But yeah, this is large, and it's in a series of connected, vaulted chambers. My theory is you and Mandi were probably held in one of the two closest to the rubble seal, which was once the old cave's mouth."

She started when Mace's flashlight beam bounced as he stuck it under his arm. He partly unzipped the neck of his tight coveralls and dug out a piece of paper.

"You did have the map handy," she said, and bent over his shoulder, holding her light, too, as he unfolded it. She clearly saw that he'd marked the dimensions of the Birth Canal: *approx. 2' X 3'.* But it was this vast series of rooms that he'd sketched most completely. "It looks like you found hills and valleys in here," she observed.

"More like false floors that suddenly open to pits or crevices," he explained. "But closer to the original entrance—opposite us that way—there are flatter floors, and that's where we need to start to see if you recognize anything. Gil and I found that the nearer you keep to the walls in here, the safer it is, just like traversing Tombstone along a narrow walk to avoid the boulders."

"At least the pits are obvious enough," she said, playing her lights ahead. "I see the first one."

"I read in Mary Drout's articles, you said that it was dark when Mandi ran from your abductors. And if she was still under the influence of some kind of drug, as you were..."

"You've reasoned it all out. I've tried to recall it, to

face it since I've come home. Earlier, I'd just tried to bury it and go on.'' She looked up into his craggy face, made even more rugged by the slant of their lights. Shadows seemed to lurk there, too, but she was suddenly bold. ''Let's go,'' she said.

Mace led the way toward the front of the cave. ''The depths of these black holes are deceptive, and you can actually feel dizzy.''

''The breeze is from the right direction, but since there's no underground stream near here, why are those ghost voices getting louder?''

''Maybe a stream we can't see runs through one of these crevices. Then, too, echoes are deceptive in huge caves.''

''You don't really believe in those hodag gremlins, do you?''

''I don't believe in saying I don't. Bad luck.''

''With Gil's fall, we've had our share already.''

''Here we are,'' he said. She wasn't sure what he meant until he explained. ''This is the flat floor where the pits and crevices end—or begin, depending on your perspective. Just beyond is the rubble from the dynamite, and I estimate the outside's only forty or fifty feet on the other side of that.''

With a sweep of his arm, he indicated a pile of rubble that seemed to slant into a more solid, arched opening.

''So Mandi and I could have been brought through here,'' she said, aligning herself with her back to the outside. ''If this is the place, we were kept around here to my right.''

They walked it together. Mace moved easily along with her; he'd obviously spent time here when he was drawing his map.

''Which would mean,'' she went on, ''that around this

curve, heading out in the dark—so it must have been night then, probably a short time before they released me—we tried to escape, and then the two kidnappers stopped us somewhere about here."

"Can you picture their faces? Body build? Anything?"

"They kept quite covered. The man I saw struggling with Mandi back at Kirkhall wore a loose sort of raincoat. One who tapped me on the chin wore gloves. But while we were kept prisoner, I only saw that one wore jeans and western boots, maybe not even the same guy. Mandi had mentioned the boots, too. The men shined light in our faces. For all the good it did me, I dove at one guy knee-high, while, I guess, Mandi turned back and ran."

"She ran inward instead of out, because they blocked the way?"

"Or else she was disoriented when the lights went out again."

"In Mary Drout's series of articles, you said that you and Mandi at first tried to feel your way out of the cave. Should we turn out the lights now?"

"No! No, I need light. Let's go farther in to see if there's anything left where we were held, although, if the cave was open then, any moron would have removed everything."

They scoured several sites because she wasn't sure of the surroundings. She felt ridiculous to think she'd find a deserted sleeping bag or remnants of a box of soda crackers in here after fifteen years. It could be the place, but maybe not.

"Jenna, I still think we should turn off our lights. We'll keep our hands on the flashlights so we can turn them right back on. You might sense this was the place, and you can try to feel your way out.''

''No! It's just stalling to keep from what we—I—have to do. Look for Mandi in the first few pits.''

''I just want this over, for both of us, but you're right. When Gil and I were here, I briefly shone a light down a few holes at random. But I knew I'd need whatever directions you could recall.''

They nodded in unison, both biting their lips to hold back tears. Then Jenna moved toward him even as he opened his arms. They locked in a fierce embrace, both breathing hard, clutching each other.

''I need you—love you!'' she cried. His kiss was devouring, almost desperate. Yet when he finally set her back, he seemed calm and resigned again, while she was only more agitated and tense. ''I keep trying not to admit it, but I think this is the place,'' she whispered. ''I've both dreaded and yearned for this for years. Let's look.''

Trembling, still breathing fast, she peered carefully over the verge of the first wide cleft. Their light beams darted down and around. There was some rock rubble at the bottom. The sides themselves looked slick with darker limestone than she'd seen so far.

''That can't be bloodstains, can it?'' she asked.

''It's just got some iron oxide in it.''

Shoulder to shoulder, they shone their lights into another, more shallow pit. When Mace's headlamp flickered out, she jumped.

''I've got to refill the carbide, that's all,'' he explained, sitting down cross-legged and shrugging out of his pack. ''It's been going a long time.''

Jenna nodded and took several steps to the next pit. Narrow, convoluted, at least ten feet deep. She sidled closer, her back along the cave wall for support. A slight overhang knocked her helmet forward to cover her eyes.

Hodags again, she thought. As she shoved her helmet back, her headlamp raked the corner of the pit. When she jerked back at what she glimpsed, she hit her head again, this time knocking her helmet off. It bounced and tumbled into the pit—atop two dust-covered sleeping bags.

Jenna's scream echoed off the stone walls, just as Mandi's had years ago.

They stood, awestruck and horrified, staring down into the pit.

Jenna finally found her voice, breathy, not her own. "The sleeping bags they must have put us in."

"They've been discarded here, or they're covering something."

"Yes." Her voice broke, and she sniffed hard to keep from bursting into tears.

"I'm going to rig a rope and go down," Mace said. "I'll be careful where I step." She nodded jerkily. She felt as if she were watching other people now, as if she stood apart from this horror.

He tied a length of Perlon cord around a boulder and let himself down carefully. Jenna, on hands and knees above, leaned over the lip of the pit to shine her headlamp and two flashlights. "What's that little white thing there—on the bigger bag?" she asked.

He bent lower to glance at it, then tossed it up to her. "A golf tee. What the hell's a golf tee doing here? And there's a funny smell, as if these bags had cologne on them. Or is that something else?"

Jenna's heartbeat kicked into a faster gear. A golf tee.

And not cologne, but the faint, sweet smell of tobacco. Yet what she was thinking was impossible.

"Anything else?" she asked, as he gingerly lifted one, then the other sleeping bag to peer beneath.

"I don't think so," he said. "The floor's flat under these bags."

But from her angle above him, when he lifted the second bag, Jenna saw that he was wrong before he did. The rough floor had a crack several feet wide, in it. And wedged in that were gleaming white bones with a skull crowned by a mat of yellow hair.

Jenna went mute. Mace grunted as if he'd taken a fist to his belly.

He fell back against the side of the pit, his arms spread as if he were clawing for a hold to keep from falling off a cliff. Jenna amazed herself by being able to react, to move. She grabbed his rope and scrambled down to him. Tears slicked his cheeks; she pressed her face into his shoulder. They clung together in a stiff, shuddering half embrace.

"It's her," Jenna whispered. "The hair."

"Yes," Mace said finally, swiping at his tears with his sleeve. "The beginning of the end of the nightmare. I hope."

Those last two words were so bitter it scared her even more. "I couldn't help her," Jenna choked out. "I didn't mean to leave her."

"None of that was your fault. Your being with her gave her comfort."

"My poor mother's going to have to get through this now. We can take Mandi out of here, really bury her. But most of all, we have to find out who put her here!"

Together, they carefully lifted both dusty sleeping bags completely away. Mace looked over the one with the big zipper especially, evidently for more possible clues. "Look," he said, shining a flashlight into the crevice where the skeleton was wedged. "A class ring—mine—on a chain around her neck."

Her throat constricted again, and she could only nod.

"We'd better not disturb any more of this evidence," he whispered. "We'll need help to get her out without...breaking her apart."

"She's broken me apart ever since that night," Jenna said dazedly. Again she felt as if this were happening to someone else, as if someone else were talking so rationally, when she only wanted to cry and scream.

"I can lead a retrieval team down here after we go to the authorities, but I'm sure your mother will think the timing's terrible."

Jenna nodded before she realized how dreadful that sounded: that recovering the body of her mother's beloved daughter and laying her to rest could ever be badly timed. But maybe, Jenna thought, amazed at her own cynicism, her mother would welcome the public closure to their family nightmare. She'd survived and even thrived during other media-intense tragedies.

"We've got to get back to Gil and help him out first," Mace said. "He'll slow us down enough, as is. I swear to you, sweetheart, we'll get her back to bury, only you know the authorities and forensic guys will be all over this first."

Jenna nodded. "Whoever brought Mandi and me to this cave is to blame for a death as well as kidnapping. Finally, we have proof!"

"And proof that whoever's been trying to scare you isn't Mandi."

In the depths of the earth, from the bottom of the pit, Jenna pressed herself back against the wall. She trained her flashlight down again so she could remember this entombment. The cave's ghost voices echoed in her ears like a litany. No running from these sounds and sights, no pretending it didn't happen or just burying the memory. She would somehow face it, grieve it, accept it.

Mace handed her the fallen helmet from where it rested at Mandi's feet. Jenna saw remnants of dark blue cloth, no doubt her sister's blouse, and scraps of denim jeans still clung to the bones. The cave had done its preservation work quite well.

"We've got to get back to Gil," Mace said. He replaced the sleeping bags over the skeleton. "Let me give you a boost out."

"It's all right. I can make it." She hand-climbed the short rope with relief and reluctance. No longer did she feel closed in by the tons of rock, but somehow, strangely unafraid of whatever else she must do.

"Wait!" Jenna said when Mace tried to tug her away. She gathered small stones and placed them near the pit to form the word *M-A-N-D-I,* then dotted the *I* with a crudely heart-shaped stone.

"They'll be back for you," Jenna said. "And now that I know where you are, I'll get the men who left you here."

21

"Mother, it's Jenna." Her hands were shaking so hard at having to break the news that the phone receiver bounced against her ear.

"So they said when they called me out of the meeting, darling. What's happened?"

"Something really amazing. It's—both good and bad. I hope you're sitting down."

"Jenna, just tell me."

"We've found Mandi's body."

Jenna had been agonizing over how to say that, all the way back from Bloomington, where the broken bone in Gil's ankle had been set and put in a walking cast. Meanwhile, Mace and Jenna had gone to report their discovery to the county sheriff, asking him to keep the news private until family members could be notified. He had agreed to sit on the news as long as he could, but considering how high profile it would be, he said he could not promise much past tomorrow morning. But by then, they hoped, Jenna's mother could fly home from the west coast and Mace could prepare to lead a caving team, including two forensic specialists, to recover Mandi's body.

"Mother, are you there?" Jenna said, steadying the phone with both hands as she leaned heavily against her kitchen wall. "I know it's a shock."

"Who is *we?* Found her body where?"

"Mace had a theory it might be in one of the caves that had been blasted shut. With another caver, he and I went down—"

"*You* went caving? And found—surely not after all this time. Are you positive?"

"It's her—her remains. The body will be recovered soon, and the police are on it, so—"

A low, keening moan, then a gasping sob.

"Mother, is anybody there who can help you?"

"No one—can help—this."

She should not have told her like this, Jenna berated herself, but she couldn't help that her mother was on a week's trip for Hal Westbrook out west. "Mother, can you come home to help us handle this—to finally grieve? And then we'll want a funeral. We've asked the police to avoid statements until you get home, but you know how things leak out."

"I can't believe this, just can't. But yes, I'll handle the public parts of it."

Of *it.* Her words echoed in Jenna's exhausted brain. How could she speak of Mandi and her murder that objectively? But perhaps she was in shock, reacting as if it were someone else's tragedy, the way Jenna had felt in the cave.

"As dreadful as this is—" she tried to assure her mother "—we now have answers, at least to what happened, if not who caused it. But now with physical evidence, we'll find out. I swear we will!"

"If you went in a cave, I believe you," her mother said, her voice quavering. "Jenna, you asked if anyone could help me. Call Garth and tell him exactly what you did—what happened. If you don't need him, I do. I'll be there in as few hours as it takes."

Without another word, the line went dead.

Yes, she was indeed going to call Garth. But not for the same reasons her mother thought.

She rushed upstairs for a fast shower. She had to scrub the grit and grime, the sweat and tears, of Mandi's tomb from her body. Her mind had been in overdrive since they'd found her. She was tempted to phone Cassie, but Mace had said he'd take care of that. Her hair still wet from the shower, Jenna dug out her friend's *Memories* notebook—the one she'd found under the dining table just before she'd gone caving. If she couldn't yet question Cassie about anything else she'd gleaned before being nearly drugged to death, this was a start.

The notebook began with lines from a poem; Cassie had always loved author quotes. This one read, *Murder may pass unpunished for a time, / But tardy justice will o'ertake the crime. —John Dryden*

The hair on the back of Jenna's neck prickled. Could Cassie mean Mandi's murder? But why would that be in a book of her own memories? Cassie must know more than she'd revealed.

Jenna found surprisingly few entries in the notebook, and even those were recent. This was not an old diary, but a very new one, even if it probed the past.

Those western boots, which Jenna mentioned, Cassie had written in her distinctive scrawl, *could have belonged to Mace, hidden in the basement when he left, and unknowingly I took them west and lost them when they could be evidence. I saw him leave the house that night after Dad told him he couldn't...his temper could flare at Dad, but surely it didn't flare at Mandi, not enough to convince me that he and Frank could have been in cahoots to shake Mandi up with a simple, little kidnapping that went wildly awry because of Jenna.*

"No, Cassie," Jenna said, closing the notebook, "it

just can't be Mace.'' The western boots must be a coincidence. She'd studied Mace MacCaman back then, and had never seen him in western boots. She was convinced, heart and mind, that he'd proved himself innocent of Mandi's death. She trusted him, loved him. ''It's not him, and I can prove it!'' she said aloud.

As she fanned again through the notebook to make certain she hadn't missed something, she recalled another notebook she'd often seen. She punched in the phone number from memory as Pretty Girl hummed loudly and curled herself around her ankles.

The phone was answered with a sprightly ''*Ridgeview Reporter,* Mary Drout speaking.''

''Hi, Mary. It's Jenna. Just checking to see if you've had any responses concerning my lost cat.''

''No, nothing, but how are you doing after that fall at Henshaws?''

''Sore all over, to tell you the truth.'' Jenna realized that she could make Mary's year—her whole small-town career—by tipping her off to Mandi's fate, but she went on. ''Let me ask you something else, then. Have you had any recent enquiries for that excellent series of articles you did on me after Mandi's loss?''

''Hmm. I gave Cassie a set. Actually, I mailed them to her when she was still living out west.''

''Anyone else?''

''I really can't say.''

''Can't, or won't?''

''Jenna, in a way it's privileged information. You know, like lawyer or doctor's privilege.''

Jenna fingered the wooden golf tee in her hand. On it, she was sure she could still smell the scent from the sleeping bags that Mace had thought was cologne, but which she had recognized as a faint, distinctive tobacco smell.

"The thing is, Jenna, I've got my hands full here today. I'm taking care of my great-niece, Samantha, while Garth sees some client in this area, and I just had to go get her off the rock slide memorial, no less. That child is giving me conniptions. Climbing on it, right up to the top."

"You mentioned doctor's privilege. Did Garth ask to see the old articles? I know you do things the old-fashioned way at the paper, so you probably never had your older work archived online. I'm guessing someone who wanted the series of articles would have to ask you directly."

"Jenna, he asked me not to tell," she whined. "And it was just background prep for treating you, he said."

"Thanks, Mary. You've helped a lot, and I'll pay you back with another long interview someday soon."

Jenna hung up and scribbled a short note to take with her. Then, since Mary had said Garth was loose in the area, Jenna looked out every window, car keys in one hand and pistol in the other, before she dashed for her van. She had told Mace she would wait here until he called, but he ought to be breaking the news to his father about now. Besides, Mace had no ties to Garth. She had to do at least this on her own.

Mace merely nodded at Rita Carlson, who jumped up from her desk as he strode into the office.

"Your father's been looking for you," she began. "He was upset you weren't home, then didn't show up at Deep Heart to oversee this morning's cutting—"

"I'm sure Clay Henshaw's happy to handle it," he said in a clipped tone.

Mace went right on into his father's office and, seeing he was alone, banged the door shut behind himself.

"Where the hell have you been?" Rod exploded, though his voice was as low as usual. He looked as if he wanted to slam a fist on the desk, but he stopped in midair. "You can't have been caving all this time!"

"I've been visiting a rock slide, one of the dynamited ones you put on the list for the government guys to blow—and don't deny it, because I checked the records."

"What in the Sam Hill are you talking about?" he demanded, but his eyes went wide and wary.

"I went caving, just like I said. I wasn't looking for cheap, macho thrills, as you always used to call them, but—"

"You can't get your butt to work Monday mornings, I'll just have Clay fill in permanent for you here."

"He'd like that. But the point is, I went looking for Mandi with Jenna, and I found her—what was left of her."

The old man's face blanched even whiter. He slumped back in his chair. Mace stepped to the front of his desk and leaned over it on the palms of his hands.

"Mandi?" Rod whispered.

"Mandi's bones, with my class ring still around her neck. She was partly covered by my boyhood sleeping bag, the one lined with red plaid flannel, with the wide zipper I always hated because it got cold at night. The one you said someone must have taken out of the back of the company truck years ago."

Mace sucked in a ragged breath and crumpled into the chair that faced the desk. He had wanted to be tough and strong through this. But he felt berserk with fear for the things he was thinking, saying, believing.

"I would never have let them pin it on you," his father said, then hacked into a handkerchief he produced from his desk.

Mace stared agape at the indirect confession. "But you let them think it might be me," he choked out. "It drove me away. You...and who was with you? Why?" he ended up shouting.

"The other man's long dead," Rod told him. "And why? Keeping the company afloat meant everything to me then, after your mother was gone. Oh hell, even when she was alive, and I've hated myself for that for years. Let's just say I was really short on cash, and it looked like MacCaman might go under, which would have ruined not only me but my staff and the entire community, which depended on—"

"So you abducted your lover's daughter?" Mace roared, jumping to his feet again. "I can't believe this! You've ruined everything—so many lives!"

"Not yours, Mace. It's made you stronger. You've taken your life back since you've been home."

Shoving his hands through his hair, Mace paced to the large glass window overlooking the mill. He fought to regain control, but his voice was as bitter as it was angry. "And then when Jenna stumbled into your harmless little kidnapping, you just grabbed her, too," he went on, "and drugged both of them. Too bad, of course, that Mandi panicked and ran, either killing herself or—"

"Yes. The fall killed her. We never meant for it to...to turn so bad."

"We'll let the forensic investigators and the county coroner determine that, won't we, because I'm taking a team down to recover her body in a couple of hours. I just thought you'd like a heads-up on this so you can get your lies all in order and hire a lawyer. And I had—

had to hear it from your mouth,'' he muttered, and turned away, afraid he'd throw up.

''There won't be any lies or a lawyer. I'll tell them all they want to know—about my part in it, anyway.''

''But who was the other man? And you never got any money out of Cynthia Kirk, did you, because she said she never paid the ransom?''

He dared to shrug. ''When things got screwed up, I never went to collect it. I assume she knows you found Mandi.''

''Jenna's probably called her to come home by now. She'll hate you more than anyone else. And you told her you loved her.'' Mace nearly spat the words.

''Loved her?'' Rod whispered, and Mace saw his father was actually crying. ''Then and now, so much.''

Jenna saw Samantha Brennan the moment she parked her van on the town square. Her hair was pulled back in a tight ponytail again, but a few, wayward blond tendrils had escaped. Jenna recognized her from photos Garth and Mary had showed her, and perhaps from her own blown-up photo in the forest.

Strange, Jenna thought, as she slowly approached the girl. She might look like Mandi, but she was acting more the way Jenna carried on when she was that age. Samantha was not climbing on the monument now but was jamming her hand over the mouthpiece of the public drinking fountain to spray the pigeons that strutted about. Glancing around to be sure she didn't see either Garth or Mary, Jenna walked closer.

''Hi! You're Samantha Brennan, right?'' Jenna said with a smile. ''I'm Jenna Kirk, Mrs. Kirk's daughter and a friend of your aunt Mary and your dad.''

''Oh, yeah, hi,'' she said, and smiled back. ''If you're

riends with them, you can call me Sammy.'' She quit praying the pigeons and wiped her wet hands on her heckered dress. She looked about six, and Jenna wonlered why she wasn't in school this Monday morning.

''I heard you were climbing the monument,'' Jenna aid. ''Aren't you afraid of high places? That top bird tatue is pretty high.''

''No, I'm not 'fraid of anything,'' she said, her frecked face lifting in an impish grin. Evidence entry number hree against Garth, and almost as good as a golf tee and obacco smell, Jenna thought. The child has no fear of eights. He'd lied.

''Those poor pigeons are afraid of getting wet, hough,'' Jenna said to keep the conversation going.

''Cats don't like to get wet, either,'' Samantha told er with a small shrug.

A new possibility hit Jenna. ''You know, Sammy, I ave a Siamese cat with really blue eyes.''

''No kidding?'' Samantha asked, hands on her hips. 'I have that very same kind, too, and she had kittens, ross-eyed, like this.''

She crossed her blue eyes and wrinkled her pert nose. However young she was, Jenna thought, Samantha Brenan would make a perfect witness against her own faher. But how tragic for a feisty, little tomboy like this ne, like Jenna had once been herself, to be without her ather as she grew up. Still, Jenna pushed ahead with er impromptu plan.

''I build tree houses in a place called the Stone Forest, nd I'd love for you to come visit me there sometime.''

''Can you keep a secret?'' the girl asked, lowering her igh-pitched voice. When Jenna nodded, she whispered, 'I was already there and saw you taking pictures. But Daddy and I were playing hide-and-seek, so I couldn't say a thing, and we had to jump back behind a tree rea quick.''

Jenna's knees almost buckled. Who would be mor skilled at psychological terror than a psychiatrist, especially one who knew personal and family secrets—an no doubt had a familiarity with and access to mind bending drugs? Her mother would pull all kinds o strings to see that this man she had trusted for so lon was punished.

''Sammy, would you give your dad a note from me as soon as he gets back here today?''

''I don't know where he went. I was 'sposed to be i school but a water main broke there. They let us out fo the day and my mom had a meeting, so I got to com with him—but I can give it to him.''

''Thanks a lot. Tell him I'll be at my tree house fo kids, where he saw me cutting limbs a couple of week ago.''

''They're real neat tree houses, and I'd like to clim up them!'' Samantha called after Jenna as she hurrie back to her van.

She drove carefully around Mother Lode where Rus had lost control. If Garth had been spying on her t terrorize her, could he have seen Russ hanging aroun and wanted him out of his way? Could Garth have cu Russ's brake line? With Russ dead, could she ever fin enough evidence to pin things on an eminent, well connected psychiatrist? The words of the note she'd lef with little Sammy spun through her brain:

> Dr. Brennan: I have finally discovered Mandi's fate, and believe *you* will need counseling. I suggest *you* simply ignore *your* part in the tragedy and forge

ahead with *your* life, burying whatever guilt haunts *you*.

But if *you* cannot, I will be waiting. Now that *you* have a daughter, do *you* grasp what *you* have done? J.K.

That, she thought, should bring him looking for her.

Nothing that went wrong had ever been the fault of the brilliant, concerned doctor. Everything had always been so carefully focused on her, so she had underlined every damn reference to the bastard. The thing was, since he'd probably been watching her for weeks, was he already in the Stone Forest waiting for her? And was his accomplice from years ago still around?

She reached into the purse beside her on the seat. Despite the warmth of the day, the gun metal felt cold, like limestone deep in the earth.

An hour later, Jenna waited for Garth Brennan in her children's tree house. She knew she was betting with her life that if he wasn't already here, her note would bring him and that her baited trap would work. She seethed with anger for his professional and personal betrayal of her and her mother. He'd even served on her mother's Right-A-Wrong executive board for years! But fifteen years ago, Garth had been a young doctor, struggling to establish a private practice. Had he been so desperate for funding that he'd risked kidnapping one of his patient's kids? Jenna knew it would take every bit of self-control she had to discuss things with Garth civilly enough to get them on her hidden tape recorder. Despite the fact that it would not be admissible in court, she intended to use it to convince her mother about him.

When Garth didn't come as quickly as she had expected, she backed up the cassette tape and started it over again. Being here in this work of her own hands and heart both pacified and panicked her, but her plan was good. It would have to work, so she had something to take to the sheriff. With merely a golf tee and a strange scent, she'd had little with which to accuse Garth Brennan when she and Mace reported finding Mandi earlier today. Even now, her proof was too tenuous to totally nail him.

"Jenna?" Garth called from the ground to make her pulse pound even more. "You up there?"

"Dr. Brennan," she answered as she stuck her head over the railing to look down. "I didn't see or hear you coming, but I guess you're pretty skilled at that."

"Should I come up?"

It infuriated her that he still employed that calm, controlled demeanor. Whatever it took, she was going to see him rattled. "I'd hate to have to shout all this down to you," she told him, speaking more quietly as he climbed the ladder in his suit pants and white shirt. He wore no tie for once, but his pipe protruded from his shirt pocket. She could smell the telltale odor of his distinctive tobacco again, as if he'd doused himself in smoke. "I know you're good at quick ups-and-downs in my tree houses," she added, as he bent his head to get in the doorway.

"What is that supposed to mean?" he asked, looking genuinely puzzled. "You—including that note you wrote—are about as easy to understand as an Arab newspaper lately."

"I was referring to that time you left a copy of *Gone with the Wind* in this tree house, and then took it back just as fast. Of course, that was only on a par with the Siamese cat figurine shuffle, and the pillow trick, to name a few. Oh yeah, I didn't mean to leave out that really clever e-mail you sent, ordering a kids' tree house just like the one Mandi and I once had. Which, of course, you learned about by reading your aunt's articles—or did I describe that in one of our so-called counseling sessions years ago?''

''Jenna,'' he said, sitting on the single bench in the room while she perched rigidly on the solo window seat, ''you're going to have to fill me in. I assumed your note meant you're blaming me for not counseling you correctly about Mandi's loss, Mandi's fate. It's not uncommon for a patient or client to blame the psychiatrist for making them face facts or their own guilt.''

''Nice try,'' she told him, folding her arms over her chest. ''You never cease to amaze me, but let's just cut the mind games for once.''

''One reason *I* wanted to see *you,*'' he said, taking out his pipe and a pouch of tobacco, ''was that I was afraid you were still having hallucinations after being drugged at that campus hangout. So far, that's my diagnosis to explain how you're acting.''

She should have realized he might come up with that. Maybe her preparations had not been thorough enough. Remembering her gun, she was glad she had a contingency plan in case this went badly. She decided to go directly for the jugular.

''Here—'' she said, thrusting the white golf tee toward him when he fished a red one out of his pants pocket to tamp the tobacco in his pipe bowl. ''Recognize this?''

''You wanted to cut mind games, so quit playing twenty questions, Jenna.''

''It's the one Mace and I found in the pit with Mandi's body, where you and your accomplice left her either dying or dead the night you turned me loose,'' she told him, pocketing it again when he leaned forward and tried to snatch it. ''You see, finding her has brought everything I've been counseled to keep repressed back to me.''

For one moment his face went completely expressionless, as if someone had erased all emotion. ''You are indeed hallucinating,'' he said, but his voice was more tremulous. ''But you mean that you believe you have actually found Mandi? Where? Does your mother know what you're claiming?''

''She'll be here soon, and the authorities are already on it.'' She was pleased to see alarm flit over his fine features. ''Mace is leading a rescue team to recover the body,'' she went on, ''and the evidence you left in that cold, dark pit with her. I should have known it was you, but I actually trusted you—and Mother did, too.''

''You really have gone out on a limb—that *is* your little company's name, isn't it?'' he asked with a sweep of his pipe around the tree house. He glanced into the corner with the storage chest, painted to look like a goldfish aquarium. She hoped he didn't notice it was ajar, wouldn't get up to look in it where she'd secreted the tape recorder. He fished a silver-plated lighter out of his pocket and snapped it open.

''No smoking here,'' she told him. ''This is a smoke-free, deceit-free zone. So if you're not going to admit to kidnapping Mandi, at least give me a clue why you've been terrorizing me. Just to help my mother out by getting me to want to leave here and go back on the campaign trail with her? Of did you want to make me need your damn so-called counseling again? I just want you to know that Cassie's interviews helped me more than you ever did!''

"Jenna, I swear to God, I have no idea what you're talking about. I believed Russ Pierce may have been bothering you, so—"

"So he bumbled in your way, and you got rid of him."

"I'm just sorry you got my daughter involved here, Jenna," he said, still maddeningly not reacting to her accusations. "I don't need your instability and warped theories corrupting her," he added, as he pocketed his unlit pipe.

"Me? You're the one who's been using her, lying about how she was afraid of heights, getting her to pose for that photo that was supposed to be Mandi come back from the dead. Well, now she *has* come back from the dead, and she's going to help the forensic experts link you to her murder."

He sighed and lightly hit both hands on his knees. "I guess it is poetic justice—that's what your little writer friend will call it at your funeral, if she recovers. Poetic justice."

"What?"

"That you died in a fall from your own tree house. Foolish girl, living alone here in the Stone Forest where accidents could and do happen. You see, your mother worried you could get hurt like that—and then it happened."

Jenna raised her voice even more so the tape recorder would get every word. "In other words, you're threatening to kill me, too? You killed Mandi, Russ Pierce, made an attempt on Cassie's life, and now me?"

"Russ—yes, but he kept getting in the way," he admitted with a shrug. "Can I help it if he couldn't make the turns in that rain—and if you chased him to force his speed up. I cut his brake fluid line, hoping something like that would happen. Russ, sad to say, was completely screwed up. I imagine he was going barefoot in the rain so he'd keep his old car clean from red mud. And what normal guy would wear an old-fashioned woman's raincoat? Sometimes his actions remind me of a mama's boy—like that weirdo in Hitchcock's movie *Psycho.*''

''The pointed hood on it looked like flowing hair,'' she whispered. ''And he ran so fast, it was like a spirit taking flight. But he was spying on—stalking me, just as he had Mandi.''

''So I ended up keeping an eye on him. See, a very sick man. But that doesn't mean you aren't to blame for his death, chasing him like that with MacCaman, as indirectly you were culpable for Mandi's unfortunate demise. You should have saved her, not come back alone, Jenna.''

That accusation, which would once have tormented her, now only infuriated her. At least she'd finally cracked his false facade of concern. ''You're the killer,'' she accused, ''and you even used your innocent daughter to keep me from learning the truth.''

He shrugged. ''She was visiting her great-aunt Mary that day I saw you taking photos in the forest. So I told Sammy we'd just play a game with you, popping out in the background, then hiding again. She loved seeing the tree houses and the stone carvings, by the way. And I just loved the way that blowup you displayed at Pioneers Day showed 'Mandi's ghost.'''

''You're the one who's sick. My mother will feel so betrayed.''

''By you,'' he countered. ''Too bad I didn't get enough of the GHB drug in you to make you comatose—or worse.''

"How did you know Cassie and I were going to the Roadhouse?"

"I was outside your window—about to put a note from Mandi on your door—when I simply overheard you calling Cassie about going there. And when I saw the place was packed with bodies, I just blended in. I had your two beers waiting for you and bribed a frat guy there to make sure you two hot chicks got those beers from an admirer. I guess he was too scared to come forward later during the police questioning and investigation."

"You—you meant to kill us both."

"Not necessarily, if you both had backed off and shut up. Cassie kept sticking her sharp little journalist's nose where it didn't belong, and I felt a certain loyalty to your mother. That book of Cassie's couldn't do anyone any good. As for you, quite frankly, I enjoyed subtly turning the screws...watching you panic—which is what I refuse to do, even now. Well, enough chatter. I'm now going to have to act decisively here, too."

Without further warning, he lurched at her across the small space between them. She tried to fend him off, but he seized her in an amazingly strong grip. Before she could cry out, he bent her right arm up behind her back and clamped his other hand over her mouth. She kicked at him, but he quickly, neatly slammed her head into the central pillar tree trunk she'd painted to look like a giraffe's neck. The jarring blow convinced her he had been the one who had grabbed and hit her over the head the night she and Mandi were taken. And that other man, the one holding Mandi—yes, he had been built like Mace. But it couldn't have been Mace that day, it just couldn't. If so, she was doomed.

"I hear you almost fell from a tree the other day,"

Garth said, mockingly tut-tutting. "Careless, reckles
with a death wish ever since Mandi was lost. So ver
sad, Jenna, but your mother will rise above a great pe
sonal loss again with my help. Perhaps she'll be the fir
vice president or even president to take her shrink t
Washington with her."

Despite the pain in her arm and head, Jenna dragge
her feet, but he pulled her through the door onto th
narrow balcony. He bent her forward over the railin
which was painted to look like a smiling green snak
She was so dizzy the snake seemed to writhe. She'd bui
this tree house lower than the others but it was still
good twenty feet aloft. And Garth was going to thro
her from it headfirst.

22

"Let her go, Brennan!" Mace ordered sharply. Stiff-rmed, he thrust the gun at the back of her captor's head. 'It's her gun, but I know how to use it—and I'm aching o."

Garth released his grip on Jenna's mouth, then her rm.

"Stand clear of her!" Mace ordered from his position prawled atop the flat roof of the tree house. It was a ood thing she hadn't added the peak and shake shingles et or Mace would have had nowhere to hide up here ut in the branches. Now, his arm extended straight to-vard Garth with her gun, he looked like some avenging ngel that had swooped down from heaven.

"Don't tell me she's got you convinced, too—or did ou do the seducing here?" Garth dared, as Mace sat p and slid carefully to the edge of the roof.

Mace ignored that. "We've got him on attempted omicide if the other accusations don't stick," he told enna. "But I think they will."

"Could you hear what he said, in case the tape didn't et it all?"

"Every word."

"You're both playing with the lives of your nearest nd dearest by setting traps," Garth accused, daring to it casually on the little porch as if he didn't have a vorry in the world. "If I go down in a splashy trial, your families are destroyed, too. You did tell her wh the other man was, didn't you, MacCaman? Or haven' you had any deathbed confessions over at the old home stead yet?''

''What's he talking about?'' Jenna demanded, takin the gun from Mace until he swung down and thudde onto the narrow deck. Garth couldn't mean that Mac had confessed to his father. She'd bet her life on Mace' innocence in the kidnapping. And he'd come through fo her. Yet Garth sounded so smug, as if he still held a the cards.

''He's talking about my father,'' Mace said. ''I wa going to tell you, but when I got here we were so rushe getting ready for the demented doctor's house call, an I didn't need you distraught over that, too.''

''Your father's taken a turn for the worse?''

She stopped talking. Her words drifted away into th trees, and her thoughts tumbled. Her head throbbed, ye seemed to suddenly clear. She recalled the little knuckl tap on her chin Rod MacCaman had given her when he' come to thank her for taking his affair with her mothe so well. It was that same odd blend of affection an muted threat that had warned her to be quiet in the cav during their abduction. And, despite the fact that Ro was now bent and frail, he and Mace had the same build That man who grabbed Mandi that awful night—for on second, he had reminded Jenna of Mace.

''No!'' she screamed. ''The other man—your father!'' As Mace took the gun back from her, Jenna sucked i great, heaving gasps. But her horror was not for Mac and Cassie's forthcoming pain and shame and not be cause her mother had been betrayed by both Garth an Rod, the men she'd most trusted.

The final piece of the puzzle had fallen horribly int

›lace. There was only one link between Garth and Rod ‹s co-captors, two men who hadn't known each other hen. There was only one person with a motive, however varped, for arranging the abduction. She was the woman vho rose above the ashes of disaster like a phoenix again ınd again for her own gain.

For this final confrontation, Jenna would be alone. The secretary from MacCaman Stone had called to say Mace's father had suffered a serious collapse at work ›ut was adamantly refusing to go to the hospital, so he'd driven him home. Mace had phoned for a private ımbulance to bring Cassie to see her father, then rushed here himself. Jenna assumed Rod was dying; she almost elt like that herself. She hadn't told Mace she feared ıer mother had masterminded the kidnapping, because ıe would not have let her face her mother alone. And she needed to do that—finally, for good.

And so, as sunset blazed and faded, she walked the ›orch of her home, waiting for her mother, her enemy. She still prayed it could not be true, that Cynthia Kirk could not in any way be involved in the living hell Jenna ıad been through for fifteen years. *Beloved betrayer,* she hought. But if such horror could be verified, beloved no nore.

Jenna thought of a million things to say, but stood nute as headlights like wolf's eyes turned in and slashed heir way through the dark Stone Forest. When the black sedan pulled up, Jenna saw Vince Sabatka was driving. She should have thought of him. Perhaps he was in on ıll this, too.

"Jenna, Jenna," her mother crooned as she hurried up he steps and hugged her daughter. Jenna stood stiffly in ıer embrace, both loathing and treasuring it.

"Was all this Mace's idea?" was the first thing ou
of her mother's mouth. Her mother led Jenna off th
porch and down the walk, as if to get out of Vince'
earshot. Jenna was surprised her mother did not seem t
want to go in the house, but this was fine with her. Any
place was equally awful for the things she had to say.

They soon left behind the pool of light from the win
dows. Yet the moon was nearly full and threw nigh
shadows of the looming trees all around them. "It coul
be a setup, you know," her mother insisted, "if Mac
was guilty—"

Jenna pulled free from her mother's arm and face
her. "Like me, he's only guilty of not putting the piece
together sooner, but Mandi and my abductors—all thre
of them—were highly unlikely suspects."

Jenna glanced back to be certain Vince had not fol
lowed. His silhouette was outlined by stark window ligh
as he sat on the porch. It suddenly seemed clear to Jenn
that someone as sinister-looking as Vince could be in
nocent, for this entire nightmare was like looking at
photo negative. The more lily-white a person's reputa
tion, the darker his—or her—heart. They kept walkin
deeper into the shadows of the trees, past Fairy Land
toward Heaven and Hell.

"*Three* suspects?" Her mother asked, apparentl
when she got her voice under control.

"Mother, just forget the spin on this. I finally force
Garth out from behind his kindly, helpful psychiatris
mask. He tried to kill me when I confronted him, bu
then confessed. He's been taken away under arrest by
sheriff's deputy for questioning. Your lover, or accom
plice, or whatever he really is—Rod—has admitted ev
erything to Mace, and is willing to testify to his part i
things to the authorities."

Cynthia stopped walking. Even in the growing gloom, her face seemed to blanch whiter. "Rod?"

"Just tell me why! Because you saw what a boost the publicity was with the rock slide, so you thought you'd try it again?"

"I told you I had nothing to do with that, and—"

"And I can't believe anything you say ever again. Your entire life is a lie, and either you're going public with that or I am!"

"You mean Garth and—and Rod MacCaman arranged to kidnap Mandi? That's what they're claiming or you're accusing?"

"I actually wanted to believe Garth had betrayed you at first. But you're the common link, the bridge between two men who didn't know each other. I suppose Rod did it for his warped love of you and Garth for money, or the chance to hang on your political skirt hems. Or was he your lover, too?"

"Not Garth, only Rod. But you're demented. What you're saying," her mother whispered, sagging back against a stone gargoyle, "is absolutely abominable. Now, I want to see Mandi's body. You have got to get over this vile, corroding jealousy that has warped you all these years—"

Jenna hit the statue so hard her hand hurt. It was either that or pound her mother into the ground. Jenna was astounded at the evil her mother had hidden all these years, worse than poor Mandi, rotting in a cave, and her own life rotting....

"Your dying lover may take your ugly secrets to his grave," Jenna cried, "but I wouldn't be surprised if Garth, at least, loves his daughter enough to try to plea bargain with the authorities. I should have realized you were the common denominator in all this. You had the intimate knowledge of Mandi's pillow collection, her Si-amese cat, our kids' tree house. No doubt you had some old recording of her signing "Happy Birthday" to her-self. Mace was with me when I got that call. Russ was dead, and even Garth or Rod would never have had that."

"I just wanted you to be with me, not out on your own in this forest of dreadful memories. I did it to get my last daughter back with me," she said, and clutched at Jenna.

Jenna darted back. "I can't bear to hear how you did anything for me. It's all been for you. I thought you loved Mandi more than me. But, really, you only loved yourself. So you can forget about putting your very best spin on what you've done, with Hal Westbrook and your adoring supporters and voters and the press. You and Garth—and Rod, if he lives much longer—are actually going to have to tell the truth for once."

"Rod's collapsed over this, hasn't he? A terminally ill man, and you and Mace couldn't spare him."

"Yes, he's bad. Mace has sent for Cassie, and—"

"I've got to go to him." She turned and ran back toward her car, shouting to Vince as she went. Jenna followed.

"Mother, you're not getting away. You're going to answer for this—"

"Shut up and get in," she told Jenna, yanking open the back door of the sedan before the astounded Vince could. "I'll need you to get Mace and Cassie away from Rod for a few minutes so I can say goodbye, tell him that he can go with a clear conscience, that I'll take all the blame. Yes, you heard me. I'll take the blame, I'll explain everything. Jenna, please," she cried, "just get in the car. I swear to you, I thought Mandi's abduction would just be a simple, quick thing. It would teach her to stop sneaking out at night and it would help my career, so I could keep Kirkhall and send both of you to college. I had no idea you'd go jumping in with both feet, that it would end in Mandi's death."

"*You* killed Mandi!" Jenna cried, pointing a finger in her mother's frenzied face. Frenzied, Jenna thought, only to get to Rod's side or to escape, not because she was conscience-stricken over what she'd done. "You can claim it was indirectly—that she ran and fell—but it was your doing! And, if Dr. Brennan's 'counseling' hadn't shut me up or scared me away, you'd just as soon have killed *me*."

A fierce determination tempered with a strange calm came over Jenna. She had no words left for this stranger. It was her mother who had been unbalanced all these years, and no one had known, especially not the desperate daughter who'd tried to earn her love. Suddenly she could not bear the sight or sound of Cynthia Kirk.

"None of that's true!" her mother screamed. "Jenna, get in this car!"

"I'll drive myself," Jenna told Vince, her voice steady. "I'll be right behind you. You're a witness now, Vince. And if this car doesn't head straight for the MacCamans', I'm calling the police from my van to track you both down."

Finally, after Cassie and Mace had spent time with their father, they came out, Mace pushing Cassie in a wheelchair. Her tear-streaked face lit to see Jenna, and they hugged.

"I'm so sorry—so sorry, Jennie. He's really dying this time. He wants to die, I think," Cassie whispered. "But I'm going to get better."

"He's been asking for you, or I wouldn't let you near him," Mace told her mother. He faced her, arms stiffly at his sides, fists clenched. "He's made the doctor step out, too, but the hospice people will be here soon. And the sheriff."

"I understand. I—and Cassie's book, hereafter," her mother said, "will testify to everything honestly and fairly."

Cynthia Kirk suddenly looked more gaunt and ill than Cassie. She squeezed Cassie's shoulder, then turned to Jenna.

"You're stronger than I've ever been. None of this was your fault."

She looked as if she wanted to hug Jenna, but spun and hurried down the hall. Oddly, Jenna thought, at the last moment her step had seemed light, almost like a girl's.

The phone rang and Mace answered. Jenna sat on the couch and just held Cassie's hands while they quietly comforted each other.

"*Time* magazine?" they heard Mace say. "How the hell did you get wind of it already? No, no statements at this time. Why don't you just call the lieutenant governor's office?"

"All her dreams, her life work," Jenna whispered, "down the drain…the pit with Mandi."

She started to cry, yet for the first time in years she felt no fear.

"Word's leaked out somehow," Mace said, coming back to join them. "I took the phone off the hook, but the vultures will probably be circling soon. Whatever Dad's done, I just wish he could die in peace. Garth and Cynthia are the ones who are going to go through hell.

Sweetheart, I don't think your mother can possibly talk her way out of this one."

He sat beside Jenna, their knees touching, and wiped tears from her cheeks. They held hands, but each reached out to take one of Cassie's thin ones, too. It reminded Jenna of the evening they'd stood out on the deck in a three-way embrace, hardly realizing what they'd really come home to face.

Mace looked at his watch again. "Time's almost up for them. I wish the sheriff would get here. I'll bet Garth Brennan's pouring out his own confession to someone else for once."

When the doorbell rang, he looked out through the closed drapes. "Sheriff Adkins," he said. "I hope he doesn't demand a deathbed confession from Dad, but if it helps to put all this to rest..."

Jenna stood as the tall, wiry sheriff came in, and Mace introduced him to Cassie. When Mace and Jenna filled him in on their parents' part in this, his thick eyebrows lifted.

"Garth Brennan's refused to talk but I bet he will now, what with your tape recording on top of all this. I already got a coupla eyewitnesses from the Limey Roadhouse set to ID his photo. You gonna produce your mother now, Jenna?" he asked, nervously reaching for a pair of handcuffs on his thick belt.

Unable to speak, she nodded. As she started down the hall to get Cynthia, Mace came right behind. When he twisted the knob of his dad's door, it was locked.

"Dad. Mrs. Kirk!" Mace called. He rattled the doorknob. "Open up, or I'll break it in."

Sheriff Adkins strode down the hall behind them. "I can have one of the officers put a shoulder to it," he told them, but Mace quickly did that himself, shoving into the room with Jenna at his side and the sheriff righ behind.

The bed was unmade but empty, and the back window was raised with the screen removed. The curtains billowed gaily in the evening breeze.

''Where are they?'' the sheriff shouted.

''My dad can barely walk. But that leads to the back deck, and stairs that go down to the side of the house,'' Mace said as they ran to look out the window. Jenna realized it was the same window where she'd seen Rod last week, standing, just staring out into the night.

The sheriff pushed her and Mace aside to look out both ways on the big deck. ''You got outside lights, get them on,'' he ordered Mace, and climbed out the window in pursuit.

Mace and Jenna watched him thud across the deck and go down the stairs. But suddenly, shockingly, Jenna felt she knew where to look.

''Come with me,'' she told Mace, and climbed through the window, too. When he followed, they saw Cassie had heard the commotion and had wheeled herself out onto the deck. She'd turned on the deck lights, which bathed the area in a bright golden glow. Jenna just nodded to her friend, then pulled Mace toward the railing that overlooked the dark ravine.

''I'm the only one who ever escaped that way,'' Mace told her, gesturing toward the rock walls. ''It's a rugged cliff.''

''But since Mandi was left in that pit…since your father's in no shape to run…''

Together, they leaned over the railing and peered into the leafy depths below. Light filtered wanly down along the ragged limestone ledges, where the sprawl of two entwined bodies gleamed as white as bone.

Epilogue

Jenna's evidence against Garth Brennan, and the fact that two college students and the Limey Roadhouse bartender had IDed him as being at the beer party the night Jenna and Cassie were drugged, was enough to make him opt for a plea bargain. Though he'd still spend years in prison, he told the authorities everything.

Jenna felt so sorry for his little Samantha, especially when she heard that the girl's mother was working day and night to make ends meet. Mary Drout kept the child every weekend, and Jenna sometimes saw her around town. Mary brought her to the dedication of the Little League tree house over at the Henshaws', and Jenna noted how little Sammy seemed so taken with Pete that she followed him around constantly. Jenna didn't say, even to Mace, how much Sammy reminded her of herself years ago, adoring Mace from afar. Jenna resolved she was going to get close to the child, no matter what Garth had done.

"A penny for your thoughts." Cassie interrupted Jenna's musings as Mace helped his sister out of the back seat of Jenna's van at the cemetery. "Thinking of Mandi?"

"Actually, no," Jenna admitted as she climbed out, too, and the three of them approached the rectangular hole into which Mandi's flower-draped coffin would soon be lowered. "But there will be many times I will—and fondly, too."

It pleased Jenna to see that the only media maven here today was Mary Drout. Cynthia Kirk's funeral had been such a circus—though she probably would have loved it—that they'd learned their lesson. Jenna was happy that today they had outsmarted the photographers and tabloid reporters. They'd announced Mandi's interment for noon today, but were here at dawn.

Mace and Jenna each took Cassie's arm, because she still wasn't walking with full strength. They all stared silently across the dewy grass and rows of headstones. Jenna had agonized over whether to bury her mother next to her father, but had finally done so, just as Rod lay beside his wife. Mandi was being buried in a new plot, one close to where the stone angel in the forest looked her way. It was a spot Jenna knew she could see from Home Tree Home. That thought comforted her. This day was not an ending but a new beginning.

"I have something I found that I want to read," Jenna told them, as they all stood in silence. Her voice broke, but she cleared her throat. "It's from a Psalm King David wrote when he was trapped in a cave by his enemies." She had it written on a piece of paper in her pocket, but she recited it: "'When my spirit was overwhelmed within me, they secretly set a snare for me. I was brought very low. You delivered me from my persecutors. Now the righteous surround me, and You have dealt bountifully with me.'"

Her voice drifted off, and she shivered at the crisp morning breeze. They stood listening to hymns of birds as if there were nothing more to be said. Mary Drout didn't scratch down a word, but put her notepad away in her big purse.

"Let me drive Cassie back home, in case you two want to stay longer," Mary volunteered. She was obviously not holding a grudge against Jenna for exposing her nephew. On the contrary, she was horrified at his part in things, and she'd not spared him in her coverage of his deeds or confession. Mary's articles on Cynthia Kirk had been picked up worldwide. "Besides, I think I better run Cassie into town and feed her up good," Mary added.

"Good idea," Cassie agreed, linking her arm in Mary's. "We can just interview each other clear through dessert." Cassie kissed Jenna's cheek, then Mace's.

The funeral director, who'd parked the hearse a good distance off, came up with his assistant. "I'll take care of everything here if you don't want to stay until she's interred. It's finished," the man told Jenna and Mace as the others left.

"It's finished," Jenna heard Mace whisper.

They thanked him and, leaving Jenna's van parked nearby for now, walked into the Stone Forest. It was a lovely early morning with the eastern sun streaming through the trees and casting long shadows from the angel and the gargoyles in Heaven and Hell. But Jenna was sure it was mostly heaven now.

They headed toward the tree houses, as if they had decided in some unspoken language to watch Mandi's burial from aloft. Mace's arm clasped her shoulders and her arm encircled his waist, so they fit perfectly against each other.

"Home Tree Home," Mace said, pointing toward her highest tree house with his free hand, "is probably just big enough for a very private wedding ceremony and an even more intimate honeymoon night. I always was intrigued by that big bed. I'd like to take you somewhere exotic, too—but I promise I won't ask you to go caving."

She clasped his waist even harder. "To marry you, I'd probably even go caving on the moon or Mars, if need be."

"Is that a yes? All we'd need is Gil for best man and Cassie for maid of honor. Why don't you let me court you as I never had a chance to, and then we'll do it."

"Your father said once he hoped you and I would build a tree house together. I'd like to think he really wanted that."

Under Home Tree Home, he turned her to him and tipped her face up toward his. The slant of the rising sun was in her eyes, but she saw her dazzling future clearly. When they climbed toward the tree house, she almost didn't need the earthbound ladder, for she could have soared.